Tell It to My Heart

USA TODAY & WSJ BESTSELLING AUTHOR

SIOBHAN DAVIS

This paperback edition © July 2023

ISBN-13: 978-1-916651-01-2

Print edition © July 2023

Critique and research by Jennifer Gibson of The Critical Touch

Edited by Kelly Hartigan of XterraWeb

Proofread by Imogen Wells of Final Polish Proofreading

Cover design by Shannon Passmore of Shanoff Designs

Cover image © depositphotos.com

Formatted by Ciara Turley using Vellum

Note from the Author

This book is recommended to readers aged eighteen and older due to mature content, including graphic sexual scenes and profanity. Some scenes may be triggering for readers. Please refer to the trigger warnings page on my website, type this link into your browser https://siobhandavis.com/triggers/

Tell It to My Heart

THE PAST

Chapter One
Sydney

A squeal slips past my lips when hands grip my waist and I'm yanked back into a tall warm body. "Where d'ya think you're going?" Jared asks in that newly deep voice that does funny things to my insides. His warm breath ghosts over my neck before he nuzzles my skin, and I melt against him.

"Art class," I rasp, not protesting when he spins me around in his arms.

Noise levels elevate as students crowd against lockers in the busy hallway, eager to grab their shit and escape West Lorian High for the weekend. I'm equally excited to leave our private school behind for a few days. Not just because I get to spend uninterrupted time with my love.

Stretching my neck to look up at my best-friend-slash-new-boyfriend, I smile at his sexy-as-fuck face. Jared had a massive growth spurt over the summer, and he's well over six feet tall now. Add that to his gorgeous face, charismatic personality, musical talent, and all-round good guy persona, and he's the full package.

To say I'm the envy of girls at school is an understatement.

Some days, I still have to pinch myself to believe he's finally mine. Years of unrequited love ended four months ago when he kissed me and confessed his feelings.

I've been walking on a cloud ever since.

"Boo." He fake pouts, and his piercing sky-blue eyes sparkle with unspoken promise.

I grin as I clutch his arms. "You know I go to Miss Elliott's every Friday after school." She used to teach Mom back in the day, and somehow, I managed to convince her to take me on as a student a couple of years ago. Jade Elliott is well known in artistic circles for her talent, her beauty, her free-spirited eccentric ways, and her reclusiveness. I don't care. As long as she helps me get a place at the illustrious art program at NYU, she can be whoever she wants to be.

"I miss you." Jared leans down and brushes his lips against mine. "I need you." Grabbing my ass through my uniform skirt, he pulls me in flush with his muscular body.

"You only saw me two hours ago in world history," I remind him though I'm secretly pleased at how much he seems to crave me. Heat crawls up my neck and onto my cheeks as I rest my hands on his chest and beam at him. Lately, things have been getting more intense between us, and I know it's only a matter of time before we go all the way. I squeeze my thighs together, like I've been doing a lot recently. It never alleviates the almost constant ache down below. "Can you come over later?" I ask, purposely feeling him up.

Jared has been working out a lot, and it shows. He goes to the gym every morning before school with Anvil, the lead singer of their band. His body is insane. Jared is all curved dips and solid muscle with a six-pack that is the envy of every jock in this place.

"Try stopping me." Grinning, he tosses waves of jet-black

hair out of his smoldering eyes before bending down to kiss me. Reaching up on tiptoe, I meet him halfway, angling my head and sighing contentedly. Strong arms wrap around me from behind as we kiss, and I always feel so protected when I'm with him. Jared's mouth glides effortlessly against mine, and my pulse races as my core throbs with potent need. My lips automatically part when his tongue demands entry, and I moan into his mouth. The outside world ceases to exist as I get lost in the only boy who has ever mattered.

My boyfriend is the best kisser in the world.

I don't care I've only kissed one other boy before Jared, and I'm not exactly an expert on kissing technique.

A girl just knows these things.

"Ahem." A familiar throat clearing pulls us apart, and I just know my cheeks are on fire as I turn to face my best friend. I'm still a little shy when it comes to PDAs.

"I think I got pregnant from that kiss," Cayenne jokes, fanning her pretty face with both hands.

"That's a physical impossibility." I snuggle into my boyfriend's side as his arm wraps around my waist, and he presses a kiss to my hair.

"Where's Vil?" Jared asks, glancing over my bestie's shoulder for any sign of his bandmate and her on-again, off-again boyfriend.

"Don't know. I'm not his keeper," Cay huffs, grabbing fistfuls of her long pink hair and wrangling it into a messy topknot as her good mood instantly evaporates.

I'm not a fan of Anvil. Period. Neither Jared nor Cayenne know he's hit on me. On several occasions over the past year. There was this one time at a freshman party last year, where I considered making out with him purely to get back at Jared because he'd disappeared with some cheerleader and I was jealous. The thought lasted for about three seconds before I discarded it. It's one thing for Jared to make out with a random stranger he'll never see again and quite another for me to make out with one of his closest friends.

Even though we were firmly in the friend zone then, I knew Jared wouldn't like it. So, I have avoided Anvil's advances. That and he's always creeped me out a little. I thought it would stop after he started dating my best friend and after Jared and I got together, but it hasn't.

I wish Cayenne would break up with him for good, even if it would be awkward. She deserves way better than that cheating asshole.

"He called practice off," Jared confirms, running his hand up and down my side. "I thought it was to hang out with you."

Cay's eyes narrow to slits, and I can almost see steam billowing from her ears. "That lying piece of shit! I asked him to walk me home so we could talk, and he said he had band practice."

Jared cringes even though I know he said that on purpose. Anvil may be his bandmate and one of his closest friends, but he doesn't approve of how he treats his girlfriend. He thinks Cayenne should break up with him too, and that speaks volumes. "Maybe he got things mixed up."

"Don't cover for him, J. Don't do that."

Pounding footsteps approach, and I sigh, already knowing who it will be.

"Miss Shaw," Dirk says when he reaches us. "You're going to be late if we don't leave now." Crossing his arms over his thick chest, my bodyguard levels me with a look. One I'm all too familiar with. The sleeves of his black suit jacket bunch with the motion, almost straining the fabric. Dirk is ex-military, and he loves barking orders at me any chance he gets.

"I'm coming. I'm coming," I murmur, shucking out of my boyfriend's warm embrace.

"Not yet you aren't," Jared whispers in my ear, and I swat his arm as I give him the eyes, silently warning him to behave. Dirk has supersonic hearing, and unlike Keaton, my other regular bodyguard, he isn't opposed to spilling the beans to my father any chance he gets.

To say Dad isn't a fan of Jared as my boyfriend is putting it mildly. He liked him just fine until we started dating, and then it's as if a switch flipped. My brothers have tried talking to him to no avail. Dad is constantly asking me to break up with him. Concerned it's too serious at our age. But he doesn't get it. He doesn't understand Jared is *the one*. I don't care I'm only fifteen. I know my own mind.

Jared is the only man I will ever love.

The only one I will ever want.

The only man I will ever marry.

"I'll see you later." I lean up and kiss his cheek. "I'll text you when I'm home."

"Love you, babe," he says, stealing one last kiss.

Jared is very romantic, and he tells me he loves me at least once a day. A girl could really get used to it. "Love you too." I smile adoringly at him before he heads off in the direction of his locker, and I walk toward the exit.

"Can I grab a ride?" Cayenne asks, looping her arm through mine as we walk behind Dick. I purposely fluff his name on occasions where he's really annoying me, purely to wind him up. He's so easy to aggravate. It never fails to get a reaction.

"Of course." Her house is on the way. Cay is one of only a handful of scholarship students at West Lorian and one of the few sophomores who doesn't have a driver. She usually walks the six blocks home. I'll be applying for my learner's permit in a few months, when I turn sixteen, and then I plan to drive her to and from school. Provided Dad will let me drive myself. I'm already preparing myself for that argument. I don't see it as a big deal. My stupid bodyguards can always tail me in the Merc or the SUV so I'm still safe, yada, yada.

"I'm done with him this time," Cay says when we are in the back seat of the Mercedes-Benz with the privacy screen up. Dirk glides smoothly out into the bustling NYC traffic as we get comfortable for the ride.

"I've heard that before." I tuck her hand in mine and send her a sympathetic look.

"He's with *her* again. I just know it."

Cay is convinced he has another girl on the side, but her boyfriend has denied it. He's been secretive with his phone, and he disappears for hours at a time with his cell switched off, which is hugely suspicious. I'm with my bestie on this. "You deserve better."

"I do." She rubs at her eyes. "I see the way Jared is with you, and I want that. I want someone who adores me and someone who means what they say. Anvil makes all these promises and always lets me down." Resting her head on my shoulder, she says, "You were right. I should never have put out. I should have waited like you."

"You can't turn back the clock, but you can change what happens from now on. He's never been good enough for you."

I know Cayenne has a chip on her shoulder because she's not wealthy like most other students who attend our school. Having a popular guy like Anvil for a boyfriend is a big deal, but she pays too high a price.

Who gives a shit if he's good-looking and rich if he's a prick? She doesn't need him to give her credibility or status. Fuck that jerk. He's not even that great of a singer. I think he pulls the band down, and they'd stand a better chance of making it without him as their front man. He's all bluster and hot air and purely in it for the fame and the chicks. Cayenne is smart enough to know this, so I don't understand why she is still clinging to a relationship that is toxic. She has a tendency to put herself down, which I hate. Along with Jared, she's the best person I know.

"Things seem to be getting serious with you and J," she adds, lifting her head and changing the conversation.

"They've been serious since that first kiss. You know I've wanted this for years."

"I mean sexually." She drills me with a look. "Have you given him your V-card yet?"

I shake my head, sending waves of long blonde hair tumbling across my shoulders. "You would know if I had." We tell each other everything. Or most everything that's important. "We've done everything but the deed."

"Why wait?" She quirks a brow. "You guys have known each other your entire lives. Your dads are best friends since college, and they know you're crazy about one another. He's a decent guy, and he loves you. He'll make sure your first time is good."

I don't tell her Jared is a virgin too because it's not something anyone knows. He's been with other girls, and everyone just assumed he was fucking them. Most of the guys I know, and some of the girls, lost their V-cards at fourteen or fifteen. At almost sixteen, it's quite unusual Jared and I haven't gone there, but we were waiting for each other. My heart was so full when he told me I almost burst with joy. "I know he will, but he wants to wait until I'm sure, and"—I chew on the inside of my mouth, embarrassed to have to articulate this, but I know Cay will understand and be as angry and humiliated as me—"my father asked him outright to wait until we're legal."

Cay's mouth hangs open, and her eyes pop wide. "Get the fuck out!"

"Truth. It's so embarrassing. I wanted to die when Jared told me."

"Your dad is so protective of you."

"It's ridiculous."

"All powerful, rich men have enemies, and I understand the need for bodyguards and extra security measures, but come on, it's Jared. He's practically a third son to your father. You think he'd be pleased his only daughter is with a guy he knows is one of the good ones."

"I don't think any father wants to think of his little girl having sex, no matter who the guy is. Jared promised him he would wait, but honestly, I don't see how we can."

"Teenage guys are total horndogs," she agrees, bobbing her head as Dirk blows the horn at some biker who cuts in front of our car.

"I'm not just talking about him." I waggle my brows and squirm on the leather seat. "I am so freaking horny all the damn time. He only has to look at me, and I'm creaming my panties. When he uses his fingers or his tongue on me, I detonate like fireworks on the Fourth of July. It takes very little effort on his part, and boom, I erupt. It's becoming very problematic."

She bursts out laughing, and I elbow her in the ribs.

"I'm being serious. Like, I'm in physical pain. I just constantly ache and throb down below. Is it like that for you?"

"Hormones are no joke, and yeah, I get those urges." She squeezes my hand. "It just means you're ready. Your body needs the release, and you should totally get Jared to rid you of that pesky V-card. Who gives a fuck what your dad thinks? It's your body. Your life. Your decision."

"Yeah, it is." It's not like Dad ever has to know. We haven't been caught fooling around in my bedroom, and we do that a lot.

Determination surges through my veins, and resolve sets in. Fuck it. I want to do it with Jared. I'm done waiting. I know he wants to abide by my daddy's wishes, but he's a walking hard-on. I'm not the only one struggling to contain raging hormones.

I just need to convince him.

Seduce him.

A grin spreads over my mouth as an idea forms, and I begin plotting.

Chapter Two
Sydney

Music plays low in the background as I make out with my boyfriend on top of my bed. Downstairs, his parents and my dad are having their usual Friday night catch-up over takeout, beers for our dads, and wine for Gladys. We joined them for food before escaping to my room. Dad reminded me to keep the door open before we came upstairs, but he never checks. He must trust Jared to keep his promise.

Fool.

Doesn't he know you can't trust teenagers? We'll tell the oldies whatever they need to hear and do what we want.

"I want you," I say in a breathy voice as I dive my hand under the waistband of my boyfriend's jeans and palm his erection. I peer deep into his eyes as I stroke his cock, loving how dilated his pupils are. Jared's face is drenched with love and lust, and I'm sure it mirrors my own. Climbing on top of him, I grind my hips onto his hard length through his jeans, moaning as almost painful desire clenches my core. Leaning down, I brush my lips over his before saying, "I want all of you, J. I want your cock inside me. I can't wait."

"Babe." He grips my hips, looking pained as he stalls my rocking motion. "I want that more than anything, but I promised your dad."

"Seriously?" I arch a brow. "Who cares? What he doesn't know can't hurt him." Pushing his T-shirt up to his chest, I trail my fingers over his cut abs, admiring the solid definition that is evidence of months of dedication in the gym.

"I don't want to get into his bad books more than I already am."

"What about getting into *my* bad books?" I snap, withdrawing my hand and scrambling off his body. "Shouldn't you be more concerned about that?" Flopping down on my back, I look up at the high ceiling and release an exasperated sigh.

Our storied townhouse in Manhattan dates back to 1830. Though it's modern in design, we have a lot of original features —like old fireplaces, ornate moldings on the ceilings and around the doors, clawfoot tubs, and even some of the original wood flooring. Mom did a lot of the restoration work herself before she died of cancer when I was five.

"Babe." Jared flips on his side and reaches for my face.

"Don't babe me," I huff, prying his fingers from my cheek.

"Sydney. Look at me."

Despite my better instincts, I turn on my side to face him.

He winds his fingers through my hair. "I love you, and I want you. Never doubt that."

"Then *be* with me, Jared. I want you to be my first and last. I want everything with you. It feels like I've been waiting an eternity to be with you." I beseech him with my eyes as I cup his cheek. "I love you so much, and I want to show you with my body. Please, babe. Don't make me beg."

"Jesus, Syd." He rests his brow against mine as his arms

snake around my waist, and he pulls me in flush to his body. Rolling his hips, he pushes his hard-on against me. "See what you do to me? I'm like this all the time. When we're not together, I'm jerking off to thoughts of you. I want you so badly, but I don't want your dad to hate me either."

"You do realize this is totally warped, right?" I ease my head back a little to stare into his gorgeous big blue eyes. "I shouldn't have to convince you. No other guy your age would give a flying fuck what my father says. They'd just do me."

A muscle pops in his jaw. "Don't fucking say that! I'm trying to do the right thing!"

"No, you're not." I grab hold of his ass and thrust my weeping pussy against the bulge in his jeans. "You're letting my father dictate our relationship. Fuck him! He doesn't get to do that. It's none of his damn business."

"It is when you're not legal! You're still a minor under his care."

I bolt upright, incensed beyond belief. "Do you even hear yourself, Jared? What the actual fuck? No one in our year is legal, and they're all fucking like bunnies! Who gives a shit? It. Doesn't. Matter." Hurt settles on my chest. "Just admit you don't want me like that if that's the truth, but stop hiding behind my dad." I jump off the bed as Jared lunges for me.

A yelp flees my lips as he manhandles me onto the bed and crawls over me. Anger flares in his eyes mixed with heat. "If you wanted to make me mad, consider it an achievement. Don't you ever fucking doubt how much I want you and love you. And don't you ever compare us to anyone else at school. We aren't like any other couple." His fingers caress the skin on my face as the hard edge of his anger fades from his eyes. "We're forever, Sydney. It's you and me for life, baby. We're making memories, and I only want them to be the best ones."

The red haze coating my eyes and infiltrating my veins

dissipates with his words. It's so hard to stay angry at him when he woos me with his dreamy words and heartfelt promises. "I just want to be as close to you as humanly possible. I want to know what it's like to feel you moving inside me. I can't wait until we're seventeen. I'll self-combust before then."

Laughter rumbles from his chest. "Are you sure you want to be an artist, because drama seems to be in your blood."

I stick my tongue out, and he chuckles.

His face dissolves with love. "I love you, Sydney Shaw. To infinity and forever." He kisses me softly, and I drag my fingers through his silky hair.

We kiss leisurely for a few minutes with him lying carefully on top of me, propping most of his weight on his arms. Jared rolls off me a few minutes later when our kissing grows in intensity. Lying on his side, he tangles his fingers in mine and briefly kisses my swollen lips. "Let's wait until your birthday. If you still want it, we'll do it then."

My eyes pop wide with excitement. "You mean it?"

"Yes. It's not easy for me either, you know. I'm trying to be a gentleman."

"I don't want you to be a gentleman. I want you to be the devil. I want you to act out every dark fantasy on my body."

"Fucking hell, babe." Jared adjusts himself behind his jeans, and I pout when he pops the button back into place. "I'm going to make a mess in my boxers."

"I can help with that." I palm his junk again.

"As much as I'd love that, we can't." He removes my hand, and I scowl. "It's too risky with the rents downstairs."

I hate he's right. Mostly, we fool around on Saturdays when the house is empty save for the staff. Dad always goes out with the Kings and their extended network of friends on Saturday nights. Oldies are so predictable.

"You are too honorable, Jared King," I say, taking his hand

and pressing a kiss to his palm. "But I guess I shouldn't be complaining. I could be stuck with a cheating asshole like Anvil." Dropping his hand, I turn over and haul ass off the bed.

"I love the guy like a brother, but Cay needs to kick him to the curb. If she doesn't do it, I'm liable to start a war with the guy." He stands, yawning as he stretches his arms over his head.

"I am encouraging her to cut him loose, but she has to make the decision." I skip over to his side. "I have something for you."

"It's not my birthday for another seven weeks." He pins me with a goofy, boyish smile that takes me back in time. An abundance of childhood memories floats through my mind, reminding me of all the happy times I've shared with this guy.

Tears prick my eyes as emotion lays siege to me. I wrap my arms around him and rest my head on his chest. "I love you, J. I love you so, so much. I don't think you properly understand it."

"Syd. I get it. I feel the same way too. I have never been more connected to any soul the way I am to you. You're my everything." He holds me close, and we don't speak for a few minutes as the emotion of the moment affects both of us.

He tips my head back a couple minutes later. "What do you have for me?" Blue eyes flash with excitement, and I fall in love with him all over again.

Reluctantly, I shuck out of his embrace. "I've been working on this at Jade's. I didn't want to say anything until it was done." I place my hands over his eyes. "Close your eyes, and don't open them until I tell you."

Jared complies, and I race into my closet where I stowed the painting earlier. Carrying the easel out to my bedroom, I position it in the center of the room, checking to ensure my boyfriend isn't peeking as I angle it where the light is best. Nerves fire at me, and a messy ball of emotion clogs my throat.

I really hope he likes it.

I put a ton of hours and effort into it, and I'm thrilled with the result.

I hope he is too.

Walking back to him, I thread my fingers in his and guide him forward, stopping at the large canvas perched on the high easel. "You can open them now," I whisper, chewing anxiously on the inside of my mouth.

Jared slowly opens his eyes, and they grow bigger as he takes in my painting of him. It was from a gig they played at the start of the summer for a sweet sixteen, held in the function room of an upscale bar. I hadn't been able to take my eyes off him the entire performance. We hadn't been together as boyfriend and girlfriend long, and I was still floating in a heavenly cocoon, hanging off my man's every word and every look.

I have always loved watching Jared play the drums, but there was something magical about him that night.

Passion seeped from his pores as he played his heart out.

My eyes had been transfixed on his hands and the way they curled around the drumsticks with confidence borne from talent and sheer hard work. Veins popped in his arms and muscles strained as he gave it his all, and I was mesmerized. I mentally captured the moment, committing it to memory. I raced home that night and sketched it out, and later, I worked on it with Jade.

It's my best ever work, and I'm proud of it. I was tempted to keep it, but it belongs to Jared. I can't explain it, but it feels like a pivotal moment in his career, and it needed to be immortalized. He should be the one to have it.

"You did this?" Jared stares at me through glassy eyes. "How did you even..." He trails off, lost for words, and I think that's a good thing?

"That image of you is imprinted in my brain. I will never forget how incredible you were that night." I brush my fingers gently over my oil painting with a soft smile. I am proud of my work. Jared is behind the drum kit, muscular arms raised mid-strike, eyes closed as he's lost in the music and the moment, his body electrified, every muscle straining, as passion takes control of him. Sweat-slickened strands of inky black hair brush over his brow and his skin is flushed with excitement.

He looks like a bona fide rock god.

It's like looking into a crystal ball and seeing his future.

"This is fucking incredible, Syd. I'm blown away. I can't even form words."

He's just staring at it in wonder, and my heart swells behind my chest. "You like it?" I shyly ask.

"Like it?" He snaps out of his fugue state and scoops me into his arms, lifting me up and spinning me around. "I fucking love it, babe. It's phenomenal. You're phenomenal. I can't believe you did this." He puts my feet down and tucks me under his arm as we stand in front of the painting. "Have you any idea how talented you are?"

"Right back at ya, stud," I tease, blushing to the roots of my hair because I'm uncomfortable with praise.

"You're going to get into the program at NYU. They'll take one look at this and admit you on the spot." He leans in closer. "It's so lifelike it's almost like a photo. You captured me so perfectly."

"You're the perfect subject, Jared. I could draw you all the time and never grow tired."

Fierce determination crests over his face as he yanks me against his chest. "Someday, you're going to be my wife, Sydney, and then you can paint me all the damn time."

Chapter Three
Sydney

I'm on a high, floating in outer space, after his statement, so I don't hear the shouting at first. But Jared does. "What the fuck is going on?" he asks as his brow puckers.

I snap out of my head and instantly frown at the ruckus wafting up the stairs.

Jared is already dragging me out of the room, and we fly down the stairs and round the corner, heading for the living room. My boyfriend slams to a halt in the doorway, and an "oomph" leaves my lips when I crash into him from behind. He pulls me protectively under his arm, and I stare with my mouth hanging open and my eyes on stilts at the scene in front of us.

Gladys King, Jared's mom, is standing on one side of our large living room, holding her hand over her mouth and crying silent tears, as she watches her husband and my father roll around the floor, throwing punches at one another. I blink several times, sure my eyes must be deceiving me. Dad and Amos King have been best friends since Amos transferred to West Lorian High his senior year. They went to NYU together. Built their business empires at the same time. Got married and started families within a year of one another. They are closer than brothers. I have never, *never*, known them to have more than the odd disagreement.

This is...shocking, upsetting.

"Do something!" Glady's implores her son.

Jared steps forward and bends over. Grabbing his dad's shirt, he pulls him away from my father. I race over to the warring men, stepping in front of my father when he makes to lunge at Amos. "Daddy, no!" It's at times like this I wish there wasn't such a huge age gap between me and my older brothers. That they weren't both married with their own homes. If Felix and Tucker were here, they'd know how to handle this.

"Get out of my house!" Dad yells, swiping at blood seeping from his cut lip as he staggers to his feet. Gripping my arm tight, he shoves me behind him. "Get the fuck out of my house, Amos, and take your family with you. You're no longer welcome here."

"Fuck you, you prick." I peek around Dad's arm, watching Jared's dad jab his finger in the air in the direction of my father. Jared inches toward me, but I shake my head. I don't know what's going on, but now isn't the time to play my hero. I have never seen my dad so enraged, and I'm scared.

"You're dead to me, asshole," Amos hisses. "If you ever come near me, my family, or my business, I will kill you. You hear me?!" Picking up a lamp, he throws it at the wall while Dad taps out a message on his cell.

Jared and I lock troubled eyes as he moves to his mom's side and tries to comfort her. Gladys sobs into her son's neck, clinging to him with a desperation that is not usual for the woman who has been a surrogate mother to me since my mother—her best friend—died ten years ago.

"I'm glad we're on the same page." Dad's cold tone sends

chills creeping up my spine. "Now get out before I have you thrown out."

Dirk and two other bodyguards come bounding into the room, positioning themselves in front of us and blocking my view of my boyfriend. Panic is doing a number on me, and I'm borderline hysterical wondering what this means for my relationship. This doesn't seem like some spur-of-the-moment argument that will pass once everyone has calmed down.

This is serious.

Some real shit has happened, and I don't think either man is going to back down.

"Escort the Kings off my property, and make it known to the full security detail that no King is allowed to ever step foot in here again."

"But, Dad—"

"Quiet, Sydney," he roars.

"Don't you dare speak to her like that," Jared says as I try to push past my father and the bodyguards to get to my boyfriend.

Dad tightens his grip on my arm, pinning me firmly to his side.

"Dad, ow. You're hurting me."

"Let her go!" Jared yells, shoving at the bodyguards as he tries to get through to me.

"Jared, no!" Gladys shouts. "Don't make things worse."

"This ends now," Dad says in a clinical tone, staring coldly in my boyfriend's direction. "You and my daughter are done."

"What? No!" I cry, fighting to get out of his hold.

"Fuck you!" Jared shouts amid sounds of commotion as the bodyguards grab the Kings and start ushering them out of the room.

"Jared!" I call out, sobbing and thrashing around as my father slings his meaty arm around my waist and holds me tight.

"Syd!" Jared calls back as he's dragged shouting from the room. "It's not over! I love you!"

That's the last thing I hear before they are physically removed from our house. My body sags against my father as all the fight leaves me.

"I mean it, Sydney," my father says, spinning me around. "You are not to see that boy anymore. He's no good for you. He never has been and especially not now."

"Why, Daddy? What's happened?"

"It's grown-up business. Nothing to concern yourself with," he says, ruffling my hair like I'm five years old again.

My anger spikes. "It *is* my business if you're keeping me away from the boy I love!"

His features soften as he loosens his tight grip on me. "It's puppy love, Sydney, and you'll get over it. You'll have other boyfriends and other loves."

"No." I bite down hard on my lower lip, throwing every ounce of hate I'm feeling into the look I give my father. "I won't have other loves. Jared is the love of my life, and you can't do this to me."

"You're fifteen, Sydney! You have the rest of your life to find the love of your life," he yells, letting me go to grab handfuls of his salt-and-pepper hair. "But mark my words, that man will not be Jared King. Over my dead body will my little girl get shackled to that family."

"What have they done? At least let me try to understand it!" I holler. It's a lie. I will never understand or accept it. If he does this, if he keeps Jared away from me, I will hate him for life. The second I'm eighteen, I'll be out of here.

"It doesn't concern you. All you need to know is they are dead to us." Removing a handkerchief from his pocket, he dabs at the blood dripping from his nose and his lip. "I mean it, Sydney. Do not try to run around with him behind my back because I will know. I don't want to punish you, but I will if I have to."

Tears leak out of my eyes and pour down my face. "I hate you!" I yell. "I hate you so much, and I'll never forgive you!" Running from the room, I vow to do everything in my power to fix this because I can't live without Jared, and no one is going to make me.

A few weeks pass, and it's living hell. Jared is still banned from my house and my life, and the only way I get to spend time with him is at school because there are no bodyguards to rat me out. A lot of the kids who go to school at West Lorian have bodyguards, and there are strict rules about them remaining outside the building during classes.

Outside of school, my bodyguards report my every move to my father. They are all on high alert and have been told I am forbidden to see Jared or any of the Kings. I managed to coax Keaton into delivering Jared's painting to him, but he made it clear it was a one-off. That he couldn't intervene and risk losing his job.

I don't want anyone getting fired because of me, so I haven't pushed it or tried anything since. But I'm getting desperate. And desperate times call for desperate measures. I've been wracking my brain, trying to think of ways I can sneak out to meet my boyfriend, but so far, I'm coming up empty.

"I hate this," I sob against Jared's chest as we steal a few precious moments in an unused classroom at lunch. "What are we going to do?"

"I don't know." His brow creases as he reaches into his bag. "But at least we can text and call one another now." He hands me a cell phone. "It's a burner. Untraceable. Just hide it someplace your dad can't find it, and don't let him see you on it." His scowl deepens. "I still can't believe he made you block my number and he's spying on your calls and messages. That is so wrong."

"Tell me about it." I slip the burner cell into an inside pocket of my bag, already knowing where I'll store it. My asshole father threatened to confiscate my cell and remove all phone privileges if he caught me unblocking Jared's number or contacting him in any way. I suspect he'd demand the school keep us apart and pull me from shared classes if it wouldn't mess with my education. Dad, Mom, and my brothers all went to NYU, and he wants me to attend as well, so he's not fucking up anything here. At least not yet. "I'm scared he's going to move me to another school."

"He can't do it mid-year. Private schools are at full capacity in the city, and they are used to wealthy benefactors. His money can't buy you a place."

"He could force me to leave for junior year."

"Let's not worry about that for now." He smooths out the lines on my brow.

"You're right. We have enough to concern us." Looping my arms around his neck, I suction my body to his and inhale his familiar citrusy scent. "I miss you so much. Snatched minutes at school just aren't cutting it for me."

"Nor me." Clasping my face in his hands, he peers deep into my eyes. "I am going to fix this. I don't know how yet, but we will find a way. Our parents are not splitting us up."

Tears stab my eyes. "I'm scared, Jared. Daddy is not acting like himself, and he seems determined to keep us apart. Every time I bring you up in conversation, he blows a gasket. He's not changing his mind."

Air expels from his mouth before he presses a lingering kiss to my brow. "I know, babe. My parents are arguing all the time, and things are shit at home. But Mum is on our side. She said we just need to be patient and wait for this to blow over."

"I wish we knew what's going on."

He winces. "I think I know."

"What? How? What is it?" The words blurt from my mouth in a rush.

"I overheard my parents arguing last night." He nibbles on his lips as his hands tighten on my lower back. Uncertainty flares in his eyes as he stares at me.

"Just tell me."

"Your dad staged a hostile takeover of my dad's company."

"What?" I shriek. "Why would he do that? Amos is his best friend. Your family is our family. I don't understand."

"I don't get it either, and I didn't hear anything else as Mum caught me eavesdropping and shooed me to my room. Dad is struggling to hold on to the business he built from scratch, and it explains why he's always at the office or on his laptop at home these days."

"Felix and Anja said nothing to me about this last week." Dad had roped the younger of my two brothers and his wife into talking to me about the situation. They said nothing about Dad's despicable act of betrayal, focusing on how important it was I broke ties with the Kings. "None of this makes sense."

"Agreed." Air whooshes out of his mouth.

"There is no coming back from this."

Slowly, he nods.

"We're screwed." In every way but the way I want.

"We're almost sixteen, and then we only have two years until we're adults. They can't stop us from being together then."

"That's two years, J." Tears prick my eyes again. "I can't handle being separated from you for two minutes let alone two years."

"We'll find a way to meet, I promise." He presses a fierce kiss to my brow. "Let me worry about this. For now, I think we need to start making plans in case Mum doesn't come through for us. Save as much of your allowance as you can. I'm already doing the same, and I'm going to actively look for more gigs for the band. We need cash if we're going to break out on our own. At least until I'm a rock star."

I love his confidence, but staking our future on him making it big is a bit of a hard sell right now. It's not that I don't believe in him. I do. Jared is talented, hot, ambitious, and hardworking. But you still need luck to make it in the music industry, and right now, the last thing either of us is feeling is lucky. "You mean it? You'd break away from your family to be with me?" I gulp over the lump wedged in my throat.

"Without hesitation."

"Me too." I answer his question before he asks it.

"Good, because I'm not losing you. They can't keep me from you forever." He hugs me tight, and I cling to him and his words. "No one is taking you away from me. I'll kill anyone who tries."

Chapter Four
Sydney

"You have a visitor," Jade says the instant she closes the door to her home behind me.

"I do?" I frown at my private art teacher, wondering what's up. This is most unusual. Whipping my head around at the sound of approaching footsteps, I gasp when Jared steps into the hallway. Dumping my book bag on the floor, I run toward him with happy tears in my eyes. My boyfriend hauls me into his arms when I crash into him, half laughing, half sobbing. Our lips instantly meet, and everything feels right in the world again. Tears cling to my lashes as I hold him close.

"Don't cry, babe," he says when we break our lip-lock. "It's killing me seeing you so upset all the time."

"I hate this. I hate being apart from you."

Pain races across his face. I wait for the accompanying reassuring words, but they aren't forthcoming today. "What's happened?" My heart thuds painfully against my rib cage, and my pulse is going haywire. I have a bad, bad feeling about this.

"You have two hours," Jade says, reminding me we're not alone. "Not a second more."

Jared crushes me against his body as he turns us around to face my teacher. "Thank you, Ms. Elliott."

Jade nods as she walks toward us. "I'll slip out the back entrance and through my neighbor's house so your bodyguards don't spot me," she says, eyeballing me.

I have no clue how Jared is here or what my teacher knows, but I'm grateful she's given us this opportunity. "Thanks, Jade."

"You don't need to thank me, sweetie." She brushes her fingers against my cheeks. "Your mama would want me to look out for you."

I cling to my boyfriend as we watch Jade exit her house via the rear door. Then Jared pulls me into the art room that is conveniently located at the back of the house, overlooking the small, well-maintained yard.

"How are you here?" I ask as he sits on the velvet couch jutted against the wall, pulling me onto his lap. My arms snake around his neck, and I toy with the ends of his hair.

"My mum took art classes with Jade too though she wasn't as dedicated as your mom." His hands tighten around my lower back. "She arranged this for me. I needed to talk to you, and this was the only safe way I could think to do it."

"Has something else happened?" Butterflies swoop into my belly as anxiety presses down on my chest.

Tears well in Jared's eyes, and I brace myself for whatever is coming.

"We're moving," he says in a choked tone.

"What?" I splutter, hoping I've misheard him.

"We're moving to England. To London."

Tears leak from my eyes as I stare at him in shock. "No," I whisper, grabbing fistfuls of his shirt. "No, Jared! No! You can't leave me."

"I don't want to." He swipes at the tears spilling from his eyes. "I screamed at my parents. Told them they couldn't force me, but the truth is, they can." He clasps my face in his hands, connecting our gazes. "My hands are tied until I'm eighteen, but I swear to you, Syd, I will come back for you the second I am able to."

"Why are you moving, and why does it have to be so far away?"

"You know Mum is from London, and she still has family there. Dad has lost control of his business." A muscle clenches in his jaw. "Your dad has ruined him. The board forced his hand, and Dad had no choice but to step down as CEO. He's sold all his shares, and he plans to start a new business overseas. They want a fresh start."

"And to put as much distance between them and my father," I surmise. "This is all my dad's fault. I'll never forgive him." A strangled sob travels up my throat as I bury my head in Jared's neck, clutching him with a desperation I feel in every nook and cranny of my body.

"It is his fault, and he's going to pay," he says in a clipped tone. "Someday, I'm going to repay him for what he's done to my family and to us."

"I won't survive without you." I cry against his neck. "How am I supposed to get through each day when you're on the other side of the ocean? At least if it was someplace in the US, we could find a way to see one another, but this is...this is..." I hiccup in between sobs.

"Heartbreaking," Jared finishes for me. His large, warm, callused palms grip the side of my face. "I promise I'm going to find my way back to you. This won't break us." Steely determination flashes in his eyes, and I wish I was as strong. I wish I shared his resolve, but an ominous sense of dread is tiptoeing up and down my spine, and I don't have a good feeling about any of this.

"It already feels like it is," I croak.

"No, baby." He slams his lips onto mine, kissing me hard and fast. "You are mine, and I am yours, and nothing or no one is going to change that. I know it won't be easy, but we will get through this. We'll focus on school. You have your art, and I have music. We use those as our outlets, and we save as much money as we can, until we're both eighteen, and then I'll come and get you. We can move away, get our own place, and tell our parents to go fuck themselves."

"That's so far away," I say, moving on his lap until I'm straddling him. "I haven't gone more than two weeks without seeing you my entire life, and that was only when we went on vacation. How will we survive two years?"

Jared's hand smooths a path up and down my spine as he attempts to comfort me. "It's going to fucking suck. I need you like I need oxygen, Sydney, but we have no choice. I've been wracking my brain all week to try to find a solution, and there is none."

"You've known all week and didn't tell me?" I knew he was extra troubled this week, but he swatted my concern away whenever I asked.

"I was trying to find a way out of this mess. I didn't want to say anything if I could find a way to stay in New York, but I can't, and now I'm telling you."

"When are you leaving?"

His Adam's apple jumps in his throat. His beautiful blue eyes are flooded with emotion as he stares at me. "Sunday."

"What? No!" Anguished cries rip from my mouth as I contemplate my boyfriend is relocating overseas in two fucking days.

"I'm so sorry, baby." He peppers kisses all over my face. "If there was any way to stop this, I would. I don't want to leave you. It's killing me inside, but it's only temporary. I need you to hold on for me. Can you do that, babe? Can you wait for me?"

"Don't talk stupid. I would wait for eternity for you, Jared. You know you're the only one I want."

"You're the love of my life, Sydney." His earnest eyes flash with a myriad of emotions. "It's you and me forever."

"What about all those English girls? They'll be all over you. How long will it take before one of them snares you?"

"I only have eyes for you." He winds his fingers in my blonde hair, forcing my eyes to his. "I have no interest in any other girl. I promise I will stay faithful to you. I would never cheat on you, Sydney. Never."

"It's not you I'm worried about," I whisper, hating we're having this conversation and that my mind has gone there. But I can't help it. Jared is gorgeous, charming, and talented. British girls love Americans, and they're going to be fawning all over his accent and throwing themselves at him any chance they get. What if they catch him when he's especially lonely and vulnerable and he gives in? How long can a horny teenage guy hold out before caving to hormones?

I need to give him something more than words to hold on to. I need him to remember how good we are together and how perfectly we fit. I know exactly how to help reinforce that message, and this time, I'm getting my way.

"Don't worry, babe. I'm yours. Only yours."

"Prove it." Grinding my hips, I thrust my pelvis against his dick. "Fuck me now, Jared. I want to give you my virginity, and I'm not waiting any longer."

"Are you sure?" His pupils dilate, and I feel his dick thickening behind the zipper of his school pants.

"Yes. I want us to experience this before we're separated. It will give us something extra to cling to."

"I don't want our situation to force this decision. It has to be because we want it."

Sometimes, I want to bang his head against the wall to knock some sense into him. "That goes without saying, J. You know I'm hot for you. I've been hot for you for months." I scramble off his lap and pull him to his feet. "Now quit stalling and take me to the guest bedroom."

Jared scoops me up into his arms, and I giggle as he races up the stairs to the next level. He opens and closes a few doors until we find a sparse bedroom that is clearly not Jade's.

I pounce on him when he turns around after closing the door, trailing my hands up and down his chest and abs as I stretch on tiptoes and kiss him passionately. My boyfriend doesn't let me down, angling his head and taking control of the kiss as his arms snake around my back. We devour one another with our mouths and tongues, and I'm a writhing mass of hormones as lust coils low in my belly and pulses in my core.

Tugging on Jared's shirt, I rip my mouth from his long enough to demand, "Take it off." Jared yanks it over his head in one skillful movement, tossing it on the ground as I begin unbuttoning my school shirt. His fingers grab the waistband of my skirt, and he drags it down my hips and over my thighs until it pools at my feet. Popping the button on his pants, I lower the zipper and drive my hand into his boxers, gripping his erection.

He hisses as he gets rid of my shirt, adding it to the growing pile of clothes on the floor, before unclipping my bra and dragging it down my arms. Cool air breezes across my chest, peaking my nipples. Jared kicks his pants away, and we remove our socks and shoes until we're standing in our underwear.

A gleeful shriek escapes my lips when Jared lunges at me, picking me up and throwing me on the bed. I bounce on the springy mattress, my eyes popping wide in anticipation as he climbs onto the bed and crawls over me.

"You're beautiful and sexy, and I can't wait to be inside you," Jared says before ducking his head and sucking one of my nipples into his warm mouth. My hips arch, and the loudest moan erupts from my mouth as he worships my breasts, paying them equal attention. Grabbing fistfuls of his hair, I hold his head to my chest, lying back with my eyes closed and savoring every flick of his tongue and the suctioning motion of his lips.

Jared moves up and kisses me. "Love you."

I wrap my arms around his neck and my legs around his waist, almost coming on the spot when I feel his hard length pushing against my pussy through our underwear. "I love you too. Please fuck me, Jared. I can't wait any longer."

His responding kiss almost steals all the air from my lungs. He fucks my mouth with his lips and his tongue in a frenzy of pent-up longing I'm feeling too. "Need to make sure you're ready, babe," he says, grinning as he slides his body down the length of mine. Hooking his thumbs in the side of my panties, he pulls them down my legs and throws them away. Resting in between the apex of my thighs, he lifts my legs onto his shoulders and dives in. A scream tears from my mouth with the first swipe of his tongue on my folds. My heels dig into his back as my pelvis lifts, and I all but shove my pussy in his face.

I love when Jared goes down on me like this. The only good thing about us not having sex before now is we're both pretty much experts at oral. I'm dying to taste him, but I'm dying to have his cock inside me more, so I let him run the show, happy to lie back floating in ecstasy.

Jared devours my pussy with his fingers and his tongue, and it doesn't take long to fall off the ledge. My orgasm shoots through me like fireworks, and I buck and writhe on the bed underneath him while moaning and whispering his name.

"I need you," Jared rasps, putting my legs down on the bed and pushing my thighs wider.

Brushing tangled strands of hair out of my eyes, I peer up at him with so much love and adoration it feels like my heart might burst from my chest. Jared's eyes are smoldering. Almost pitch-black with lust as he lines up his straining cock to my entrance.

"Fuck me now. I'm ready."

Chapter Five
Sydney

With the crown of his dick notched at my pussy, he leans down and kisses me sweetly. "Tell me if it hurts and I'll stop." Excitement mixes with concern in his eyes, and I tenderly cup his face.

"I love you, and I trust you." I already know it's going to hurt. Cayenne gave me a full blow-by-blow account of her first time so I know what to expect.

"You're my everything, Sydney," Jared says as he thrusts inside me.

Pain rips through my core as he plunges through my innocence, and I wince.

Jared stops. Concern is etched upon his face as he holds himself still inside me. "Do you want to stop?"

I shake my head. "No, baby. Keep going." My pussy walls hug his throbbing cock, and we both whimper. "I love the feel of you inside me." It's true. I might be in pain, but I'm awestruck at the feeling of fullness knowing I'm connected to my boyfriend in the most intimate way.

Jared moves slowly, and I can tell it takes effort to be gentle.

The vein in his neck throbs, and his jaw is pulled tight as he slowly pumps in and out of me.

Gradually, the pain eases, and I loosen up, wrapping my legs firmly around his waist and yanking him down on top of me. I kiss him passionately while arching my hips and urging him to move. "Go faster," I rasp in his ear. "Harder. Faster."

"I'm not going to last long, babe."

"I don't care. Just keep going."

Jared pumps another few times, and then he cries out as I feel his hot seed fill me up. Tears stab my eyes. A mix of happy and sad. Wrapping my arms around him, I hold him close as he collapses on his side.

"Syd." His voice sounds choked as he sweeps hair back off my face. "Are you okay?"

I beam at him as I snuggle in closer. "I'm perfect." Not exactly true. A raw ache throbs in my core, but I don't care. I have never felt closer to another living being, and I wish I could stay in this bed with Jared nestled around me and in me forever. The thought is a wake-up call. I pinch his nipple and grab hold of his ass cheeks. "How long will you need to go again?"

His lips curve at the corners as I feel him thickening inside me. "I'm ready whenever you are, babe." Jared flips me over onto my stomach, gently placing a pillow under my head as he lifts my legs and spreads my thighs. Positioning himself at my pussy, he eases inside me slowly this time, from behind, and a contented sigh leaks from my lips. I know I'm going to struggle to walk tomorrow, but I don't care.

If this is all the time we have left, I'm going to make the most of it.

After we're finished, we take a shower together, washing one another as the clock ticks down. We dress in tense silence, the magnitude of our imminent separation weighing heavy on both of us. Jared holds my hand firmly in his as we make our way back downstairs.

Jade appears in the music room a few minutes later. A sob swims up my throat, bouncing off the silent walls.

Sympathy splays across my teacher's face. "I'll give you a few minutes to say your goodbyes," she says before slipping back out to the hallway.

"We should run away," I blurt, clutching his shirt and holding on to him. "Let's just pack our bags and sneak out tonight."

"And go where, baby?" Jared tips my chin up with one finger. "There is no place we can run where your father won't find us. He's got some of the best IT brains working for him. We'd be no match for them. And even if we could outrun them, we don't have enough money to last long."

"You can get gigs, and I'll get a waitressing job or something."

"I love you." His eyes glisten with unshed tears as his lips brush against mine. "It's tempting to run. Don't think I didn't think of that first, because I did, but I won't derail your future, Syd. You're too talented an artist to throw it all away. I want you to go to NYU."

"That's probably a moot point now, anyway." I trail my fingers back and forth across the nape of his neck. "Father won't pay for college when I leave with you at eighteen."

"You'll get a scholarship, and maybe I'll have had a lucky break by then."

"I can't do this," I sob, flinging my arms around his neck and suctioning myself to his body. "I can't live without seeing you. It's going to kill me."

"I know, babe. Believe me, I know. It's killing me too." He presses a fierce kiss to my lips. "But we can do this. We're strong enough to get through it. Just think we'll be together forever as soon as we're old enough to make our own decisions."

"I'm scared." I rest my brow against his, peering deep into his eyes. "I'm scared you'll forget all about me and find someone else."

"That won't happen, babe." He holds me tight, almost crushing me to him. "You and me were written in the stars. Our mums predicted it. You are the only girl for me, Sydney. Please don't ever doubt that." He eases back a little, staring me straight in the eyes. "This is going to be hard, but don't lose sight of what we mean to one another." Lifting my wrist, he presses his lips to my soft skin and delicious tremors dance up my arm. "You are my forever girl. It's you and me for eternity." Delving into his pocket, he removes something silver and drops it onto my palm.

Tears prick my eyes as I pick it up with gentle fingers. It's a Tiffany locket in the shape of a heart.

"Open it," he says, removing something from his other pocket.

I pry the locket open, and my heart swells inside my chest. "I love that picture of us," I say over my sniffles as I smile at the photo taken a few months ago at a sweet-sixteen party. We have our arms locked around one another, and we're wearing matching lovesick grins.

"Me too. I got one framed, and it will be going on my nightstand so your beautiful face is the last thing I see every night and the first thing I open my eyes to every day."

"I love it." I fling my arms around his neck again. "I love you so much, J."

"I love you too, babe, and I'm going to ensure everyone knows it." He eases out of our embrace, and I watch as he straps a leather wristband on his left wrist. A silver panel on top of the leather bracelet is engraved with Sydney 🩶 Jared and my heart melts.

A knock on the door claims our attention. "Jared, it's time," Jade says. "You need to leave before Sydney's protection detail starts asking questions."

"Just one minute," Jared calls out, pulling me to my feet as he stands.

"I don't want to say goodbye," I cry, circling my arms around him and resting my head on his chest.

"Then we won't. This isn't goodbye. This is just an obstacle on our path to forever."

I smile through my tears. "Spoken like a true songwriter." I know Jared has written tons of songs because I have helped with some and he played some other songs for me first before showing them to the guys. "I know this is doubly hard for you because you have to leave the band." I straighten up and cup his cheek. "I'm sorry for being so self-absorbed. I know this is worse for you." He is leaving everything and everyone he knows and loves behind. It's going to be a massive adjustment for him, and I need to pull my big-girl panties up and stop making it harder.

"It's not a competition. It won't be easy for me or you, but I trust in us."

I nod, stretching up to kiss him.

Jared tightens his arms around my back as he dips me low and kisses the living daylights out of me. "Let that keep you going until I can kiss you again," he says when we come up for air.

"I love you," I say as Jade opens the door.

"Not as much as I love you." Jared lifts me off the ground in a bear hug. "Stay strong, beautiful."

"I'll try." I'm fighting tears again when he puts my feet back on the ground.

"We'll talk or text every day, and as soon as I can manage it, I'll come visit."

"Promise?"

"I promise."

With one final kiss, we separate. Wrapping my arms around my waist, I hug myself and shiver as a chill tiptoes the length of my spine. Tears roll down my cheeks as I watch my love walk away.

Jared turns around in the doorway. Tears pool in his eyes, and his voice is choked with emotion when he says, "No matter what happens, always remember how much I love you." He blows me a kiss, and then he is gone, taking a large chunk of my heart with him.

Chapter Six
Sydney

I scream into my pillow, muffling my frustration, after I check my burner cell for the umpteenth time today, and it still displays no new messages or calls. It's been one month since my boyfriend moved to London. One month since the day that was both the best and worst day of my life. I don't regret giving Jared my virginity, but I hate the memory will always be associated with our tearful, painful goodbye.

A knock on my bedroom door forces me to sit up. "Come in," I say in a deadpan voice, expecting one of my brothers. Dad is at a loss what to do with me, and he's been calling in reinforcements because I refuse to speak to him or even acknowledge him. He has ruined my life, and I'm never speaking to him again. Hence why my brothers are showing up on a biweekly basis. Not that it matters. I'm not close to Felix or Tucker, and I barely know their wives. My brothers were fourteen and sixteen, respectively, when I was born, and the age gap was too large. Both were at NYU when Mom died and then out making their way in the world. They were never here when I was growing up, so there was no time to form a bond.

They are virtual strangers. I don't know why Dad thinks I will listen to them.

"Earth to Sydney Shaw." My best friend snaps her fingers in front of my face, yanking me from my inner monologue.

"Oh, it's you."

"Wow." Cayenne flops down on the bed beside me. "Way to make a girl feel wanted."

"Sorry." I hug her briefly. "It's not you. I'm glad you're here. I just thought you were Felix or Tucker. Dad's been sending them up to *talk sense into me*." I use my fingers to make air quotes.

"Fuck him. Fuck them all," my bestie loyally states.

"My sentiments exactly." Grabbing a pillow, I pull it into my body and lie on my side as I check my cell again.

"Still nothing?" Cay asks.

I shake my head as pain stabs me in the heart. "I don't understand it. Apart from our call when he first arrived in London and daily texts the first week, I haven't heard a word from him. It's been complete radio silence. He hasn't even posted anything on social media. It's as if he's disappeared off the face of the earth. It doesn't make sense. I thought maybe his parents had found his secret phone, so I've been emailing him too, and nada. No reply. I'm really worried. What if something has happened to him?"

"I'm sure he's okay. He's probably just busy getting settled into his new house and new school. It doesn't excuse the lack of contact though, and I'm pissed on your behalf."

"Jared would never be too busy for me. Something doesn't add up." Even with the difficulties posed by the time difference, I know Jared would find an opportunity to reach out to me at least once a day.

"Give me his number and his email. Let me try reaching out to him."

"I doubt he'll respond to you if he hasn't responded to me, but I guess it can't hurt to try." I send his contact details to Cayenne's phone, and she busies herself sending him a text and an email while I scroll through my phone, swiping over the succession of texts and calls I've made to my boyfriend on a daily basis since he moved overseas. There are literally hundreds of calls and messages, and that's before I count the emails I've sent him.

"There. Done." Cayenne repockets her cell.

"Jared promised he would text or call every day, so why hasn't he?" I muse out loud.

"I don't know, babe, but try not to worry. We'll get to the bottom of it."

If only it were that easy.

Another week passes without any word, and I'm plotting ways I can buy a plane ticket, steal my passport from Dad's safe, and fly to London to check up on my boyfriend. This is not like Jared. He doesn't make promises and not keep them. Something is wrong. I feel it in my bones.

"Wow, Sydney, you look amazing," Anvil says, his gaze raking over my much thinner frame with obvious interest. Leaning against his locker, he smirks as he blatantly checks me out.

He's such a creep.

Cayenne scowls at him, and I hate we have to involve her ex. Jared moving gave her the push she needed to end things with the cheating bastard. She only approached him today because he's our last hope. Jared didn't reply to Cay either, and I'm desperate enough to reach out to Anvil in the hope he has heard from him.

"Have you heard from Jared recently?" I ask, crossing my arms over my chest and ignoring his attempts to fuck with his ex's head by flirting with me.

"Yep." A smirk ghosts over his lips as all the blood leaches from my face.

Nerves fire at me from all angles. "When?"

"He sent me a text over the weekend." His grin expands as my heart plummets to my toes.

If he's texting with Anvil, it means he's purposely avoiding me. I don't understand it. Why would he do that?

"Here, I'll show you," Anvil adds, whipping out his cell phone.

Cay loops her arm through mine, confirming she fears the worst too.

"It seems he's having a blast in London. All the ladies love his American accent," he says, shoving his cell in my face.

Pain eviscerates me on all sides as I stare at the picture through stinging eyes. It was obviously taken at a party or a bar because the lighting is low and there is a crowd in the background who appears to be dancing. But it's the foreground image that is laying siege to my heart and making it difficult to breathe. Jared has his arms around two stunning brunettes, one girl on either side of him. His grin is wide, his face bleeding happiness, as if he hasn't a care in the world. The girls are smiling at the camera like it's Christmas morning and they've just unwrapped a surprise gift.

Bile swims up my throat, and an anguished cry escapes my lips as I shuck out of Cay's embrace and flee to the bathroom.

I barely make it to the stall in time, bending over the toilet and throwing up. Tears roam freely down my face as I expel the meager contents of my stomach. Pain stabs me repeatedly in the heart, and the crushing pain in my chest is so severe it feels like I'm having a coronary.

"Here." Cay hands me a wad of tissues when I finish vomiting, leaning over me with concern etched on her pretty face. I hadn't even heard her come in.

Slumping on the floor, I lean against the wall and sob.

My bestie joins me, stretching her legs out as she folds one arm around me. "It might not be as bad as it looks."

I bark out a bitter laugh. "I think it's exactly how it looks."

"Jared isn't the cheating type, and he's devoted to you. I bet there's an explanation." She pauses for a few beats. "But if there isn't, if that's legit what it looked like, I'm plotting a gruesome death for him and finding you some prime eye candy to hook up with and rub his nose in it."

"He's changed his mind." Defeat underscores my tone as I rub my eyes. I'm fucking pathetic. Crying over a guy who has tossed me aside so easily. "He lied to me. I bet he never had any intention of coming back for me. He said what he knew I needed to hear and enough to let me know he arrived safe, and now he's cut all ties."

"It doesn't make sense."

I clamber to my feet. "It makes perfect sense now. He's deliberately not talking to me. He must have blocked my cell and my emails. He's moving on with his life, and he doesn't give a fuck what it's doing to me."

Cayenne stands. "You don't really believe that."

"If you'd asked me yesterday, I would have loyally defended him, but that photo paints a very different picture." My lower lip wobbles, and I'm fighting tears again. "I never would have thought him capable of such betrayal, such cruelty, but there is no other explanation." My hands ball into fists at my side. "I'm such a fool. It's obvious all his loving words were lies. He was probably cheating on me when he was here. He *is* best friends with Anvil after all."

Hurt splays across Cay's face, and I feel like a bitch. "Sorry," I whisper, taking her hand. "That was low. I didn't mean it."

"I know you didn't, and it's not like you're lying. Anvil *was* cheating on me, and I enabled it by constantly forgiving him. I just can't believe Jared would be so deceitful. It doesn't seem to be in his nature."

"We didn't know him, Cay. We only knew the side he showed us."

Slowly, she shakes her head. "I'm not buying it. You *do* know him. You've known him your entire life. He wouldn't do this to you."

"I want to believe that. I want to believe everything we shared and everything I know about him to be true, but how do I dispute that photo? You saw it. He looks happy. He's not moping around miserable like I am. I always suspected my feelings were greater than his. He was going off with other girls for years before we got together when I couldn't even look at another guy because they weren't him."

"He told you he was terrified of ruining your friendship and he didn't think you returned his feelings, especially when you didn't seem bothered when he kissed someone else. Do you think he made all that up?"

"I don't know," I say, exiting the stall. Classes have already commenced, so the bathroom is empty, thankfully. We'll be reprimanded for skipping class, but I couldn't care less. The last thing I need is this getting out at school. I'll be the biggest laughingstock. I wouldn't put it past Anvil to share that photo because he's a prick. Most girls in our grade dislike me because I snared Jared. This will only give them ammunition to gloat, and my life will become even more unbearable.

"I don't know what to think anymore," I say over a sigh. "The Jared I thought I knew would never have abandoned me like this. To think I was worried his parents had done something to him." I scoff as I wash and dry my hands and then rinse my mouth out with water. "I'm the biggest idiot. I can't believe I gave him my V-card. Maybe that's what it was all about. He just wanted sex, and after he got it, he moved on."

"You need to talk to him. He's the only one who can confirm the truth."

"How?" I throw my hands in the air as I turn to face my friend. "How can I speak to him when he doesn't answer my calls, texts, social media messages, or emails? And I won't be sending any more. Not now I know he's out partying and hooking up with other girls. Only a moron would continue chasing a guy who clearly wants nothing more to do with her."

I rub a hand across the tightness in my chest, smothering another wave of tears. "How do I come back from this, Cay? He's the one, and I've lost him. My heart is broken, and I don't know how to go on without him. He's been a huge part of my life for so long, and now there's this big dark void, and I fear it's sucking me in and going to suffocate me." Despite my resolve, wracking tears burst from my mouth as I fall apart in my best friend's arms. "It hurts so much." I push the words past the messy ball of emotion clogging my throat. "It feels like I'm dying."

"I'm so sorry, babe." Cay hugs me close. "This is the worst part, but it will get better."

Chapter Seven
Sydney

Another couple of months pass without any word from Jared. My sixteenth birthday comes and goes and nada. Not a peep from him. I'm forced to accept the truth. He is no longer mine. He lied to me. Forgot or chose to abandon the promises he made.

After that day when Anvil showed me the photo, my emotions veered all over the place. I spent days clinging to hope, reminding myself the Jared I knew was the real deal and believing there was some logical explanation. Our parents wanted to separate us. It's not inconceivable to think they have done something. But we have burner cells our parents know nothing about, and our relationship is only a blip in the greater scheme of things. I can't imagine they would go to this much trouble to break us up. So, I do a complete three-sixty, and my mind swings to the only other explanation.

Jared is avoiding me on purpose.

He has blocked me on social media, but my emails, texts, and calls don't bounce back meaning he has received them but has chosen to ignore them.

It makes my blood boil.

Days when I let thoughts like that fester, I chastise myself for continuing to dream and focus on the facts. He has chosen not to reply to my many communications, which confirms he didn't really care about me. Not in the way I care about him. When he said he loved me, he never meant it. Not if he can move on so quickly and so callously.

Dad is losing his patience with me. My schoolwork is suffering because I can't concentrate for shit, and I've lost all interest in my classes and studies. My clothes hang off my much thinner frame, and my pasty skin and sunken eyes make me look like death warmed up. Even on days when I can force some food into my mouth, it doesn't take long before I'm vomiting it back up. I'm not doing it purposely, but it's like my body has lost the will to live, and it's rejecting anything that lands in my stomach.

I don't give a fuck about my appearance or the whispered words and finger-pointing that follow me around the hallways of West Lorian High. It's hard to care when I feel so empty and lost. Hurt and anger are eating me from the inside out and I just want it to stop. I want to stop missing someone who clearly isn't missing me. But how do you shut your emotions off? How do you switch from one emotion to another? How do you force yourself to feel something at times when you feel so numb inside?

The only thing I find comfort in is art, and I spend hours sketching and painting in my room now that Dad has canceled my private lessons with Jade. He told me he'll re-enroll me when my grades improve. I wish it was incentive enough, because I miss Jade, but it doesn't help. Nothing does. I'm drowning without Jared, and I hate myself for being so goddamned weak.

"Mutt is throwing a party Saturday night," Cay says, unpeeling the wrapper from her protein bar as we sit across from one another in the cafeteria. "We should go."

"No thanks," I say, lifting the soup spoon to my lips. Gnawing hunger claws at my insides as I drink the tomato-and-basil-scented liquid. My stomach churns, and I place a hand over it, rubbing my sensitive tummy in the hopes it will settle it. I'm making an effort to eat because I'm physically ill, thanks to all the stress of recent months. No guy is worth developing an eating disorder over. But food tastes off, and nothing goes down easy.

"You can't pine away forever. It's time to get back out there. Jared isn't moping around behind closed doors."

"I'm aware," I snap, not relishing the reminder. That photo is imprinted in my brain, and I suspect it will be for a lifetime.

"Don't bite my head off. I'm just trying to help. You're throwing your life away over a guy who doesn't deserve it." Cay leans across the table and lowers her voice. "Fuck Jared. He's an asshole, and he doesn't deserve you. You're the best person I know, Sydney, and I'm worried about you. You're wasting away, and you're depressed." Tears fill her eyes as she reaches across the table to take my hand. "Don't let him do this to you. I'm begging you. Please."

"I can't help how I feel. If I could snap out of it, I would."

"You should speak to a therapist," she suggests, squeezing my hand. "Maybe you need to go on antidepressants."

I shrug. "Dad won't agree to anything until my GPA improves," I say before swallowing another mouthful of soup. A grimace spreads across my mouth as it lands heavily in my stomach.

"What's wrong?" Cay's brow puckers.

"Taste that." I slide the soup and spoon over the table to her. "Does it taste off to you?"

My bestie tastes the soup without hesitation. "Nope, it tastes good."

"Really?" I rub a hand over my queasy stomach again, praying the few spoonsful I've managed to eat will stay down. "Everything tastes weird to me these days. I'm trying to eat, but even the smell of food nauseates me, and my stomach is super sensitive. I swear I'm not starving myself on purpose." Those first few weeks after Jared left, I had zero appetite, and I didn't even attempt to eat. But it's not like that now. Now, I want to eat, but I can't. I may have broken something irreparably inside me.

"Babe." The panic underscoring Cay's tone alarms me. Her face has turned deathly pale, and I jump to the obvious conclusion.

"You feel sick too? Told you there was something wrong with the soup."

"I don't feel sick." She gets up and claims the seat right beside me. "How long has this been going on?" she whispers.

"What?" I ask, completely perplexed.

"Getting sick. Food tasting weird, smelling weird."

I shrug. "I don't know. A couple months? Maybe more? Why?"

"I don't want to freak you out, but Juniper had those symptoms when she was expecting my niece. Could you be pregnant?"

Time stands still, and our surroundings evaporate as her words slam into my brain. Panic bubbles up my throat as I grip the edge of the table. "Oh my god."

Cay swallows. "When was your last period?" she whispers as I frantically try to remember.

"I don't know," I admit, rummaging in my bag for my cell.

"I can't remember having one recently, but that could be stress, right? Stress can impact your period."

"So can sex."

I don't even bother drilling her with a look as I fumble with my cell, pulling up my calendar and scrolling through it. Blood rushes to my head as I scan back through the months with a lump in my throat. "Oh fuck, Cay. Fuck, fuck, fuck." I clamp a hand over my mouth as reality dawns. I stare at my best friend in a shocked daze. "My last period was two weeks before I had sex with Jared. We didn't use anything. I haven't had a period since."

God, we were so stupid.

I was stupid.

I haven't even once stopped to consider the fact we used no contraception. I'm not on the pill because my father refuses to let me go on birth control until I am seventeen and can legally have sex.

Tension bleeds into the air as the weight of my discovery settles on both of us.

"Let's go." Cay grabs our bags and pulls me out of my seat. "You need to take a pregnancy test."

We sneak out of school through the rear entrance as it's the only way to ditch Dirk. I plan to return to school before the last bell so my bodyguard never knows I skipped class. I can only pray the school doesn't call my dad.

After we buy a few different tests, we head to Cay's house. Her mother works, her younger siblings are at school, and her older sister, Juniper, goes out with her baby daughter, Callie, every afternoon, so we have the house to ourselves. I pee on the sticks, wash my hands, and return to Cay's bedroom to wait for the results to show.

"What are you going to do if it's positive?"

We both know these tests are just a formality. Since Cay mentioned it, I've been connecting all the dots in my head. I'm pregnant. I feel it in my bones. I'm such an idiot for not considering it before now. I've been so heartsick I never stopped to think there could be another reason why I was hormonal and so sick and tired all the time. Even though I've lost weight, my stomach isn't as flat as it used to be. I have a little belly. That should have been my light bulb moment, but it wasn't.

I feel so gullible. Naïve and stupid. And so afraid. "My dad is going to kill me, especially when he finds out the father is Jared."

"We need to find a way to contact him."

"We've been over this already, Cay. He's not communicating with me or you."

"We could ask Anvil to—"

"No." I cut across her instantly. "We are not telling that weasel a goddamn thing. He didn't hesitate to share that picture with everyone at school. He can't be trusted."

"I'm not suggesting we tell him the truth. Just ask him to message Jared to contact you. That it's important."

I shake my head. "That would be like waving a red flag under the nose of a bull. Anvil will sniff a story and try to uncover the truth. No one at school can find out."

Cay sucks in a sharp breath as her arms fold around me. "Look at the tests," she whispers.

Even though I already know what they're going to say, it still requires huge amounts of inner strength to look over at her bedside table where the three tests are situated. I clutch her arms tight as all three confirm my pregnancy.

I can't speak over the emotion wedged in my throat and

pressing down on my chest. Initial numbed shock gives way to potent emotion. Sobs wrack my slight frame as I fall apart in my best friend's arms. This can't be happening. I'm only sixteen. I can barely look after myself. How am I expected to look after a baby? "I want my mom," I cry through blurry tears. "I want my mom."

She would know what to do. Mom would take control and help me make sense of this. Why did she have to die? Why hasn't she been here for me? I was so little when she died that I barely remember her. But it doesn't stop me missing her. Key milestones are always the hardest. Growing up in a house full of men was no picnic, and it was largely just Dad and me. Dad struggles to show his emotions, but he did his best. Until recently, I never doubted his love or the efforts he took to protect me.

Since that shit went down with the Kings, Herman Shaw is different. It's like a stranger is wearing his skin. He's colder, less affectionate, and he is quick to lose his temper.

For the first time in my life, I am afraid of my father.

Afraid to tell him his little girl got knocked up by the son of his new enemy.

A chill creeps up my spine, and a full-body shudder works its way through me. "This is bad, Cay. So freaking bad. I can't tell my father." I shuck out of her embrace and turn around to face her on the bed with my legs crossed. "He will go crazy."

"You have options," she softly says.

"I'm keeping it." There is no hesitation despite my initial concerns. "I don't care I'm only sixteen and not ready to be a mother. I'll learn." My hands gravitate to my stomach, and I carefully place my palms there. "J may no longer love me, but I love him, and I already love our baby." I eyeball my friend. "This innocent baby doesn't deserve to die because we were dumb. I don't fault anyone who makes the decision to get an abortion. That is their decision and their right, just like this is mine. I could never abort Jared's baby. I want it."

"Then we need to make plans. Starting with finding a way to tell Jared." Her lips purse. "I don't care whether he's moved on. It takes two to make a baby, and he has a responsibility now. To both of you. You won't be alone. You'll have me, but he needs to be involved too."

"Even if he doesn't want me, he will want his child."

I hope.

It's not like I can claim to know him anymore.

"I can't keep this from him. At the very least, he needs to know."

THE PRESENT

Chapter Eight
Sydney

"Happy birthday, cuz!" Ashley shrieks through the screen of my cell phone, almost damaging my eardrums.

"Thanks though I'm trying to forget I'm twenty-six," I reply, racing around the kitchen of my penthouse apartment, tidying it up before I have to leave for work.

"Twenty-six is far from ancient, Syd. I thought you were all about embracing life these days."

"I am," I say, closing a drawer with my hip before I slurp the last dregs of my coffee. I stare at my cousin's pretty face as we video chat. "Twenty-six means I should probably start adulting now, and I'm really not ready for it."

"You do you, babe," my cousin says as loud rock music suddenly blares in the background. California is nine hours behind Italy, which means it's close to midnight on Friday night, and Ash is probably hosting a party. She's famous for them. "Ares," she shouts over her shoulder at one of her husbands. "Turn that down. I'm trying to talk to Sydney."

The music dies, and my ears give silent thanks. "Sup, Syd?"

Ares says, popping his head over Ash's shoulder. "How's Florence treating you?"

"Florence is good. Great. When are you guys coming for a visit?"

"As soon as things die down here, we'll be on a plane. Promise," Jase says, materializing on the other side of my cousin. He drapes his arm around her shoulders, and Ares glares at it like he'd love to chop the limb off his body. I don't know how my cousin does it. I can't manage a relationship with one guy for more than a couple months, yet Ashley makes marriage to three alphas look like a cakewalk.

"Did you like your flowers?" Chad asks, elbowing Ares out of the way. Ares lets loose a slew of expletives as he disappears from view, and my lips curve at the corners. There is never a dull moment in that house.

"I love them. Thanks. It was really sweet of you guys to remember my birthday." Along with the flowers, there were several expensive gifts—all carefully chosen by my cousin with my taste in mind.

Ashley is the only member of my family I talk to regularly. I hear from my brothers at Christmas, and I received birthday cards and gifts this week, but that's our only contact. They have never made any effort with me, so why should I make any with them? I feel bad my nieces and nephews don't know me very well, but it's not my fault their fathers have always sided with my asshole dad instead of sticking up for me. They bought into the whole "Sydney is troubled and can't look after herself" bullshit Herman Shaw successfully peddled for years.

I know I didn't help my cause by going completely off the rails. In my defense, I had legit reasons. I haven't touched drugs in six years, and I don't drink alcohol to excess anymore. I have turned my life around. I moved overseas. I live alone, and I'm financially independent. I eat well and exercise. I have a tight-knit group of friends. I paint. And I adore my job at the art gallery.

The only thing missing is love, but I've long ago given up on that.

Before my mind can go *there*, I move my phone around to show Ash and the guys the gorgeous lily and rose bouquet propped stylishly in one of my large glass vases. "They're beautiful, and my apartment smells amazing."

"Woah! Who are the other flowers from?" Ashley inquires, a devilish glint appearing in her eyes.

"No need to get excited. They're from Giorgio."

"I thought you kicked him to the curb?" Ash scrunches up her nose.

"I did." I heave a sigh.

"And that's our cue to leave," Jase says. He blows a kiss at the screen. "Happy birthday, Syd."

"Have a good one, sweetheart," Chad adds, also blowing me a kiss before both guys disappear.

"Are you having second thoughts about Gio?"

"Nope. He's just having a hard time letting go."

"Aw, the poor guy. He must not have gotten the memo my cousin's a heartbreaker."

I snort out a laugh as I place a tablet in the dishwasher and switch it on. "Hardly."

"Apart from 'he who shall not be named,' have you ever not dumped a guy or been left heartbroken?"

I pad through my open-plan living, dining, and kitchen area and along the hallway toward the bedrooms. "My heart wasn't exactly intact after that fiasco with Hunt."

"Puh-lease," Ashley scoffs. "That was a fake arranged marriage, and you were never into Sawyer."

"This is a non-conversation anyway. Why are we discussing this?" Propping my cell on my bedside table, I strip off my silk nightdress and wrap a towel around my body.

"You haven't moved on," she quietly says. "I hate that for you."

I shrug, trying to ignore the usual stabbing pain in my heart anytime I think of Jared. "I don't need a man to be happy. I'm content in myself, and it's taken me a long time to get to this place."

"I'm proud of you, but I want you to experience love. No one deserves it more than you." Ashley is the only other person, besides Cayenne, who knows exactly what I've been through. I only told her recently what went down when I was sixteen, and she was shocked and disgusted. She's never had much time for Dad anyway, but she hates his guts almost as much as I do now.

"I don't know if I'll ever feel that way about anyone again or if I even want to. I'm not short of dates, and if I want sex, I can find it. For now, that suits me perfectly. I've got to go, Ash," I say, glancing at the time, "or I won't make it to work on time."

"I'll call you next week at our usual time."

"Love you. Thanks for calling, and thanks for the birthday flowers and gifts."

"Love you too. Enjoy the rest of your day, and don't work too hard!"

Forty minutes later, I bounce from my apartment building located above Ponte Vecchio with a spring in my step. Summer in Florence is magical. Actually, year-round in Florence is magical. When I was first researching locations in Italy to relocate to, a couple years ago, I focused on seaside towns. I always daydreamed about a little house by the ocean, but then I happened across Florence, and I fell in love with the city known as the birthplace of the Renaissance. It's over an hour's drive to the nearest beach, but I didn't let that sway me. I just knew Florence was the place for me the minute I found it.

It's not surprising, really, when it's been voted the most beautiful city in the world in the past and it's renowned for art, architecture, and fashion. You won't find skyscrapers here—only an abundance of carefully preserved classic and neoclassic buildings, pristine streets you could eat your dinner off, stunning gardens and parks, and the great dome of the Cathedral of Santa Maria del Fiore, which stands proudly above all other structures in the thriving city. Giotto's Bell Tower is the highest vantage point to view the city, but it's not quite as tall as the dome that dominates the city skyline.

One of my favorite things to do is wander around the Piazza della Signoria, a distinctively medieval square that showcases stunning historic buildings dating back centuries. Palazzo Vecchio, a palace that was once the center of Florence, looms over the square like a majestic ruler with its tall tower and impressive architecture. Elaborate ceilings and the most exquisite frescoes line the walls inside the ancient palace. I usually stop first for a latte and a pistachio-cream *cornetti* before I explore the magnificent sculptures housed in the Loggia dei Lanzi and admire the sublime skill of the master craftsmen who created the Fountain of Neptune.

Some of Florence's and Italy's most famous painters have walked these streets before me, and I can almost feel their ghostly hands guiding me to explore their impressive city. This place is an artist's paradise. From the wealth of art museums and galleries to the myriad of stunning scenery to spark every imagination and the eclectic mix of the creative community, no place has ever felt more like home. Outdoor painting is a regular occurrence for me. Whether it's painting one of the city's lush gardens, an ancient monastery, the palace, one of the oldest buildings, or the Ponte Vecchio—the famous old bridge that arches over the river Arno—with its quaint collection of shops on either side, which makes it feel more like an enclosed road than a bridge, there is no shortage of inspiration.

Florence feeds my soul.

It's been a breath of fresh air for me.

Strolling around the city is like stepping into the past. You can feel the history all around you though it's equally modern in sophistication. I don't even have a car. I have a bicycle, and I walk a lot. The small boutique gallery I work at is only a ten-minute walk from my penthouse, and the city center is a twenty-minute walk.

Everything is on my doorstep, and I love how free I feel here. Cay visits several times during the year, but I suspect I will see less of her now Jerry has popped the question and they're planning their wedding for later in the year.

I smile as I pass tourists on the bridge, not minding how crowded the city gets in the summer months. It never feels as claustrophobic as New York.

Though I miss The Big Apple, it will never be home.

Too many bad memories are attached to the city for me to ever feel happy there again.

Chapter Nine
Sydney

Salt water from the Arno lingers in the air as I make my way over the Ponte Vecchio, basking in the glorious sunshine as I smile and wave at the people passing by. Scents of coffee and fresh pastries tickle my nostrils as I pick up my pace and head toward the Neptune Art Gallery building. Named after the famous fountain at the Piazza della Signoria, it occupies prime real estate a couple blocks from the bridge. The building dates back to 1554, and it has a gorgeous courtyard and garden that we make use of during the summer for outdoor showings.

"*Buongiorno*." Francesca, the owner, greets me with a kiss and a mimosa when I step inside the air-conditioned gallery. "*Buon compleanno*."

"*Grazie*." I kiss both her cheeks.

"Are you sure you don't want to take the day off?" she asks as I head toward the staff area at the back of the large showroom.

Although I am fluent in Italian, thanks to my language degree from NYU, we mostly speak English for Gemma's benefit. Gemma is from Liverpool, and she started working here eight months ago. She didn't know a word of Italian when she first arrived, but she came highly recommended by a London gallery where she had worked post-graduation. She knows a few words now, but we have gotten into the habit of speaking English for her benefit. Gemma is three years younger than me, and I have taken her under my wing—she's good people and a good friend. We have found a little ex-pats crew to hang around with and some Italian friends too.

"Heads-up," Gemma says, emerging from the staff room carrying a small, gift-wrapped box. "I have it on good authority that Giorgio will be dropping by shortly to surprise the birthday girl."

A groan leaves my lips. Gemma is casually dating one of Gio's friends, and I'm hoping it won't become awkward. I ended things with Gio six weeks ago, after a few months of dating, but he seems determined to win me back. He's a charming, good-looking guy. An architect with his own firm. I like him, and I would have been content to date him for a while longer if he hadn't started talking about marriage and telling me he loved me countless times a day. I realized it would be unfair to string him along, when I know I won't ever return those feelings, so I broke it off. But he seems to think he can change my mind, and nothing I say deters him.

"Speak of the devil," Gemma mutters under her breath, jerking her head over my shoulder.

Smoothing a hand down the front of my sleeveless knee-length teal silk dress, I turn around and smile at my approaching ex. He looks handsome, as usual, in his gray suit and light-blue shirt. Warm brown eyes latch on to mine as Gio closes the distance between us, carrying a bottle of champagne and a cake box. "*Bella.*" He leans in and kisses me on both cheeks. "Happy birthday, Sydney." His English is precise, perfected at the best local private school and supplemented with personal lessons.

"Thank you, Gio."

He hands me the gifts one at a time, and I thank him profusely while stating he really shouldn't have gone to all this trouble. He already sent me flowers, so this is definitely overkill. Still, it's super sweet and very indicative of the kind of man Gio is. Someday, he will make some woman very happy. I wish it could have been me, but I can't force feelings where they don't exist. I would insist on refusing the gifts, but that would hurt him, and I can't do it.

"You're a good friend," I say, licking my lips as I ogle the delicious freshly baked cake from my favorite bakery.

He frowns momentarily before his features smooth out. "I was hoping to take you out for dinner tonight."

My heart sinks. Guess there is no avoiding an unpleasant conversation. "That's a lovely thought, Gio, but I'll have to decline. I already have plans."

"Perhaps another time?"

"I don't think so," I softly say.

"You're not going to change your mind, are you?"

I shake my head. "I'm sorry."

"Don't be, *bella*." He brings my hand to his lips and gently kisses my fingers. "I appreciate your honesty. I had to try."

"I meant what I said, Gio. It's not you."

"It's the American. The one who broke your heart."

My cheeks pink. I told him that in confidence, and I don't appreciate him blurting it out in front of my colleagues, even if I know there was no malicious intent. At least I didn't give him Jared's name or tell him the hot drummer from Ruminate is the one who ruined me for all others. That would have been infinitely more embarrassing.

"Yes. I wish you all the best, Gio. Thank you again for the

gifts, but I need to get ready. The doors open in twenty minutes."

"Take care, Sydney." His shoulders slump as he walks away, and I feel like the world's biggest bitch.

"He's a decent guy. I'm glad he finally got the memo," Gemma says, the words coming out clipped and nasally in her distinctive Scouse accent. She cocks her head to one side. "What American was he talking about?"

I knew she wouldn't let that go.

"Just someone from my past. He's not important."

Her lips twitch. "If you say so."

"I do."

Deciding to drop it, at least for now, she takes the champagne and cake box from my hands. "At least we've got champagne to toast the birthday girl with later before we head out on the town." Waving the bottle in the air, she waggles her brows, and I wonder what mischief she has planned for tonight. I gave her free rein to organize my birthday night out because she loves event planning. "I'll put these in the fridge."

The morning flies by, and the gallery is busy. Though most are just tourists browsing, we sell one of our bigger pieces, by a new local talent who is going to blow up fast, which is cause for additional celebration.

Francesca is busy on calls with a couple of VIP prospective clients, so I'm flitting around the gallery, attending to a million and one things, while I try to nail down the final details of the big exhibition we're hosting in six weeks.

Riposa arrives and our door closes for a couple hours, giving us a much-needed breather.

Francesca, Gemma, Ricardo, and Felipe sing happy birthday to me, and then we cut the cake, all huddled around the front desk area. Licking my lips, I'm just about to devour my slice of cake when the buzzer sounds, alerting us to someone outside the gallery.

"It's probably a tourist who doesn't understand *riposa* means we're closed, like every other shop and business in the middle of the day," Gemma says, rolling her eyes.

A lot of businesses close for three hours, and most employees head home before returning to their workplace later. Usually, Gemma and I go out for lunch or make lunch at my place and either eat it sitting at the table on my terrace or we head to the park with a picnic basket. It's busy today, so we're all taking advantage of the downtime to catch up on admin and stuff.

"He's early." Excitement lights up Francesca's face, and I'm guessing it's one of the VIP clients she was talking to on the phone this morning. "I'll let him in." Quickly smoothing the wrinkles out of her designer skirt suit, she lifts her shoulders, thrusting them back, and strides confidently to the door. We can't see who it is from here because we don't have a clear view of the entrance, but all will be revealed in due course.

Francesca greets the client, and the responding voices are male and female.

The oddest sensation washes over me, and I wet my suddenly dry lips, keeping my back to the entrance, unlike my coworkers who are straining their necks and trying to see who it is.

Footsteps approach, and my heart is racing like crazy.

What the fuck is up with that?

"We're interrupting. I'm sorry," a man with a deep male voice says. "We can come back at the prearranged time."

All the blood drains from my body when I hear his voice. I grip the edge of the desk as my vision blurs, my head spins, and my body sways. His voice is deeper than I remember, but I would know it anywhere. Not just because I've heard him speak in countless interviews over the years.

Never moving on from the boy who became a massive rock star, adored and admired by millions of people around the globe, is its own form of torture.

No matter how hard I have tried to forget Jared, it's impossible when his face is plastered across social media and his words dominate the airwaves.

"That won't be necessary," Francesca says in her professional voice. "It's my gallery manager's birthday today. We have more than enough cake, and I'm sure Sydney won't mind sharing."

Shock is splayed across Gemma's face, and her cheeks are flushed. Our male colleagues are equally excited, but they hide their reaction better. We were joking earlier that the new clients were rock stars because a host of them are in town for the MTV awards. I hadn't checked the lineup, because what are the fucking chances I move to Florence and the man who has haunted my dreams for years shows up in my neck of the woods? You couldn't make this shit up if you tried.

Gemma is giving me weird eyes, and I know I'm being rude not turning around or responding to Francesca's statement, but I physically cannot move. I am rooted to the spot and shaking all over as pure terror shoots through my veins. Without conscious thought, my fingers wind around the silver Tiffany locket resting on my collarbone.

This cannot be happening.

"Sydney?" A rough quality spears through Jared's tone, and I hear him take a step closer. "Sydney Shaw?"

Gemma's eyes pop wide, and I feel eyeballs on me from both sides.

Shit, shit, shit.

Briefly, I close my eyes and beg my body to get with the program.

I can do this.

I can act unaffected.

I've had experience faking it with the best, and I just need to put on the show of a lifetime.

There will be plenty of time to fall apart in private after he's gone.

Ignoring the shocked and curious gazes of my friends and coworkers, I plaster the biggest faux smile on my face and turn around to face the boy who ripped through my heart like a juggernaut.

Chapter Ten
Sydney

With my heart hammering against my rib cage, I lift my eyes and stare at my ex, keeping a forced pleasant smile fixed on my face.

Fuck.

Fuck.

Jared looks so incredibly hot in the flesh, and it's not fair.

No man should be that talented *and* that good-looking.

A tight black T-shirt molds to his broad shoulders and carved chest and abs. Sculpted biceps and toned, tanned, tattooed arms give new meaning to arm porn. A few leather bands encircle one wrist, a flashy expensive watch is strapped to the other, and a silver chain adorns his neck. Custom fit dark denims hug muscular thighs and lean legs. Blinding-white Nikes cover his feet, looking like he just plucked them off a store shelf.

The last time I saw him, Jared was still a boy in transition. But he's definitely all man now. Unlike his two bandmates, Jared wears his hair short. Shorn tight at the sides and long on top and at the front with disheveled strands of inky black hair brushing his brow. His jawline is sharper, his skin golden from the sun. Defined cheekbones, full lips, and the stylish layer of black stubble on his chin and cheeks only adds to the appeal. Jared is one sexy beautiful man, and I hate how my traitorous fingers itch with a craving to explore his exquisite face and tempting body.

Startling blue eyes, the color of the sky on a bright summer's day, gaze back at me, and it's like rewinding time. Memories flit through my mind despite the walls I've thrown up around my head and my heart. Jared's presence is larger than life, and it's bringing everything to the surface again.

Pain floods every part of me, and it's a miracle I'm still upright.

Looking at him hurts. It shouldn't after all this time, but it does.

It raises so many questions I never had answers to.

It reminds me of everything I lost and how he was the catalyst for my life turning to shit.

While I've been checking him out, his eyes have been roaming over me too. My pulse throbs in my neck, and it takes considerable effort to hold his stare and not betray any emotion. Inside, I'm a tornado about to wreak havoc. Rage is mushrooming inside me, fueled by the constant pain of his abandonment and betrayal. On the outside, I wear a mask of professional coolness as I inwardly question the nerve of him to stand before me like he didn't destroy my world and almost ruin me to the point of no return.

How fucking dare he stand there checking me out, probing my face, like he's trying to pry the truth from my head as if he is owed anything by me?

Tension is thick in the silent air, and it's obvious to everyone we have history.

"Do you know her?" the tall woman clinging to Jared's arm

asks, her ice-blue eyes narrowing in suspicion as she stares at me.

Even if her heavily accented voice didn't give her away, I would know who she is. We all do. Her face has been plastered everywhere since she started dating one of the hottest rock stars on the planet.

Vittoria Russo was a barely known model until she started dating Jared and he catapulted her into the spotlight. Long brown hair hangs in pristine sheets down her back as she straightens her six-foot frame to full height. With her broad shoulders, long legs, sharp facial features, and a cutting expression, she looks like an Amazonian warrior minus the tan, fighting skills, and requisite muscle tone. Her long white silk dress hugs her slender body, leaving nothing to the imagination. Thin with small breasts, pert nipples poking through the fabric of her dress, minimal hips, and the barest dip at her waist, she epitomizes that androgynous shape the fashion industry seems to adore these days.

It's like Jared purposely set out to find someone who looks nothing like me. Except for above-average height, we have nothing in common.

"Jared." She enunciates the vowels as she digs long mani-cured nails into the bare flesh of his arm, claiming his attention.

Jared breaks our face-off to look at his fiancée. "Did you say something?"

I feel Gemma's eyes boring a hole in the side of my face, but I avoid looking at her.

"Do you know this girl?" Vittoria hisses, lifting her other hand to Jared's arm, ensuring I get an up-close view of the ostentatious rock on her ring finger.

"Our parents were friends when we were kids," Jared explains, leaving out the most important part of our history. "I haven't seen Sydney in over ten years." His eyes drill into hers as he snakes his arm around her back and holds her close to his side.

"What a funny coincidence," Francesca says over a glowing fake grin, eager to get the meeting back on track, no doubt.

"I'll tidy this up so you can show the clients around," I say, pleased my voice is even and devoid of the turmoil churning in my gut.

A muscle clenches in Jared's jaw as he swings his gaze back to mine. His hand tightens around his fiancée as he levels a glare in my direction.

Like, what the fuck?

What gives him the right to glare at me?

My natural instinct is to glare back, but Francesca would kick my ass all over Florence if I cost her such a lucrative client. His smirk is firmly in place as he leans in to kiss Vittoria's cheek. I'm tempted to throw the cake in his face, but I wouldn't waste good cake on that lying, cheating asshole. Visions of lunging at him and clawing my nails down his face race through my mind, and it's tempting. So fucking tempting. But this job isn't worth losing over my piece-of-shit ex.

Smiling sweetly at the loathsome couple, I say, "Enjoy your viewing," and I grab the cake and stride with confidence toward the rear of the showroom with my coworkers hot on my heels.

Setting the plate down on the counter in the staff room, I grip the edge and count to ten as I close my eyes and try to talk myself off the ledge.

The door shuts with a soft snick, and I brace myself for the interrogation that's sure to come.

"Babe, are you okay?" Gemma asks, coming up alongside me. Her voice is laced with curiosity and concern as she deposits plates and silverware on the counter.

"No," I truthfully admit. I'm not in the habit of lying to my friends or colleagues.

"Wild guess," Felipe says as I turn around. "He wouldn't happen to be the American Giorgio mentioned earlier?"

I give him a curt nod, and Gemma's eyes pop wide.

"You were with Jared Dempsey?" she blurts, shock and awe littering her tone.

I'm glad the door is closed and these old walls are thick. "I knew him as Jared King. Dempsey is his stage name," I admit, hating how my voice trembles. Dempsey is his mother's maiden name and I'm guessing he chose to use it for privacy. Not that it matters. Unless you live under a rock, you know who Jared is whether you know him as Dempsey or King.

"Here." Ricardo hands me a tumbler of amber liquid. "For the shock."

"Thanks." I knock the whiskey back in one go, welcoming the burn as it glides down my throat into my belly.

Gemma guides me to the small table, and I join my coworkers in sitting around it. Three sets of expectant eyes wait for me to elaborate. "We grew up together. He was my best friend, and then he became more. Our parents had a falling out, and he moved overseas with his family, and our relationship ended acrimoniously. I haven't seen him since." I haven't told any lies, but it's not the full truth. I will tell Gemma if she asks in private, but I don't know Felipe or Ricardo well enough to divulge the harsh realities of my breakup and the downward spiral it sent me on.

Gemma levels me with a knowing look. One that says "I know there is more to this story and I want all the deets." I subtly nod as the door opens, and Francesca steps into the room. "Jared is very interested in Amadeo," she says, eyeballing me. "I understand there is some personal conflict, but you know his work best, and I'd like you to talk Jared through the piece he likes."

Of course, he would home in on my recent local find.

Amadeo is a young male contemporary artist with huge talent and massive potential. A famous celebrity buying one of his works would be a big deal, and it could open the door to his success. I cannot say no. To my boss or my favorite artist, so I stand, willing myself to keep it together.

"No problem," I lie, fixing a fresh fake smile on my face as I head out of the staff room with Francesca.

Jared is standing in front of my favorite painting, wearing an intense expression as he examines the vivid masterpiece with his arms folded over his chest. Beside him, Vittoria is typing away on her cell, looking pale and disinterested.

"As I was saying," Francesca says, coming to a stop on Jared's left. "Sydney discovered Amadeo, and she knows his work best. She can talk you through his thought process and help you to choose the perfect painting for your new home."

"Paintings," Vittoria confirms, sliding her cell in her purse and wrapping her arms possessively around her fiancé. "Our house in Florence ten thousand square feet. Lot of rooms to furnish." Her English accent is clipped, her words uncertain.

"Perhaps if you tell me which rooms you are looking to furnish and what the aspect and lighting is, I can suggest pieces that might work," I supply.

"I like this one," Jared says, not taking his eyes from the large canvas in front of him. "What does it mean?"

Stepping up beside him, I focus on the magnum opus hanging on display. "This is Amadeo's signature piece. His largest and most intricate work. His best to date and my personal favorite from his collection." I clear my throat and avoid looking at Jared as I attempt to explain the meaning behind the striking painting. "Naturally inquisitive from an early age, Amadeo strives to provide meaning to the abstract, the undiscovered, and the inexplicable in our world."

I move closer to the painting, spellbound by it like always.

No matter how often I stare at it, it still takes my breath away. "His father is a neurologist and a scientist. Growing up, Amadeo became fascinated with the complexities of the human brain. He has studied thousands of brain X-rays and scans and various forms of brain injury and disease. This work depicts his attempts to understand the various facets of the most complex organ in the human body."

"What does each image represent?" Jared asks, his eyes skimming across the different painted images of cross sections of the brain. There are more than fifty, in various colors and patterns, bursting across the canvas in a way that draws the eye.

My lips twitch. "That's the beauty and intelligence of this piece." Hovering my finger over one image, I air trace the word embedded in the swirling matter. "Each image represents a different emotion, or movement, or sense. A varied behavior or sign of intelligence. It is Amadeo's attempt to understand something no human has ever fully understood. Because it's a puzzle, so is his work. Embedded in each image is a word that describes what it means to him."

"I don't see words," Vittoria says, "but I like the colors."

It could be my imagination, but I think Jared winces.

"Do you know each word?" he asks, turning to stare at me.

I shake my head. "I have spent hours inspecting this painting up close, and I have only managed to decipher a few."

"He doesn't want it to be decipherable," Jared surmises. "Amadeo wants everyone to find their own meaning behind it."

I can't stop the smile ghosting over my mouth. "Yes. It's a highly personable piece. Amadeo's hope is that whoever buys this painting will find hidden meaning or altered meaning."

"It can change to reflect different periods in a person's life," Jared correctly guesses again.

I bob my head. "It's meaning will vary over time. What one person sees will be different to another."

"I love it," Jared says, staring in awe at the work. "I'll take it."

"Excellent." Francesca can barely conceal her excitement. The commission will be considerable. "I'll ask Gemma to print out the paperwork. Sydney can answer any questions you may have," she says, throwing me to the wolves before walking off.

"Do you still paint?" he asks without taking his eyes from the Amadeo.

"Yes."

Vittoria's eyes narrow to slits before she rakes a derisory look over my body. My middle finger twitches, so I shove my hands in my pockets to contain any rash outbursts that might cost me my job.

Jared turns to look at me, pretending not to see the scowl on his fiancée's face. "Are any of your paintings here?"

I shake my head.

"Why not?"

"My work isn't for sale." Francesca has offered me an exhibition on several occasions, but I always decline. Her praise and belief in me bolstered my confidence, but I'm not ready to put myself out there. I may never be. And I'm okay with that. I paint in my free time and work a job where I help other artists to fulfill their dreams. That is more than enough for me. Compared to the cage I was living in for years, this is the ultimate freedom. I get to choose what I do with my life, and right now, I'm exactly where I want to be, doing what I love.

"Wasn't that your dream?" His eyes pierce mine, searching and searching, but he'll never find whatever it is he's looking for.

"Dreams change, and I'm no longer that girl."

You made sure of that.

I think it, but I don't say it, working hard to school my features into a neutral line. It was easy to get caught up in my passion for art and for Amadeo's work and to temporarily forget who this man is to me and what he's done.

"That's probably not a bad thing." The glare is firmly back on his face, and inside I'm screaming and throwing punches at him.

Why does he seem angry at me when I'm the only one entitled to that emotion?

If this was any other situation, I'd be spitting in his face and kicking him in the balls.

I have often wondered what would happen if I saw him again. How I would react. What we would say.

Never in a million years did I predict it going down like this.

I remember the headlines a couple of years ago announcing Jared's engagement after only a few months of dating. It devastated me. That was already a dark time in my life. When Father had forced me into marrying the son of his business partner. The marriage was fake, yet Sawyer and I had slept together the night of our wedding, and I had thought maybe it wouldn't be so bad. Until he rejected me, leaving me alone in his soul-sucking obsessively clean penthouse with a head full of depressing thoughts and every mistake I'd ever made in my life replaying on a loop in my brain.

I'd cried myself to sleep most every night.

I'm sure Sawyer thought it was over him. But he was barely a blip.

It's always been about Jared.

No matter how hard I have tried to evict him from my head and my heart, he stubbornly refuses to leave, claiming squatter's rights and the intent to reside there permanently.

I hate him. I truly do. But hate and love toe a very fine line, and the love I had for him has never gone away.

It's pathetic. Every time I think of him, I feel like that foolish, weak, gullible fifteen-year-old who gave everything to a guy who toyed with her emotions.

I also remember, as clear as if it was yesterday, him telling me I was the only one and I'd be his wife someday.

I guess there is no end to his cruelty.

A new layer of pain joins the bubbling hatred swirling in my veins as I watch his model fiancée digging her proverbial claws in her man. She may as well hold up a sign reading, "He's mine. Back off bitches." I wonder if there's a reason she seems insecure. Maybe Jared got a taste for cheating as a teenager and he no longer knows the meaning of loyalty and faithfulness? I'm sure he has groupies throwing themselves at him wherever he goes and sex on tap.

I should probably feel sorry for her, but she's too calculating and transparent to deserve any pity.

I'd like to say I'm shocked Jared has ended up with someone like her, but it's just further proof I did not know him like I thought I did.

Or perhaps it's karma finally come to collect. It would serve him right.

"Honey." Vittoria clutches his arm tight as she bends over and fake gags.

"Shit." Jared crouches down, concern etched all over his face. "What can I do?"

She dry retches, her face turning pale, and all the blood leaches from my skin.

"Can we go?" she pleads, stumbling against him like her gangly giraffe legs are about to go out from under her.

"Of course." Jared looks over at me as he props his fiancée up, holding a firm arm around her shoulders as he tucks her protectively into his side. "Could you arrange for Francesca to email the paperwork to my assistant? She has my business card."

"No problem." A lump rises in my throat.

"Please keep secret," Vittoria says, resting her head on Jared's chest as she pins me with a smug look. "No one knows about baby." She palms her flat stomach, confirming my suspicion, and something inherent dies inside me. "Or we bought house in Florence to raise family."

She might as well have taken a chainsaw to my heart.

It would probably hurt less.

Somehow, I force myself to nod as I clutch my locket and desperately try to hold myself together. At least until they leave and I can break down in private. Standing rooted in place, I watch Jared lovingly cradle his pregnant fiancée against his chest and escort her out the door with a stabbing pain in my heart.

Chapter Eleven
Jared

After helping Toria into the back seat of the chauffeured car, I slide in beside her and ask the driver to crank the AC to the max. Grabbing my backpack off the floor where I left it, I remove the ginger biscuits, paper bag, and a bottle of water. "Here," I say as my girlfriend lies down on the seat, resting her head on my lap. "Tor, you need to sit up and wear your seat belt."

"Sick," she mumbles, clutching her stomach and dry heaving.

"It's not safe," I admonish, gently lifting her into a seated position and strapping the belt around her. Traffic is crazy in the city, not helped by the influx of crowds who have descended on Florence for the awards ceremony tomorrow night. "Lean against me," I suggest as I hand her the paper bag. I hate seeing her so sick, and it seems almost constant since we found out she's pregnant a month ago. I don't know who coined the phrase morning sickness, but it's woefully inadequate. Try all-morning and all-night sickness, and it would be more accurate. At least in Toria's case.

She's not handling it well. I'm doing my best to help, but I haven't been around much. That will end with our last show in five weeks, and then I'll have more time to take care of her.

I rub her back as she dry retches into the bag. She hasn't eaten anything today, and this can't be good for the baby. We have three days at home in the US, after the awards show, before the last leg of the tour kicks off again, and I plan to see her ob-gyn and demand he do something to help her. Toria has never been a big eater, but lately it's a joke.

"I fucking hate this," she says in her heavily accented tone, leaning her head against my shoulder and snatching the water from my hand.

I offer her the ginger cookies, but she shakes her head.

"It won't last forever. Most women's nausea ends after the first trimester." I've been reading a pregnancy book I bought online in my downtime. It would be helpful if I could ask my mother or my sister for advice, but Mum and Heather despise Toria, and I'm waiting until the last possible moment to break the news to them.

Which reminds me.

"You shouldn't have mentioned anything about the baby at the gallery," I say, rubbing her back. I don't think Sydney would say anything to anyone, but it's clear I don't know her anymore. When she wasn't acting indifferent, I didn't miss the hostile looks thrown my way. Or the way all the color drained from her face when Toria blabbed about the baby.

What the fuck right does Syd have to look at me like I'm her worst enemy? If anyone has a right to play that card, it's me. I'd like to say, after ten years, I'm over her betrayal, but it would be a lie.

Sydney Shaw stuck her claws in me as a young kid, and I've got the scars to prove it. Hurt scores my chest as I think of her, and how amazing we were together, like always. I still don't understand why or how it all went wrong. Why she did what she did. I don't think I'll ever get over it. As long as I live, I'll carry that pain with me.

I was willing to give her everything.

I laid it all on the line, and she lied to me.

Broke my heart without a second thought.

She was right when she said that girl was gone.

I learned that lesson the hard way.

"I saw the way you looked at her. It's *her*, isn't it?" Toria spits out the words like they're poison.

When I proposed, I felt it was only fair to warn Toria of my limitations and what she was signing up to. I didn't mention Sydney by name or tell her the full story, but Toria knows I'm incapable of loving her because my heart was torn apart as a teenager and there's still a gaping Sydney-shaped hole in it. That's not the only reason I'll never love her, but there's no point dwelling on it. The baby changed everything. I can't shirk my responsibilities to her or my unborn child even if I look at that monstrosity on her ring finger and feel like throwing up.

This is not what I planned for my future, but such is life.

"Answer me!" she snaps as the driver turns the corner that leads to the five-star hotel we're staying at.

Only the fact she's pregnant with my kid holds my temper in check. "Yes, she's the one."

"She's fat." I don't know if it's a model thing or a Vittoria Russo thing, but she measures everyone by the sum of their looks. It's her least endearing quality, and if I'd seen it when we first started hooking up, I would have tossed her to the curb without hesitation.

"She's not, and what has that got to do with anything?" Sydney has the perfect body. Slim with curves in all the right places. The girl I loved and adored has grown into a stunningly beautiful woman with grace and confidence. Even though I still hate her for what she did to me, I can't deny the pride I felt as she talked passionately and intelligently about the painting I bought.

"She needs understand place."

"I don't know why we're discussing this. I haven't seen her for ten years, Tor. She's my past, and there was no need to rub the baby in her face." I know that's exactly why she said it.

"She thinks she better than me."

I don't respond to that because she wouldn't like what I have to say. "We need to keep the news contained. I thought you were in agreement?"

"I am." She glares at me before drinking from her bottle. "I want work long time. Felicia and Anna cannot know." Felicia is her agent, and Anna is her booker. They won't be pleased to discover their star new signing is knocked up even if the baby is mine.

"Don't tell anyone else." I warn her as the car pulls up to the private staff entrance of the hotel where Toria's bodyguard waits to escort her to our suite.

"You won't see her." She drills me with a look. "I forbid."

Toria is not my fucking keeper, and she can fuck off trying to tell me what to do. I'm biting my tongue nonstop around my pregnant girlfriend these days because most every word out of her mouth irritates the shit out of me. Grinding my teeth to the molars, I purposely ignore her and get out. After walking around the back of the car, I yank the door open almost pulling it off its hinges. "I will talk to you later," I say through gritted teeth after handing her off to Tom.

Toria scowls, flipping me the bird as she stomps off with Tom flanking her.

Rubbing a tense spot between my brows, I slide into the back seat, pop my AirPods in, and settle in for the half-hour journey to the Unipol Arena where Linc and Wilder are waiting for me to rehearse.

My mind wanders to Sydney without permission. Pain tightens my chest as a host of memories floods my mind. I can still remember how she smelled—like wild berries and jasmine. How she tasted—sweet as honey. My hands twitch as I recall the feel of her silky soft skin under my fingertips. Blood rushes south as I mentally revisit the only time I was inside her. A shiver cascades over my skin. We were only kids, and I didn't have a clue what I was doing, but it's still the most intimate sexual experience of my life. My most precious memory.

Until her actions stomped all over it.

I rub at the pain in my chest, willing it to go away.

How could I look at her today and still want her after everything she did?

I don't know. I don't have any answers.

Maybe it's time I asked for them.

***

"Dude, what the fuck?" Linc asks after we finish our rehearsal and sound check. We're only performing one song tomorrow night, but that didn't stop me from fucking up several times. "What was that?" he adds with a frown. Our bassist is right to question me. I'm normally solid, but that was my worst performance in years. Usually, music helps me to get out of my head, but nothing could blow the cobwebs of the past from my brain today.

"I'm sorry." I drag a hand through my messy hair. "I've got a lot of shit on my mind. I'll get it together before tomorrow." I haven't played as badly as that since I was a cocky teen who thought he knew it all.

"What's going on? Trouble with Tor?" Wilder asks. Our

lead singer and guitarist clamps a hand on my shoulder as we exit the stage, all of us nodding at the female artist who is up next.

Linc snorts. "That's an oxymoron if I ever heard one."

At one time, I'd bite his head off for his disrespectful comment. Maybe, if I'd listened to Linc, I wouldn't be in this mess. He didn't like her from day one. He was immediately suspicious of her motives, and he thought the arrangement was a bad idea.

"My past has returned to haunt me, and it's fucking with my head," I admit as we make our way through the busy backstage area, surrounded by our team of bodyguards. "I saw Sydney today," I clarify when I spot their perplexed expressions.

"We need a drink for this conversation," Wilder says, high-fiving some dude in an MTV shirt as we pass by.

"Fuck yeah," Linc agrees, lighting up a smoke as we duck our heads and exit via the side entrance.

Twenty minutes later, we are hidden away in an old man's bar in some small town on the outskirts of Florence. No one has so much as looked in our direction, and I like the anonymity. It's rare these days. As much as I craved fame and success—and I was gaga for it in my youth—it gets old real quick. I would pay good money to be able to go about my business in private, but those days are long gone.

"This town reminds me of the shithole I'm from in Boston," Linc says, dragging on a joint as we share a bucket of beers.

"This isn't a shithole. You want the real authentic Italian experience, try visiting Toria's hometown. That puts the shit in shitty."

I knew she grew up poor, and I thought I was prepared, but the crumbling, run-down two-story house she was raised in was worse than anything my vivid imagination could conjure. As difficult as Toria is, I've got to admire her fighting spirit. To claw her way from a poor Italian town to become one of the brightest lights in NYC is no small feat. It can't have been easy, and it took balls.

Her parents were lovely and very welcoming when we dropped by yesterday, en route to our hotel from the airport, but I was shocked as shit at how little they have. I thought their only daughter was sending money home, but it doesn't look like it. Unless Mr. Russo has a secret gambling or prostitution addiction, or Mrs. Russo is hiding some money-sucking hobby.

Tapping out a text to my assistant, I ask her to obtain their bank details for me so I can wire them some money directly. I'm not sure I trust my girlfriend to transfer the money if I gave it to her. Toria has embraced the lifestyle of the rich and famous with gusto, and she has expensive tastes. While she is earning decent money, and she has more than enough to live well, she is constantly tapping me for cash. It's really grating on my nerves along with most everything else she does.

"That explains a lot," Linc drawls before swigging from his beer. His long dark hair is tied back in a ponytail. A necessity in this heat.

"Cut the girl some slack. She's Jared's baba mama." Wilder is often the peacemaker these days, which is funny as fuck because the dude was crazy as shit when we first got together as a band. We were only kids then. Nineteen years old thinking we were gods. Man, we were so fucking naïve. Those early years were insane. Post heartbreak, I threw myself into the rock star lifestyle with enthusiasm. Drink, drugs, sex. Rinse and repeat.

Keith OD'ing and almost dying was a wake-up call for

Wilder and me. Linc joined us temporarily while Keith attended rehab, but he chose not to return, and Linc became a permanent part of Ruminate. We're lucky we all gelled. In a lot of ways, the three of us are a better team than we were with Keith. A lot of bands I know hate one another, and it's just a job. The three of us are close. Close as brothers, and there isn't much these guys don't know about me and vice versa.

It's why it works.

Why our star is ascending higher and higher.

'Cause we're tight.

We look out for one another.

And we make awesome fucking music together.

"I stand by what I said." Linc scrubs a hand across the thick growth on his chin and cheeks. "I don't trust her, and I think you should have stuck to your guns. You're miserable as fuck, man. It's no way to live."

"You're hardly a ray of sunshine," Wilder comments, arching a brow as he sweeps his long dark-blond hair back off his face. The ladies all love our leading man. Helps that he's pretty to look at, has a deep husky voice, and shares DNA with rock legend Ryder Stone.

"I own my misery," Linc says. "I left the best thing that ever happened to me behind for this gig. I should have nailed Presley down before skipping town. Married the fuck out of her when I had the chance. Nothing I can do about it now, short of murdering that Kennedy prick."

I snort out a laugh. "I doubt killing her husband would win you any favors or help get Presley back in your bed."

"I'm being facetious on purpose, jerk face." Linc flips me the bird before he drains his beer and reaches for another one. "We all know my situation is irreversible, but yours isn't. Especially if you bumped into Sydney again. This is your opening, man."

The guys know all about her. She's been my muse and the inspiration behind most of the songs I've written. In the same way, Linc channeled all of his heartbreak into the lyrics he wrote during his dark time. All of us have loved and lost and used those feelings to create magic with our music.

"Where did you meet her?" Wilder props his ankle over one knee.

"She works at the art gallery I visited today."

Wilder's brows climb to his hairline. "With Toria?"

I nod.

"Shit." Linc whistles under his breath. "What I wouldn't have given to be a fly on the wall for that meeting."

"She told her about the baby, and I swear Sydney turned as white as a ghost."

"It must have been a shock seeing her after all these years."

"Yep." I knock back a mouthful of beer and grab a few nuts, popping them in my mouth.

"How did she look?" Linc asks, leaning forward on his elbows.

"Fucking beautiful, but I'm not surprised. Sydney has always been a looker."

"Got any pics?" Wilder asks, smirking, and I throw some nuts at his face.

"What? You think I took selfies with her? Tor and me and my ex?"

Wilder chuckles. "How sharp were Toria's claws?"

"Sharp enough to easily shred glass."

"Ouch."

"You should talk to Sydney." Linc eyes me somberly. "This is your chance to find out why she did it."

"I'm not sure there's much point. I thought if I ever saw her again she'd show remorse, maybe rush to apologize, but she looked at me like she hated me. As if I was the one who broke her heart and not the other way around."

"Huh." Wilder grabs a handful of nuts from the bowl. "That's weird."

"I have always felt there was more to it," Linc says, stretching his arm across the back of our booth. "It never made sense to me. Girl sounded crazy about you. Maybe it didn't go down how you think it did. What if there's more to the story?"

"Like what?"

Linc shrugs. "I don't know, and you won't either unless you ask her. All I know is this. If I had another shot with Presley, I'd grab it with both hands."

"I have a pregnant fiancée," I remind him. "Wanting answers to something that has puzzled me for years is not the same as a second chance. That ship has sailed. Even if there is an explanation, I don't think I can ever forgive Syd for what she did."

"So, get closure," Wilder suggests, lighting up a blunt. "Find out what really happened after you left for London, and then put it behind you."

Linc nods. "If it was me, I'd be swinging by that gallery on my way home and demanding answers. I wouldn't leave until I got them."

Chapter Twelve
Sydney

"You want me to get that?" a man with a sleep-heavy deep voice asks as someone repeatedly bangs on my front door, rousing me from slumber. My eyes pop wide in a flash. It all returns as the bed dips and Gio leans over me, smiling like all his birthdays and Christmases have come at one.

Barely touching any food at my birthday dinner.

Drinking my body weight in wine.

Bumping into Gio and his friends at the nightclub.

Dirty dancing with my recent ex and inviting him home.

Fucking his brains out all night as I attempted to blot Jared and his pregnant supermodel fiancée from my mind.

I'm a goddamned idiot.

My stomach lurches the same time I notice the painful pounding in my head and icky taste in my mouth.

It's been years since I went on a bender, and now, I'm paying for it.

This is why I don't get trashed.

The hangover is never worth it.

What was I thinking? The last thing I need is to regress or slide back down that slippery slope. I have worked too hard to drag myself into the light to return to the darkness.

Jared will not break me again.

"Baby, you want me to get the door?" Gio purrs, running his fingers back and forth across my collarbone.

"No." Flinging the covers off, I grab the nearest item of clothing off the floor—his light-blue shirt—and yank it down over my nude body. "Stay here. I'll get rid of whoever it is."

And then it'll be your turn.

I cringe at my thought, but it's the truth.

A night of hot sex doesn't change things. Gio and I aren't a good fit, and I'm a selfish bitch to have reeled him back in when he had just let go.

This is why I am normally careful with alcohol. I cannot be trusted to make the right decision when I'm drunk.

The pounding continues as I race down the hallway and past the kitchen, rubbing my sore head and fighting nausea as alcohol sloshes in my stomach.

I yank the door open without looking to see who it is. "What's so—" The words dry up as I stare at Jared with my mouth trailing the ground.

While I try to calm my beating heart, he slowly drinks me in. From the knotty bedhead I'm sporting, down over the loose shirt which hits me mid-thigh, and along my naked legs to my bare feet and the chipped glittery red nail polish on my toes.

I bet Vittoria never steps out of bed looking less than immaculate. My mood sours as the thought lands in my head, igniting the anger that is never far from the surface. I snap out of it, refusing to ogle the rock god standing in my doorway looking far too good for this hour of the morning.

Not that I know what hour it is. It could be after midday, for all I know. I never set an alarm on my day off.

"What are you doing here, and how did you know where I live?"

Jared removes his designer shades, piercing me with clear crystal-blue eyes. "We need to talk, and I got your address from the British girl at the gallery."

I am going to murder Gemma with my bare hands.

"I have nothing to say to you," I lie, folding my arms over my chest.

"We both know that's not true." He leans against my doorway, flicking strands of hair out of his eyes. "We are long overdue a conversation. Ten years overdue."

"It should stay in the past, just like our lo—friendship," I correct, inwardly cursing my tired hungover brain for almost blurting the L-word.

"Don't rewrite history, Syd. We both know what we meant to one another." A muscle ticks in his jaw. "Or at least what you meant to me."

"What the hell does that mean?" I narrow my eyes.

"Exactly what it sounds like. It was an instant case of out of sight, out of mind for you, right?" His fists clench into balls at his sides, as I see red.

"Are you for real?" My pitch elevates a notch as I full-on glare at him now.

"Don't give me that bullshit, Syd! And fuck off looking at me like I murdered your cat. The only person who has a right to be angry is me." He thumps a hand over his chest, right where his heart beats.

"You're fucking delusional!" I snap. "All those drugs you consumed have clearly addled your brain, and I need this crap like a hole in the head." Pain rattles around my skull, and my stomach churns uneasily.

"You were never quick to judge, but I guess that's just something else that's changed."

I jab my finger in his chest. "Fuck you, Jared. You don't get to show up on my doorstep and throw shade at me. Just go."

Air whooshes out of his mouth. "Look, I think we both need to take a step back. I didn't come here to argue with you."

"Could've fooled me," I harrumph.

"I came here for answers." His eyes plead with me for understanding that is in limited supply.

"What does it even matter? We were just kids, Jared. Kids who thought they were in love, but what the hell did we know about life or love at fifteen?"

There's a lot of truth mixed in with the lie. We were completely ignorant of the world, but I still know what I felt in my heart was the real deal. Standing before him only confirms it.

Jared King will forever remain the love of my life.

I wish it wasn't true, but try telling that to my heart.

It wants who it wants. I haven't ever been able to understand it. It should be puppy love. It should have been easy, after all this time, to forget him and move on.

But I can't.

I have tried.

And I can't do it.

I hate him as much as I love him.

I know we will never be together, yet it makes no difference.

My heart still beats only for him.

Stupid, cruel organ.

"I know what I felt," he says, sadness threading through his tone. "We might have been inexperienced in the ways of the world, but I knew I loved you. I would have waited forever for you, Sydney."

"You didn't even wait six weeks!" I yell, rage battering me instantly on all sides.

"What?" His brow puckers. "What the fuck are you talking about?"

The photo of him with the two brunettes resurrects in my mind in vivid Technicolor, and vicious pain spears me through the heart. "Please go, Jared. I can't do this. I can't go back there. I can't relive it all again. I barely survived the first time."

He takes a step forward. "Sydney, something doesn't add up, and I think it's time we got to the bottom of it."

"It's too late." I shake my head and sigh. "What benefit is there to dragging all that shit up again? You've moved on. I've moved on," I lie, noticing how his gaze falls to the man's shirt I'm wearing again. "Just let it go."

"I can't, Syd." He reaches for me, and I fall back, almost stumbling over my feet. I can't let him touch me. I don't want to find out what his touch would do to me after all this time. "At least give me closure."

"Sydney?" Gio calls out from behind me, and I briefly close my eyes. I was wondering how long it'd take for him to make an appearance. "Is everything okay?" he asks.

Casting a glance over my shoulder, I force a smile on my face as he pads quietly toward us. "I'm okay. Jared is just leaving."

Gio's mouth pulls into an instant frown until he takes a proper look at the guy standing in my doorway, and shock splays across his face. He must not have heard the gossip yet. "You're Jared from Ruminate," he says, coming up alongside me.

"You have me at a disadvantage, mate." Jared's tone is clipped, his expression tight.

"Giorgio Pedina." Gio thrusts his hand out, and it's a little surreal watching them shake hands. "I'm a big fan of your music."

Oh, for fuck's sake.

I level a glare at Gio as he snags my waist and jerks me into his side. I should push him away, but I don't. Maybe if Jared believes I have a boyfriend, he'll back off and forget about taking a walk in the past.

Jared nods, forcing a smile. "Thanks, man. We appreciate the support." Refocusing on me, he ignores Gio completely. "I'm just asking for a few minutes of your time. Please, Syd. If I ever meant anything to you at all, do this one thing for me."

"If you ever meant anything to me?" I shout, losing the tenuous hold on my control as I shuck out of Gio's hold. "Fuck you, Jared King." I shove him, letting the full extent of my pent-up anger run free. "You were my everything! Don't pretend like you didn't know that! When did I ever give you the impression I wasn't serious? I had our whole future mapped out! I even used to imagine our wedding!" I snort out a derisory laugh as I shove him again. "I was so stupid. So fucking pathetic. I let you trample all over my heart, and it almost killed me."

Pain, sadness, and confusion wash over his handsome face. "Syd, I—"

I cut across whatever he was about to say. "How dare you act like I'm the one who's in the wrong when you were the one who broke every fucking promise you made to me!"

"That's the thing, Sydney, I didn't." His Adam's apple bobs in his throat as he reaches for me again.

"Yeah, right," I scoff, wetting my lips. "Now who's rewriting history?"

"It sure as fuck isn't me!" he yells, stepping closer.

Gio does me a solid and yanks me back. His eyes narrow at Jared. "I think you should leave. You're upsetting my girlfriend."

I should correct Gio. But, of course, I don't. Right now, getting Jared out of my apartment takes priority.

"Sydney, please, I'm begging you. I need closure. Don't you need closure too?"

There will never be closure for me. That's what he doesn't understand. "Why do you need closure, Jared? Surely you got that years ago when you turned your back on me. Why does it matter now? You're engaged with a baby on the way. Do us all a favor and let this go. I know I have." I can't look at him as I tell the biggest lie of all.

But I cannot do this with him. I'm tempted because I have so many unanswered questions, and it seems like something is amiss. Yet, I can't go back. I can't remember it all. It has the power to undo everything I have fought so hard to come back from.

"You heard her. It's time to leave," Gio says, tightening his arm around me.

"If I leave, Syd, this will be it."

His eyes beg me to reconsider, but I'm not going to kiss him on the cheek and tell him I forgive him so he can get on with his life and pretend like I never existed. Maybe it's petty. Maybe I should be the bigger person and just talk to him. Forgive him and try to put it properly behind me, but I can't risk my sanity. Spending any time with Jared, especially a shared walk down nostalgia lane, will only hurt, and I've been hurt enough.

It took me a long time to learn how to prioritize myself. To understand it's not selfish to put *me* first. It's what I need to do now before I fall apart and undo all my progress.

"Goodbye, Jared." I say the words I didn't want to say all those years ago. "I hope you have a good life."

Chapter Thirteen
Jared

I wander the busy nighttime streets of Florence with my head down low, hoping the ball cap is enough to disguise me from rowdy revelers who spill out of bars and clubs, laughing and joking and having a good time. The city is bursting with energy, as mobbed as if it was the middle of the day, and the air crackles with electricity. The usual summer crowd is swollen with additional tourists and music lovers, thanks to the MTV awards.

The event went well tonight. Somehow, I managed to keep my shit together to perform flawlessly. I should be out with Linc and Wilder, celebrating our best album win, but I'm not in a celebratory mood. Toria is furious. She wanted to party, and when I declined in favor of returning to our suite at the hotel, she assumed it meant I was down to fuck. When I rejected her, *again*, she turned crazy, throwing shit at me, and that's when I made my escape.

A grimace spreads over my face. I don't know what I'm going to do about my situation, but it can't continue. Something has to change before I sink into depression. I think my bandmates are right—I made a mistake proposing to her. I thought I could do this. I want to, for my unborn child's sake, but I'm already miserable as fuck. Toria is too, and I don't see how this will work. It's not fair on either of us to force something that's never been there.

I *should* want to fuck my gorgeous, pregnant, horny girlfriend, but I can't bear the thought of touching her or her touching me. I haven't wanted her like that for some time, and it's only gotten worse since I saw Sydney again. Touching anyone but Syd seems like a betrayal. Which is all kinds of fucked up. Not least that we ended over a decade ago. Sydney screwed me over big-time and left my heart in pieces at my feet. I owe her no loyalty, so why am I feeling the things I'm feeling?

Sydney hates my guts, and I don't understand why.

It's driving me crazy. Clawing at my insides and tearing strips off my heart and my sanity.

Why is she acting like I betrayed her when it was the opposite way around?

My feet move of their own accord, and a bitter laugh leaves my lips when I find myself at the river's edge, at the entrance to the quirky bridge with the shops on either side. I didn't consciously head in this direction, but it's no surprise my heart has led me toward my ex's apartment. Sydney made herself very clear earlier, so I doubt she will entertain me as a late-night guest, but it's like I'm being pulled by an invisible rope as I step foot on the bridge and start walking.

Sydney doesn't want anything to do with me. She drilled that point home this morning. She's moved on with that smug, preppy, Italian jerk with his shiny white teeth, manicured hands, and neatly styled hair. I bet he irons his boxers and flosses religiously.

Tool.

He is all wrong for Sydney.

But what do I know anymore?

The girl I fell in love with, the girl I still carry with me in my heart, seems to no longer exist.

I have no clue who Sydney is anymore, and it hurts.

I thought bleeding my heart into my song lyrics would purge the pain from my heart, but it lingers. No matter what I do, I cannot forget her or properly move on. I wasn't lying earlier when I said I needed closure. Maybe if I understand how and why it all went wrong, I can finally start letting her go and move forward without the ghost of our relationship haunting me at every turn.

Stopping when I reach Sydney's four-story apartment building, I lean back against the wall across the road and look up at the roof. I wonder if she's home or if she's out with that pretentious prick. Rubbing a hand across the tightness in my chest, I angle my head back and stare at the terrace that wraps around Sydney's penthouse. My heart does a funny little jump when I spot faint light on the furthermost terrace and clock the shadowy figure leaning against the railing, staring out at the city below.

Her long golden hair blows in the breeze, and I wish I could see her face to know what she's thinking. Her posture is relaxed but rigidly so. I wonder if she's been obsessively thinking of me, the way I've been obsessively thinking of her, since our unplanned reunion yesterday.

As if I called out to her, she turns her head in my direction, and my breath stutters in my chest. I stare up at her, and she stares back at me, and my heart thumps wildly within the confines of my chest cavity. I can't read her face in the dark and from this far away, but I'm hoping she realizes it's me. I remove my ball cap in case I look like some creepy stalker and keep my gaze trained on her.

How did we get to this place where we're virtual strangers?

Although I am still angry at her for what she did, sadness and regret are the two most overriding emotions I've been feeling these past two days. It wasn't supposed to be like this. We weren't supposed to live apart.

Hurt flays me from the inside when Sydney disappears from the terrace. I drop my head and shove my hands in the pockets of my jeans, willing the anxiety pressing down on my chest to disappear. I draw exaggerated breaths, in and out, in an attempt to get my shit together. What the fuck is happening to me?

"Jared." Sydney's distinctive tone tickles my eardrums, and I raise my head. She is standing at the entrance to the apartment building, leaning against the doorway with her hands clasped in front of her. She jerks her head and steps sideways, holding the door open in invitation.

Gulping back nerves, I stride across the road and bound up the few steps until we're face-to-face. Her features are illuminated under the soft beams of the overhead light, and she's not shielding anything from me. Pain mixes with anger, fear, regret, and longing, and I can relate. I have felt every combination of those emotions in recent days.

"You were right," she says in a croaky tone of voice. "We need to talk. I need closure too."

"I love your apartment," I say as I follow Sydney out through the double doors and onto the main terrace. Those are the first words spoken between us since the doorway downstairs. Tension was thick as we walked up the three levels to the penthouse. I had taken the opportunity to drink all of her in. Wearing a long, floaty, white, sleeveless dress, she is like some ethereal being. Innocent yet worldly-wise. Beguiling and guarded. Stunningly beautiful but completely off limits. Her gorgeous hair hangs in soft waves down her back, begging to be touched. Slender fingers brushed against the banisters as we walked, and I never thought I'd be jealous of a piece of wood, but I was.

"I'm only renting, but it's the first place that has properly felt like a home." Her words yank me from my head, and I focus on the here and now. Sydney gestures for me to take a seat on the L-shaped gray wicker couch as she sits in front of the matching glass-topped coffee table and sets an empty wineglass down beside her half-filled one.

Claiming the seat beside her, I ensure to leave adequate space between us so I'm not crowding her. My butt sinks into the soft, gray-patterned, padded cushion as I admire the outdoor area. Sydney has potted plants and flowers dotted all over the tiled floor, interspersed with candles and stone ornaments. A gray wrought-iron table and four matching chairs reside on the other side, situated perfectly to admire the stunning view over the river below and the sprawling city beyond. The dome and bell tower are visible in the distance, and I wish I didn't have to leave tomorrow so I could spend some time exploring.

"Would you like a glass of wine?" she asks, lifting the bottle of Sancerre from the silver cooler.

Piercing emerald eyes pin me in place. Flawless sun-kissed skin, full lips, high cheekbones, and a heart-shaped face complete her stunning features, and she is truly mesmerizing. She doesn't have a scrap of makeup on, and she is exquisite. Stunning beyond belief. I was completely gone for her as a kid. In awe of her vibrant personality, her clear ambition, and her good looks, but it is nothing compared to the woman sitting beside me now. I have no words to describe how utterly compelling and completely gorgeous she is.

"Jared?" she asks again, and I realize I've just been staring at her like a creeper.

I shake my head, declining her offer. I usually only drink wine if I'm out for dinner, and I'd rather keep my wits about me tonight.

"Please join me. Otherwise, I'm liable to drink the entire bottle myself, and I'd really rather not."

Her words contain hidden meaning, and I arch a brow in silent question.

Her expression turns forlorn. "Alcohol and I have a checkered past." Sadness coats her tone and her pretty features.

"I'll take a glass."

Relief smooths out her face as she pours me a healthy glass and hands it to me. Our fingers brush in the exchange, sending fiery tingles shooting up my arm. She yanks her hand back like I just electrocuted her.

"What did you mean? About alcohol." She can't be implying what I think she is because it wouldn't make sense.

Bitter laughter bursts from her full lips. "You have no idea who I am anymore, Jared. If you did, you'd realize you had a lucky escape."

She looks so fucking sad, and it guts me. Sydney was always full of life and so determined. She let nothing stand in the way of her goals, and she wasn't one to put herself down either. I hate hearing the defeat and self-loathing in her tone. I equally hate the thought I might be someway responsible for it, even if I am still totally in the dark. "I would never think that. I probably should, but it's not how I feel inside. If you've listened to any of my songs, you should know that."

"I try not to. It's too painful," she says, before taking a sip of her wine.

Time to rip the Band-Aid off. There is no point in pussy-footing around the subject. I drink a mouthful of the crisp white wine before asking, "What happened to us, Syd? Why did you give up on me?"

She whips her gaze to mine, eyes blazing. "Why did *you*?"

I lean forward, peering deep into her eyes. "I didn't, Syd. I didn't give up on you. Not until it was clear you had given up on me."

"You stopped communicating with me after a week. *One freaking week*, Jared! You totally ghosted me after that." Pain skitters across her face as she lifts her wineglass to her lips.

"Nope." I shake my head. "I most definitely did not. I wrote, called, or texted most every day for ten months, Sydney. Even when I heard nothing back from *you!*"

She almost chokes on her wine. After composing herself, she says, "What are you talking about? I wrote to you constantly, and you never replied. Not even when I told you about—"

"Told me about what?"

"Nothing." She chews on her bottom lip in an obvious tell.

I move a little closer and tentatively place my hand on her knee, over her dress. "Syd."

"Drop it," she hisses, avoiding looking at me.

Tension bleeds into the air as we both contemplate what has just been revealed.

"Are you telling me the truth, Sydney? Were you still contacting me?"

She turns to face me with glassy eyes. "Why would I lie after all this time? What would I have to gain?"

"Exactly. Why would I?"

"This doesn't make any sense," she whispers, swiping at an errant tear that leaks from one eye.

"Tell me what happened after I left." It is hard to remain calm when my brain is churning all kinds of thoughts, but lashing out won't help.

"I didn't hear from you after that first week. There was radio silence, but I kept texting, calling, and emailing you, and nada. I never heard from you again even though I continued communicating with you for months until I was forced to give up when it was abundantly clear you were never going to reply."

Her confession shocks the shit out of me. All this time, I thought she didn't care. That she had given up on me immediately. "I don't know why I never received your calls or messages, but I swear I had not given up on you. After that first week, I continued sending texts and emails, and I called you every day, but you never picked up."

Shock splays across her face as she stares at me. "I never received anything from you. I swear."

"Hang on a sec." I pull out my cell as an idea occurs to me. "I rarely use my old email account anymore, but I still have it connected to my phone," I explain as my fingers race over the keypad. I type in my password, and the inbox loads. Sydney quietly sips her wine as I go into the sent items and filter it by year. I'm relieved the log is still there. I'm guessing randomly using the account over the years has kept it active. "I have a different phone now, so I can't show you the hundreds of calls and texts I sent, but I can show you this." I hand her my phone, and she takes it with trembling fingers.

Tears flood her eyes as she scrolls through pages upon pages of sent messages, all timestamped to prove I'm telling the truth.

"What happened, Jared?" she whispers, turning to look at me. "Why did I never receive any of these?"

"I can't explain it." Though I'm starting to form some theories. "I tried to come see you one time," I add, dragging a hand through my hair. "I was going crazy not hearing from you and panicking that something had happened. I begged my parents to let me visit, but they told me I had to forget about you. I was so angry at Mum. She'd promised she was on our side, but it was a lie. Anyway, when it was obvious they weren't going to let me see you, I booked a flight and ditched school for the airport. I didn't even have a bag. I didn't care. I just needed to see you. To know you were okay."

"What happened?" she asks, tucking hair behind her ears.

"The school called my parents when I didn't show, and they used my cell to track my location. Dad showed up at the airport and dragged me out kicking and screaming." I grind my teeth to the molars as I revisit the scene in my head. "I was so angry and so frustrated. I refused to speak to my parents after they confiscated my passport and secured it in their safe." I grab fistfuls of my hair. "They sent me to a boarding school for the last two years of school."

"Oh my god." Her eyes startle wide.

"It was hell. A fucking prison. You couldn't get in or out of the grounds without parental permission, which my parents refused to give. We weren't allowed access to social media or cell phones, but I did have email, and I continued emailing you constantly." It took me a long time to speak to my parents after I graduated school and relocated to L.A. I was really angry at them for sending me to that hellhole.

"Jared, I was doing that too. I hadn't given up on you. Not even when I knew you were hooking up with other girls, I—"

"Woah, stop there, sweetheart. What other girls? There was no one but you. I told you that, and I meant it." I see the disbelief in her eyes, and it kills me. "There weren't any other girls."

Her lips purse. "Don't lie to me, J. I saw the proof."

I wave my hands in the air. "I don't know what you saw, but it wasn't proof."

"He showed me the picture!" she snaps, shoving my phone

at me and wrapping her arms around herself. "It broke my heart," she sniffles.

"What picture? I have no clue what you're talking about."

"The one of you with your arms around two pretty brunettes. You were out partying, and you looked happy, while I was miserable as fuck and feeling like a goddamned fool!" She glugs wine like it's water while I wrack my brain to try to remember what it could be.

Then it comes to me. "Sydney, they were my cousins. Lynn and Lucy."

"What?" she splutters.

Placing a hand over my heart, I say, "I swear on my sister's life that is the truth. Ask Heather if you don't believe me. She'd flown in with her husband to attend the party. It was Lucy's sixteenth birthday, so it was a big deal. I remember getting that picture taken, but how did you see it?"

Her brows knit in confusion. "You sent it to Anvil, and he showed me."

"Anvil?" I roar, instantly enraged. "How the fuck did he get it, and were you already screwing him by then?"

Chapter Fourteen
Sydney

"What?" An anxious fluttery feeling invades my chest, and I feel like I might puke. "Of course, I wasn't screwing Anvil. I hated his fucking guts."

A red haze coats Jared's gorgeous blue eyes. "Don't fucking lie to me!" He stands, grabbing fistfuls of his hair as he paces. "I know about you and him."

All the blood drains from my face. "There was no me and him," I truthfully admit.

"Stop fucking lying!" He drops to his butt, pulls his knees to his chest, and buries his face in them.

Pain eviscerates me from all angles. He knows, and I can guess who told him. I am ashamed. I'd like to say it's my most shameful moment, but there are much worse things I've done. Setting my wineglass down on the coffee table, I rise and walk to the end of the couch, sinking onto the tiled floor across from Jared with an ache in my heart.

"Anvil told you," I quietly say.

Jared lifts his head, stabbing me with tortured eyes. "He emailed me a photo."

My eyes pop wide. That backstabbing, double-crossing asshole. "I didn't know there was a photo." I palm my queasy stomach, thinking of the other vulnerable photos and videos of me that are out there somewhere in the world. Acid churns in my gut, and I'm regretting my wine consumption on an empty stomach.

"You were asleep. Naked in his bed."

"Not his bed," I whisper. "It was a party."

His mouth pulls into a sneer. "Like it fucking matters!" he barks, and a fresh wave of shame washes over me. "While I was locked away in a boarding school, dreaming of you and counting down the days until I could be with you again, you were fucking my ex-best friend."

"I wasn't. It was a one-time thing, and I—"

"How could you do that to me, Syd?" His eyes fill with tears, and I'm horrified. "Seeing you with any other guy was always going to hurt, but Vil? Why him?"

"I was out of my mind. High and drunk. I don't even remember how it happened, just that I woke up beside him and threw up everywhere," I whisper, biting on the inside of my cheek to stop the scream dying to break free.

His expression alters in the blink of an eye. Fear swims in his gaze. "Did he rape you?" He crawls over closer. "I swear I'll fucking kill him if he did."

Excruciating pain flays me on the inside, and I tuck my knees into my chest and hug my legs, desperately praying I keep it together. "No." I shake my head. "I might not remember it, but it was consensual. Cay was there. She saw it going down. Tried to stop me, but I pushed her away."

The only time Cayenne and I stopped speaking was then. She was furious with me because I slept with her ex but angrier over how I was behaving. I lost my will to live during that time, and I was completely out of control. My best friend tried everything to get through to me, and her avoiding me for four months was her form of tough love. Cay was appalled when I told her the real reason for my wild behavior, but it was on me for not telling her sooner.

Silence descends, and it's not the comfortable kind.

"I'm sorry," I say. "I thought you'd given up on me. That you'd been fucking other girls for months. I assumed we were over, and there were extenuating circumstances."

His head whips up.

"Not that it's an excuse, but..."

"He told me he was going to move in on you," Jared admits, shocking the shit out of me.

"What? When?"

"We had a big argument just before I left for London. Vil was pissed I was ditching the band."

"You didn't have a choice," I remind him.

"He didn't care. Said I could get emancipated."

"New York doesn't have a statute for emancipation. Remember we researched it when our parents told us we couldn't see one another anymore? You can only file an emancipation motion in conjunction with another case."

"I told him all that. Said if it was an option I'd have done it so I could stay with you. That's when he started threatening me. He said he was going to steal you away. He swore before the year was out you would be his."

"What a dick." I rub at a tense spot between my brows. "He was always jealous of you. You were talented and clearly going places. He hated you were more popular than him at school."

"He was in love with you," Jared says.

I shake my head. "He just wanted what you had."

"I saw the way he looked at you. I think he only got with

Cayenne to make you jealous in the hope you'd ditch me for him or to stay close to you."

I clear my throat and admit something I should have told my boyfriend back then. "He hit on me a few times."

Jared's spine stiffens, and a muscle pops in his jaw.

"I always shot him down." I rush to reassure him.

"Why didn't you tell me?" he asks in a gritted tone, scrubbing his hands down his face.

"Because I didn't want the band to break up over me. I knew it would start World War Three."

"You still should have told me."

"I know." I hug my legs tighter. "I should have done so many things differently, but I was a lost, scared kid trying to survive."

"I was in so much pain after he sent that picture. For years, I tortured myself imagining you with him."

"I swear it was only that one time, and if I'd been sober, I would never have gone there. I despised the guy."

"I believe you."

His words wrap around my heart like a comfort blanket. "Thank you, and I'm sorry for the pain it caused you. I hate that I fed into his scheme to hurt you."

"I looked him up about five years ago," he says. "He's working a day job in insurance and playing shitty bars at night with his equally shitty band. Got some girl knocked up at eighteen, and he married her." A frown creases his brow as bile swims up my throat. "He looked miserable as sin in all the photos online, and I got satisfaction from it. Petty maybe, but he did me dirty. He knew what fucking you would do to me, yet he had to drive the knife in deeper. He knew that photo would gut me, yet he still sent it."

"I am really sorry, Jared." Now I know he wasn't cheating on me, I feel even worse about sleeping with his ex-friend and bandmate. Although I hated I had sex with Anvil, I remember thinking at the time I hoped Anvil would tell him. I wanted Jared to hurt as much as I was hurting. But I had it all wrong. So wrong. "If it helps, I was disgusted with myself, and I made sure to avoid him. It got easier after I was expelled from West Lorian."

His eyes almost bug out of his head. "You got fucking expelled?"

"Yeah. Wasn't my finest hour. As punishment, Dad sent me to the public school around the corner." That's when my descent into anxiety and depression really took root. If Dad had wanted to save me from myself, he should have sent me anywhere but there.

He winces. "I can't imagine you there. It was rough as fuck."

"It was hell on earth, and it only made things worse."

"Go back to the beginning again," Jared says, and I'm glad we have moved past Anvil. It's one of my biggest regrets, and I don't want to dwell on it. "I need to understand things from your perspective."

"Like I said, I was trying to reach you, but I thought you had tossed me aside almost immediately. I sank into a deep depression."

That's putting it mildly. I should tell him about the baby, but it's only going to hurt him, and what good will it do now? We can't rewrite history. Jared is expecting a baby with another woman. Engaged to another woman. There is no benefit in sharing this truth—it would only be painful, for both of us, and he'll get closure without it—so I work around it.

"I was a mess without you," I truthfully admit. "I was crying all the time, and then I just wanted to blot it all out, so I started doing drugs and drinking myself into a stupor. My grades dropped. I got expelled. I got arrested for shoplifting a couple times. Dad was so mad. He told me continuously how much of a disappointment I was. Stopped me from going to art class. Forced me to attend the public school where I fell in with a shady crew. I barely graduated. I only attended NYU, to study languages, 'cause Dad pulled strings. Spent the first couple college years in a drugged-up-drunk haze until I almost overdosed, and it brought me to my senses."

I'm watching all manner of emotions play out over Jared's face as I talk. "Fucking hell, Syd. I had no idea. I should've come for you at eighteen instead of moving to L.A. to make my rock star dream come true. I should have stuck to my guns. If I'd come to you, we would have discovered the truth much earlier, and I could have been there for you. Helped you get through it. I let you down. I failed you." He crawls over beside me, gently clasping my head in his hands. "I can't believe you almost overdosed." Tears well in his eyes again. "I can't imagine a world without you in it."

"I didn't want to live. I was in agony." Tears cascade down my cheeks. "My world was so empty without you in it." It's cruel to let him believe his absence was the only reason I self-destructed when that's not the full truth. But I can't tell him the rest. He will only feel more guilty if he knows what I was forced to endure. And I'm sure there would be rage, loss, grief, and most likely a need for vengeance.

Maybe if he wasn't starting a family with another woman, I would tell him. A big part of me believes he has a right to know we lost a baby and to understand all the ways in which my father plotted to keep us separated and how Herman Shaw failed to protect me. But we can't rewind the clock. We can't do anything about it now. Purposely hurting him with this infor-mation, at what is a happy time in his life, feels wrong.

What he doesn't know can't hurt him.

"I'm sorry, Syd."

"It's not your fault. You didn't know."

Oh so slowly, he circles his arms around my shoulders, watching me to ensure it's okay. We should not be doing this, but I'm fragile after unlocking the vault to my memory bank, and I need his comfort right now. His scent swirls around me as heat from his arms sinks into my chilly bones, and it just feels so right being with him like this. I rest my head on his shoulder as we quietly contemplate all we have learned tonight.

I'm exhausted and incapable of any more truth talk, but there is one thing that needs to be said. "My dad did this. He kept us apart," I say, eyeballing him.

Jared slowly nods. "It's the only explanation that makes sense except I think my parents must have been in on it as well."

"My dad was the one with a company full of IT specialists," I remind him. "He clearly had someone tamper with or redirect my calls, texts, and emails. None of them bounced back meaning our numbers weren't blocked."

"He must have discovered your burner cell and had someone redirect all communication from your cell and email to mine. And then any incoming mail and calls from that number, and my main number, redirected to the same place because my messages to you didn't bounce either."

"I reached out to you on social media too."

He frowns. "You know I'm not a big fan of social media, but I did occasionally log into my profiles, pre-boarding school, and there was nothing there." A muscle pops in his jaw. "My parents must have done something."

"I don't think your parents were involved. Dad could easily have had someone hack into your profiles and block me without you realizing." Jared is a disaster with social media, so he would not have noticed anything amiss unless he knew what to look for.

"I wouldn't be too sure." Jared presses a kiss to the top of my head, not even realizing he's done it.

It would be so easy to stay here with him like this, but it would only be pretend. He has a pregnant fiancée, and my heart is vulnerable. Shucking out of his embrace, to avoid further temptation, I climb to my feet and head back to the couch. "I don't know about you, but I definitely need a drink after tonight's revelations." I flop down on the couch, reaching for the bottle of wine.

"Have you fallen off the wagon?" he asks, rising elegantly to his feet. "Have I done this to you?" Remorse flashes in his eyes.

"No. I still drink, but I know my limits. As long as I stick to them, I'm fine. I haven't touched drugs in over six years. I went to rehab during summer break before junior year and got clean."

"Good for you." He reclaims his seat beside me. "I bet that wasn't easy."

I top off both our glasses, emptying the bottle, and hand his glass to him. "It wasn't, but almost dying put things into perspective."

"I would never have forgiven myself if you'd died."

"It wasn't your fault, J. I own my mistakes and take responsibility for my behavior."

Our relationship ending, and the fallout from the baby, was the catalyst that set me on a destructive path, but it wasn't either of our faults. Two years of therapy has taught me I wasn't responsible for the things that were done to me. While depressed and traumatized, I made a slew of bad decisions, and even though I was incapable of making the right ones because I wasn't of sound mind, I still need to own what I did. I had to accept that before I could forgive myself and move on.

The people who were supposed to care for me let me down.

My father failed to protect me. Instead, he set out on a controlling path that meant even after I got cleaned up I was permanently depressed because he kept me in a cage and refused to let me out.

"My parents sent that photo to Vil," Jared seethes. "They must have because I sure as fuck didn't, and I doubt your dad stole the picture off Mum's phone and sent it to Anvil from my phone. Even with his IT knowledge, I don't know if that's possible."

"I'm sure it is." I was married, albeit briefly, to a tech genius, and Sawyer explained that with the right skills there isn't much a hacker can't do. Although this was ten years ago and technology wasn't quite as sophisticated, so maybe Jared is right. "I don't think it's a big stretch to believe my dad was spying on your parents. They hated one another. It was the whole reason your family left the US."

"I don't fully understand it, but either that was a ruse or it was the truth and both sides were working independently to separate us."

I still think it was all my dad's doing, but there's no point arguing over it. It's a moot point now. "Why? Why the fuck did it matter to them?"

"That's the million-dollar question." Jared leans back, knocking wine into his mouth, and I try to ignore how sexy he looks as he drinks.

He's only wearing a plain white tee with dark denims and sneakers, but he looks incredible. Jared is the kind of guy who could wear a trash bag and make it sexy. It's hard looking at his gorgeous face, knowing I no longer have the right to freely touch and kiss him. What I wouldn't give to run my fingers through the stylish stubble on his chin and cheeks, trace my tongue along his plump lips, or drag my fingers through all that messy black hair.

"Will you ask your father?" He pulls me back into the moment.

I shake my head. "We don't talk."

"At all?" He sits up straighter.

"Nope. He didn't care for me the way a father should. I hated him for the part he played in separating us. He was very controlling when I turned rebellious, and he made my life a misery. When I finally broke free, I told him he was dead to me and I never wanted to see or hear from him again."

"I'm sorry you went through that."

I shrug because it's water under the bridge now.

"But I'm really proud of you for all you have achieved. I know you had a different dream, but look how far you've come? You're an accomplished manager in a reputable gallery in one of the most artistic places in the world."

"I'm proud of me," I admit. "There were times I didn't think I could ever break free. I have worked hard for the life I live, and I never take it for granted."

"I need to take a page out of your book."

I arch a brow. "You're living your dream. You get to make music for a living, and you're adored the world over. Is it not what you thought it'd be?"

"Don't get me wrong, I love it, and I love the guys. They're like brothers to me, but fame and lack of privacy is a bitter pill to swallow at times. I don't mean to sound ungrateful, because I know I'm so fucking lucky, but sometimes it's too much."

"I can't relate, but I can imagine it's hard. I wouldn't like photographers chasing me everywhere." Because of who my father is, I often get photographed if I attend a public event, but it's vastly different to having paparazzi following my every move. I would hate that.

"It was awful when Dad died four years ago. They camped outside my house for days."

"I read about Amos, and it saddened me. He was taken far too young."

Jared finishes his wine and sets his glass down on the coffee table. "Yeah, he was. He had a heart attack three days before his sixty-third birthday. It was a big shock."

My tongue darts out, wetting my lips. "I thought of reaching out to you then, but you were this big rock star, and I didn't think there was any point in rehashing the past."

"Funnily enough, I almost called you then." His sad eyes fix on me. "We hadn't spoken in years, yet the only one I wanted by my side at the funeral was you."

"I would have been there if you'd asked me to come."

"They stole our future from us, Syd. Our parents did this to us. I'm not sure I can ever forgive my mother."

"She might not have known, J. This could all be my dad's fault, or maybe both our dads were involved," I tack on the end because he seems convinced his parents played some part. Except I just can't see Gladys doing anything to hurt her son or me.

"I'm going to confront her. After the last leg of our tour, I'm going to demand answers."

Gently, I place my hand on his. "Don't." Pain claws its way up my throat as I force these next words out. "Let the past stay in the past. We know now we didn't give up on one another. It's sad we never made it, but it took me a long time to learn how to look back without regret. To focus on the future and moving forward. We have enough answers to give us closure. You have a different life to lead, and so do I."

"It's not fair." His voice is choked with emotion. "They had no right to ruin our relationship."

"Life isn't always fair, but some things happen for a reason."

"I would never have let go, Sydney." His fingers thread through mine. "I didn't willingly give you up."

"Nor I you." I cling to his hand, fighting tears. "But we've got to willingly let it go now. Don't dredge up the past, Jared. It won't do any of us any good."

Chapter Fifteen
Jared

"You need to eat," I tell Toria, working hard to leash my frustration as I stare at her. She's seated across from me by the window of the plane, sulking as she looks everywhere but at me. "If not for you, for the baby. I can ask what else they have on board if this isn't to your liking," I add, wondering what is wrong with the chicken salad the air steward, Lydia, produced for my difficult girlfriend.

"Not hungry." She pushes the plate away, and my eyes lock on Wilder's. My bandmates are seated in front of us on the private jet. The seating is arranged in little sections of four—two recliner seats on each side with a high table in between. Our manager and our three assistants are traveling with us too, seated across and behind Toria and I, but the rest of our crew flew commercial.

I exhale heavily, not having the patience for this today after fuck-all sleep last night. "Tor. You have to stop starving yourself. It's not good for you or the baby. You need to at least try." I slide the plate across the table until it's back in front of her.

In a lightning-fast move, she grabs it and throws it at my

head. I duck down at the last second, narrowly avoiding impact. A shrill cry emits behind me, and I turn around, discovering Felicity, Linc's assistant, wearing said chicken salad.

"Are you hurt?"

"I'll probably have a goose egg," she says, rubbing at her brow, "but I'll live."

"Shit, I'm sorry." I move to get up, but Daria gets there first.

"It's fine, Jared," my assistant says. "I'll help Felicity get cleaned up." Daria narrows her eyes at my girlfriend before helping her friend from her seat, and they disappear into the bedroom with en suite bathroom at the rear of the plane.

"Was that really necessary?" I glare at Toria.

"Yes," she hisses. "You don't understand." She pinches nonexistent fat on her hips and her stomach. "I can't be fat. Career over!" She waves her hands in the air in an agitated fashion.

"You can't hide your pregnancy forever."

"If I don't eat, can hide it long time."

"If you don't eat, you'll die. My baby will die!" I snap because I am sick of hearing this bullshit. Toria refuses to tell her manager or booker she is pregnant, which I think is a mistake. They are booking her for projects months out, and they won't be happy when she shows up with a noticeable baby bump. I know she has nausea to contend with, but spending the past few days with her has made me realize a lot of that is made up. She is adept at faking it to avoid eating, and I'm the sucker who's been falling for it.

God strike me down for this thought, but why the fuck did the condom burst when I was with this woman? I would give anything to be having a baby with anyone but her.

There, I said it.

I have finally admitted it to myself.

I don't want to have a child with this spoiled, whiny, selfish bitch who is already putting herself before our unborn baby.

Things will have to change, and I'm going to be the one to do it. I won't sit by and watch this woman starve my child.

Leaning over the table, I work hard to control my anger, but it's challenging. "You will feed my fucking baby, or I will take your selfish ass to court and have you charged with child neglect."

"Try it, asshole! I will tell world you hit me!"

Linc leans over his seat and barks in her ear, "Try that shit, honey, and we'll bury you. By the time we're done, you'll be ruined. No one threatens our brother." Linc's gaze bounces between Wilder and our manager, Brian. "You both heard that, right?"

They nod.

"I heard her as well," Lydia says. "If you need me to sign something after we land, I'd be happy to." It's no surprise Lydia is standing up for me. She has flown with us for years, and she knows the band. There is no love lost between her and my girlfriend. Toria seems to ignite that reaction in most women.

Toria glances over her shoulder, shooting the evil eye at Lydia.

Linc eyeballs Toria. "Pull that bullshit, and we'll hang you out to dry. We all heard you threatening Jared."

"I think everyone needs to calm down." Brian climbs out of his seat and comes over to us. Our manager is skilled at putting fires out and God knows he's had to put a lot of them out in the seven years he's worked with us. He smiles softly at Toria. "What would you like to eat, Vittoria? I'll ask Lydia if she can make it for you."

"Fruit and water."

I barely contain an eye roll. It's hardly substantial, but I'll consider it a win if she consumes any food.

I ignore my scowling fiancée as Brian speaks to Lydia.

After she hands Toria a bowl of chopped fruit and a bottle of water, Lydia cleans up the mess on the floor. I make a mental note to send her some flowers when we land. Daria and Felicity return to their seats, and things finally settle down in the cabin.

"Is she asleep?" Wilder asks an hour later as I exit the bedroom at the back.

"Yes."

"Thank fuck." Linc hands me a beer, and I gladly accept it as I drop into the leather seat beside him. "You deserve a fucking gold star for putting up with that shit," he adds, keeping his voice low. Everyone else is snoozing, but we don't want them to overhear our conversation.

"She's a handful," Wilder says.

"She's a conniving cunt," Linc adds, making no apologies for not mincing his words. "Please tell me you've come to your senses because I cannot sit back and watch you fuck up your life by tying yourself permanently to that woman."

"I second that," Wilder agrees. "I know you want to do the right thing, Jared, but marrying her is not it."

"I know. You're right. I can't go through with it."

"Halle-fucking-lujah." Linc taps his bottle against mine.

"You know I only proposed because of the baby," I whisper. "I didn't want my kid growing up in a broken home, but it would be worse growing up in a household where his or her parents hate one another. I can barely stand to look at Toria. There is no way I can marry her."

"I don't envy you breaking the news." Wilder winces.

"I'm going to wait until after we finish the tour. I'll hire a nurse to keep an eye on her, and I'm going to talk to the ob-gyn about my concerns. When I return, I'll sit her down and tell her I'll be there to support her during the pregnancy and I won't abandon my child, but that's as far as my commitment extends. I'll give her the house in Florence and get a legal agreement drawn up for joint custody and child support. I'll ensure she wants for nothing, so hopefully that will mean she won't contest it."

"That's more than generous," Linc says, lighting up a joint. "But I'm telling you now that woman will not go easy. She'll fight you tooth and nail and try to squeeze every penny she can from you."

"Get your lawyers involved ASAP," Wilder advises.

"I'd go as far as siccing a PI on her," Linc adds. "I don't trust that woman especially after what she just said."

<hr>

Sydney

"Oh, Syd, my heart breaks for you," Cay says as we FaceTime Sunday night. Jared's already on a plane back to the US, leaving me to pick up the pieces of my newly shattered heart all alone again. It's an uncharitable thought. I was the one who told him to leave the past in the past and move forward with his life. It's not like I could have asked him to stay with me. He has a new life. A new family. There is no room in his life for me anymore.

"I feel like I'm fifteen all over again and he's just broken my heart," I admit.

"I'd like to say I'm shocked your father did that to you, but nothing that prick does surprises me anymore." My bestie tosses long purple locks over one shoulder as she lies on her stomach on the king bed she shares with her fiancé, Jerry, at their new apartment in Pacific Heights. They moved from New York a year ago after Jerry got a promotion at work, and he was transferred to the Wells Fargo HQ in San Francisco. Cay is self-employed, and she set up a new aromatherapy practice at the marina. I have yet to visit, but my bestie is totally enthralled by San Fran and living her best life.

"I should have realized it back then."

"Your dad had only just started showing his true colors. You would never have thought that of him, and neither would I."

"True." I swing my feet up on the couch on the terrace, sipping my sparkling water. It's tempting to hit the *vino*, but it won't help. I need to keep a clear head to decide where I go from here.

"How did Jared handle the news?"

"He was upset too. He thinks his parents were involved. He swears he didn't send any photo to Anvil, and I believe him."

"That lot give parents the world over a bad name."

"For sure. And all because of something my dad did. Why did Jared and I have to pay the price for my dad's betrayal? It's so unfair. But dwelling on all the what-ifs won't help me. I've got to let it go. Let him go. Maybe now I can put him behind me."

"I'm not sure how easy that'll be when he moves to Florence with his wife and child."

"I know." I release a resigned sigh. "It's been playing on my mind a lot today. If he was a regular person, the chances of bumping into them would probably be slim."

"But he's a famous rock star, she's a famous model, and interest in them and their kid is going to be through the roof."

"Exactly," I concur with my best friend as I lean back and cross my feet at the ankles. "They will be photographed everywhere, and there'll be no escaping them locally. Everyone will be talking and gossiping about them."

"Not to mention, Jared knows where you work, and so does that bitch. I'm betting she'll be a regular visitor to the gallery, just to rub your nose in it."

I told Cay all about her reaction to me, and Cay is convinced Vittoria feels threatened. Which is ridiculous when she's the one wearing his ring and carrying his baby.

"He's ruined Florence for me now," I admit though it's not Jared's fault. It wasn't premeditated. It is what it is. "I can't stay here."

Cay bolts upright, her eyes widening with excitement. "Come here!" she shrieks. "Oh, please, please, Sydney. Move to San Fran! I miss you so much, and I don't have many friends here, and it would be so awesome if my bestie was close by again. There's a real artistic vibe here and plenty of galleries and museums you could apply to. You could even get a house by the beach like you've always wanted!" She bounces on her bed, and I laugh. Her enthusiasm is infectious.

"I wasn't ever planning on returning to the US, but California is far enough away from New York I could consider it."

Cayenne's shriek is so loud it brings Jerry racing into the bedroom in a panic.

"Jesus, love, I thought someone was murdering you in here or something," he says, scooping a jumping Cayenne into his arms.

"Hey, Jerry."

"Hi, Sydney." Cayenne's big beefcake of a fiancé waggles his fingers and waves at me as he cradles my bestie in his arms.

"I'm trying to convince Sydney to move here. Help me." She playfully swats Jerry's chest.

"I said I'd consider it, Cay, not that I'm committing."

"Pssh." She rolls her eyes. "We both know I'm totally convincing you to move to San Fran." Another squeal escapes her lips. "I haven't been this excited since Jerry proposed."

Clinging to her fiancé, she leans in close to the screen. "This feels right, Sydney, admit it. I know you're feeling it too."

"I'm admitting nothing until I've had time to think about it. It's been an emotionally draining day, and I need time to clear my head." Between breaking Gio's heart again, talking with Jared after all these years and learning the truth of the past, and old memories resurfacing, I'm destroyed and in no position to make life-changing decisions.

Her expression softens. "It's been a lot, I know. And I won't pressure you, babe. But at least consider a trip here before you make up your mind on where you're moving to next."

"I can do that."

"I'm here for you, babe." She wriggles in Jerry's arms until he puts her down, and then she shoos him out of the room. I shout my goodbye as he waves over his shoulder at me. "I can't begin to imagine how you must be feeling right now. I know it's dragging everything to the surface again, but don't let it suck you back in."

"That is easier said than done. I'm feeling so much again. It's hard seeing him and not remembering everything. I still love him, Cay," I quietly admit. "I know it's wrong. He doesn't belong to me anymore, but I can't help how I feel. It's still him. I suspect it always will be."

"You don't know that. It just feels like it because it's all so raw again." She props her cell up, on her bedside table I'm guessing, and lies on her side on her bed. "You have come so far, Sydney. I'm proud of you for getting your life together. It wasn't easy after all you've endured. I'm glad you got some closure with Jared, but don't get sucked in again. I think it's time to fully let go, and I think you need your bestie by your side to help you through it. Whether it's here or you're some-place else, know I am going nowhere. I will help you through this. I promise."

Chapter Sixteen
Sydney

"Thank you so much. I couldn't have done this without your help," I tell my bestie and her fiancé after we finish unloading the boxes from the moving truck into my new beachside bungalow.

"I'm amazed you managed to relocate from overseas, buy a new house, purchase furniture, and get a new job all within two months, Syd," Jerry says, lifting his palm for a high five. "You're a miracle worker."

"Don't underestimate a woman when she's trying to get away from a man," Cay teases.

I roll my eyes at my bestie as warmth spreads across my chest. "Come here, you big teddy bear." I yank Jerry into a hug whether he wants one or not. "Thank you. For helping me and for loving my best friend. I'm so happy Cayenne found you."

"He's the best." Cay snuggles into her man as I step away.

"He's a keeper," I agree.

"I'm thrilled you're here, Syd. This move is going to be the absolute best thing for you. I feel it in my bones," Cay adds.

"I agree," Ashley says, wiping her hands down the front of

her jean shorts as she steps out of my house. "I'm so excited we're living close to one another."

I wouldn't call a three-hour drive close, but I know what she means. Half Moon Bay is much closer to Lowell than New York is. "I can't wait to hang out more often." I smile at my pretty cousin.

"Bring your husbands next time," Cay says, waggling her brows. "I'm dying to meet them. Syd says they're all total smoke shows."

Ash smirks. "Did she now?!"

"I've got eyes in my head. You know they're all hot AF. Own that shit, cuz. You did good."

"Yeah, I did. Didn't I?" Her smirk transforms to a dreamy smile.

"And that's my cue to leave," Jerry quips, removing the truck keys from his back pocket.

"You're *my* smoke show." Cay grabs a fistful of his shirt and yanks him into a searing-hot kiss.

Ash and I pretend to fan ourselves when they break apart, and Jerry leaves a contented man. He is driving the moving van back to the city while his fiancée stays with me for the weekend to help with the unpacking.

"He's one of the good ones," Ash confirms as we wave Jerry off and head toward my new house.

"I never thought I'd ever fall in love," Cay truthfully admits as we enter the hallway. "And then, bam, I ran into Jerry on the street, and it was like being struck by lightning."

"Aw, I love that." Ash squeezes Cay. "Now, we just need to get this one fixed up." She jabs her thumb over her shoulder in my direction.

"I'm a lost cause. Don't waste your energy on me."

Ash quirks a brow as we walk past stacked boxes in the hall

and gravitate toward the kitchen. "Why do I get the feeling this so-called-closure you talked about hasn't happened?"

"Because you can't control your heart with your head, no matter how much you might try," Cay says, lifting a box onto the island unit in the middle of my large airy kitchen. "Did you ever meet Jared?"

Ash and I lift boxes onto the large wooden table and begin unpacking dinnerware.

"I met him a couple times when I visited with my parents at Christmas," Ash explains. "But it was years ago."

"Then you'll know he's not easy to get over," Cay explains, unwrapping bubble wrap from a ceramic dish.

I had all my kitchen ware, art supplies, and personal items shipped from Florence, paying a premium to have it expedited, but I needed to buy all new furniture as my apartment in Italy had come fully furnished, so I didn't own anything. I still don't have everything I need, but I focused on the main rooms—the kitchen, living room, my bedroom, and my art studio.

The minute I discovered the large sunroom at the back of this house, which faces the oceanfront, I knew this was home for me. The four-bedroom, five-bathroom, four-thousand-square-foot bungalow isn't directly on the beach, but I have a private walkway to it through the small, wooded area behind my house. My property is on a slightly elevated plot, so I can see the beach and the ocean from the sunroom and the adjoining dining room.

The lady who sold me this place was an avid gardener, and the stunning rear gardens are a bonus. I can't wait to entertain on my patio and to paint outdoors. I still pinch myself to believe this is mine.

It's always been my dream to live by the ocean, and now I'm doing it.

Although I was sad to leave my life and my friends behind in Florence, I'm excited to be beginning a new chapter.

This feels incredibly right. Like I've always meant to be living here. Although I adored Florence and had come to call it home, it's only now I'm here I realize it was a temporary stopgap. My first home but not my forever one. Half Moon Bay feels like my endgame.

"Have you heard from him?" Ash asks, carefully stacking white dinner plates on the table.

I shake my head. "I haven't heard from Jared since the night we talked in Florence. Not that I was expecting to. We didn't leave it like that." Thankfully, I've been busy managing the relocation, but that doesn't mean he hasn't been on my mind.

Because he has.

A lot.

"My heart hurts for you, babe. I still can't get over everything Uncle Herman did." Ash's eyes narrow to slits. "My offer stands. Just say the word, and I'll have someone look into it."

"I appreciate it, but I don't want to look back. It's in the past where I want it to stay."

That's not quite the truth. I have been reconsidering options in the two months since the full truth was revealed, and it raised everything to the surface again. It's all so raw, and it's reignited my anger. I just don't want to involve my cousin. Ashley went through something recently. Mostly stuff she hasn't told me, because she can't, but I know it was some heavy shit. She's newly married and still grieving her loss, and I don't want to drag her into my crap.

If I'm going to do anything about it, I'll go to Sawyer and Xavier. I know they'd help, and this is what they do for a living.

But it's not something I'm ready to decide quite yet.

"I still think you should have told Jared that part," Ashley adds.

"It would only hurt him. I want him to be happy even if it's not with me."

"I saw the news online," Cay says before her lips pull into a tight line.

"What news?" Ash's gaze dances from me to Cay.

Pain stabs me through the heart. "Vittoria's pregnancy has hit the headlines. I'm surprised you didn't hear it on the radio on the drive here. It's all I see when I turn on the TV and my social media feeds are full of it." The sooner they move to Florence, the better.

"I thought they wanted to keep it a secret?" Cay muses, remembering what I told her of that day at the gallery. "She only has a teeny bump. I'm sure she could have disguised it for longer."

For someone who is four and a half months pregnant, Vittoria is tiny. You would barely know she is pregnant. "Someone in their entourage probably blabbed," I surmise. "They were completing the last leg of their tour, and someone must have noticed and sold them out."

"I don't think so." Cay empties that box and lifts a second one, leaving the contents for me to decide where they go. "From what I've read, she was in L.A. the whole time they were touring."

"Can we change the subject, please. It hurts too much to think of him having a baby with her when ours was stolen from me."

"Aw, babe," Cay says as they both rush to my side and hug me.

A sob rips from my mouth. "Sorry," I whisper as tears roll silently down my face. "I'm trying to move on. I thought it would be easier after I knew he didn't purposely abandon me, but it's harder. We would be together if our parents hadn't kept us apart. That should be me having his baby. I should be the one wearing his ring, and it fucking hurts."

I fall apart, letting weeks of pain run free as I lean on my cousin and my best friend for support. After a good cry, I feel a little better. Not cured. I doubt I will ever get over losing Jared and our baby, but at least I've purged some of my emotions.

We make quick work of the kitchen, and the girls move on to the living room while I head to my bedroom to tackle it.

Hours later, as nightfall encroaches, we call time-out on the unpacking, order takeout, and escape outside with a bottle of wine.

"Man, it's so peaceful here." Cay rubs a hand over her full belly and kicks her legs up on the empty chair across from her. "Maybe we should have bought here too."

"You love your apartment, and it's in a fabulous location. Neither of you have far to travel for work."

"It's only a fifty-minute drive for you," she reminds me, swirling the white wine in her glass. "That's a workable commute."

"Yeah, but I'm only working part-time at the museum, and I won't be driving in rush hour."

"That makes a big difference," Ash agrees, topping off our wine in between texting her husbands.

"You and Jerry can come here on the weekends if you want to unwind. I have plenty of room."

"You might regret offering that." Cay smirks as she clinks her glass against mine.

"You know I won't. You're family."

"Maybe, next weekend, if it suits, we could do a barbecue here. Jerry could invite Logan. It'd be more casual than a double date."

"Cay." My tone warns my bestie. She's been trying to set me up with this guy Jerry works with, but I'm having none of it.

I have enough on my plate without adding another complication to the mix.

"You need to get back out there, babe. You're not going to sink into another Jared-induced depression on my watch. Logan is hot. He's totally your type. And he's a fucking sweetheart. I think you'll love him."

"What harm could it do to meet him on your terms?" Ash suggests, gulping back wine. "If you don't gel with him, it doesn't have to go any further."

"Maybe you're right."

What is the point in clinging to memories of a lost love who has moved on? This is a fresh start. Another chance to start over, only this time I know exactly where I stand with Jared. There is no point pining over a man who will never be mine. Maybe throwing myself into the dating scene is what I need to put Jared behind me once and for all.

He's not mine to love anymore, and I need to start accepting the harsh truth.

It's time to prioritize *my* happily ever after.

I see how happy Ash and Cay are, and I want that for me.

"Set it up," I decide, raising my glass in a toast. "To new beginnings."

"To new beginnings." Cay and Ash grin conspiratorially as we clink glasses, and I sincerely hope this means I have turned a corner.

Because I desperately need it.

Chapter Seventeen
Jared

I storm into my Bel Air house with steam billowing out of my ears. "Tor!" I roar as I stomp down the hallway, stopping to throw my keys in the bowl on the hall table. "Where are you?" Popping my head into the kitchen and the living room and finding it empty, I take the stairs two at a time, heading for my master suite on the top level. My anger mushrooms with every step, and I'm fit to explode. My ex-fiancée is testing my patience to the limit, and I'm close to cracking.

We returned from our tour two weeks ago, and I immediately broke things off. The sense of utter relief was enormous. It was like this giant boulder lifted from my shoulders. Predictably, Toria pitched an epic hissy fit, screaming and crying and shouting threats when throwing things at me didn't work. I'm glad I took Linc and Wilder home with me for the confrontation. I had a feeling I would need witnesses.

I told her to take whatever time she needed packing up her stuff even though it shouldn't take long as she only moved in after I proposed. But she's still here, and she's already playing games. I know she has her apartment in downtown L.A.

because she'd signed a lease for a year, so it's not like she has nowhere to go. If she didn't, I would have found her some place to live. I'm not heartless, and I already told her I would ensure she is well looked after.

"Tor!" I yell again as I race down the hallway toward my bedroom. "Fucking answer me!" She fired the nurse I hired even though she had no right to do it as I'm the one paying her wages and she reports to me. The poor woman refuses to return even with my offer to triple her already generous salary.

Toria managed to traumatize her in *a fucking week.*

I rue the day I ever let my publicist set me up with her. If I'd said no, I would not be in this mess.

The door to my bedroom slams open, and my fists clench at my sides when I see the state of the place. It's like I've been burglarized. Piles of clothes fight for floor space alongside empty vodka bottles, overturned takeout cartons, stale, half-eaten doughnuts, crumpled pizza boxes, and used tissues. Drawers are pulled out, the contents tossed haphazardly over the floor. One of the drapes has been torn from the top, and it's hanging precariously off the pole. Several windows display cracked panes of glass.

I would probably be happy she's eating, even if it's a ton of junk food that's bad for the baby, except the sight of alcohol has me fit to throttle the selfish bitch. Tapping out a message to my assistant, I ask her to send a medical team, the cops, my lawyer, and Toria's lawyers to my house ASAP. I want this documented officially, and then I'm taking Toria to court to fight to protect my unborn child. This is fucking unacceptable.

My rage only accelerates when my ex saunters out of the en suite bathroom, completely naked, and proceeds to fling her arms around me. "Baby," she slurs, trying to kiss me. "I missed you."

Taking care to be gentle, which is harder than it might

seem, I lift her away from me. "Don't touch me, Tor. I am not yours to touch anymore."

"Imma not leaving." She sways as she pierces me with a venomous look. "You'll have evict me. See how fans like that!"

"You're drunk," I snarl, taking pictures of my ruined room.

She flips me the bird.

"You're hurting the baby. This is not fucking okay, Tor."

"This your fault." The waterworks start. "You did this to me. Ruin my body." She waves her hands up and down her naked body. "Ruin career."

"No," I say, scooping a black cotton dress up from the floor, scowling as I spot burn marks on my expensive rug. Was she fucking smoking?! "You did that to yourself."

I wonder what she said to my housekeeper to keep her out of here because downstairs doesn't look like this. I might think she hadn't left this bedroom except I know she's the one who leaked the news of her pregnancy to the media, and I'm guessing she did that in person because she wouldn't want any phone records tracing back to her.

"I know you tipped off the media."

It makes no sense. All along, she's been refusing to eat because she was worried about her career, so why would she out herself? Linc thinks this has been her plan all along. He thinks she got pregnant on purpose to trap me, and I am coming around to his way of thinking. Linc says not telling her manager and booker she was pregnant was strategic so they'd fire her when she showed up to jobs pregnant. He thinks she plans to milk me for every cent, and I threw a wrench in the works when I dumped her manipulative ass. So this is Plan B. Fall apart and pin the blame on me. Portray herself as the injured party. I knocked her up and then kicked her to the curb, and she turned to drink in a way to purge her pain. Make me out to be the bad guy when I am bending over backward to take care of her even if I fucking hate her guts, and at this point, I do.

Unfortunately, our PR people think she can garner sympathy by putting this spin on it. They have warned me to be cautious, as have my lawyers. Right now, my priority is my baby, and I will do whatever is necessary to protect my unborn child from his selfish, reckless mother.

"Put that on." I hand the dress to her.

"No." She throws it back at me, cupping her slightly enlarged breasts and pinching the nipples. "We fuck and make up."

I'd rather fuck a guitar.

Grabbing fistfuls of my hair, I pace the room and try to contain the turmoil raging inside me. She's riling me up to trick me into doing something she can throw back at me, and I can't let her.

"I have people on the way," I say, working hard to remain calm. "It's no skin off my back if you want them to see you naked. Knock yourself out, sweetheart." I turn and walk away as she screams and cries, ducking as something comes flying at my head.

I call Wilder on my way down the stairs. He lives closer to me than Linc. I should have asked them to come with me after we left the recording studio, but I hate having to ask them to drop everything to deal with my shit. Still, this has proven I need someone with me every time I am with Toria. I need witnesses because she's a crazy bitch, and she's capable of doing or saying anything.

Wilder arrives the same time the medical team does, closely followed by the cops and our two legal teams.

It's a fucking shit show. Tor puts on the performance of a lifetime, and she's taken away in an ambulance. She refused a breath test, but it doesn't matter. Everyone could see she was intoxicated. My lawyers took contact details from everyone on the scene, and they'll get statements. They also made everyone sign an NDA before they left. It's important we keep this contained, but it's a moot point if Toria continues blabbing to the press.

"I suggest we amend the paperwork to say she can stay in this house for the duration of her pregnancy, provided she agrees to a full-time nurse, agrees to take proper care of herself, abides by normal house rules, and she won't do anything that would injure or pose a risk to her unborn child. We can ask for biweekly sobriety and drug tests. If she disagrees, we go to court," my lawyer says as we discuss the situation in my dining room. Everyone but John and Wilder have left at this point.

"Okay." I exhale heavily. "Also amend it to say when she has given birth she must choose where she wants to live. If she wants to remain in L.A., I will sign over this house to her, but I'll be selling the Florence one. I'm not giving her both."

"You're not legally required to give her either one," John says, making notes on his phone. "This place is massive. You could sell it and buy her something smaller."

"She'll be taking care of my son." *I hope.* We discovered we are having a boy at the last scan. "I want them to be comfortable."

John removes his glasses and looks at me. "We could consider petitioning the court to grant you full custody. After what I witnessed upstairs, I think you'd have a decent chance of getting it. She seems unhinged."

"I thought the courts didn't like taking children from their mothers."

"They don't, but if there is a risk to the welfare of the child, they will."

"I don't want to take her baby from her. Unless it's absolutely necessary, and then I'll fight her tooth and nail for full custody." I'm hoping her maternal instincts will kick in when she delivers our child, but I'm not holding my breath.

"Let's play it by ear," John says, wrapping up his stuff. "I'll get the amendments made and have a fresh copy couriered to her legal firm first thing in the morning."

"Thank you."

He clamps a hand on my shoulder. "Stay strong, son, and I suggest you pack your bags and be gone before she's let out of hospital."

I land in London one week later, after some of the most stressful days of my life. Toria is determined to play hardball, but she fucked up by getting drunk and trashing my house. She clearly wasn't expecting me home yet, and I'm glad she messed up. I have a chance to stop this now before she damages our unborn child. The hospital took blood, and we have official proof she was intoxicated. Unfortunately, it's not enough to petition the court. There are no laws that restrict pregnant women from drinking, and it's not even considered child neglect if the drinking is constant or to excess—which it should be in my opinion.

Drugs are a different story. California is one of dozens of states that criminalize taking drugs during pregnancy. While none were found in her bloodstream, I don't trust her not to resort to cocaine. Toria is obsessed with her appearance, and she won't continue drinking because of the potential weight gain. There is a high risk she will resort to coke instead. I know she does it. It's part of the lifestyle, but hell will freeze over before I let her snort snow while carrying my child.

Unlucky for her, I have pics of her doing lines. We used it to threaten her. She had no choice but to agree to biweekly alcohol and drug testing and a day and night nurse. I've also got a full-time security detail protecting-slash-spying on her. Her lawyers convinced her to agree for her own safety. Now word is out, we're both being hounded by the media and chased by paps. I got a clause added to the legal agreement to say if she deliberately sabotages the relationship with the nursing team and drives either lady away, we will petition the court to have her sentenced to a care facility for the remainder of her pregnancy. Proof of drug use, along with her volatile personality, should be enough to take her to court on the grounds of risk to the fetus.

The fact she agreed means she considers it a real threat, and at least I have something to hold over her now.

I'm sure she's spitting blood, but I haven't been alone with her since the confrontation at the house to know. When we met at the lawyer's office to sign the agreement for the remaining period of her pregnancy, co-parenting, custody, and child support, she was on her best behavior, and there was barely a peep out of her.

I know she's biding her time. She's going to up the ante and try her best to destroy my sanity and my career, but for now, the situation is under control.

I wonder what Sydney is making of all this. As far as the public at large are concerned, Vittoria and I are still engaged and expecting a baby. Our PR people want to hold off on announcing the breakup because I'll look like a callous jerk for breaking up with my pregnant fiancée if it comes out so soon after the baby news.

I wish I could fly to some remote island, with no internet and no paparazzi, and escape from my troubles. It's tempting, but I can't leave Cali for more than a few days because I don't trust Toria. I'm worried she's going to try to kill herself or end the pregnancy, but my bandmates disagree. They think she's after my money and the baby is her golden key.

I hope they're right. At least my son will be safe if that's her agenda.

A car greets me at the airport, and I'm lost in thought on the drive to my mother's home in Chelsea. I haven't been able to stop thinking about Sydney and everything that transpired years ago. God, I've missed that woman so much. A few hours in her company, and I'm lovesick all over again. We were so good together. I don't care we were only kids. It was the real deal.

I knew then what I know now—she is my forever.

I'm going to fight to win her back.

Nothing else matters to me but her.

I'm so fucking pissed at the things her father did and annoyed at myself for not looking her up when we turned eighteen. I played right into Vil's hand, reading more into that photo he sent and using it as the basis for turning my back on the only girl who has ever mattered.

I need to know if my parents were involved. Hence why I'm here.

"Darling." Mum rushes out to greet me. "I'm so glad you're here." She holds my arms and looks me over. "You look like shit, and it's no surprise." Her lips purse. "I did not like hearing I am to be a grandmother on Sky News."

"I was going to tell you, but the media beat me to it."

"Come in and tell me everything." She loops her arm through mine as we climb the steps and enter her three-story townhouse.

She bought it with the divorce settlement from Dad—later supplementing her portfolio with a villa in Portugal, a beachside property in Barbados, and a condo in New York—which happened seven months after they sent me to boarding school—

and she's lived here alone ever since. She doesn't seem short of male company, regularly jetting to luxurious destinations with various younger men. Some are even younger than me, but I don't judge. It's her life, but I can't help feeling they are just using her for her money. I wish she'd find a new husband. She must get lonely, and I don't like thinking of her so far away from me and my sister, all alone in this big house.

I confide everything about Toria and the baby over ham and cheese sandwiches, scones with jam and clotted cream, and English tea.

"Jesus, Jared." Concern is etched all over her face. "I always knew she was a manipulative little bitch, but she's certifiably nuts. You're right to be worried about the baby."

"She's almost five months pregnant. We're more than halfway through, so I just need to hang on and get her safely through the rest of the pregnancy."

"Oh, Jared. You poor sod. You're fucked. She's your baby's mother, and you'll be dealing with her tantrums for years, my boy. I wish you had knocked up anyone but her. She puts Naomi Campbell to shame with her antics."

Truth. She's chucked far worse things than cell phones at my head. "It wasn't intentional. Trust me."

"Are you even sure it's yours?"

"She had a paternity test. It's mine."

"What can I do to help?" Mum asks, propping her elbows on the table and her chin in her hands.

"I'm not sure there's anything you can do yet, but if you could come to the US for a while after the baby is born, I'd appreciate the help."

"I'll be there with bells on. Heather will help too."

Heather lives in Boston, and she has her own family, so I'm not sure how often my sister will be able to visit, but I know if I asked her she'd be on a flight straightaway.

"I didn't just come to tell you about Toria and the baby. I wanted to ask you about something else."

"Let's grab some beers and sit in the garden," she suggests, and I don't protest.

Ten minutes later, I'm enjoying the late August sunshine in Mum's garden, nursing an ice-cold beer.

I clear my throat and eyeball my mother as I say, "I saw Sydney recently."

Her eyes pop wide, and then I see it. Fear. Panic. And something else. She's quick to hide it, but I saw, and it tells me enough to confirm my suspicions.

"Oh, how lovely," she says when she recovers. "How is she?"

"Cut the crap, Mum." I grind my teeth to my molars as I level her with a sharp look. "I'm sick of all the lies, and I want the truth. I want to know what exactly you did and why you purposely sabotaged my relationship with Sydney."

Chapter Eighteen
Jared

"I did it for you." Her lower lip wobbles, and her hand shakes as she lifts the beer bottle to her mouth.

Rage charges through my veins, and I grip the side of my chair in an attempt to calm down. "I knew it! I fucking knew it," I snap. "You sent that picture to Anvil from my phone, didn't you?"

She gives me a curt nod. "I suspected Herman was intercepting your calls and texts to Sydney, so I had to get creative. I heard you arguing with Anvil shortly before we left New York. I knew he was planning to make a play for her. I knew if I sent him that picture he would jump to the obvious conclusion, and I knew he'd show it to Sydney."

"Why, Mum? Why would you hurt Sydney like that? She was like a daughter to you! You practically raised her after Michelle died. Did her feelings mean nothing to you? Did mine?" I drain my beer and throw the bottle against the wall, watching it shatter into smithereens, as anger pummels me from the inside.

"Are you done?" Mum's tone is firmer, and she's more in control.

"Not even fucking close!" I hiss.

"It hurt me to hurt Sydney. I did love her as if she was my own flesh and blood. She was such a sweetheart. Having to walk away from her was one of the hardest things I've ever done especially because I knew I was leaving her with that... that fucking psycho!" Unnamed emotion flits across her face. "I have felt huge guilt for years."

"So you should. He made her life hell. She doesn't even talk to him anymore. That's how bad it was."

She at least has the decency to look ashamed. "I'm genuinely sorry to hear that, but I had to make a choice, Jared." Leaning across the garden table, she takes my hand. I snatch it back immediately and glower at her. "He threatened your life," she admits. "He warned me if I didn't keep you away from his princess he would kill you and hide the evidence."

Bitter laughter slips from my lips. "Come on, Mum. Surely you didn't fall for that."

"Mock me all you like, but I know what that man is capable of. The threat was very real."

I lean forward. "Why did he do it? Why take over Dad's company and try to ruin us?"

"I'm not sure you're ready to hear that truth."

"Goddamn it, Mum!" I slam my fist down on the table. "Enough with the lies! Just tell me!"

"Your father had an affair with Michelle Shaw," she blurts, and my jaw slackens.

"What? When?"

"It started when you kids were only toddlers. They were carrying on right under our noses for years. They were planning to set up home together until Michelle got cancer and

Amos dumped her." A cruel sneer spreads over her lips, and I never would've thought Mum capable of such naked hostility.

"I don't believe you."

She barks out a laugh. "No, of course, you don't. You thought your father could do no wrong, but he was a cheating asshole who couldn't keep it in his pants. Michelle was not his first affair nor his last."

Shock races through me. "Are you telling the truth or embellishing it because the man is not here to defend himself?"

Hurt splays across her face. "I guess I did a better job of shielding you than I realized. Ask Heather if you don't believe me. Your older sister saw a lot of it. She knows the truth."

"Why did you stay with him? If he was cheating on you, why didn't you leave?"

Tears pool in her eyes. "Because I loved him. I knew most of them meant nothing, but that was before Michelle. She was my best friend. Our kids were best friends. Our husbands were best friends. How could she do that to me?" She's full-on crying now, and some of my anger fades.

I circle my arm around her shoulders. "It was a double betrayal. I can't imagine how that must have felt. Did you confront her?"

Mum sniffles and pulls away. "I didn't know at the time of her death. I only found out years later." She swipes at the dampness under her eyes. "Herman was getting work done in the house. The workmen found a box when they pulled up the flooring in his bedroom. It contained letters, shared between his wife and my husband, along with damning pictures and other mementos of their secret relationship."

"Herman didn't know either?"

She shakes her head and swallows a mouthful of beer. I take the opportunity to go inside and grab two fresh ones.

I sit back down and slide a bottle to her side.

"He was devastated." Mum stares into space as she talks. "Herman idolized his wife. He was obsessed with Michelle, sometimes to the point she felt smothered. I have never seen a man more in love with his wife than Herman Shaw. Her betrayal changed him, and not for the better."

"He wanted revenge. That's why he did it."

Air expels from her mouth. "Yes, and he planned it methodically. He continued pretending to be your father's friend for over a year while he plotted to ruin his life. He wanted to take everything from him so he would know similar devastation." She averts her eyes and picks at the label on her bottle. "Your father found out before he could put his full plan into place, and well, you saw how that turned out."

She wets her lips. "It's why we left. We were terrified Herman would physically harm us." She turns to face me. "He was acting crazy, and he wanted you nowhere near his daughter. He considered you to be a chip off the old block. He was convinced you would turn out to be a philanderer like your dad. He made death threats against you, Jared. I know you're struggling to accept this, and I understand how it sounds, but that man is pure evil. We hadn't realized it before, or maybe what your father did sent him over the edge. Either way, I wasn't taking any chances. You are my son, and I had to prioritize you over Sydney. I'm not saying it's right, but I did what I had to do."

She drains the rest of her first bottle and instantly starts drinking the second.

"Did Dad know about the photo?"

She shakes her head. "He wouldn't have approved. He loved Syd, and he was worried about her."

"Thank fuck someone was. Pity he didn't do anything about it." I scrub my hands down my face as I try to grasp the seriousness of what she's telling me. Sydney told me her father became controlling, and I get the sense she was holding stuff back. When I factor that in, it doesn't sound so farfetched.

"I understand, Mum. I don't forgive you for it, but I understand why you did what you did. I still don't know how you could turn your back on her knowing that. Did you even check in on her?"

She hangs her head, and I have my answer.

"You could have gone to the authorities and reported him."

"On what grounds, Jared?" She knots her hands on top of the table. "I couldn't go to the police without any proof, and we were afraid of what else he could do to us. He was an extremely well-connected businessman, and he had skilled technologists working for him who could ruin people with a few strokes of their keyboards. We couldn't take that risk. He had already robbed your father of his company, and we lost half of our wealth when we were forced to sell our shareholding at a rock-bottom price. We had enough to reestablish ourselves here, and that had to be a priority. You're going to be a father soon. Then you'll understand."

"You could have gone to her when she was eighteen and helped Sydney to get away from him, or you could have told me then what you'd done, but you didn't plan on ever telling me, did you?"

Her expression is resolute as she looks at me. "No. As long as Herman Shaw is alive, you are not safe if you go near his daughter."

Harsh laughter rumbles through my chest. "Herman Shaw might have been able to control my life when I was a teen, but I'm a grown-ass man now with powerful contacts and resources of my own. He doesn't get to dictate what I do now."

"No, Jared." Mum clutches her chest. "Please don't pursue anything with Sydney. He'll kill you!"

"Not if I kill him first." I drain my beer, placing it down on the table this time. I'm eerily calm as I stand. "You need to understand something, Mum. I love Sydney. I have loved her my whole life, and I'm done living without her."

I'm not sure how I'll pull it off. I don't know if Sydney still has feelings for me, how serious things are with her boyfriend, or if she's willing to give me a second chance. If I can convince her to let me back into her life, there's the obvious elephant in the room. Even though I'm no longer in a relationship with Toria, she is still having my baby. That won't be easy for Sydney to accept, whether it's now or after my son is born. But I'm hoping we can find a way to make it work because I want her back for good. That future I have always wanted is there for the taking, and I'm going to fight with everything I have.

Sydney belongs with me.

We can be a family.

Sydney would be a positive maternal figure in my son's life and, if I end up getting full custody, his future stepmother.

We can make lots of beautiful babies together.

The thought of watching Sydney's belly swell with our child brings out the Neanderthal in me as well as a jealous possessive side I have only ever felt with her.

"If you love her, you'll leave her alone, Jared. No good can come from this. Please. I'm begging you."

I thump a closed fist against my heart. "I am done living with this hole in my heart. A few hours in her company, and it reinforced what I have always known. Sydney is it for me. She's the love of my life. Nothing and no one is keeping me from her again. Herman can send his goons after me. He can try to ruin me. I don't fucking care because I'll throw everything right back at him. All that matters is Sydney. I wasn't there to protect her last time, but I'm sure as fuck going to be there for her now. If Herman comes for us, he'll regret the day he crossed me, and that's a promise."

Chapter Nineteen
Sydney

Warmth fills my chest as the sun crests the hazy blue sky, shooting glorious rays of buttery sunlight over the land below. Languid waves lap the sandy shore, ebbing and flowing with unhurried grace. The Pacific Ocean is peaceful at this time of morning, and the fresh salty air cleans my lungs and clears my head. Sitting back in my chair, propped in front of my easel, I admire the rugged beauty of the green Santa Cruz mountains in the distance. My gaze flits from my canvas to the awe-inspiring sight in front of me as I attempt to capture the sunrise in all its magnificence.

You haven't lived if you haven't experienced sunrise. It's magical.

One of my favorite things to do now is get up early to paint or walk on the beach just as day is breaking. Apart from a few joggers, walkers, and fellow sunrise worshippers, the beach is usually pretty deserted at this hour. It feels like I'm the only person in Half Moon Bay, and I adore the serenity and the feeling of being at one with nature and the world.

In the month since I moved into my bungalow, I have tried

my best to embrace my new life to the fullest. I'm enjoying my shared museum manager's role at the Legion of Honor, the foremost fine arts museum in San Fran. Working part-time keeps it from becoming too stressful, and it gives me plenty of time to paint as well as work on getting my house fixed up exactly the way I want it. I've been painting it myself, taking time to live in the space before deciding on the right décor.

I've even been out on a few dates with Logan. He's a nice guy. Attractive. Charming. Interesting. While there are no major sparks, I'm giving it a chance. I owe it to myself to try.

Humming quietly to myself, I dab my brush at the base of the horizon on my canvas, adding a few orange tones to mirror the view in front of me. I'm engrossed in my work, so I don't see the jogger until he's almost on top of me.

Exaggerated breathing and the pounding of sneakers on the sand breaks my concentration, and I look up, my mouth instantly slackening as the man slams to a halt, staring at me in equal shock.

It's been three months since I last saw Jared in the flesh. The very last place on earth I thought I'd find him is here.

His Adam's apple bobs in his throat as he looks at me. He's shirtless, wearing only sneakers, flimsy running shorts, and a sheen of glistening sweat on his broad shoulders, toned abs, and defined chest. There is no missing the ink covering both arms and dancing across the top of his chest or the fact his nipples are pierced. A tempting layer of dark hair trails invitingly under the waistband of his shorts, reminding me Jared is all man now. Defined V-shaped indents at his hips are testament to dedication in the gym.

Jared King is the full package, and I'd challenge any woman not to fall at his feet if he showed up looking like this. Dragging his arm across the sweat beading at his brow, he cuts through the sand as he strides toward me with visible purpose.

My heart beats faster, and weird things are happening in my stomach and lower unmentionables.

Worryingly, his impact has not lessened. I'm as enamored with him as I've always been. In a few seconds, it feels like all my progress has been undone. How I ever thought I could get over this man is beyond me.

There is no getting over losing someone like Jared.

I don't think I'll ever get past it.

"Syd?" Jared comes to a standstill in front of me, hovering behind my easel. "What in the world are you doing here?"

"I could ask you the same thing." Setting my paintbrush down, I stand, feeling at a disadvantage when he's looming over me. I jerk my head behind me. "I live back there."

His eyes almost bug out of his face. "Since when?"

"I moved in a month ago."

A slow glorious smile spreads over his mouth, and his entire face lights up. Bathed in a halo of early morning sun, he looks like a bona fide Greek god. No guy should be this good-looking. It's unfair to the rest of the male race.

"I have a flight booked to Florence on Friday," he admits. "I'm glad I bumped into you. I'd be pissed to travel all that way to see you, only to discover you're right on my doorstep."

A frown creases my brow. "Why would you be coming to Florence to see me?" He must mean to put the finishing touches on his new house there.

"I have a lot to catch you up on." He comes around to my side, and his smile expands as his gaze skims over my painting.

Anxiety churns in my gut, and I chew on the inside of my mouth. I'm always antsy showing anyone my work.

"Wow, Syd. This is fantastic." He lifts his smiling face to mine, and I almost drown in the depths of his gorgeous sky-blue eyes. "You haven't lost your touch."

"Jared, what's going on right now?" I just put it out there

because I'm thoroughly confused. "How are you here? I don't understand."

"I live a few houses down there." He stretches his arm to the right as all the color drains from my face.

"What?" I blurt, instantly fighting tears. This cannot be happening. "I thought you lived in L.A.?"

"I did." He rubs the back of his neck. "I mean, I do. I still have my house in Bel Air, but I bought a place here recently. Only moved in three days ago. I wanted to escape all the noise in L.A. but still be close enough I can commute easily for work. I bought a helicopter, and I'm planning to take flying lessons so I can eventually pilot it myself."

Everything he says, after he confirms he's living here, floats over my head. All my hopes for a fresh start evaporate, and I'm close to losing my shit. I refuse to break down in front of him. I don't want Jared to see what this revelation has done to me. Abandoning my things, I turn and run toward the private path that leads to my house, needing to get away from him before I fall apart.

Jared calls after me, but I can't focus on anything but getting away from this new hell.

"Syd, stop!" He takes hold of my elbow, and I almost face-plant the ground.

"Get away from me!" I cry, trying to shuck out of his hold as I lose control of my emotions.

"Not until you tell me what's going on." Concern is etched all over his face as he watches the silent tears roll down my cheeks. "I've upset you. Tell me what I did?" he asks more quietly, loosening his hold on my elbow but not letting go.

"You're moving here with your family, Jared. I would've thought it's self-explanatory." I bark out a laugh. "I moved to get away from you! I literally just bought a house here, and now I'm screwed. Fuck my life!" Tipping my head back, I shout at the sky. "What the fuck did I ever do to deserve this?"

"Sydney." Jared's tortured voice wraps around me, and it makes me mad. What does he have to be upset about?

"What?" I snap, eyeballing him as I silently erect walls around my heart and suck all the tears back into my eyes.

"You moved from Florence because of me?" Disbelief threads through his tone.

"Did you seriously think I could live there knowing you were planning to raise your family there? You might have moved on, but I have struggled. I'm still struggling." I'm too pissed to shield the truth from him. He needs to know so he'll stop freaking moving to wherever I live.

Something close to relief flares in his eyes. "I haven't moved on." He steps in closer, peering deep into my eyes. "I have never gotten over losing you, Syd. My heart still beats only for you."

I feel sheer joy for about five seconds until I remember. Horror washes over me as I stumble back, fixing him with a sharp look. "Does your fiancée know this?"

"She's not my fiancée anymore."

I blink repeatedly and tug at my ears, sure I must have misheard him. "What?"

"I ended things with Toria."

"Why? When?" I croak. My mind is a jumbled mess.

"The minute I came off tour, and because I don't love her. I never have. It's only ever been you, Syd. It's only you." His soft tone is laced with heartfelt emotion, and I'm a firework about to detonate.

This can't be real, can it? "What about the baby?"

"I won't abandon my son. I have a co-parenting agreement in place with my ex, but that's my only involvement with her going forward." He stares at me expectantly, unaware I'm a mess inside and incapable of speaking. "Say something," he pleads.

"I don't know what to say," I whisper, rubbing at my chest.

"It's only one of the things I wanted to catch you up on." He drags a hand through his messy hair. "Can we talk? Properly talk? How about breakfast at my place? I make a mean omelet." He flashes me a grin.

My mouth opens and closes. I'm speechless. My head and my heart are in a tailspin. "I don't know if that's a good thing."

"Please, Sydney." The grin fades. Anguished blue eyes plead with me. "I spoke to Mum. I've got stuff to tell you about the past. About your dad. I'm just asking for an hour of your time. Can you spare me that?"

***

"Go and see what he has to say for himself," Cay says after I have calmed down. I was like a raving lunatic when I first video called her. "I don't see how there's any harm in it."

"This has thrown me." I flop down on my bed and sigh. "Do you think he was telling the truth? There is nothing in the media about them breaking up. Maybe he lied to get me to his place."

"This is Jared, Syd. I know we don't know him anymore, but he was never a liar. I don't see how it would serve his agenda to do so now. Just go and find out what he has to say, and then call me immediately. I don't care what time it is. I'll give my cell to my assistant so she can interrupt me if I'm with a client."

"I'm scared," I whisper.

"Why?"

"What if he's telling me the truth? What if he hasn't moved on? What if he still has feelings for me?"

Her features soften. "You mean what if you might get what your heart has always wanted?"

I nod.

"That wouldn't be a bad thing, Syd."

"So much time has passed, and we're different people now. It might not work. I might get my heart broken all over again."

"Your heart has never mended. Either this is meant to be or it'll give you the closure you need to move on."

"Maybe."

"No matter what happens, I'm here for you. Take it one step at a time, babe, starting with getting answers, and we'll figure it out from there."

Chapter Twenty
Jared

"I thought we could eat on the deck unless you'd rather sit indoors?" I say as Sydney surveys my vast kitchen with inquisitive eyes. She looks beautiful in her soft-pink knee-length dress with a white cardigan. Wedge sandals adorn her feet, elongating her long slim legs and making her look even taller. Blonde strands tumble down her back in silky sheets and she's wearing minimal makeup. She's a breath of fresh air in a world drowning in fakeness. It's no wonder I've never been able to forget her.

"The deck is fine." She turns to look out the floor-to-ceiling windows that wrap around the rear of my two-story house, offering an ocean view that is to die for. I still can't believe we've both ended up here.

I'd say it's fate, but I believe fate is what you make it.

She steps outside, and I follow carrying a tray with orange juice, coffee, omelets, croissants, and fresh fruit.

After we are settled at the table, seated beside one another, overlooking the beach, I pour her a coffee, serve her a plate with a mushroom, spinach, and cheese omelet, and tell her to help herself to the rest.

"Want to see something cool?" I ask, removing the remote control from the pocket of my shorts.

"Sure." Her pretty eyes dart to my face before quickly looking away.

Pressing the button, I watch her eyes widen as the wooden fencing around my property retracts, revealing the clear bullet-proof polycarbonate fencing behind it.

Her mouth trails the floor, and I chuckle.

"I had to install fencing all around the perimeter and implement other security measures when I bought this house," I explain.

"That makes sense," she murmurs. "I bet you have all kinds of groupies, crazies, and stalkers harassing you."

"I could tell you a few stories," I say over a grimace. "Privacy is important to me. I wanted to ensure my house was safe, but I didn't want to miss out on the spectacular view. The interior designer I hired came up with this solution."

"It's genius."

"I think so."

"The things money can buy," she murmurs as she cuts her omelet into even-sized chunks.

"I know I'm fortunate. I never even experienced life as a struggling musician like most wannabe rock stars 'cause Mum insisted on buying me an apartment in L.A. and giving me a generous monthly allowance."

Sydney cocks her head to one side, tracing a slim finger around the rim of her mug. "I thought my dad ruined your father's business?"

"Oh, he did. My parents lost a lot of their wealth that time, but dad built a successful new business in the UK, and it must have done okay as Mum got a very generous divorce settlement."

"I only heard about the divorce from media reports at the time of your dad's death," she quietly says.

"They divorced a few months after they enrolled me in the boarding school from hell."

"That must have been hard."

I shrug. "Guess it's no surprise their marriage was a casualty. Things were pretty shit after we left New York." This is the perfect opportunity to share what Mum told me, but we haven't eaten yet. I know she's going to be upset, so I selfishly say nothing for now.

Silence descends, and we're both lost in thought, but it's not awkward. Scooping some omelet into my mouth before it goes cold, I stare at the calming rolling motion of the waves as they hit the shore.

"Wow, this is yummy," Sydney acknowledges after a mouthful of omelet. Her mouth is practically watering as she enthusiastically scoops up another forkful of my creation.

"You're welcome."

"When did you learn to cook?"

"I didn't." I smirk. "I can cook this, spaghetti bolognese, and beans on toast. That's about it. Unless you count cooking anything frozen as a special talent."

She grins. "That sounds more like the Jared I know." Her smile fades as the words register, and I hate it.

"I didn't get much opportunity to learn how to cook," I admit as she returns to her omelet. "I was too busy with the band and you when we were younger, then I was in boarding school, and when I moved to L.A., I existed largely on takeout or ready-made meals. Now, I mostly eat out or live on frozen food and the limited meals I can cook."

"I followed your career," she admits in between bites. "I wasn't surprised you made it, only how quick it happened."

"I caught a lucky break. I was only in L.A. three months when I met an A&R guy at a bar where I was playing with a crappy band I'd hooked up with shortly after arriving. He spotted something in me and asked if I was interested in auditioning to join a band already signed to Torment's new label. I hit it off instantly with Wilder and Keith, and the rest is history."

"I'm really proud of you, J." Her stunning emerald eyes glisten with emotion. "Even if I was mad at you for abandoning me, I never stopped being proud of your accomplishments."

"I wished you were with me all the damn time," I admit.

She levels me with a knowing look. "Yeah, I'm sure you wanted a girlfriend tied to your hip when you were out partying and hooking up with celebrities and supermodels."

"I won't deny I enjoyed the trappings of fame, but it was all transitory. A blur of nameless faces and bodies." Her mouth pulls into a grimace, but I'm not apologizing for my past. I was a red-blooded nineteen-year-old man when we hit it big. I was single and pining for the girl I lost. Doing everything I could to try to numb my heartache. I buried myself in drink, drugs, and pussy, but it never worked. "None of them were you."

Finishing her omelet, she reaches for her OJ, and I watch her mind churning as she drinks. She swivels on her chair to face me. "Is that the truth? Were you really thinking of me?"

I nod. "Constantly. You're embedded in here"—I tap my temple—"as much as you're embedded in here." I place a hand over my heart.

"Yet you never came for me."

Shame surges in my veins. "I thought you betrayed me with Anvil, Syd. I thought you didn't give a shit about me. I was hardly going to come chasing after you even if my heart couldn't let go."

Slowly, she nods. "Yeah, I get that, to a certain extent." Her eyes pierce mine. "I never forgot you either, Jared," she says in a raspy tone. "I tried really hard, but I couldn't move on."

Inside, I'm throwing a party. We have a mountain to climb, but knowing she still has feelings for me is what I've been hoping for. All would've been lost if she no longer cared, so this is huge. Momentous.

Taking a risk, I reach out and place my hand over hers on the table. She goes rigidly still. "We have lost so much time. I hate all the years we were apart, and I'm hoping we can make up for it now."

Pulling her hand out from under mine, she looks down at her plate for a few seconds. I chew the last piece of omelet and spoon some fruit onto my plate, along with a croissant, while I wait her out.

"I can't even consider that, let alone discuss it," she finally says, lifting her head. "It's been more than ten years, Jared, and you just broke up with someone you've been engaged to for two years. A woman you're having a baby with. I really don't see how there is any room for a discussion of us picking up where we left off."

"I wasn't engaged to her for two years," I clarify after munching on a strawberry. "I only proposed when she told me she was pregnant. We were only engaged for three months. That's it."

"Don't lie." She glares at me. "I remember the magazine headlines when you got engaged. I'd only just gotten married, so I know exactly when it was. I was miserable already, and those headlines nearly pushed me over the edge."

Acid crawls up my throat at her admission and my heart

stops for a few beats. "You are married to that guy?" I choke out.

Her brows knit together. "What guy?"

"The prick in Italy," I hiss.

"I'm not married to Gio. He's only an ex-boyfriend. And for the record, he's not a prick." Relief sinks bone deep as she levels me with a scathing look.

"If not him, then who?"

"Sawyer Hunt."

"Should I know who that is?"

Sydney dollops fruit onto her plate as she talks. "I forgot you're no longer up to speed with New York life. Sawyer's dad owns Techxet, a global billion-dollar tech company. Sawyer went to West Lorian too though he was a few years younger than us. He's a tech genius in his own right, and he runs his own IT consultancy company now with his husband."

"Husband?" Curiosity underscores my tone.

She sighs as she reaches for a croissant. "It's complicated, and it doesn't matter. The marriage didn't last long, and it was annulled. It wasn't real. Our fathers forced us into it."

"What?" I almost fall off my chair. "What do you mean you were *forced* into it?"

"I told you my father turned controlling. That was one aspect of it. He made me marry the son of the man he was entering into a merger with. It was that, or he was going to cut me off and kick me out with nothing."

"I'm going to fucking kill him," I say through gritted teeth.

"Get in line."

"I mean it, Syd. How did he even get you to agree?"

She pins me with a warning look. "I'll tell you some other time. It's not important. Your baby momma, on the other hand, is."

To say I'm shocked would be an understatement. That I

didn't know isn't surprising. I'm sure there must have been media coverage, but I wouldn't have seen it. I was probably overseas touring at the time, and I'm not on social media. Our PR people handle our online presence, and I avoid reading headlines. I don't even have any of the usual social media apps on my phone.

I don't want to know what shit is being spouted about the band, and I have never searched for Sydney for fear of what I'd find. If she'd still been with Vil, I didn't want to know.

It can't hurt me if I'm not privy to the facts.

It was a stupid strategy. I'll admit that now. I should have checked. Then maybe I'd have had the balls to go find her.

It's easy to blame our families for ruining our relationship, but we both let it go without checking up on one another after we became adults.

I try not to harbor regrets, but I regret not going after Sydney.

She tears off pieces of croissant, popping them in her delectable mouth as she waits for me to explain about my ex.

"My relationship with Vittoria was one of convenience," I admit, sipping my coffee in between talking. "My publicist, Amanda, suggested it. She knew I was fed up with the scene, yet I needed dates for events. Toria was, at that time, friends with the daughter of a woman who is like a sister to my publicist. Liza asked Amanda for help in launching Toria's fledging modeling career. It seemed like a win-win. She'd get noticed on my arm, and I had a steady date when I needed one."

"You were clearly sleeping with her," she says, putting her empty glass down. "So, it obviously became more."

"Not really." I shift on my seat, crossing my ankles at my feet. "We fucked whenever we saw one another which was usually a couple of times a month. It meant nothing to me. I know that sounds harsh, but it was just sex." Average sex, at best. Looking back now, I don't know why I even bothered. "I didn't have any romantic feelings toward Toria. Back then, she seemed sweet, but I know now it was all an act."

"Did she catch feelings for you?"

"Honestly, I don't know." I scrub a hand down my face. "She says she did, that she does, but she's a pathological liar, and I don't believe a word that comes out of her mouth anymore."

Sydney is quietly contemplative. "You let the media think you were engaged on purpose."

I nod. "I didn't care either way, and it was fantastic for Toria's career. Bookings were flying in, and she was in high demand. That's when things started to change. I'd been on tour for months. We were in Europe first before coming home for the US leg. Toria flew in for a gig in Sweden, but I didn't really get to talk to her. It was a flying visit, purely to feed the media machine. She made more of an effort to visit when I was back on US soil, and she was different."

"In what way?" Sydney asks, wiping bits of pastry off her fingers onto the plate.

I fucking love she has an appetite and she's not afraid of eating in front of me. Just goes to show how much of Toria's bullshit I've had to deal with over the past two years. "She was demanding and very vocal if she didn't get her way. She talked down to people. Said nasty, hurtful things. Whined if I didn't drop everything when she wanted me. Expected expensive gifts and for me to pay for everything. Flirted with other guys in front of me and then got enraged when I wasn't jealous."

I wasn't even fucking her much back then, the novelty having long since worn off.

"When she suggested she move in with me, as if we were in a permanent relationship, I knew it was time to cut her loose.

The day I went to break it off with her was the day she told me she was pregnant."

Sydney's eyes pop wide. "And you proposed to her?"

"Yeah. It was a stupid move. To be fair, I was completely caught off guard, and I did what I thought was the right thing. I knew almost immediately I'd made a mistake, but I thought I should follow through to give my son a chance at a proper family life. But I couldn't tie myself to that woman in marriage. I can't stand to be in the same room as her, let alone share a bed. We haven't even fucked since we got engaged." It's not for lack of trying on her part.

"A son? You're having a boy?"

"Yeah." I can't keep the smile off my face. "We found out recently."

"That's...congrats." She forces a strained smile before averting her gaze, staring out at the ocean.

Pain pounds in my chest. "I know it's hard, but—"

"There are no buts, Jared." Sadness splays across her face when she looks back at me. "How would you feel if I was currently pregnant with another man's child?"

I gulp over the lump in my throat. "I would hate it. I would hate it wasn't mine."

Tears cloud her vision, and I hurt because she hurts. "Exactly," she whispers.

"I wish it was you." I thread my fingers through hers. "I wish that so bad."

"Yeah." She pulls her hand back, swiping at a lone tear that falls from her eye. "I wish it was too, but it's not, and there isn't anything you can do to change it."

"I want you back, Syd." I lean toward her. "I know this isn't ideal, and I know it's asking a lot, but I need you in my life. I'm done living without you." I take both her hands in mine, going out on the ultimate limb.

Go big or go home, right?

"I love you, Sydney Shaw. You're still my ride or die. We belong together. I know it won't be easy, but please, can you give me another chance? Can you let me prove to you my love is real?"

Chapter Twenty-One
Sydney

"Jared, you cannot just...drop all of this on me and expect me to jump into your arms," I say as a riot of emotions plays havoc with my insides.

"Why not?"

"Isn't that a little presumptuous on your part?" I narrow my eyes.

"Yes, but I only get one shot at this, Syd. I fucked up once before, and I'm not doing that again. Even if you don't love me anymore, I will win back your heart."

"And here I was thinking you were remarkably humble for a famous rock star." I finish my now lukewarm coffee as I eyeball him, purposely avoiding the L-word.

"Tell me what I need to do?" Sincerity radiates from his eyes. "Whatever it is, I'll do it." Vulnerability plays across his face, reminding me of the younger version of himself. It's hard to stop my heart from melting, but I can't give in just because he's decided he wants me back.

"You're still as impatient as ever."

"Guilty as charged. You know me. When I want something,

I go for it, and I give it my all. I want you, and I'm prepared to do whatever it takes to have you back in my life." Claiming my hand again, he brings it to his lips, placing a feather-soft kiss on my knuckles. His eyes remain locked on mine, and it's intense.

My entire arm is tingling, and I already know it would be so easy to fall back into his arms, but it's not so easy to pick up where we left off. "We were kids then, Jared, and we're very different people now. Who's to say it would work?"

"As long as we love one another, we'll make it work."

"And what about Vittoria and your son?"

"She will only be in my life as the mother of my child. She has a set role."

I yank my hand back. "That's a little callous, Jared. I know this wasn't planned, and she may be difficult, but it took two of you to create a new life, and you can't turn your back on her."

"I'm not." He claws a hand through his hair, sending waves of inky black strands over his brow. "I'm going to ensure she's well cared for, and I'll be involved every step of the way for the duration of her pregnancy."

Pain spears me through the chest. "There's no room for me in that equation."

"Of course, there is." He leans forward, propping his elbows on the table as he pleads for understanding that is nonexistent. He can't fully contemplate how excruciating it would be for me to be with him while another woman gives him a child. "I have plenty of downtime for the next year. We won't be touring again for at least eighteen months, and we have ten months to deliver our next album to the label. We already have half the songs recorded, and we're making progress on the rest. If you're worried I won't have time for you, I swear I do. You'll be my priority, Syd. You and my son."

Every time he says the word, it's like a dagger through my heart. He doesn't get it. He can't because he doesn't have all the facts. Something I would have to reconsider if I let him back into my life. "I can't do it, Jared. I can't be with you when another woman is carrying your child, and you shouldn't ask it of me."

Air rushes out of his mouth. "I know it's a lot to ask, but I can't rewind time and change what's happened. If I could, I'd go back to our sophomore year and do everything differently."

Leaning my head back, I tip my chin up and close my eyes, basking under the subtle September sun. My head is a battlefield, charging enthusiastically into war with my heart. If it was as simple as love, we'd no longer be talking. We'd be tangled in the sheets and one another.

But it's not that simple.

It's as complicated as it can be.

And I can't rush into anything and risk undoing all my hard-won independence.

"She's only got another three and a half months to go. If she even goes to full term. It's not that long."

My eyes pop open. "Then we can wait. It's the respectful thing to do." That's if I can even accept the situation after the baby is born. At least this way, it gives me time to come around to the idea and to see if getting back together with Jared is really what's best for me. Love isn't always enough.

"Toria has nothing to do with what happens between you and me, Syd. It's none of her business."

"She won't see it that way! You only recently broke up with her! Her hormones are probably all over the place, and I won't be that woman. The one who stabs another woman in the back when she's low. And think about your career? What would your fans think? They'll hate me!" God, what was I thinking even considering this? I stand, ready to be done with this conversation. "I can't be under a spotlight, Jared. If I'm with you, everyone will want a piece of me, and that's not me. I like anonymity. I like a quiet life, and I'd like to keep it that way."

"So that's it?" He climbs to his feet, looking equally upset and angry. "You won't even consider it?"

"I didn't say that." I rub at my sore temples. "You've just sprung all this on me, and it's a lot to take in."

Compassion is written all over his face. "I'm sorry. You're right. I'm pressuring you without even giving you time to think about it." He steps right up to me, gently brushing his fingers against my arm. "I've just missed you so much. Spending time with you again is like no time has passed. Like we were never separated. It's hard to be in your presence and not touch you or kiss you."

"We spent more time as platonic friends than romantic partners," I remind him, in case he's forgotten.

"Then let's be friends again." His eyes twinkle as if the idea has only occurred to him. "It will be torturous, but let's go back to the beginning. Please, Syd," he adds when he senses my warring emotions and thoughts. "Just let me get to know you again. I promise I won't pressure you. We'll just hang out, like old times, and see where things lead."

"I'm making no promises, Jared."

"I'm not asking for any." He flashes me a confident grin.

"If anything was to develop, it won't happen until after your son is born."

"Okay." His grin expands, and I glare at him.

"I mean it, J. No funny business."

"Scout's honor." He does a two-finger salute, and I roll my eyes.

"You were never in the scouts."

"I'll be honorable, Syd. I swear." His fingers wrap gently around my arm. "You're too important to mess this up. Whatever you need is yours. I promise I will let you set the pace."

"Friends, Jared. We're just friends."

"For now." The grin is back in full force, and I wonder what the hell I've signed up for.

"I can't believe your mother had an affair with Jared's dad," Cay says on Saturday night as we prep the salads in the kitchen while Jerry mans the grill outside.

"It kind of explains some things even if I was loath to believe J when he first told me."

"You could always ask your dad?" she suggests, tossing the salad leaves in basil-scented olive oil.

"I want nothing more to do with that man, and I'm not sure I'd believe anything he says anyway."

"What about your brothers? They're older than you, and they might know."

"I'm not close with them. You know that. If Tucker and Felix don't know, maybe it should stay that way. I don't remember Mom. I was too little when she died, but they have lots of fond memories of her. Why take that away?" I say as I remove the baked potatoes from the oven.

"You shouldn't carry the burden alone," she adds, dressing the salad with cubed feta, olives, and sliced tomatoes.

"It's not a burden. It's just another piece of the puzzle," I say as the doorbell chimes. "One I suspect I'll never be able to complete." Wiping my hands on my apron, I remove it and straighten the front of my dress. "Do I look okay?" Knots form in my stomach as I bite on the inside of my cheek.

Cayenne beams. "You can spout this friendship crap till the cows come home, but I'm not buying it. You're positively glowing, Sydney."

"Why are you so happy about this?" I ask as the doorbell chimes again.

"I'll get it!" Jerry strides inside and heads toward the hallway.

"Why wouldn't I be?" She takes my trembling hands in hers. "We know Jared. Deep down, we know who he is. He's a good guy. You've been in love with him your whole life, and he's still in love with you. I understand there are obstacles, and the timing isn't quite right, but you're going to figure it out. I just want you to be happy, babe, and he's always been your happy place."

"He has a lot to make up to me."

"I do," the man himself says, appearing in the entrance to the kitchen with Jerry hovering beside him. "I know I need to win back your trust, and I'm determined to do it."

I try—and fail—to not notice how hot Jared looks in his dark jean shorts and light-blue shirt that is rolled up to the sleeves, showcasing the ink covering both arms and his toned, tan skin. His hair is tamed back off his face, the stubble on his chin and cheeks is neatly trimmed, and he smells incredible as he leans in to kiss me on both cheeks. "Thanks for inviting me. You look beautiful." His eyes roam appreciatively over me as he hands me a large bouquet of flowers and a bottle of Sancerre.

"Thank you." My cheeks feel like they're on fire, and I bury my nose in the fragrant petals to conceal my blush.

"Cayenne." Jared grins. "It's so good to see you. You look great."

"I could say the same to you, rock star," she replies, treating him cautiously because that's what besties do. "But we won't feed your ego. I'm sure it's already larger than Mars."

Jared cracks up laughing as he bundles her into a hug. "I hear congratulations are in order," he says, letting her go and glancing between her and Jerry. "When's the big day?"

"We're having a winter wedding in early December," Cay says. "Play your cards right, and you might score an invite."

"I would love to be there." He smirks as he eyeballs Jerry. "I didn't think there was a man on the planet brave enough to take this one on. You've got big balls, mate."

"Shut it." Cay slaps his chest. "He's a lucky bastard, and you both know it."

I give the guys beer and shove them at the grill so Cay and I can finish the salads and set the table. It's a little chilly tonight, so we're eating at the large table in my kitchen. I have a dining room, but it's for more formal occasions, and I want tonight to be relaxed.

Apart from early morning jogs on the beach, I haven't seen Jared since we bumped into one another on Monday. He's been flying in and out of L.A. daily to work on the album with his bandmates while I took on two extra shifts to cover when my co-manager came down with a stomach bug.

I decided on an impromptu barbecue because Cayenne and Jerry were planning to visit this weekend, and I knew Cay would go out of her way to orchestrate a meet and greet with Jared unless I set something up.

All week, I've been thinking about what he said. About my mom and his dad, the revelations about his relationship with Vittoria, and his declarations of love. My emotions have been veering all over the place, so I've made an appointment with a therapist. I need to talk it all through, and therapy has helped me enormously in the past.

"I'll get the guys," Cay says, heading outside to the grill while I arrange the bowls with the various salads, bread, and the potatoes in the center of the table. I grab a couple of bottles of sparkling water and some red and white wine and bring it to the table as the others come inside.

Jared sits beside me on one side while Jerry and Cay sit across from us. Conversation is casual and lively as we eat.

"This pasta salad is divine." Jared compliments me for the umpteenth time on the food. "You'll have to teach me how to make it."

"It's easy. Not much to it at all."

"For you, maybe," he teases. "We've already determined I'm a bit of a lost cause in the kitchen."

"That sounds like a challenge if ever I heard one." Cay waggles her brows.

Jared smirks. "I'll make you a deal." He stabs me with his gorgeous blue eyes. "If you'll give me a few cooking lessons, I'll teach you how to play the drums."

"Who says I want to learn?" I quirk a brow.

Jared laughs. "Try pulling the other one, darlin'." He tweaks my nose. "You may be all grown up"—his gaze roams over me, lingering briefly in certain places—"but you're still the same girl who used to beg me for a turn on my drum kit."

"Only so I'd get to spend more time with you," I truthfully admit. "I had, *have*, zero interest in learning how to play the drums."

His face softens as he peers at me with blatant adoration. "You never told me that."

"I was trying to seduce you." I giggle.

"You can seduce me anytime, beautiful." His pupils are dilated as he lifts my hand to his lips and kisses my knuckles.

"Jared." My tone contains warning. "You promised."

He clears his throat and slowly lowers my hand to my lap. "I did, and I'm trying, but you make it so hard. Pun intended." He whispers the last words, but Cay has supersonic hearing.

She bursts out laughing. "That was cheesy as fuck."

"It hasn't even been a week, J." I purse my lips. "Try harder."

Chapter Twenty-Two
Jared

I glance up from my drum kit in time to see Ryder step out of the control room. A few seconds later, he enters the live room where the guys and I are warming up before we record our new song. "Jared, would it be okay if I gave Zeta your home address?" Ryder asks, walking across the hardwood floor toward me.

"Sure, but what's up?"

"She wants to send Toria a baby hamper, whatever the fuck that is." He shrugs and smiles.

I eyeball Wilder. "Didn't you tell him?"

As well as being Wilder's older half-brother, Ryder is also lead singer and guitarist for Torment and the co-owner of Torment Records, the label our band is signed to. This recording studio in downtown L.A. belongs to the label, and Ryder is very hands-on, often popping in to check on proceedings. Clearly, he takes a special interest in his brother's band, so we see a lot of him when we're in town.

I still have to pinch myself that I'm signed to one of my idol's labels and he's now a good friend. As a teen, I worshipped

Torment and aspired to be like Ryder. It's ironic I ended up here, but I couldn't be happier. The guys know what it's like to be shafted in this industry, and they genuinely care about the acts signed to their label. They are fair and flexible, and it feels like family. I can't see us ever signing with anyone else.

"Haven't had the chance," Wilder replies, fingers stalling on his Fender Telecaster as he lifts his gaze to mine.

"What don't I know?" Ryder folds his arms over his chest and a serious expression materializes on his face.

"I broke things off with Toria."

"Should I say I'm sorry?"

"Hell no," Linc pipes up. I was wondering how long it would take him. "You should throw a party and celebrate his freedom. That woman is nothing but trouble."

"Are you okay?" Ryder's concern bleeds through his tone.

"Yeah. I'm not happy I'm having a baby with Toria because she's shown her true colors lately, and it's not pretty, but I won't abandon my child. I'll be there every step of the way for my son."

"Let me know if I can do anything."

"I will, thanks. And if Zeta wants to send the baby hamper, tell her to go ahead. Toria is living in my Bel Air place at least until the birth." I'd like to say I'm sure it'll be appreciated, but with my ex, who the fuck knows?

"Jared bought a new place out in Half Moon Bay. We're getting the grand tour later," Wilder confirms.

"You're welcome to join us. Zeta too if it's not short notice."

"She's not here. She's visiting her sister with the kids for a couple of days."

"Then you should definitely come unless you have plans tonight."

"Sounds good." Ryder nods as he backs up. "I'm heading to the office for a bit, but I'll be back later. Have a good one."

A few hours later, we call it a wrap on the seventh song for our new album and make our way to the roof after saying our goodbyes to the producer and sound engineer.

We stride across the asphalt to the helipad where my helicopter and pilot are waiting. I'm itching to get home so I can see Sydney. Ryder is already seated, and we climb in beside him for the fifty-minute flight to Half Moon Bay.

After I show the guys around my new house, I tap out a message to Sydney to see if she's home yet. She replies immediately, confirming she'll be over in thirty minutes. I send her the takeout menu, telling her to pick what she wants so I can place our order while we wait for her. "Tell me what you want," I say, handing another couple of menus around to the guys as we drink beers at my kitchen table. Ryder has a soda because he doesn't drink alcohol anymore. "Sydney will be here shortly," I confirm as I return to the kitchen. The guys are looking forward to meeting her.

"Who's Sydney?" Ryder asks.

"Jared's lost love," Linc supplies before I can.

Opening an overhead cupboard, I remove a bag of chips and a large bowl.

"Is she the one you write about?" Ryder inquires.

"She's the one," I confirm, dumping the chips in the bowl and bringing it to the table.

"This is the girl from New York?" Ryder remembers something I said in passing when I was drunk years ago.

"Yeah. I bumped into her in Florence, and it helped me decide to end things with Toria." Claiming a seat beside Wilder, I help myself to a beer. "We ended up having a heart-to-heart, and it made me realize I was never going to get over her and I didn't want to."

"Get this," Wilder says, brushing his long hair out of his face. "She moved back to the US and bought a house just up the road."

"Is that why you moved here?" Ryder asks.

I shake my head. "I didn't have a clue she'd left Florence. It's pure coincidence. One I'm fucking ecstatic about. I couldn't have planned this better if I tried."

"Dude, do I have to remind you you've been friend zoned?" Linc says before stuffing his face with chips.

"It's only temporary until after the baby is born. We're getting to know one another again."

"She still has feelings for you?" Ryder asks before tipping some soda into his mouth.

I can't contain a smile as I nod.

"Good for you."

"It's early days, and I'm not sure if things will work out, but I'm hopeful."

My phone pings with a text from Sydney, and I wonder if her ears are burning. I break our conversation to call in an order with the local Thai place, leaning back against my kitchen counter while I watch the guys shoot the shit. When I'm done, Wilder and Linc have headed to the garden to check out my retracting fence, leaving me alone with Ryder.

He takes a stool at my island unit and stabs me with a solemn expression. "Zeta and I spent seven years apart," he says. "I can't help thinking how similar our situations are, even if the circumstances were different." Ryder met his wife Zeta in juvie of all places. After they got out, he left to protect her, breaking both their hearts. They ended up reconnecting years later when she was sent to interview Torment by the magazine she worked for. Theirs was a rocky road, by all accounts, but they're happier than ever. Ryder adores his wife and his family life.

"I want what you have," I truthfully admit. "I want to win back my girl, marry her, and start a family."

"The minute Zeta reappeared in my life, I was determined to get her back. I'd never stopped loving her. I was forced to walk away from her. It wasn't by choice."

"Same." I hop up on a stool beside him. "How did you do it? How did you win her back? I'm starting from scratch with Sydney, and I already feel like I'm fucking up."

"Zeta friend zoned me too at the beginning. We had to learn how to be friends before we could be more, but it was challenging. I just wanted to be with her."

"Yep. I can relate."

"I was a goddamn mess back then. It's a miracle I won Zeta over because I fucked up real bad on so many occasions. I'm just grateful she was so understanding and forgiving. I wouldn't be where I am today if it wasn't for my wife."

"She's a good woman." I have met her a few times over the years and she's good people. It's blatantly obvious Ryder and Zeta are solid. They have an amazing relationship, one that isn't usual in celebrity circles. These days, I admire Ryder for more than his music. "Any advice?"

"Put in the work and let Sydney set the pace. In my experience, women don't want extravagant gestures."

He clearly hasn't met my ex.

"It's the small things that count and being there for her when she needs you," Ryder adds. "Show her you care through your actions, not expensive gifts, and be real with her, Jared. Don't be afraid to be vulnerable. If you want her back in your life, she needs to know the man you are today. Don't try to fake it. Show her who you are now, warts and all."

"I think you missed your true calling in life. You're better than any therapist. I feel like I should be paying you."

He shrugs. "I'm older and wiser, and I've had a lot of time to reflect on my mistakes. I went through hell before I found my heaven, but it was worth it."

"Thanks for the advice. I appreciate it."

"Anytime, Jared. I hope it works out."

"Me too."

"Flowers don't hurt either," he adds with a grin. "I give Zeta flowers on more than just her birthday or our anniversary, and she loves it. If the way to a man's heart is through his stomach, the way to a woman's is with flowers."

"If it works, I'm getting that inked on my body."

"If it works, I might just give up the music business and become a therapist to the stars," he quips.

My cell phone pings with a notification from the security system, and I call up the video feed of the gate. Sydney is carrying a cake box and a bottle of wine, looking adorably nervous as I press a button to let her in.

"Wow. You should see the look on your face right now." Ryder chuckles. "You are fucking smitten, man."

"I am crazy in love with this woman. Sydney has always been it for me."

"I can't wait to meet her."

"I forgot to tell her you joined us too, but she'll be cool," I say, jumping off the stool and heading to the door.

Butterflies dance around my chest when I open the door and see her approaching. My smile is instant when I see her beautiful face. She's wearing a gorgeous orange-red dress that is fitted on top with a frilled hem over her chest and straps that tie in a bow on her shoulders. It flows softly from her waist to her calves with a similar frill at the hem. Plain white tennis shoes adorn her feet. Her blonde hair is braided on top, almost like a hair band, and the rest of her golden locks hang in soft waves over her shoulders and down her back.

She is effortlessly stunning, and I'm already a puddle at her feet. I smile as she steps up to the door. "Hey, Syd. You look beautiful."

"J. You look good too." She leans in to kiss my cheek, and the scent of wild berries and jasmine tickles my nostrils, sending my senses into overdrive.

"You still wear the same perfume," I blurt because I've got zero chill.

Two pink spots bloom on her cheeks. "I wear others, but Marc Jacobs is still one of my favorites."

I wonder if she wore it for me. As that thought lands in my mind, my gaze lowers to her neck, and my heart swells when I find the silver locket resting against her collarbone. "I like that you still wear my locket." My heart had swollen to bursting point at the gallery that day when I saw her clasping it around her neck. I lift my eyes to hers.

"I rarely remove it."

Ryder mentioned vulnerability, and I see it now on Sydney's face. This is what he means. Opening up and shielding nothing from her.

I extend my right arm where a few leather bands are wrapped around my wrist, singling out a particular one.

"You have yours too."

I run the tip of my finger over the engraving of our names on the silver panel of the leather band I bought the same time I bought her locket. "I couldn't always wear it, and mostly I didn't want to. This was just for us. And I was afraid of it breaking, but it's one of my most treasured possessions."

"Are we naïve trying to replicate the past?"

I stare deep into her eyes, wishing I could lace my fingers in all that thick golden hair, pull her face to mine, and show her with my lips there is nothing naïve about reclaiming the spark that has never died, but I'm not going to pressure her before she's ready.

I will be her friend.

The best fucking friend she's ever had, and when she's ready for more, I'll give it to her.

Shoving my hands in the pockets of my jeans to ignore the urge to touch her, I shake my head. "We're not replicating the past. We're starting over. It's a clean slate. We're writing a new chapter."

Chapter Twenty-Three
Jared

Her full lips pull into a smile. "I like that. I—"

The buzzer rings, cutting her off mid-sentence, and I move to check the monitor. I step aside to let her inside and buzz the delivery guy in at the gate.

"I made dessert." She hands me the box. "And I brought wine."

"I have a wine cellar in my basement unless you forgot that part of the tour," I tease.

"I remember, but I didn't know if you had any Sancerre."

I smile at her in amusement. "I might have ordered a few boxes during the week."

Her mouth hangs open. "A few *boxes*?"

"I want to ensure I always have your favorite wine on hand," I say, peeking into the box.

"It's tiramisu," she confirms. "If you'd been home last night, I would've let you watch me make it. It's one of the easiest desserts."

We haven't started our cooking lessons yet, but we have penciled in time on Saturday to begin. "For you, maybe." My stomach rumbles appreciatively as I gaze upon the gorgeous creation with hungry eyes. I set it and the bottle of wine down on the hall table as the delivery guy parks outside.

"For you, too. I'll make a chef out of you yet."

If it means I get to spend more time with her, and I can learn how to cook a romantic meal, then sign me up.

Stones crunch on the driveway as the delivery guy gets out of his van and stalks toward us. His eyes pop wide when he notices me. I use a credit card in the name J. King to purchase stuff so I can stay under the radar. I know it won't take long for details of my new home to leak to the press, but I'm enjoying the anonymity while it lasts.

"Ugh, delivery for Mr. King," the young guy says, stuttering a little.

Sydney smiles softly. "I'll take that." She takes the two bags from his trembling hands as we watch his cheeks burn brighter.

"You know who I am."

He bobs his head. "I'm a big Ruminate fan. I've been at every L.A. event since I turned fifteen. My mom wouldn't let me attend before then."

"Your mom sounds smart, and thanks for the support. We appreciate it." I quickly tap out a message to the guys. "Would you like an autograph?" I offer, and his eyes almost bug out of his head.

"Yeah, that'd be cool." His head whips over my shoulder at the sound of approaching footsteps. His eyes widen farther, and he looks like he's about to piss his pants. "Oh my god. You're all here," he blurts as Wilder and Linc approach. "This is the best fucking day ever."

Sydney smiles at my bandmates as she steps aside to let them get to the door. Pulling a notepad and pen from the drawer of my hall table, I scribble my signature before handing it to the guys.

The delivery dude looks fit to burst he's so excited, and I love it. This is what it's all about. Making the fans happy. I try to never forget they are the reason I live my dream. "Would you like a photo?" I ask, and the guy almost keels over.

Wilder and Linc chuckle.

"For real?" His tone has elevated a few notches. "Yeah, thank you so much. This has just made my day. My whole life really."

"Aw, I love that." Sydney smiles at him as Wilder hands him a page with our autographs.

"I'm gonna get this framed," he says, handing his cell to Sydney.

"You should," she agrees, placing the bags with the food down as we step outside and surround the guy. She snaps a few pics before handing it back to him with an even bigger smile.

"I love you guys even more now," he says, hugging his cell to his chest like it's precious treasure. "Thank you so much."

"You're welcome," Wilder says.

"Give me your name and address, kid, and we'll get some merch sent out to you," Linc says, handing him the notepad on his phone.

"Best. Day. Ever." The kid taps in his details with a wild grin.

"Do me a favor, mate, and don't tell anyone where my house is."

"I promise I won't. I'll just say I bumped into you at the mall or something."

"Have a good one, dude." Wilder hands him a fifty as a tip.

It's a miracle he doesn't shit his pants as he leaves, and I hope to fuck he makes it back to the takeout place without crashing.

"That was adorable." Sydney beams at all of us as we come

back into the hall. "You guys are super sweet to do that for him."

Linc snorts out a laugh as he grabs the takeout bags. "Babe, we've been called a lot of things, but super sweet is a new one."

"Own it, Lincoln," she says as if they haven't only just met. "Because that was one of the nicest things I've ever seen."

"It's easy to think all fans are nutjobs," Wilder says, closing the front door. "Because you only hear about the crazy ones, but the majority are cool. We wouldn't be here without them."

"Fact," I agree, lifting the cake box in one hand and the wine in the other.

"It's nice to finally meet you, Sydney," Wilder adds as we walk toward the kitchen. "This guy has talked about you for years."

"Cheers, mate." I flip him the bird.

"You're his muse," Linc supplies because the assholes are determined to ensure I have no game.

"Sydney already knows." I'm glad I told her now.

"I do, and it's great to meet you both."

We turn into the kitchen where Ryder is still sitting at the island unit, now drinking a bottle of water.

"Oh my fucking god!" Sydney's high-pitched tone and the way she grips my arm almost has me dropping the box and bottle in my hands.

"What's wrong?" I turn to face her, confused when I spot her dilated eyes and both hands clamped over her mouth.

Linc laughs as he dumps the bags with our food on the island unit. "It's the Ryder Effect."

I watch the blush creep up Sydney's neck and onto her cheeks when she lowers her hands and stares at Torment's front man. "I can't believe you're here. I'm such a big fan, and this is surreal," she gushes.

"Seriously?" Wilder pouts. He loves his brother to death,

but a little jealousy rears its head from time to time. "You didn't bat an eyelash when you met us, and you're gaga for my brother?"

"Blame this guy." She jerks her head to the side while keeping her gaze locked on Ryder. "Jared was a massive Torment fan as a kid. I was a massive Jared fan, so anything he loved I tried to get behind. It wasn't a chore with Torment. I loved you guys, and I might've had a few Ryder Stone posters on my walls."

If he wasn't happily married, and I didn't know Sydney still loves me, I might be sporting a case of the green-eyed monster myself in this moment. But a starstruck Sydney is priceless. Especially after what just went down at the door. She's almost as awestruck as the delivery guy, which is funny as fuck.

"I'm flattered." Ryder climbs off his stool and comes toward us.

"I don't usually fangirl, but I wasn't aware you were here." She narrows her eyes at me. "J failed to mention it."

"It was a last-minute thing."

"Some warning might've been nice."

"Then I would've missed the show." I smack a kiss to her cheek. "You're adorable."

Realizing she's clutching my arm in a death grip, she lets go and walks over to Ryder with her shoulders back, exuding quiet confidence. She extends her hand. "It's an honor to meet you."

"The honor is all mine." He shakes her hand and smiles.

Wilder is huffing and muttering under his breath as he walks past to the kitchen table.

"Aw, Wilder, I love your music, and you're an incredible musician and singer too. Them's some talented genes in your family."

"For sure," I agree, putting the dessert and the wine in the fridge. "Do you want a glass of wine now?" I ask her as I remove plates from the cupboard and silverware from the drawer.

"I'll wait until after we've eaten," she says, coming over and taking the plates.

Conversation flows freely at the table as we enjoy the sumptuous takeout. Sydney finishes her meal and helps herself to bits of mine, and it's so comfortable having her here. It's like she's always been part of my crew. The banter is flying as she teases the guys, and they tease her back. She got over her shyness with Ryder pretty quickly too.

After tidying up, we move into the living room, and I put music on in the background as we relax on my large leather couches with our drinks. Sydney squeals when she spots the Amadeo painting I bought in Florence hanging on the wall at the back of the opposite couch. "When did that arrive?" she asks, getting up to walk around to it.

"Yesterday. I hung it immediately because I couldn't wait to see it on my wall."

"It looks amazing. I need to send him a pic. He'll love this." She spends ten minutes explaining the intricacies of the painting and the thought behind it to the guys, gushing about the artist who she says is going to set the art world on fire. I hope she's right. It means my investment will be worth a lot more in the future. Only Ryder seems remotely interested, but my bandmates are polite as they feign enthusiasm.

We settle on the couches again and shoot the shit. Syd is sipping her second glass of wine and bobbing her head to the music. Predictably, Linc lights a joint and passes it around.

"No thanks," Syd says when it comes to her, immediately handing it off to me.

"You don't smoke?" Linc inquires before blowing smoke circles like the show-off he is.

"Not anymore. I had a big issue with drugs when I was

teen. Went a bit crazy for a while. Cleaned my act up when I was twenty, and now my only vice is a couple of glasses of wine."

"I went a bit crazy for a while too." Ryder admits something that is common knowledge. He didn't shy away from telling the world his truths, earning the steadfast loyalty of his fans for life. His battle with addiction is not a secret nor is the reason why he fell down a dark hole. But that's a story for another day. "I don't touch alcohol or drugs anymore. My personality is too addictive. It's all or nothing for me."

"I'm like that with drugs," Sydney admits, unconsciously shifting closer to me on the couch. I'm not complaining. "I won't even touch a joint. It's a slippery slope, and I'd rather not fall back down it."

"Amen to that." Ryder nods, and his gaze is full of admiration and understanding.

"We can stop if this is bothering you," Wilder offers.

Linc scowls.

I doubt a day passes when he isn't stoned.

"That's not necessary. I can handle a bit of weed though I'm not sure I could handle the full-blown rock star scene." She looks sideways at me.

"I don't do much of that anymore," I explain, sliding my arm around the back of the couch behind her. "And I'd never put you in a situation you were uncomfortable with."

"I know."

I have a feeling the baby issue isn't the only hurdle I'll have to overcome with Sydney. She's not exactly a fan of the rock star lifestyle and the lack of privacy that comes with it. "We won't be touring for ages, and we're lying low right now, so it's not anything you need to worry about yet."

"I know that too."

An awkward tension bleeds into the air, broken a few beats

later by Linc. "You're a really talented artist, Syd. It's a shame you don't paint for a living. I bet you'd kill it."

Sydney laughs a little. "Um, thanks, but how would you know?"

"I fucking love that portrait of Jared, and I can't believe you painted it at fifteen," he replies.

Sydney turns to me. "You still have the painting?"

"Of course." I reach out and pull an errant strand of hair away from her brow. "You didn't seriously think I'd ever get rid of it, did you?"

"I don't know." She wets her lush lips. "I guess I thought it was back in London at your mom's or something."

I pull her to her feet. "Come with me." Clasping her hand in mine, I lead her into my small home studio where her painting hangs on the wall beside some of our framed gold and platinum awards. "I had it framed years ago, and it comes with me wherever I set up home. I had it in my bedroom in the apartment when I first moved to L.A., and it was the focal point in the living room of my Bel Air house."

"You seriously painted that at fifteen?" Ryder asks, coming up behind us. I didn't realize the guys had followed us.

"I did." Sydney steps up to it, examining it in more detail.

"She drew it from memory," I explain. "I didn't even pose for it."

"Wow, that's even more impressive," Wilder says.

"I was always drawing Jared," she admits, reaching a hand out to touch the painting.

"You made him look better than in real life," Wilder says, and I flip him the bird.

"The energy jumps off the canvas," Ryder supplies. "There's an almost magical quality to it."

"That's how Jared always looked to me," she murmurs, a little lost in her head and maybe the past. "I could never take my eyes off him when he played. As soon as you put drumsticks in his hands, he became this other person. I used to think of him as a magician because he makes magic with his hands."

Her words and the dreamy expression on her face penetrate deeply, cementing her permanent hold on my heart. Hearing her talk about me like that will never get old. Knowing she supports my passion has always meant everything to me. I don't even know if I'd be where I am now if she hadn't encouraged me from day one. She has always believed in my talent, like I have always believed in hers.

"Oh, yeah, baby, yeah," Linc says in his best Austin Powers voice, gyrating his hips.

Sydney rolls her eyes and fights a smile. "I said with his hands, not his cock, dipshit."

Wilder grins at me, and I know that look. He's pleased she has fit seamlessly into our circle in a way my ex never did.

Anyone that can handle the enigma that is Lincoln Lee is a keeper.

"You make me look good, and the painting is incredible. Better than any of the artwork I've bought over the years," I say, softly squeezing her hand.

"I suppose it's not bad."

"Not bad?" Linc almost screams. "It's fucking awesome. I want one." He steps up beside her, flashing me a mischievous grin over his shoulder. "Can I hire you to paint me? I'm thinking in the nude. Just me, my guitar, some JD, and quality weed."

"Nice fucking try, mate. Not happening."

"I wasn't asking you."

"I don't do commissions," Sydney says, still staring at the painting.

"Why not?" Wilder asks. "I bet you'd clean up." His eyes pop wide. "We can help spread the word. I've just had an awesome idea." His excited gaze bounces between us. "Sydney should paint the band, and we can use it for our new album cover."

"That's a fucking genius idea," I agree, looking at the boss man to see what he thinks.

"I love it," Ryder concurs.

"Would you do it?" I ask.

Sydney finally turns away from the painting. "I don't know."

"Think about it," Ryder says. "There's no pressure. You could drop by the studio, take a look, see if it's something you vibe with."

"I'll reflect on it," she says, and that's as much commitment as she's prepared to give right now.

Chapter Twenty-Four
Sydney

Jared rings the bell before letting himself into my bungalow with his key. We swapped house keys last week because we spend most every evening together at either his place or mine. I also have a fob and code for his front gate and the code for his security system. His footsteps thud in the hallway, and I try to quell the butterflies running amok in my chest. It's the same every time I'm with him, and I don't know who I'm kidding with our friendship pact. It's getting harder and harder to be around him and not want more.

Another couple of weeks have passed, and it's almost one month since Jared and I discovered we were neighbors and agreed to restart our friendship. Some days, it's hard to imagine the time when he wasn't in my life.

"Hey, Syd." Jared's handsome face swims into view as he enters my kitchen. He holds up a grocery bag. "I got the ingredients."

"Good stuff." Our few cooking lessons have gone well. Jared even cooked the oven-baked salmon fillets with spicy tomato rice recipe for me last weekend, and I was impressed.

He's a quick study and an eager student. Depositing the bag on the island, he leans in to kiss my cheek, like always.

Like always, I silently swoon.

"I noticed some oil under your car," he says, pulling back somewhat reluctantly. "When was it last serviced?"

"I don't know. I bought it secondhand when I got to San Fran."

"Did you purposely not buy a new car?" he asks, unpacking the supplies.

"Yes. I think new cars are such a waste of money. I got that way cheaper, and it's only two years old. It's virtually new."

"That's a very practical way of thinking."

Removing two bottles of water from the fridge, I throw one to him. "I had to learn to be frugal. Dad had total control over my money for a few years. I hated running everything by him, so I learned to get by on less."

"He's a prick," Jared snaps, scrubbing a hand over his jaw. "Who does that to his own flesh and blood?"

"When I was out of control and spending every penny on drugs, I understood it," I say, taking some chopping knives out of the drawer. "But after I was clean and sober, he needed to trust me again, and he refused to do it. The only reason I have any independence is because Sawyer insisted on giving me the agreed settlement per the prenup, and he paid it directly to me. He also hooked me up with my own bank account and helped me to move overseas. Without his support, I would have been lost."

"I can't believe your dad cut you off like that." He uncaps his water and takes a swig. "He's a fucking multimillionaire! Why would he treat you like that?"

"I have given up trying to work it out, and I refuse to give him headspace anymore."

"It's fucked up," he says, rounding the unit and standing beside me.

"Yup."

"I'm glad Sawyer helped you. I guess I should stop feeling so envious and resentful of him."

My brows climb to my hairline. "You're envious and resentful of Hunt?"

Sincere blue eyes, awash with emotion, pin me in place. "He got to see you walking down the aisle in a white dress."

"It was fake, and the whole day was kind of miserable." A lump rises in my throat. "All our guests were congratulating me and telling me I was beautiful, and my husband hadn't even noticed, let alone made any comment. That night, I had to practically beg him to fuck me. After, he left immediately and later said it was a mistake." I have put that whole sorry episode behind me, but thinking back to my wedding day and night always makes me sad. I wish I could wipe the memory from my mind as easily as we wiped the marriage from the record books.

"What?" Jared says in a clipped voice. His jaw pulls taut.

That was the absolute last thing I should have said to him, especially when he has a sharp chopping knife in hand. "It's in the past. It doesn't matter now," I say as I remove the chicken breasts from the packaging.

"It fucking matters, Syd." He puts the knife down. With tender fingers, he clasps my face, and I almost forget how to breathe. "Fake or not, it was still your wedding day. He should have gone out of his way to ensure you were comfortable, protected, and felt cherished. He didn't have to love you to acknowledge how beautiful you were. I haven't seen any photos." A visible shudder works its way through him. "But I don't need to see any to know you were the most stunning bride to ever walk the earth. How dare he do that to you. I will knock that guy the fuck out for treating you so disrespectfully."

Tears prick my eyes, and it's hard not to react to his caring words and his protective manner, but I force them away. No more tears is my new motto. "He made up for it in other ways. He's a good guy. I think you'd like him."

His mouth opens and closes a few times, and then he drops my face and puts a little distance between us.

"What?" I probe. "Say what you were going to say."

"I shouldn't," he says, picking the knife up again and beginning to cut the chicken into cubes.

"We agreed on total honesty, J. Don't hide shit from me."

"Okay, but you asked for it," he says, putting the knife down and giving me his full attention. "I will make sure you know how loved, adored, cherished, and beautiful you are when you walk down the aisle to *me*. I will spend all night worshipping you with my fingers, my tongue, and my cock, and you sure as fuck won't have to beg for it. You'll be damn lucky if I ever let you leave our bed, and there wouldn't be a single part of me that would ever, could ever, regret it." His eyes drill into mine. "How's that for honesty?"

I'm stunned speechless as lust coils low in my belly, and I throb down below. When Jared and I had sex before, we were clueless kids. Now he's an experienced man with intimate knowledge of a woman's body. A rock star with the notches on his bedpost to prove it. I can't find it in me to hate all who have come before when I know the next time we fall into bed he's going to blow my mind, decimate my heart, and ruin my body for eternity.

Is it wrong that I can't wait?

No. I internally chastise myself. Jared and I sleeping together, getting back together, is not a forgone conclusion. He's still having a baby with another woman, and I still don't know if I can ever deal with it.

My ardor instantly cools.

"Have you nothing to say?" he asks in a gruff voice.

His eyes are dilated when I look at him. "You're right, I shouldn't have forced you to tell me."

He opens and closes his mouth again, but this time, I don't ask. I have learned that lesson.

"So, about your car," he says as he resumes chopping the chicken. "I'd like to take a look at it tomorrow. Check out that oil leak."

"Sure," I say, placing the vegetables on the second chopping board. "Thanks."

He sets his knife down again. "Can we forget I said anything?" he asks, and I detect hurt behind his words. "I don't want to ruin things. Not when they've been going well."

"You haven't ruined anything, and I'm sorry if I hurt you. Honestly, I'm a little speechless. That was incredible to hear, J. My heart is overflowing, and I'm all choked up. I just need some time to process everything."

"I get it, and you have nothing to apologize for."

I turn on some classical music as we prep the meat and vegetables, lowering it down as I explain the recipe for creamy chicken pesto pasta.

We work companionably, side by side, but I'm acutely aware of his presence, his scent, the warmth rolling off his body, and just how manly he is. Sounds cheesy, I know, but I can't explain it any other way.

He's just...all man.

My mouth is dry as I watch him toss the chicken and veg in olive oil, his fingers working overtime to coat every piece. Muscles flex and roll in his tanned, inked arms and it's the most delicious arm porn. Visions of those skilled hands gliding over my naked body float through my mind, and I discreetly squeeze my thighs as heat floods my panties.

"Sorry," he says when his hip accidentally brushes against

mine, sending fiery tremors zipping through my already over-heated body.

It snaps me out of my lust-fueled mind. "You can, ah, toss them in the skillet to brown them a little, and then we'll put them in the oven."

Jared moves to the stove, and I sneak a quick peek at his rear profile. Broad muscular shoulders and a toned back fit snugly under his T-shirt. Jared is the only man I know who regularly strips his sweater off in Cali in October. His ass molds perfectly to the expensive denim before it curves over solid thighs and lean legs. Sizzling sounds fill the air, and I inspect my body to ensure the sounds aren't coming from me because every inch of skin feels like it's on fire.

Damn this man. And so much for snapping out of my lusty daze.

"Syd." Fingers snap in my face. "Earth to Sydney."

"What?"

His lips twitch. "I've browned the meat and veggies and transferred it to the oven dish."

"Wow. How long was I drooling?"

He barks out a laugh, and I want to punt kick myself up the ass for speaking the thought out loud.

"You can drool as long as you want, Syd. You know I'm good for it." He flashes me a cheeky smile that takes me back in time.

"Shut it." I playfully jab him in the ribs. "I meant daydreaming not drooling. As if."

His knowing grin says it all, and the only person I'm fooling is myself.

Chapter Twenty-Five
Sydney

I come home a few days later to find my car jacked up and Jared propped underneath it. I lightly tap the hood so he knows I'm home. "Is it safe for you to be under there?" I ask, concern underscoring my tone. I'm worried the car might drop on top of him and crush vital organs and bones.

He slides out on some roller thingy with a wide smile. "I know what I'm doing," he says. "Before I was shipped to boarding school, I spent every Saturday working with my uncle at his garage. I can't claim to be a mechanic, but I know my way around a car."

"So, what's the damage?" I prop my elbows on the hood.

"It's nothing serious." He hops to his feet like a gazelle, and I'm jealous. Last week, I could barely get up after weeding the garden for a couple hours. Jared stopped by when I was elbows-deep in my flowerbeds, and he insisted on helping. Like he insisted on helping me paint the last two bedrooms. I can't deny he's handy to have around.

"Your oil pan was leaking," he says, wiping his greasy hands on a dirty piece of cloth that looked like it might have been white at some point. "I took it out, cleaned it, and then replaced it and tightened the bolts."

"You're a man of many talents," I stupidly say.

A grin spreads over his gorgeous mouth. "You haven't seen the half of it."

I roll my eyes. "I walked straight into that one."

"Doesn't mean it's not true." He waggles his brows, and I shake my head, laughing.

"I topped up your oil and water and did a couple of other checks, but all looks good."

"Thanks, J. I owe you. Would dinner work?"

"I'm famished. Dinner sounds great." He swipes his arm across his brow, smearing it with a streak of oil.

"Come," I say, extending my hand, then thinking better of it when I see the greasy marks on his hands and oil under his fingernails. "Time to get you cleaned up."

"You're offering to clean me?" His eyes dance with excitement as he leans in. "All of me?" Jared is the biggest flirt. He always has been. He just can't help it.

"Hold your horses, Casanova. I'm offering my bathroom for you to clean up."

"Well, that's disappointing."

"You're incorrigible."

"Only with you."

"You're also really sweet. Thanks for helping with my car, my garden, and my house."

"It's not a chore. You know I love spending time with you." Mischief skips over his face. "And you also know I'm great with my hands."

"Oh my god." I slap a hand against my brow. "Make it stop!"

He holds up his dirty palms, chuckling. "I'll put you out of your misery. I'm going to head home. I need a shower and a fresh change of clothes. What time is dinner?"

"Say an hour?"

"Works for me. Bye, babe."

My eyes pop wide. He hasn't called me that in years, and it's not appropriate even if it does make my heart spike.

"Sorry. It slipped out." He doesn't look the least bit sorry. He's not even pretending.

"It's fine." I don't want to make a big deal about it. "Go get your smelly ass in the shower, and I'll see you later."

I'm just plating our dinner—chicken parmigiana with noodles and side salad—when Jared saunters into the kitchen with one hand behind his back.

"Something smells delicious," he says, rubbing his free hand across his flat stomach.

"If you like it, I can show you how to make it on Saturday."

"Sounds perfect." He hands me a bouquet of mixed flowers. "For you."

My heart swells as I smile at him. "Thank you. They're beautiful."

"Not as beautiful as you."

Heat blooms in my cheeks. "Can you set the table while I put these in water?" I ask, deliberately ignoring his compliment as I hand him silverware and glasses to take to the table. Some nights, we eat at the island unit, but most nights, we eat at the table in the kitchen. It has a lovely view over my garden and the ocean in the background.

I place the flowers on the counter before extracting a glass vase from the cupboard and filling it with water.

"About Saturday. I was hoping you might come to the city

with me and watch us record. You could bring your sketch pad if you like?" he says as he fixes two place settings.

I carry the vase to the table, placing it in the center as I mull over his offer. I grab our plates next and set one down in front of him.

"No pressure," he adds, examining my face carefully. "You don't have to paint the band. It was just an idea."

"I've been thinking about it, and I'm equal parts excited and nervous. What if I mess it up?"

"The album isn't releasing until next year, and they'll have backup. It's the norm in the industry. None of us would ever force something on you that'd make you uncomfortable."

"I know, and I appreciate that." I settle into my seat across from him with my dinner. "Cay and Ash think it's a fantastic idea. They're encouraging me to give it a shot."

"So, come on Saturday, and see what happens. There are no expectations."

"Okay. I'll come. I'm dying to see you perform again."

"I'm dying for you to watch me."

We share a cheesy grin. "Okay, I'm in," I say, cutting a piece of chicken.

After dinner, Jared insists on cleaning up while I grab a quick shower and get changed. When I emerge from my bedroom, he has a movie lined up and a bottle of wine on ice in the living room. Sitting on the couch beside him, I raise a brow as I stare at the screen. "*The Mortal Instruments.* Really?"

It instantly takes me back in time. To one of our first official dates. I remember how we spent so much time making out in the back row of the theater we barely saw any of the movie. So, Jared took me again the following week, and we did our best to keep our hands off one another and watch the movie. It was only semi-successful, which is how we found ourselves back at the theater a few days later where we managed to watch most of it on our third attempt.

It became an instant favorite. Mostly because of the memories attached to it. All those teenage feelings rush back to me as I stare at the guy at my side, trying so desperately to reclaim the happiness our parents stole from us.

My heart swells with love for Jared. Moments like this remind me he's still the same guy deep down underneath. The boy who was my everything is the man who wants to be my everything and more.

Jared shrugs before stretching his arm out on the couch behind me. "You were addicted to this movie when it came out. I haven't watched it in years. It popped up when I was scrolling, and I thought why not." He reaches for the remote. "We can look for something else."

I grab his hand, stalling the motion. "It's fine, J. Leave it," I say with a lump in my throat. "Let's see if it's as good as we thought it was as kids."

I switch off the lights, putting the tall lamp in the corner on so it's not completely dark, and settle down to watch the movie with my ex. Jared keeps a running commentary during the movie, scoffing at the obviously fake tattoos, some of the dodgy hairstyles, and sometimes cringey dialogue. I haven't laughed this hard in ages. We polish the bottle of wine off, and I'm nicely relaxed.

During the course of the movie, he ends up moving closer to me until our arms are brushing and our thighs are touching. Neither of us moves, and it's at that point I stop paying attention to the screen and start focusing on every breath that expels from his mouth, every movement of his face, the way his hand slides up and down his thigh, and the way he constantly wets his lips.

I turn rigidly still when his fingers toy with my hair, unsure if he's aware of it or not. My back is stuck to the couch, and my pussy pulses with need, reminding me I haven't had sex in four months. My little electric friend just isn't cutting it these days.

I should not be thinking these thoughts in Jared's company, but it's all too common these days. The man is sex on a stick, and I deserve a medal for ignoring our clear chemistry and resisting temptation.

The credits roll, forcing me to move, and I welcome it. I was dangerously close to throwing caution to the wind and doing something stupid like pouncing on him. I can't forget he has a pregnant ex and a baby on the way. It's enough to throw ice water over my libido and end all sexy ideas.

"What did you think?" he asks after I've turned the overhead light back on.

"I still like it, but it's definitely not as good as the show."

"You've watched it too?"

"Yeah. All three seasons."

"Same."

The unspoken sentiment isn't voiced. It doesn't need to be said. In our own ways, we were finding ways to cling to our past and one another.

He clears his throat. "The show is way better. I like the cast better, and they have more time to develop the story. The movie tried to squeeze too much in."

"I agree."

"We were approached last year to provide the theme song for a movie, but we had to turn it down because our schedule was too tight. We were gutted."

"I'm sure the opportunity will arise again."

"Hopefully."

"Do you want a coffee for the road?" I ask, climbing to my feet.

"I'll make it." He pulls me back down. "Do you want your usual chamomile?"

"Please." I smile at him.

He jumps up and rounds the couch. "Coming right up," he says from behind me, leaning down to press a sweet kiss to the top of my head.

When he's gone, I sit with my silent thoughts, acknowledging how easy it's been to have Jared back in my life. We have settled seamlessly into a new routine. We don't do anything exciting. Mostly we hang around our houses and the beach. Entertain our friends on occasion. Take regular weekly trips together to the grocery store. It's all been pretty mundane, and it should be boring.

But it's not.

I wake every day excited to see him.

This past month has given me a taste of what it would be like to be with him, and I don't dislike it.

Not one little bit.

My mind keeps returning to Toria and his son.

It hurts.

It fucking kills.

I know I'm going to have to tell him the truth soon. I see the way he looks at me whenever he mentions his ex, which isn't often, but I'm betting he thinks I'm being a bitch because I know I come across as disinterested and resentful. It's not fair to him, and I know it hurts him.

I just don't see how I can get past this. It's not like I can force myself to not feel these things. I can't help it.

"You look like you're a million miles away." Rounding the couch, he hands me a mug with my tea.

"I was." I cup my hands around the mug, siphoning its warmth.

"Am I allowed to know what has you so lost in thought?" He reclaims his seat beside me with his coffee.

"I was just thinking about Vittoria and the baby."

"What about them?"

"You haven't mentioned anything in weeks."

"Because it seems to hurt you," he quietly says.

"It does."

"I'm sorry."

"Please don't apologize. Not about that."

"I'm actually glad you brought her up." His jaw tightens. "We had her six-month checkup at the ob-gyn's last week, and she threw a hissy fit after we left the building." He places his coffee down on the table and drags a hand through his hair, emitting a heavy sigh. "I'm afraid to say this to you in case you tell me it's not worth being my friend, but I'm afraid not to say it in case you get caught in the crossfire."

"Just tell me," I say before sipping my tea.

"Word has gotten out about me living in Half Moon Bay. It's only a matter of time before they discover my house. Then I'll have fans showing up and the odd paparazzo. We spend a lot of time together, and I want to keep you safe. From fans, the media, and especially my ex."

"What exactly are you saying, J?"

"I'd like to hire you a bodyguard and install some security features at your house."

"No." I vigorously shake my head. "Absolutely no to the bodyguard. You know how much I hated them growing up."

He leans forward, pleading with his eyes. "It wouldn't be like that. He wouldn't be there to spy on you, just to keep you safe. He'd be in the background, and you'd barely even know he was there."

"*I'd* know he was there. It would make me paranoid, and it feels too controlling."

"I could never do that to you. I just want to know you're safe."

I take a moment to consider his request before replying. I know it's coming from a good place. I'm not sure how I feel about the need for it. I hate my association with him means I have to take extra precautions, but it's not his fault. "What kind of security measures do you have in mind?"

"A fence like mine around the perimeter of your property, an alarm system, and some outdoor cameras. A gate with code entry too."

"I'm paying for it," I say.

"No way. You only need this because of me. I'm paying for it. Please don't fight me on this. Just let me take care of you. I'll sleep easier at night knowing you're protected."

Only a fool would say no to extra security. It's a dangerous world we live in, especially the one Jared inhabits. If I'm going to be in his life, I have to accept some things will have to change. Starting with this. "Okay. If that's what you need to feel reassured, I have no objection to it. But the bodyguard is a hard no."

Chapter Twenty-Six
Jared

"That's a wrap," our producer says, giving us a thumbs-up from behind the glass in the control room as we lay down our ninth track for the new album. We're way ahead of schedule, and it's a nice feeling.

"Thank fuck." Linc places his guitar against the wall before palming his stomach. "I'm starving, and not just for food." He waggles his brows and licks his lips, and Wilder laughs.

"You're such a cliché," Syd proclaims not lifting her head from her sketch pad. She's been in the live room with us most all day, drawing nonstop in between bopping her head in time to the beat.

I have loved having her here. It's been nostalgic for both of us. We've shared plenty of lingering looks, and things are definitely heating up between us, but I haven't drawn attention to it. I'm letting my girl set the pace, but I'm hoping we'll be on the same page soon. Keeping my hands off her is a challenge that is growing more and more difficult. Sydney has slotted effortlessly back into my life the way I knew she would. I'm an impatient prick, and I'm itching to officially make her mine.

I want her permanently in my life.

In my house.

In my bed.

"What good is being a rock star if I don't enjoy the perks?" Linc retorts, pulling a crumpled packet of cigs from his back pocket.

"You're a pig." There is no heat behind Sydney's words, and she still hasn't lifted her head from her pad.

"Love you too, honey pie." Linc smirks as he saunters over to the couch Syd is sitting on. His features soften as he leans down to look. "Fuck, that's awesome."

Setting my signature sticks down, I stand, stretching my arms above my head and arching my back to loosen the stiffness there.

"It's only a rough draft," Syd replies, chewing on the corner of her mouth as I walk toward them.

I flop down beside her on the couch as Wilder places his guitar on the stand and ambles toward us. "Lemme see," I demand, pressing my body against her side as I crane my neck.

The three of us praise her incredible work as Syd quickly flicks through her sketch pad showing us various drawings. "They are all superb, but the first one is my fave," I confirm, flipping back to it.

"Mine too," Wilder concurs. Linc nods, puffing away on his cig.

"I have spent the most time on it because I like the energy," Syd supplies, narrowing her eyes critically on the drawing. "But there are a few others that might work better for a cover. I'm going to put my top three on a short list and spend some time working on them. Then I'll show you guys, and you can pick the one you like best." She closes the pad over, looking adorably anxious as she peers up at me.

"You're going to do it then?" I can't keep the smile off my face.

A delightful blush stains her cheeks as she nods and visibly swallows. "I think so. I mean, it'll be up to you guys and Ryder. You might not like any of them."

"That's a virtual impossibility," Linc says in between drags. "I already love them."

"You're gonna kill it, babe," Wilder agrees, pressing a quick kiss to Sydney's cheek.

My scowl is automatic as is Linc's burst of laughter. He almost chokes, snorting out more laughter when I flip him the bird.

Sydney looks bemused as her gaze bounces between us. "Sometimes it's like wrangling toddlers at dinner time around you three."

"I couldn't agree more," Ryder says, stepping into the room with a familiar brunette on his arm.

"Sis." Wilder launches himself at Zeta, scooping her up and lifting her legs off the ground as he spins around.

"Put her down, asshole." Ryder is smiling as he stares at his brother swinging his wife around the room.

"You're as crazy as our eldest." Zeta grins as she clings to her brother-in-law's arm when Wilder puts her feet on the ground.

"How is my man Zan?" Wilder asks, pressing a kiss to Zeta's temple.

"Trouble," Ryder says with pride. He tucks his wife into his side, and they share a loving look.

"We wouldn't have him any other way. All the kids are great," Zeta says as her curious gaze moves to the couch for a split second. "Etta asks for you all the time."

"Love my princess," Wilder says of Ryder and Zeta's nine-year old, and it's the truth. He dotes on his niece. "I'll come visit soon. I promise."

"She'd like that." Zeta smiles at Sydney. "Wes took Cory and Zander camping last weekend, and they are pestering him nonstop to do it again. Maybe Etta would go next time if you're there."

Wes is Wilder's other brother. He's three years younger and he works in marketing for a top advertising agency. Ryder is always trying to entice him to come and work for Torment Records, but I think he likes working independently of his family, and I respect that. He's a great uncle to all Ryder's kids, but he has a close bond with the boys.

"I'll talk to Wes, and we'll line something up," Wilder confirms as Zeta moves toward us.

Sydney rises the same time I do. "I'm Zeta." Ryder's wife thrusts her hand out. "You must be Sydney."

"I am." Syd shakes her hand. "It's lovely to meet you." She leans in closer to me as she speaks with Ryder's wife, and I love that she's naturally relying on me for support. Slinging my arm around Sydney's shoulders, I smile at Zeta. "I'll try to keep my fangirling to a minimum as I already made a scene when I met your husband, but I am a massive, massive fan of the work you've done with Savage Mania. "Forever True" is one of my absolute favorite songs, and I was screaming with joy when you won the Grammy for it."

Ryder's wife is a talented songwriter, and Zeta was pivotal in Savage Mania's success. We got our first big gig supporting them on their world tour, and they helped to launch our careers.

"That is really sweet of you to say." Zeta beams at my girl. "Thank you so much."

"Sydney is only telling the truth, love." Ryder wraps his

arms around Zeta from behind. "You're one of our top songwriters. Own that shit, babe."

"I wish I had more time to write," Zeta laments, "but life is hectic with the kids, and I help with our charity. It doesn't leave much time for anything else."

"Sydney used to help me write songs back in the day," I supply.

"Jared." Sydney uses a cautionary tone that stirs my dick.

"What?" I arch a brow as I peer deep into her gorgeous green eyes.

"It's hardly the same thing. Zeta is a Grammy-winning songwriter, and I used to pluck a few words from my head to help you finish your lyrics."

"Don't dismiss your input or your ability. You have a good ear for music. It's probably the artist in you."

She shrugs, still not easily accepting praise.

"You're both talented ladies," Linc says, stubbing his cigarette out. "And I think it's time we toasted to that." He rubs his hands as mischief alights in his eyes. "Let's party."

Sydney leaves with Zeta to get ready at a local salon while we use the facilities at the studio to shower and change before heading to a local bar to wait for the girls. I'm on my second beer when they finally show up, and I almost choke on my tongue when I see Sydney. She's wearing a one-shouldered, tight-fitting, red and gold minidress that hits mid-thigh with skyscraper gold stilettos that make her legs look super long and super slim. Her gorgeous blonde hair is pulled back from her face in a high ponytail, highlighting her exquisite bone structure. She's wearing more makeup than normal, but it's been artfully applied, and it looks subtle.

She looks like rock royalty, and I'm ready to bow to my queen.

She takes my breath away as she walks confidently toward us with her arm looped through Zeta's.

"Fuck. Me," Linc murmurs, and I dig my elbow into his ribs without taking my eyes off my woman. I haven't even noticed what Zeta is wearing, but I'm sure she's equally stunning as she's a beautiful woman too.

"Hey." Sydney smiles, somewhat shyly, when the women reach our table.

I stand and lean in to kiss her cheek. "You look incredibly beautiful and so fucking sexy," I whisper in her ear. I feel like fist pumping the air when she visibly shivers.

"Thanks." Tinkling laughter leaves her lips. "I might be a little tipsy. We had champagne at the salon, and I forgot I hadn't eaten since breakfast."

We didn't stop for lunch today as we wanted to finish our set early to enjoy a night on the town. It's been ages since I've gone clubbing in L.A. It hasn't been my scene for a long time, but I want to experience everything with Sydney. To make memories in place of the ones that were denied to us. "I should have ordered you lunch."

"Stop it." Her eyes rake over my tall frame, and it's an effort not to puff out my chest when her eyes darken with lust. "It's not your responsibility to feed me. I would've gotten lunch if I'd been hungry."

"Speaking of food, our table at the restaurant is ready," Ryder says, linking his fingers with his wife's.

My fingers itch with a craving to hold Sydney's hand, but I shove my hands in the pockets of my jeans instead, keeping close to her side as we exit the bar and head in the direction of the restaurant Ryder reserved for dinner.

"Are you okay?" I ask as we walk side by side, trailing the others.

"I'm great." Her beaming smile is genuine, and I return it.

"You seem to have bonded with Zeta."

"Oh my god." Her eyes light up. "I just love her!" She hooks her arm in mine, and I'm not sure she realizes she's even done it. "She's so fun. She invited us to their house for dinner, and we swapped numbers and everything."

I make a mental note to send Ryder's wife some flowers. I know Syd was a little nervous about tonight, and Zeta seems to have single-handedly erased all her anxiety. Sydney's obvious joy does funny things to my insides, and I fight the urge to sweep her into my arms and kiss the living daylights out of her. "Zeta is good people," I say. "I had a feeling you two would gel." I hold her close, darting to the side as a dick on a scooter whizzes by us.

"She's really down to earth and so gracious about her talent."

"Like someone else I know."

Her cheeks pink, and I smile, almost floating on a cloud as I walk with the girl of my dreams to one of my favorite restaurants. "How did you like it in the studio today?" I inquire.

Her face animates again. "I loved it." She clings to my arm tighter. "I'm in awe of you. Of all of you. You're such incredible musicians. Thanks for letting me be a part of it today. It was amazing."

"It was special having you there." Toria had zero interest in our music. Unless it benefited her, she didn't want to know. I love how much enjoyment Sydney gets from seeing me happy and living my dream. She is happy if I'm happy and vice versa. It's that simple between us. It's only when others are added to the mix it gets complicated.

"I know I've said it before, but I am so fucking proud of

you, J. You did it." Tears prick her eyes, and I wish we weren't on a busy street with nosy bystanders staring so I could envelop her in my arms and never let her go. "You did what you set out to do. It's mind-blowing and inspirational."

"It all means nothing without you," I softly say, knowing I'm close to crossing a line.

"I'm here now." Her eyes are determined as they latch on mine. "And I'm not going anywhere."

Chapter Twenty-Seven
Sydney

I'm having the fucking best night of my life. To think I was worried leaving Half Moon Bay this morning. Afraid I wouldn't fit into Jared's world or that I'd get papped and incur Vittoria's wrath, but it's been smooth sailing. The guys are fucking legends. In the studio and as human beings. Wilder and Linc are amazing guys, and they already feel like good friends. I can see how the three of them work so well together. There is no pretense. They are honest and vulnerable with one another, and it's blatantly obvious they are as close as brothers. I'm so happy for J that he has them. I've been chatting with Ryder and Zeta a lot tonight too, and it's like I've always known them. Jared is surrounded by good people, and it helps to alleviate some of my concerns about the rock star lifestyle.

I'm buzzing from more than just the champagne and great company.

I'm feeling invigorated. Alive in a way I haven't felt in a long time.

Being in the studio today was magical.

I don't have the words to describe it, but I just vibed with the atmosphere and the creativity swirling in the air. I haven't sketched like that in forever. It's like my fingers were on fire. Whether it's being around Jared again, the music, or a combination of the two, it feels like I'm getting my mojo back. I'm itching to draw and paint and seriously considering giving it a go as a full-time career. Seeing the guys bouncing ideas off one another and how passionate they are when playing has inspired me. Maybe it's time to spread my wings and pursue my artist dream. I'm going to create the best fucking cover for Ruminate's album and then see where it takes me.

Right now, I feel like I can achieve anything my heart desires, and I'm happy. Truly happy for the first time in ages. I know there are obstacles to overcome, but tonight I feel confident I can get past it.

"Let's dance." Zeta pulls me out of the booth in the VIP area of the club we came to after dinner, dragging me toward the busy dance floor.

We have fun dancing, giggling, and singing while avoiding the grabby hands that occasionally wander our way. It's therefore no surprise when Ryder and Jared materialize at our sides a short while later. We naturally split into two couples, and it's not long before I'm bumping hips and brushing arms with my sexy ex.

The beat changes to a sultry, sensual number, and the room darkens when the overhead lights are dimmed. Jared slides up behind me as I shimmy my hips and throw my arms out to the side. I'm acutely conscious of his every movement as we dance, drawing closer and closer with every sway of our bodies. I'm on fire. Every nook and cranny in my body is on high alert as my hands roam over my body, and I grind my hips in tune to the music.

Behind me, Jared flexes his powerful body, keeping only a minuscule distance between us. He's about to come out of his skin too. I can feel the sexual tension exuding from his pores, and I get braver, brushing against his body as we dance a seductive dance. When his talented fingers caress my bare arms, sweeping up and down my sensitive flesh, I bite down on my lower lip to trap the moan dying to burst free.

Heat rolls off him in waves as he presses firmly against me from behind, all pretenses gone. We grind and shimmy against one another, clutching at each other as our mutual arousal elevates to dizzy heights. Shivers dance over my overheated skin, raising goose bumps, when he moves his mouth to my ear. "You are mesmerizing tonight." His arm slides around my waist as he holds me flush against his toned body. "I want to tear every guy in this place from limb to limb for daring to even look at you."

His jealousy and clear possessiveness shouldn't turn me on, but it does. Pressing my ass against the bulge straining his zipper, I reach an arm around to grip the back of his neck. Tilting my head, I pull his face down to mine and direct my lips to his ear. "They can't have me," I rasp.

"Can I?" His sky-blue eyes are glimmering with barely contained desire as he braves the question while maintaining eye contact.

Our eyes lock in a sinful battle, and my heart is pounding superfast in my chest. Need flares in my core as my pussy clenches and unclenches. Lust pools low in my belly, and I'm struggling to not give in to what we both want. I can't keep fighting our connection. Jared has always been it for me. This is what I have craved for years, so why am I refusing us what we both want?

Keeping my eyes glued to his, I slowly nod, conveying everything I want to say with a heated look.

Yes, J. Yes, you can have me.

Take me. Take me now.

Reclaim me and make me yours.

Jared twirls me around and clasps my head in his large hands, resting his brow against mine. "I love you, Sydney Shaw. I love you so fucking much."

"I love you too."

Tears glisten in his eyes as we stare at one another. Tension is ripe in the air, and though I want him, I can't forget where we are. I ease my head back, and he straightens up. "Not here."

Clutching my hand, he leads me off the dance floor with urgency lacing each step. My heart is ping-ponging around my chest, and the vein in my neck is thrumming in expectation. My panties are soaked, and I wet my suddenly dry lips as Jared pulls me into a dark alcove shielded from prying eyes on both sides. Pushing me up against the wall, he cages me in with his muscular arms. My heart thumps frantically as blood rushes to my head, and I feel a little dizzy.

He leans into my face, his hungry gaze lowering to my mouth before dancing back up to my eyes. "I need to know you are serious about this, Syd. I can't be with you and then return to the friend zone. It would kill me."

"I want this, J." I clutch a fistful of his shirt. "I'm done living in denial."

"Are you sure, Syd?"

"I am." Steely determination threads through my tone. I grip his shirt tighter as my eyes drop to his tempting lips before I drag my gaze back up his face. "I am not drunk. I'm in control, and I know what I want." I worry my lower lip between my teeth as I prepare to spill my truth. "I want you. I have always wanted you. There won't be any time where I won't want you. You're it for me, J. You always have been."

"You took the words right out of my mouth. I love you so fucking much." He grips my chin, forcing my face up a little. "What about my career and Toria and my son?"

"Those are things for us to work through but not insurmountable." We need to have a heavy conversation, and I need to share the things I've been holding prisoner in my heart. We can't have a future without confronting the rest of the past. But that doesn't need to happen now. It can wait until tomorrow. It's better if we have that conversation completely sober and in private. If he doesn't kiss me soon, I'm likely to self-combust.

"You are my world, baby." His grip loosens on my chin, and his fingers sweep reverently across my face. "I will move heaven and earth to make you happy because you are everything, Syd. I never want you to regret choosing me."

"I won't. As long as you kiss me now." I yank him in closer until our faces are almost touching. "I need your lips on mine stat."

"Never beg, my queen," he says, brushing his lips fleetingly against mine. "What you need you shall have." His eyes flare with heat as his lips crash against mine in a potent display of longing and possession, and I am here for it.

Our reconnection is explosive as we devour one another in the shadowy alcove with a roomful of people just outside. Jared holds the back of my head, directing the angle of our kiss, as he ravishes my mouth with his lips and his tongue. I cling to his wrists, kissing him back with the same intensity as fire rages inside me. Kissing him again feels both familiar and new. Jared the man is a more skilled kisser than Jared the boy, but I still stand over my assertion.

My man is the best kisser in the entire world.

Fact.

I melt against him as his tongue roams the inside of my mouth, and his hands drop from my face to go exploring. Every brush of his fingers against my body is like lighting a fuse, and I'm writhing and moaning as he presses against me, rocking his hips in a circular fashion and grinding his erection against my core through our clothes. A squeak leaves my lips when he lifts my leg and wraps it around his waist so he can thrust more accurately against my pelvis. I see stars as his thick shaft brushes against my pussy, and I grab handfuls of his ass, pulling him in closer to me.

"J," I rasp, peppering kisses against his face as his fingers creep up the inside of my thigh. "I need you."

"Need you too, baby." Jared dusts feather-soft kisses all along my neck and my collarbone, and if he keeps it up, I'm liable to come without him even touching my cunt. I hiss when he abruptly pulls back and carefully places my leg on the ground. "Don't pout, beautiful." He sweeps a finger along my swollen lips. "I'm taking you home so I can worship you the right way. I'm not fucking you against a wall in a nightclub where anyone could see."

Well, when he puts it like that, I can't complain. I thread my fingers in his. "Take me home and make me yours again, J."

We head back to the table to say our goodbyes, and Jared calls his driver to meet us at the rear of the club. I refuse to hold his hand as we make our exit, fearful someone will take a photo of us.

One of Jared's bodyguards meets us downstairs, and we follow him along what appears to be a staff hallway. Several men and women wearing the signature black-and-white uniforms line the hallway to say hi and gawp at the famous rock star. A few inquisitive gazes are directed my way along with some hostile looks.

"I'm going to call Amanda, my publicist, in the morning," Jared says, keeping his voice low as we approach the door. "She'll issue a press release tomorrow confirming my broken engagement. I'll call Toria and tell her about us."

"Okay." I heave out a sigh. "But I don't want anything made public between you and I until after the baby is born. I don't want to be portrayed as a home wrecker or be disrespectful to Vittoria." She's a selfish manipulative bitch, and I don't like her, but I don't want to embarrass her in front of the world's media. She is still the mother of Jared's child. The usual pain ruptures in my chest, but I'll have to find a way to deal with it. My first therapy session this week went well, and I plan to attend weekly until I get a handle on my emotions. It hurts that the man I love is having a child with someone else, but I'll get over it.

He wants me, not her.

And that little boy is half Jared. I know I'll be able to love him because he shares my love's DNA. With time, I'm confident I'll be able to get past this, and then, hopefully, we'll be able to have a child of our own. One that won't be stolen from us this time.

The instant the bodyguard opens the rear door, all hell breaks loose. Flashes go off in my face as Jared yanks me into his body, pushing my head down to his chest and cradling me close as we fight a barrage of photographers who were clearly tipped off we were leaving.

I'm jostled and shoved as Jared fights his way through the heaving crowd. I keep my head pressed to his chest even though I can barely breathe, but I'm too terrified to move. The last thing I need is my face plastered all over the internet, but I doubt there's any way to stop it from happening now. My breaths are oozing out in panicked spurts, and butterflies are running rampant in my chest. Blood pounds in my ears and rushes to my head, and I'm vaguely conscious I'm shivering all over.

"Fuck off," Jared snaps, alternating that response with "No comment" as he's bombarded with questions.

"Who's the blonde, Jared?"

"Does Vittoria know you're cheating on her?"

"Are you fucking both of them?"

"Is it true you're in an open relationship?"

"Is she a groupie?"

"Do you share her with your bandmates?"

"I said fuck off," Jared roars as I'm shoved into the back of a car. I keep my head down, too afraid to look up, as I hear an angry commotion outside. The seat bounces with the weight of a body, and then the sounds are muffled when two car doors slam violently shut. "Get us the fuck out of here," Jared barks.

Hands reach for me as the car shoots forward, the driver keeping his hand pressed on the horn as he navigates away from the club. "Syd. Baby." Jared gentles his voice as he lifts me up and onto his lap. "It's okay. I've got you." He holds me close, rubbing a soothing hand up and down my back.

I cling to him as I try to control my erratic heartbeat and calm my trembling limbs.

"I'm so sorry, babe. Some asshole tipped them off."

"The alleyway was clear when I came inside to escort you, sir," a man says, and I'm assuming it is the dark-haired bodyguard.

"They arrived seconds before you came out," another man says, and he must be the driver. "I didn't even have time to warn you."

"It's fine," Jared says, sounding defeated. "There isn't anything you could've done. We know the drill." He dots kisses into my hair. "Put the privacy screen up," he says, and a few seconds later, a soft whirring sound tickles my eardrums as the screen moves into place.

Wetting my dry lips, I lift my head from his chest and brush hair off my face. Worried eyes meet mine. "We shouldn't have gone out. I'm so sorry, Sydney. I never wanted to put you in the line of fire. That club is well frequented by celebrities and known for their discretion. I have never had anything like that happen before in there. We thought it was the safest place to go."

"It's not your fault. You didn't force me to go." I knew the risks, and I still went out in public with him. It was a bad judgment call. and I'm the one who will pay the price. I slide off his lap now I'm calmer and strap myself into a seat belt.

"Does this change things?"

I peer into his troubled eyes as all the earlier euphoria completely disappears. "I want to say no because I know this comes with the territory, but that was scary shit, J. I'm not unaccustomed to the media, but that was a whole other level."

"It's why I wanted you to have a bodyguard." His tone is soft, and it's not a dig.

"I hate the thought of it. I hoped the extra security measures would be enough, but they only protect me at home." After I agreed, Jared had guys over the following day installing my new gate, alarm system, exterior cameras, and the snazzy retracting fence. "It's going to be a shit show. Everyone will think you're cheating on Vittoria, and I'll be blamed for your broken engagement. Fuck." I bury my head in my hands, second-guessing myself all over again. How did I think I could do this?

"I'm sorry. What can I do?"

"I'm not sure there's much you can do." I lift my chin and eyeball him. "The damage is done now."

"They might not have seen your face or be able to identify you." He's clutching at straws, and we both know it. If they got a clear pic of me, it won't take long for them to figure out who I am. Jared sighs and scrubs his hands down his face.

"I'm pretty sure every pap got a good shot of us when the door opened." I rest my head against the window, watching the streets of L.A. whiz by as the driver heads toward the studio where Jared's helicopter awaits.

"I'll do damage control. I'll call Amanda when I get home, and we'll come up with a plan. Try not to worry."

I snort out a laugh as I fix him with an incredulous look. "That's an impossibility, J. I'm fucked. My life as I know it is over, and I'm not sure I'm strong enough for what comes next."

Chapter Twenty-Eight
Sydney

The following morning, I clasp my hands around my mug while I sit outside on my patio, bundled in a thick cardigan, staring out at my colorful garden and the ocean beyond, as my thoughts churn violently. What started out as one of the best nights last night turned into one of the worst. The return journey to Half Moon Bay was silent and tense. Both of us were lost in thought and melancholy. All trace of our earlier passion was gone, and there was no recovering the night. Neither of us were in the mood any longer. Jared walked me home, pressing a soft kiss to my lips after promising he was going to fix this.

But I don't see how.

A shudder works its way through me, and it's not from the gentle October sea breeze. I'm too chickenshit to check out social media, but I'm plagued with all kinds of horrors, thanks to my vivid imagination. Even the familiar sound of waves crashing to the shore and the brisk salty tang in the air fail to soothe me today. I'm terrified to step foot outside my door and grateful I don't have a shift at the museum until Tuesday. I'm not sure what awaits me when I leave the comfort and safety of my home. Or how long it will remain my private haven.

Finishing my coffee, I head inside to my art studio and attempt to paint, but I find no solace in creativity either. I swipe my finger across my cell phone, preparing to call Jared, but I think better of it. I need to know what's happening, and I'd rather talk with him face-to-face. I can't hide in my house forever.

I grab a quick shower and change into jeans, sneakers, and an oversized hoodie before snatching my keys and setting out on foot to Jared's house. Nerves fire at me from all angles when I take that first tentative step outside my front door. My shoulders slump, and I relax a smidgeon when there is no baying crowd lying in wait holding pitchforks and screaming for my blood. Maybe Jared's PR people worked some magic and got the story killed. It's probably wishful thinking, but I'm clinging to it.

Exiting through the side gate at my front entrance, I race across the road heading in the direction of Jared's house. Déjà vu slaps me in the face when I pass by a familiar Mercedes SUV with tinted windows, and all the fine hairs lift on my arms. Normally, I wouldn't notice, but this model has a gold trim and distinctive custom wheels, and I'm pretty sure I've seen it parked outside my house on a few different occasions in the past few weeks.

It could be a paparazzo, but my gut says it isn't. If someone knew about me weeks ago, there would already be speculation online, and there's been nothing.

It's not a pap, but someone is clearly spying on me.

Motherfucker.

Rage infiltrates my veins as the thought lands in my head. My hands ball into fists at my side as I quicken my pace and snarl into thin air. I fucking told Jared I didn't want a body-guard, and he went behind my back and hired one anyway. That is way out of line, and I'm ready to rip him a new one as I run the rest of the way to his house and let myself in.

"Jared!" I roar, slamming the door with force behind me. "Where the fuck are you?" I race down his hall, poking my head in his studio, living room, and dining room, but they're all empty. I find him in the kitchen, sitting on a stool at the island unit with his cell in his hand and a resigned expression on his face. He cautions me to be silent with bloodshot eyes as an unfamiliar woman talks ninety miles an hour on the line.

I shoot daggers at him with my eyes before I turn and grab a bottle of water from the refrigerator. It's tempting to reach for something stronger, but that's a slippery slope. I pace the room as the woman—his publicist I assume from the nature of the conversation—discusses strategies to minimize the damage.

So, I guess the word is out after all.

Awesome.

Unable to listen to it anymore, I head out to his terrace and drop into a chair, grimacing as I sip my water and wonder what the hell I'm going to do now. The door slides open behind me a few minutes later, and tension bleeds into the air when Jared claims the seat beside me.

I grind my teeth to the molars and grip the arms of the chair so tight I break a nail.

"You're upset," he says in a gruff voice, breaking the silence first.

"Ya think?" I turn and smother him with a glare. "I expressly told you I didn't want a bodyguard, and you still went and hired one!" I narrow my eyes. "That is a massive invasion of my privacy. I don't care if it was for my protection. I made my feelings clear, and you ignored them."

His brow puckers as he scrubs a hand along the stubble on his chin and cheeks. "What are you talking about?"

"The fucking car camped outside my house!"

"Fuck." He drags a hand through his disheveled hair. "It must be one of those scumbag photographers."

"It's not," I snap. "I've seen this car around on other occasions."

He reaches for my hand, but I snatch it away before he can hold it. Hurt splays across his face. "Syd. I swear to you I have not hired a bodyguard. I wanted to, but you made your feelings clear, and I respected your wishes."

I stare into his earnest features, and I see nothing but the truth. Some of my irritational anger eases. "You swear that's the truth?"

"If there's a guy outside your house, babe, it's not any bodyguard I hired. I planned to talk to you again today about hiring one, but I swear I'd never go behind your back. I wouldn't do that to you. Please say you believe me." He bravely reaches for my hand again, and I let him thread his fingers in mine as the intense heat of my anger completely fades.

"I believe you." I tighten my hold on his hand. "I'm sorry," I add. "I shouldn't have jumped to conclusions. I know you wouldn't act without my permission. I'm really on edge today after last night, and I just flipped." I feel bad I ever thought J would do that to me.

"It's okay." He rubs soothing circles on the back of my hand. "You're not the only one on edge."

"So, the cat is definitely out of the bag?"

"I'm afraid so."

"Maybe it is a photographer after all." Maybe he's been watching and waiting for something to kick off before reporting on what he knows. Shit, shit, shit. This could be about to completely blow up in our faces.

Air whooshes out of his mouth and strain creases the corners of his eyes. "I thought we were in the clear, at least for now. I've been on the phone with my publicist and her team for hours. There are reports and gossip online, but no one has named you and none of the pics I've seen show a clear shot of your face. We got lucky with so many flashes. The first images are all blurry and not enough to identify you."

"That doesn't mean someone hasn't figured it out."

"If the word was out, there'd be a horde of vultures camped outside your house." He stands abruptly. "I don't even like the thought of one. I'm going to give that shithead a piece of my mind."

I tug on his arm, pulling him back down. "Let's park that for a minute. I want to know what your PR people are suggesting."

"Amanda says the best strategy is to come partially clean. I've just approved her to release a statement saying my relationship with Toria was always casual and we were only briefly engaged. It confirms we broke up two months ago and I'm supporting her fully during her pregnancy and we have agreed a co-parenting arrangement. It also confirms I was not cheating on her."

"What about me?"

"This is where I disagree with Amanda. She doesn't want to mention you now. She prefers to downplay it and say you're an old friend. I think she's wrong. I really want to keep your name out of it, but it's only a matter of time before they find out. I prefer to get ahead of it and say we are childhood sweethearts who have recently reconnected and we're enjoying spending time together again. But I won't do anything without your agreement. If you'd rather we keep it vague, that's fine by me."

"Ugh." Wrenching my hand from his, I rub at a tense spot between my brows. "This is a nightmare."

"I'm sorry, Syd."

"Please stop saying you're sorry. I know you are, and it's not your fault." I stare absently out at the ocean, struggling to make sense of the warring emotions in my head.

"Is this it for us?" he quietly adds, strain evident in his voice. "Have you decided I'm more trouble than I'm worth?" Pain slices through his tone, and I hate it.

"No. I haven't decided anything. I just need some time to wrap my head around it. I don't want to commit unless I know I can deal with it. Right now, I'm not one hundred percent sure." I swivel on my seat and clasp his hands in mine, peering deep into his worried eyes. "I meant what I said last night, J. I love you, and I want to find a way to make this work, but I'm terrified this is bigger than I can handle."

"You're worried about falling off the wagon?"

"A little."

He pulls me onto his lap in one swift move as if I weigh nothing. "It will be different this time. I'm here for you, and I won't let anyone hurt you. I promise."

"What about Vittoria?" I circle my arms around his neck. "Does she know?"

He winces, and I brace myself for it. "She called me screaming bloody murder a few hours ago. I barely got a word in edgewise before she hung up on me."

"She'll know it's me."

He nods. "She already suspects, but I didn't have a chance to say anything because she was just shouting and cursing at me in multiple languages."

"Maybe we should get ahead of this before she does." Right now, I'd rank a scorned woman above cutthroat paparazzi on the list of things to worry about.

He nuzzles his nose against my cheek. "Take the day to think about it. We can let my first statement settle and then address the question of my mystery woman later."

"Okay. I'll mull it over and talk to Cay. I'll let you know later." I hop off his lap and extend my hand. "Come on. It's time to confront the asshole in the SUV outside my house. Let's get ahead of that too."

Chapter Twenty-Nine
Sydney

"**S**yd! What the fuck?!" Jared yells as I jump out in front of the SUV, and a screeching noise tortures my ears when the driver slams on the brakes.

"He's not leaving until I know what's going on." I bang my hands on the hood of the car, all riled up again at the thought someone has been following me around without my permission. I know it was reckless to lunge in front of a moving car, but I want answers, and I want them now.

"You almost gave me a coronary." Jared levels me with a stern look as he stalks toward the driver's door. "We'll be having words about this later."

"Open the fucking door, J, and pull that asshole out." The fact he was preparing to speed off when he saw us approaching confirms he is up to no good.

Jared tugs on the driver's side handle, but the asshole has locked the door. J hammers on the glass, bellowing out threats while I remain in front of the car, stopping him from moving. "Face us like a man, dipshit, or I'm calling the cops."

Jared removes his cell and taps on the keypad, preparing to

call 911, when the engine cuts out. He jumps back as the door opens, shock rendering him speechless when polished black dress shoes land on the asphalt and a large broad man heaves himself out of the SUV.

"What. The. Fuck?" Jared's gaze bounces from the man to me as I slowly round the hood and come up to them.

"Dirk?" I gasp, staring at the man who was one of my bodyguards as a teen.

"Hello, Sydney." He flashes me a nasty grin I'm all too familiar with. It's been years since I last saw him, and the years haven't been kind to him. His dark hair is now speckled with thick strands of gray. Pronounced lines at the corners of his eyes and his mouth age him more than his years, and he's carrying at least an extra fifty pounds. Not ideal if you're employed in the security industry.

"What the fuck are you doing here?" I plant my hands on my hips and glare at him.

"I see your vocabulary hasn't improved."

Jared growls low, stabbing Dirk with a menacing glare, but he remains quiet, and I'm glad he's letting me handle this.

I cock my head to the side and smirk. "My attitude hasn't either. At least when it comes to my father. I presume he's behind this?" I'm working hard to leash my anger, and it's challenging.

Dirk nods.

"How long have you been spying on me?"

"I've been *protecting* you for the past seven weeks." He cracks his knuckles, and if it's meant to be threatening, it's laughable.

"Protecting me from what exactly?" I arch a brow.

His gaze darts to Jared, and my eyes bug wide.

"You cannot be serious." My glare deepens. "I don't need protecting from Jared!"

He shrugs. "Take it up with your father. I'm just following orders."

"Get the fuck out of here," Jared snaps, slinging his arm around my shoulders and drawing me into his side. "And don't come back. If you harass my girlfriend again, I'll call the cops and have you arrested for stalking."

An inordinate thrill rushes through me when he calls me his girlfriend, and I feel like I'm fifteen all over again. It's more than a little presumptuous, as nothing is agreed between us, but I'm not about to argue the point in front of my father's lackey.

"Like I said, take it up with Mr. Shaw."

"Oh, trust me, I will." I'm seething, and while I don't relish talking to my father, I will do it to stop this bullshit.

"Scram or I'm calling the cops." Jared tightens his hold on me as he levels Dirk with a warning look.

"I'll be seeing you around, Sydney," the jerk says as he climbs behind the wheel.

"Go to hell, Dick. If I see you near my house again, I'll shoot you and claim self-defense."

He pins me with an irritating grin before yanking his door shut and peeling out of our neighborhood.

"What the fuck is going on, Syd?" Jared pulls me into his arms.

Resting my head on his chest, I inhale his comforting scent, wondering the same thing. "I don't know, but we're going to find out."

"Sweet pea, it's so good to hear from you," Herman Shaw says, his booming voice projecting around my kitchen where I have him on speakerphone. Jared is beside me, and we agreed he'd remain silent while I talk to my estranged father. "I have missed my little princess."

"Quit the bullshit, Herman, and don't call me that. I'm not your little princess anymore."

"You'll always be my princess, Sydney," he says in a softer tone.

I grip the edge of the counter hard. "You lost the right to call me anything with your controlling ways, and I see you still haven't changed."

A pregnant pause ensues before he clears his throat. "Dirk is there to keep you safe. You're in danger, Sydney, and if you think I haven't been protecting you these past few years, then you're more naïve than I realized."

Jared glares at the phone, and his mouth opens to defend me, but I shake my head, silencing him. This is my fight, and I'm doing this my way. "You're a paranoid freak, Herman," I say in a cold tone. "And if you don't stop harassing me, I'll take out a restraining order. You're not the only one with powerful contacts and friends in high places."

"Everything I do, I do for you, pumpkin."

Again with the fucking names. When I was a kid, I adored my father and I loved how big his love felt. Now, I wonder if he has always been manipulating me and I was just too young to understand it.

"Controlling every aspect of my life was for me?" I snarl, losing the tenuous hold on my emotions. Every time I talk to my father, this happens. He enrages me. He drags me back to that dark time in my life, and I hate it. I hate him.

"I was protecting you then like I'm protecting you now."

"I don't need protecting!" I yell.

"If you're hanging around with Jared King again, then you most certainly do."

Jared and I share an exasperated look. "You're certifiable,

Herman, and I'm done with this conversation. Call your hound dog off, or you'll be sorry."

"Come to New York," he blurts. "I'll send a plane. I'll tell you everything I didn't back then." Desperation is transparent in his tone.

"You're too late. I already know. Gladys filled us in."

The growl that crawls down the line has me jerking back in instant fear.

"Whatever that fucking bitch has been saying is bullshit, and you need to stay away from her, Sydney."

"I know Mom had an affair with Amos and you destroyed his business in retaliation."

"That's only part of it, sweet pea," he rasps. "I know you hate me, and I know I've given you good reason to, but just hear me out. I'll tell you everything."

"The time to tell me everything was back then." I hate how my voice wobbles. Jared stands and comes up behind me, circling his arms around my waist and offering physical comfort.

Leaning back against him, I cling to his arms and siphon some of his strength. "You ripped me away from the only boy I have ever loved. I still remember how you scoffed at me. The things you said and did. I will never forgive you for it, and I don't want to hear anything you have to say. Actions speak louder than words. Your actions spoke volumes, Daddy." A sob swells in my throat. "I love Jared, and there is nothing you can say or do that will ever take me from him again."

"Sydney, please. I—"

I hang up before he can spew more lies.

Jared turns me around on the stool, holding me close as I wrap my arms around him and cling to him with a desperation I feel deep in my bones.

"He's fucking crazy," he says after a few beats, smoothing a hand up and down my hair. "Mum was right. He's dangerous." He tilts my chin up. "I know how much you hate the idea of a bodyguard, but I'm scared for you, babe. There's Herman, Toria, and the news that's sure to break soon. Please let me assign a couple of guys to look out for you. I swear you won't even know they're there. And I'd like to talk to my lawyer. John will know what to do about your father. He can't get away with stalking you like this."

There is no point fighting something that is inevitable. "Okay. I won't fight you on it anymore."

"Thanks, babe. I will breathe easier knowing my guys are shadowing you and keeping you safe."

"Leave my father to me." I've had an idea I think might get Herman Shaw off my case once and for all.

"Are you sure?" he asks as his phone pings in his pocket.

I nod. "If anything changes, I'll let you know."

Jared leaves after his call from Ryder. He needs to attend to some business in L.A. It's probably for the best. I didn't want to call Sawyer while Jared was here. He's still irrationally jealous when it comes to my ex-husband. Can I even call him that when our marriage was annulled? I don't know.

I head into my art studio as I wait for the call to connect.

"Sydney. Long time no speak. What's up?" Sawyer greets.

"It's been a while." I prop my butt against the table in my studio as I talk to my ex. "How is Xavier?"

"He's good. Still drives me crazy, but that's nothing new. We can't complain. Business is booming."

"That's actually why I'm calling. I wanted to hire you to do something for me."

"Are you in trouble?" His voice instantly turns sober.

"No, it's nothing like that. It's my father." I give him a quick rundown of the situation, and he listens attentively as I explain. Sawyer knows I was rebellious in my late teens and that my father put me in a cage, but he doesn't have the details, and I need to fill him in now. I don't tell him everything. Just the pertinent information he'll need to do some digging.

"Damn, Syd. I knew Herman was controlling, but that takes things to a whole new level."

"He's irritational, and he won't stop unless I force him to."

"What do you need me to do?"

"Can you dig into the past? See if you can find out exactly what went on between my parents and Jared's and see if you can find something I can hold over Herman? Something that will get him off my back for good."

I could go the legal route, but Dad has connections and resources, and it would probably be a waste of both our time and money. It would also end up in the public domain, and I don't want to give the vultures any extra ammunition to come after me. This calls for a creative strategy. One Herman Shaw will understand and abide. "I am sick of dealing with his bullshit. I have worked hard to get where I am. Jared and I have a chance at real happiness, and my father is not going to interfere. I won't let him ruin this for me again."

"Leave it with us. If there is something to find, we'll find it."

"Thanks, Sawyer."

"Anytime, Syd. You know we look out for our friends. I'm glad you called me."

"I probably should have done this sooner." I already feel relieved. Xavier Daniels is one of the best hackers in the world, and Sawyer Hunt has mean tech skills too. There isn't much those two can't do.

"We'll get to the bottom of it. I guarantee it."

I hang up and spend the afternoon painting, committing

some time to working on the sketches of the band, while I mull over what to do about the press release, considering all the ways my life will change once I'm outed as the new woman in Jared's life. It won't be easy. No matter how the PR people spin it, I'm going to be painted as the villain. But that will happen now whether I'm with Jared or not. I've said I won't let anyone come between us again, and that includes me.

So, really, there isn't any decision to make.

I have to accept this comes with loving Jared. This is his world, and I just have to suck it up and get used to it.

It's going to be hell—at least it will be at first—but I'll get through it as long as I have Jared by my side. Some other scandal will happen to divert attention from us, and when his fans see our relationship is serious, I hope they'll come around to me.

It's like a weight has been lifted from my shoulders when I make the decision. It feels right. As does finally opening up to Jared about our baby and what happened after. We can't take our relationship to the next level until he knows.

It's going to devastate him, but he needs to know.

I try calling Jared a few times, but it goes straight to his voice mail. We didn't make any plans for later and I don't know if he'll be back from L.A. in time for dinner. I'm hoping he will so I can unburden myself. Now I have made the decision to go all in, I just want to get it over with. Then we can finally start healing and start making plans for the future.

I head to the kitchen to make meatballs, playing music on my cell and humming to myself as I sip a glass of wine and prepare our meal. I can keep the meatballs warm in the oven until Jared shows up and then put some spaghetti on.

A nervous smile curves the corners of my lips when the buzzer sounds a few minutes later, and I wonder why Jared is buzzing to be let in. He must have left his fob at home. But when I check the monitor, it's not my beau waiting at the gate.

It's Logan.

His car is parked at the curb behind him as he stands in front of my gate, looking confident and handsome in a fitted navy suit.

Shit.

I nibble on my lip as I contemplate pretending I'm not home. But he can see my car in the driveway, and it wouldn't be a very nice way to treat the man. He's been on my list to call. He's left a couple of messages asking me out, and I haven't returned either of them. I'm not sure if Jerry said anything to him about Jared. Either way, he deserves to know, and there's no better time than the present. I buzz him in and move to the front door to greet him.

"Logan, this is a surprise." I smile softly as he approaches.

"I hope you don't mind me dropping by unannounced, but I had a client meeting in the area, and I thought now might be a good time to talk."

"Sure." I stand back to let him in. "Come on in to the kitchen."

Chapter Thirty
Jared

I rub at the tight pain in my chest as I open Syd's front door, my rotten mood instantly perking up when delicious smells of garlic and tomato hit my nostrils. This is just what the doctor ordered after the afternoon from hell.

I slam to a halt in the doorway to the kitchen watching Sydney throw back her head and laugh at something the guy facing her says. "Who the fuck are you?" I blurt, venom spewing from my tone.

"J." Sydney spins around, gulping and tucking her hair behind her ears in a nervous tell. "I didn't hear you come in."

"Obviously."

"I'm Logan." The guy steps forward with his arm outstretched.

Call me petty, but I cross my arms over my chest, glare at him, and ignore his hand.

A muscle clenches in his jaw as he lowers his arm to one side, but he keeps a polite smile fixed to his lips. "Sydney and I have been dating."

Sydney cringes, and I can't keep the hurt from my face. She

mentioned nothing to me about any other guy. As far as I was concerned, she hasn't been with anyone since the pretentious prick in Italy. Guess I was wrong.

"Don't let me interrupt then," I snap, spinning around on my heel.

Fuck her and whatever game she's playing. I storm toward the door as she calls out after me.

"Jared, wait!"

I yank the door open and stride outside, my boots crunching on the gravel driveway.

"It's not what you're thinking, J, please wait." She catches up to me and tugs on my arm. "Jared, I know what that looked like, but—"

"Save it, Syd!" I bark. "I'm not in the mood to hear it after the day I've had. Just leave me alone." Wrenching out of her hold, I exit her property and return home.

She shows up thirty minutes later carrying a ceramic dish which she places on the island unit where I'm nursing my second glass of JD.

"Jared, I'm so sorry."

I stare at the amber liquid in my glass and ignore her.

"Logan works with Jerry. I had three dates with him before we met on the beach. I haven't seen him since though he has left me some messages. I was planning to call and tell him I'm with you now, but he just showed up at my door unannounced, and I figured I'd let him down in person."

I lift my head and pierce her with heavy eyes. It's been an exhausting couple of days, and I'm barely holding it together. "Did you fuck him?"

"No." She vigorously shakes her head. "It wasn't like that."

Exhaling slowly, I release some of the tension from my shoulders. "Why didn't you mention him?"

"It didn't occur to me. It wasn't ever going anywhere." Slowly, she comes up behind me on the stool and wraps her arms around my waist. "The truth is, from the moment you showed up on the beach you are the only man I've thought about."

I grip her hand and rest my head back against her shoulder. "I'm sorry for overreacting."

"No." She spins me around on the stool and cups my face. "This is on me, not you. I should have told you about him, and I should've texted to say he was at my place. I never want to cause you pain, Jared."

"It's clear we have some trust issues to work through." I haul her into my arms, badly needing a hug. Sydney always grounded me, and I need that now. Clinging to her, I inhale her scent and absorb the feel of her soft curves against me, instantly feeling some of the stress seeping from my body.

"Yeah, but we'll get there." She holds me tight as one hand inches up my back and into my hair.

Her touch feels so fucking good, and it's exactly what I need. I briefly close my eyes and memorize the moment.

"I'm all in, J." She tips my head back so we're eye to eye. "We have shit to work through, but I'm one hundred percent committed to you. I have wanted to be with you from the time I was a little girl, and that has *never* changed. It never will. You're it for me."

Tears prick my eyes, and it feels like I'm drowning in emotion. "I need you, babe." I hug her again. "I need you real bad."

"What's wrong?" she asks, easing back to look at my face. "You're trembling, J."

"I got arrested this afternoon."

"What?" Disbelief is etched all over her face. "Why?"

"Toria went to the cops claiming I hit her. Clearly someone

did as she has a black eye and some bruising on her face, but it wasn't me."

"That fucking spiteful, jealous, selfish shrew!" Poison pours from Sydney's eyes. "She's lucky she's pregnant because, otherwise, I'd be over there beating the shit out of her until she confessed to lying."

A smirk graces my lips, and it's a miracle I can smile at a time like this. "Is it wrong I wish I could see that? Or that seeing you all riled up kind of turns me on?" There's no kind of about it, but now isn't the time or place.

"I'm not lying. Someone needs to teach that despicable woman a lesson. How dare she fabricate claims when other women are subjected to domestic abuse and often not believed? It makes my blood boil. Not to mention if she set the assault up to frame you, she risked harm to her baby. That woman is legit insane, and she deserves to be locked up."

"She's dangerous," I agree, all hint of humor fading at the reminder of how careless she is with the new life growing inside her. "And this is only the start of it."

"When is she alleging this happened, and do you have an alibi?" she asks.

"Thursday night."

"We were together all night. I'll make a statement, and they'll have to dismiss it then."

"No." I shake my head. "I'm not dragging you into this. John has a few tech guys he works with already on the case. They'll retrieve footage from the video cameras outside the yoga studio where she alleges the assault happened, and he'll take camera stills from my house to prove I was at home and not in L.A. He'll make it go away. The guys are also going to give statements to confirm she threatened to do this a couple months ago."

"She can't be trusted with your baby, J." Concern trips over her face.

I sigh. "I know." I rest my head on her chest. "It's a fucking clusterfuck to end all clusterfucks, and it's all going to play out in public."

"We'll get through it, and we'll find a way to get you full custody. If we can prove she's lying, maybe you can charge her for making false claims and trying to damage your reputation. Perhaps we can use it to show her state of mind and how she poses a risk to your unborn child."

I love how she's naturally including herself in the equation. When she said she was all in, she meant it, and I'm relieved. The only reason part of me feels like this will be okay is because Sydney is in my corner. I honestly don't think I could do this alone. "The guys think she wants money," I admit, running my hand up and down Syd's spine. "I haven't ruled out offering to pay her off in exchange for full custody."

"She won't get away with this, J. I refuse to let her win whatever fucked-up game she's playing."

I tilt my head up. "I love you."

She leans down and kisses me sweetly. "I love you too."

It's late, but I'm starving, so Syd heats up the food she brought. I wolf down the scrumptious spaghetti and meatballs, and then we cuddle on the couch, half-heartedly watching TV as I attempt to de-stress. I need to get my shit together. Sydney seems antsy, and I sense she has something additional on her mind, but when I ask, she tells me it can wait, and I don't push it. I'm not sure I could handle more crap tonight.

We fall asleep on the couch, and I wake a couple hours later when an icy chill crawls over me from behind. Very carefully, I lift my sleeping beauty and carry her to my bed. We lie side by side, in our clothes, on top of the comforter, and I pull a thick blanket over us and promptly fall back to sleep.

"J." My shoulders shake as I'm roused from sleep. "J, wake up. Your phone is going nuts."

My eyes pop wide in alarm, and I reach for my cell as I curl my other arm around Syd, keeping her close. The clock on my phone reads six a.m., and this can't be good.

"It's about time," Amanda snaps when I pick up.

"What's happened?" I deadpan as resignation settles in my sleep-heavy bones.

"That little bitch leaked your arrest and her assault to the press." There is no love lost these days between Amanda and the woman she set me up with. I know she feels guilty for my predicament, which is ridiculous. It was still my decision, and I was the idiot who chose to fuck the crazy psycho and subsequently knocked her up. My situation is all on me.

"It's blowing up everywhere," she adds. "I need you to come in ASAP."

"Fuck."

Sydney's worried eyes latch on to mine.

"Is Sydney mentioned?"

"No. The new reports are all about your arrest for assaulting your poor sick pregnant fiancée and how you've been cavorting with other women. It does not paint you in a good light, Jared."

We didn't get to release my statement yesterday as efforts were immediately diverted in the wake of my arrest. It would've helped if I'd had the first word, but there's nothing I can do about it now except do damage control. "Call a press conference. I'll make a live statement, but I'll need to run everything by John first."

"Agreed. I'll set it in motion, and both of you meet me at TR HQ. I'll call Ryder and the guys too. A visible show of support will help."

"Okay. I'll see you in a couple of hours." I hang up and rub at my tired eyes.

"I heard," Syd softly says, propping up on an elbow. "What can I do?"

"Stay indoors and stay safe." I wrap my arms around her and hold her close. "Everything is going to come to the surface now, and it's not going to be pretty."

"I can make a statement, and this will all go away."

"No, babe." I peer deep into her eyes. "I want to keep you away from this for as long as I can. Let me get rid of this bogus claim first, and then we'll put out a press statement about us after we've proven my ex is a manipulative bitch and a complete liar. We'll garner sympathy then. If you are outed as my girl at this time, you'll be lynched, and I'm not having it. You are not going to be the one to pay the price."

"Okay. Whatever you think is best."

As much as I'd love to stay in bed all day with Sydney in my arms, cocooned from the harsh reality outside my window, I can't. It's time to deal with Vittoria Russo once and for all.

"Whatever you do, Jared, do not lose your cool out there," John says as we stand in a room to one side of the hotel ballroom where the press conference is due to shortly take place. I've spent most of the day locked in lengthy and often heated discussions with my lawyer, the label's legal team, my PR people, the label's PR people, Ryder and the other co-owners, and Wilder and Linc, thrashing out the best strategy. It's been decided I will fully confess the nature of my relationship with my ex and deny her assault allegations.

"Run through it again, Jared." Amanda casts a scrutinizing glance over my attire. She wanted me to wear a monkey suit, but fuck that. I won't pretend to be someone I'm not. I'll go out there in my black shirt, ripped jeans, and scuffed boots, looking like the rock star I am. They can take what I have to say or leave it.

"I'll be reading my statement, Mandy. I don't need to go over it."

"Humor me," she says, and I barely resist the urge to roll my eyes.

"I'm going to state how our relationship was one of mutual convenience and I only proposed when Toria told me she was pregnant because I thought it was the right thing to do for my unborn child. When it was obvious it wasn't going to work, I ended things, ensuring mother and baby are well taken care of with agreed provisions for the duration of the pregnancy and for the future. While I can't divulge the nature of our agreement, thanks to a rock-solid confidentiality clause, I can confirm I have no plans to abandon my baby or the mother of my child even if we are no longer in a relationship. I have to be careful not to cast aspersions on Toria's character and just stick to facts, which also include that I have never laid a hand on her and I was at home in San Francisco when the alleged assault took place. Something that will be proven beyond doubt in due course. I will categorically deny assaulting her now or at any other time. Okay?" I dart a glance at my publicist.

"Far from it, but stick to the script, and you'll be fine."

"Don't let the press heckling get to you," Ryder cautions. "They'll try to anger you so you blurt something you shouldn't. Just go out there. Read the statement. Show the appropriate emotion. Then thank them for coming and leave."

"We're going up there with you," Wilder says, approaching on my left.

"Thanks. I appreciate the support."

"We've got your back, man," Linc adds, slapping me on the

shoulder. "And anything else you need to take this crazy bitch down, it's yours."

"Put the TV on!" Amanda shrieks, startling everyone. She glances up from her cell phone with shock splayed across her face. "CNN. Now!" she barks at some poor nervous-looking intern as she runs toward the wall-mounted screen at the back of the room.

"What's going on?" I ask as I stride toward her.

"Did you know Sydney was going to do this?"

Panic rushes to my head. "Do what? Is she okay? What's happened?"

"Watch." Amanda drags me in front of the TV as the others crowd around and behind us. My jaw trails the ground when I spot my girlfriend on the screen, and I have a feeling I know what she did. A flurry of emotions swirls inside me, and I swallow hard over the lump in my throat.

The reporter clears her throat, glancing between the camera and the scene going down behind her in front of the police building in downtown L.A. "Breaking news in the sensational allegations made by model Vittoria Russo against Jared Dempsey. In an unexpected development, a woman has come forward providing an alibi for the Ruminate drummer. She's just about to make a statement, and we're bringing this to you live from LAPD HQ."

A hush descends on the press crowd assembled in front of Sydney as she steps up to a microphone. Two unfamiliar men in charcoal-gray suits stand to her left and two cops in uniform on her right.

My heart is pounding in my chest as Sydney clears her throat and begins. "Good evening, my name is Sydney Shaw, and I am a longtime friend of Jared Dempsey. Jared and I have known one another since we were born as our families were close growing up. We recently reconnected after several years of no contact. I met Jared and Vittoria Russo in Florence at the time of the MTV awards. Back then, Vittoria and Jared were engaged, and I was in a relationship with another man."

That's not technically true. Syd had explained how she'd broken up with the pretentious prick prior to their subsequent one-night stand. I doubt the guy would come forward to dispute it. He was bang in love with my girl, and it'd only be splitting hairs anyway.

"I moved to San Fran a couple of months later," she continues. "It was a big surprise to discover Jared had bought a property close to mine and to find out he was no longer engaged to Vittoria or in a relationship with her. We resumed our friendship, and it recently became more. At no time did Jared ever cheat on Vittoria. In fact, he has gone above and beyond to provide for her and his unborn baby. He will be fully involved in his child's life, and he has already signed a co-parenting agreement with his ex."

She looks up from the page in her hand, staring directly into the camera. Her face shines with determination and confidence, and I've never been prouder. She's so fucking beautiful, and my heart swells with the knowledge she is finally all mine. We've been given a second chance, and I don't intend to waste it. I'm going to devote the rest of my life to worshipping this amazing, brave, selfless woman and ensuring everyone knows it.

"I know the kind of man Jared is," she says. "He is caring and compassionate, and he protects his loved ones with his whole heart. He would *never* assault any woman, and he did not assault Vittoria Russo because, at the time of the alleged attack on her, he was with me at my home. I have provided the police with video evidence from my property as well as a sworn statement confirming he was with me for the duration of the time the assault is alleged to have occurred. I don't know Vittoria at all, so I can't claim to understand her motives, but I can tell you with one hundred percent certainty that Jared Dempsey was not the man who assaulted her. Thank you. I have nothing more to add."

The gray-haired man at her side nods, and then he takes her elbow and escorts her away from the building as the press bombards Sydney with questions. The cameras trail her all the way to a blacked-out Land Rover, and I only relax when she's safely inside the car and it's peeling away from police HQ.

"I'm fucking marrying her if you don't," Linc says.

"Get in line," Wilder adds, smirking.

They're such assholes. "If it was up to me, I'd have a ring on her finger right now, and I'd be marching her up the aisle as soon as I could get a license."

"You're going to turn me gray," Amanda exclaims, turning around as the TV is turned off. She jabs her finger in my direction. "Do not go and marry that girl until this circus has died down. I have enough fires to put out already."

"Sydney just did you a huge favor," Ryder says, coming up to us. "But I hope to fuck the fans appreciate the gesture for what it is."

"I want to make some additions to my press release," I say. "Get me it and a pen."

Chapter Thirty-One
Sydney

"I guess it's official now, huh?" I say, snuggling into Jared's side on the couch. He held a press conference shortly after my statement was aired and confirmed he was in love with me in front of a packed crowd. Can't lie. It made my heart beat like crazy and my pussy ache with longing.

"Yep." He nuzzles his face into my neck as his arms tighten around me. "The whole world knows you're my girlfriend now."

"Cay says everyone is going crazy and opinion is pretty evenly divided." For my mental health, I am going nowhere near social media.

"You won a lot of support standing up for me." Jared's hands sweep up and down my side, his fingers brushing against the edge of my breast in a way that makes it difficult to concentrate. "Our fans love you protected me from Toria's lies. And several high-profile women's charities have denounced her for making false allegations. The people who are sticking up for her, despite no charges being brought and the case being dismissed, are not true fans. They can't be if they are claiming we're the ones lying."

"Some people are nuts," I rasp, clenching my thighs together as he peppers kisses along the column of my neck, and delicious tremors coast all over my body. "It's obvious she lied in a very malicious way. How can anyone believe a word that comes out of her mouth now?"

That lying cunt made a statement a few hours after Jared's press conference saying she is under enormous stress, her hormones are all over the place, and she's heartbroken to have been cheated on and abandoned by the love of her life. She says the trauma made her delusional and that's how she was convinced it was Jared who assaulted her outside the yoga studio. Now she's claiming it's a Jared lookalike. If Dr. Phil was still airing, I'm sure she'd be making an appearance on the show. They'd lap that crazy shit up big time.

"There will always be people who overlook shit staring them in the face. Those are the people focusing on how I abandoned my pregnant fiancée for another woman even though that's not how it went down."

"Is it enough to go after her legally for full custody?"

Jared sighs against my ear, and his hands stall on my body. "I don't know. That will be my next battle."

I scramble off his lap and stand. "Take your shirt off and lie down."

He waggles his brows and licks his lips. "I like where this is going."

"I'm going to massage you. It's been a stressful few days, and I want to help loosen some of that tension in your muscles." I wiggle my fingers and smile. "You're not the only one with magical hands."

He climbs to his feet and reels me into his arms. "Thank

you for what you did. It feels so good to have your support. To know I'm not alone in this."

"It felt good to do it. You're *mine*, J. I protect what's mine in the same way you do." I was seething after his conniving ex went to the press. I still don't understand why she didn't rat me out. Maybe she was planning to blackmail Jared by threatening to reveal my identity. Or she was timing it to make a few bombshell announcements one after the other. Either way, I wanted to steal some of her thunder.

I took back some control, and it feels good.

It's all out in the open now, and I got Jared off the hook.

Even the ton of reporters camped outside both our houses hasn't dampened the euphoric feeling swirling through my veins.

"I won't ever tire of hearing that." He playfully pinches my ass.

"Good, 'cause you can't get rid of me now, rock star." Snaking my arms around his neck, I lean in and kiss his full lips. I love that I have free rein to kiss and touch him now. We still need to have that other conversation. I'm dreading it. But I can't keep putting it off.

Which reminds me.

I break our lip-lock, laughing when he pouts. "I did something else I need to tell you. If you don't like it, I'll tell Sawyer and Xavier to drop it."

"I have a feeling the massage is meant to make me more pliable."

I laugh again as he starts unbuttoning his shirt. "If that was the case, I would have waited until after. There is no ulterior motive. I just want to help you destress."

"Okay. Lay it on me."

I have a hard time keeping my eyes on his face as he continues unbuttoning his shirt, slowly baring his delectable chest and abs. Damn. I want to lick every part of his body and then go back for seconds and thirds.

"Syd." Jared smirks, knowing exactly where my mind has gone.

I blink to clear my head. "I called Sawyer yesterday and asked him to dig into my dad. To find dirt I could use to get him off my back. I called him back today and said there was a new priority. I asked him to investigate Vittoria to see if he can find anything we can use to our advantage."

He goes preternaturally still, and I worry I've just fucked up. "I'm sorry," I blurt. "I should have asked you first. I—"

He silences me with a passionate kiss that curls my toes. His bare chest brushes against my clothed one, sending lusty tremors cascading over my body. His large palm possessively holds the back of my head while his other hand rests on my lower back as he controls our kiss, and I'm here for it.

I'm panting like I just ran a marathon when we finally surface for air. "Not that I'm complaining, but what was that for?"

"I love the way you love me. Having you go to bat for me is everything, Syd." He stares adoringly at me. "You're everything."

"You're not mad?"

"Not even a bit. It's a smart move. One I should have done before now. I just wanted to give her the benefit of the doubt."

"That's because you're a good person. But we've got to up our game, and if we have to be stealthy to beat her, then that's what we must do."

Jared pounces on me, and I squeal as he tosses me on the couch and crawls over me. His shirt is quickly discarded, and he leans down in all his bare-chested glory. I'm enraptured, and my body moves of its own accord, my legs wrapping around his waist as I yank him down to me. His lips descend in a hard claiming kiss, and we're devouring one another as my hands roam up and down the velvety-smooth skin of his back.

I whimper into his mouth when his fingers find their way under my silk blouse and begin exploring. Every touch is like flames searing across my skin, and I'm writhing and moaning like someone who hasn't had sex in years. Deft fingers unbutton my blouse as we continue kissing. My jean-clad legs naturally part, and I almost come undone when Jared presses his pelvis against mine, the feel of his erection straining against his zipper and pushing into my core nearly enough to send me shooting to the stars.

When his mouth finds my nipple over my lace bra, I close my eyes and arch my back, stuffing him full of my breast. Liquid lust floods my panties when he pulls my bra down and his hot mouth suctions on my hardened tip. "J," I moan.

"Baby, I'm so hot for you." He thrusts his hard-on against me. "Feel what you do to me."

Baby.

The word registers in my lust-addled mind, and though I don't want to, I know I need to stop this before it goes any further. I'm internally crying as I gently shove his shoulders. "Stop. We need to stop."

Lifting his head, he frowns as he studies my face. "What's wrong?"

Tears stab my eyes as I contemplate all I have to tell him. "We need to talk," I whisper as I cling to his shoulders. "There is something from the past I haven't told you. Something you need to know before we take this to the next level."

His eyes probe mine for a few beats before he nods. He fixes my bra into place and lifts up off me. I sit up straighter, refastening the buttons on my blouse as Jared bends down to retrieve his shirt.

"I have a feeling I might need alcohol for this conversation.

Want anything?" he asks, sliding his arms through the sleeves of his shirt.

"Water, please." There is no way I could stomach alcohol right now. I'm already praying the takeout we consumed an hour ago doesn't come back to haunt me. I bite down on my lip as I kick my sneakers off and nestle into the corner of Jared's couch with my knees tucked up to my chest.

"You're scaring me, Syd," he says when he reenters the living room and sees me curled into myself.

"There's no easy way to say what I have to say. No way to protect you from pain," I admit, accepting the bottle of water as he hands it to me.

He sits down beside me and takes a swig from his beer. "I sensed you were holding something back."

I maintain eye contact as I nod, willing my frantic heart to calm down. I wipe a sweaty palm down the leg of my jeans. "I didn't want to keep this from you, but when you were with Vittoria, I thought the right thing to do was to say nothing. It was in the past. I believed you were happy and it might put a dampener on things." I chew anxiously on the inside of my cheek before I take a mouthful of water.

"I'm imagining all kinds of things," he admits, reaching out to hold on to my leg. "Just tell me."

Tears cloud my vision, and pain spears me through the chest. An errant sob rips from my throat.

"Syd." Jared fixes me with tormented eyes. He puts my water and his beer down and pulls me into his lap. "Whatever it is, I won't judge."

I'm trembling all over as I slide off his lap and sit beside him. I can't sit in his lap and tell him these things. It's going to kill him. I bury my face in my hands as I try to compose myself enough to blurt the words out.

His arm glides around my shoulders, and he presses a tender kiss to my temple. "I love you."

"I know, and I love you too." I peer at him with tears in my eyes. "This is so hard. I tried to tell you. Back then, I was calling and messaging and emailing. I needed you." Another sob wrenches free. "I was so scared and so alone."

His eyes widen as alarm skates over his handsome features.

"I was pregnant," I whisper, watching all manner of emotions overtake him. "I was pregnant with your baby."

Chapter Thirty-Two
Sydney

Shock splays across Jared's face as he stares at me. I can only imagine the kind of thoughts spinning through his head. "I found out months after you were gone," I continue while he tries to process the revelation. "I hadn't been eating, and I was feeling sick all the time, but I just thought it was heartbreak."

"Pregnant?" he chokes out, holding me tighter. His eyes lower automatically to my flat stomach. "You were carrying my baby?"

I nod as silent tears stream down my face.

He pulls me into a hug, holding me as I sob into his chest. He's shaking all over. "What happened?" he asks in a low tone. "What happened to our baby?"

The dam breaks, and I fall apart. I have talked this all through in therapy. It took me years to handle my emotions, yet I'm still a mess as I relive it all. "Herman forced me into an abortion," I choke out over my tears.

"He what?" Jared's icy tone chills the air.

Rubbing the tears from my eyes, I try to pull myself

together to tell him the rest. I latch on to my anger, and it's easier to stop the tears. "He confronted me a few days after I took some pregnancy tests. Said he found one in the trash. I accepted that back then, but now I know it was because he intercepted my messages to you. He told me he was taking me to see this ob-gyn contact of his to get checked out." My lower lip wobbles as I struggle to hold on to my rage. "The doctor knocked me out, and when I woke up, he told me the abortion had been a success and I could go on with my life now without the burden of having a kid at sixteen." My hands ball into fists. "He acted like he was doing me a favor."

Red-hot rage washes through me like every time I think of Dr. Mulligan.

"I'm going to kill him. Both of them." Jared hugs me fiercely as he spews fire from his eyes.

"Herman tried to look shocked when I came out crying and hitting him. As if it was news to him. Then he told me it was for the best and took me home where he attempted to buy back my affection with new clothes and paint supplies. He tried to coax me to go on vacation, and he even offered to let me go back to Ms. Elliott's classes, but nothing worked. I was empty inside." I stare off into space as I remember how desolate I felt at that time. "I was in so much pain. I already loved our baby. I wanted it even if I thought you didn't want me."

"I would have wanted it too." He smooths a hand up and down my spine, and I lean into him in a way I wish I could have done back then. "Just like I've always wanted you. Oh my god, Syd. I can't believe this." He cradles my face in his hands, and I'm not surprised to see such potent emotion staring back at me through glassy eyes. "I hate you had to go through that alone. I want to burn the fucking world down for what you endured, but I'll start with that doctor and your father. They're not getting away with this. How dare they do that to you! To us."

He presses a fierce kiss to my brow. "Jesus, Syd. It's no wonder you've struggled with Toria and the baby. I'm so sorry." He dusts kisses into my hair. "I'm so fucking sorry."

"Knowing she was carrying your baby was hard enough, but seeing how little she cares infuriates me. I never thought I'd hate anyone the way I hate Herman and Dr. Mulligan, but Vittoria is right up there. How can she ignore something so precious? I would literally give anything to have your baby growing in my belly. I wanted him or her so badly." Tears roll down my face again, and Jared is crying now too.

I don't know how long we stay locked in an embrace, but it seems like ages before we dry our tears and break apart. "Are you mad I didn't tell you sooner?" I ask, looking up at him.

He shakes his head, looking so sad it makes my heart ache. "No, babe. I'm not mad at you."

Looking down at my lap, I nibble on my lip, trying to pluck up the courage to tell him the rest. "There's more," I whisper, and he turns rigidly still. When I lift my head to stare at him, I can tell pain is transparent on my face. It's flaying me on the inside, filleting me from all angles and impossible to hide.

Jared's face bleaches of color as he patiently waits for me to spit it out, already understanding this is going to be bad.

"Dr. Mulligan violated me." I clutch my throat and dig my nails into my flesh. "I had to return for a few checkups. He said it was to ensure I developed okay because I'd had an abortion so young." I bark out a bitter laugh. "I couldn't understand why I was always drowsy and confused when I returned from those appointments or why I couldn't remember anything." I briefly close my eyes as the images flare in my mind. "At my third checkup, I woke up in his office to find two strange men standing over my naked body groping me. I was on the bed with my legs in stirrups, and one man had his fingers inside me while the other man was fondling my breasts." I wrap my arms around myself to ward off the tremors overtaking my body. "Dr. Mulligan was filming it with a camera on a tripod."

Jared's Adam's apple bobs in his throat, and he's digging his nails into his palms so hard beads of blood bubble to the surface.

"My head was fuzzy, and my limbs wouldn't cooperate properly, but I knew what was happening. They hadn't strapped me down, and I went crazy. I grabbed the speculum on the table beside me and stabbed it in one of the men's cheeks, then I overturned the table, and I was screaming and making as much noise as I could. His secretary burst into the room, and I could tell she was shocked. The two men fled through a side door, and I heard her threatening the doctor. My adrenaline rush disappeared then, and the next thing I remember is Dad carrying me out of there."

"Please tell me he murdered those sick bastards."

Another harsh laugh bursts from my mouth. "He didn't believe me."

Jared's head whips around. "What?" he says through gritted teeth.

"I told him what happened, and he told me I must have imagined it because I was drowsy. He brushed it off completely. Said I should just put it out of my mind because it hadn't happened. I told him the secretary would corroborate my story, but he said she had moved overseas."

Jared stands and grabs fistfuls of his hair. "I swear to God, Sydney, if your father set that up, he's a fucking dead man. I don't care if I do time for it. Herman Shaw is going to pay for this." He falls to his knees in front of me, crying. "I hate I wasn't there for you. If I'd been there, none of that would have happened."

"Don't do that. Don't blame yourself. The only ones to blame are my father, the doctor, and those despicable men." A shudder works its way through me, and I hug my body tighter. "I wanted to die, J. I had no idea what those men had done to me or what videos existed or how many other sick pricks had watched me being violated while I was unconscious. I don't know whether I was raped or not. I don't know what happened. I go through phases where I consider it lucky I don't know, and then other times, I think it would be better if I did. Maybe it wasn't as bad as I've imagined. I turned to drugs and drink because I couldn't live with myself. I had lost you, had our baby stolen from me, and I'd been sexually abused, and my father wouldn't believe me. I didn't want to live. I pushed myself to extremes, and the more it angered and worried Herman, the further I pushed it. I did shit to embarrass him on purpose, like shoplifting. I lashed out physically. I got in fights with girls at school. I punched my brothers when they tried to intervene."

I slide to the ground beside him. "I slept around, and I felt nothing. I was numb when guys were inside me. It took me a long time to find any enjoyment in sex."

"That's how you ended up with Vil."

I nod. "That wasn't an isolated incident. I regularly woke in strange houses, in strange beds, with strange men. After I almost died that time in college, Herman took matters in hand. He had a full team of bodyguards shadowing my every move. He took all my bank cards off me and only gave me the bare minimum. Everything else was purchased for me by his secretary. He arranged it so I finished my degree online, isolating me from the campus and my friends. After that, I had a succession of shitty jobs I kept getting fired from because I didn't give a fuck about anything. I was clean then but still so empty inside. Forcing me to marry Sawyer was the last straw, but I had no choice. It turned out to be a good thing though. Sawyer helped set me free."

I wipe the tears from his cheeks. "I've only felt like I'm

truly living these past few years. Before that, I was in hell. Even though I was happier, a hollow part inside me still remained because I'd lost you and our baby. I think I'll always have that empty part inside my heart, but it's better now I have you back."

"Jesus, Syd." He presses his brow to mine. "I had no idea. While I was out there living my dream, you were trapped in a nightmare."

"I don't blame you for any of it anymore, J. I hated you for a long time, but now I know the truth. I blamed me for a lot of it too. I had choices to make, and I made the wrong ones. I could have chosen a different path, and maybe Herman wouldn't have been so controlling if I hadn't gone off the rails." I shrug, feeling lighter even as I feel weighed down with emotional trauma. "But I can't turn back the clock. Years of therapy have helped me to deal with my emotions and own my mistakes. I won't ever forget our baby or the things done to me, but I can't dwell on them any longer. It was eating me alive. I try to focus on the present and take it one day at a time."

I run my fingers through his hair, smiling softly. "I'm yours, and you're mine, and that's all that matters to me now. I want the past to stay in the past because it's the only way we'll have that future we always talked about. I know you're in shock. It's been a lot to take in. I know you want to hurt Herman. To make him pay. I did too, for a long time, but it won't help. It can't undo the things done to me. I chose to let it go and focus on healing instead. My father will die a lonely old man in his bed, and that bastard doctor got what was coming to him."

Jared's eyes pop wide in silent question.

"He died in a fire years ago. It made the headlines, and I remember partying that night and celebrating his death." I rest my arms around his neck. "Karma definitely worked in his case."

"Herman has a lot to answer for," he says through gritted teeth as he hauls me into his lap.

I go willingly this time. "He does, but we need to leave it in the past; otherwise, we won't ever let go." I brush my lips against his. "I want to move forward with you, not back, Jared. Nothing good would come from confronting my father. The bastard will rot in hell for his sins, and I'll be celebrating the night he dies too."

Chapter Thirty-Three
Sydney

I blink my eyes open as daylight slips through the cracks in the blinds in Jared's bedroom. We were both too upset last night to part, so I didn't raise any protest when he took my hand and led me upstairs. Nothing happened. He didn't even get the massage I'd offered. Instead, we fell asleep under the covers wrapped up in one another, and we've barely stirred all night.

Jared is still out cold, and I rake my gaze over him slowly, noting the bruising shadows under his eyes and how it looks like he's frowning even while sleeping. He's been under so much stress lately, and he's carrying too much on his shoulders. I know he's going to take what I told him to heart. To blame himself for failing me. I wish I could help to alleviate it, but he's got to work through it himself. I've had years to come to terms with the forced abortion and the subsequent sexual assault, and I still have bad days, so I know it's not easy.

Jared is a protector, and he's going to be hard on himself. It doesn't help he's expecting a baby with a woman he can't stand.

I'm sure it's all playing on his mind and he's wondering why our baby was taken when he's having a baby with someone who doesn't seem to want the child except for how she can use her son to manipulate Jared into doing her bidding.

I wish Vittoria Russo was wiped from the planet.

She's a scourge, and if she thinks I'm going to sit back and let her threaten my boyfriend again, she has another think coming.

Whatever Jared needs from me, he has it.

If he requires me to strap on armor and head into battle on his behalf, I'm already there.

In a weird way, it's given me a new purpose. Everything I thought my life would be when I first moved to San Fran is already changing but in a good way.

My eyes move to the framed photo beside his bed, and I find myself melting like the first time I noticed it. It's a picture of us as a young couple, taken the night of a sweet-sixteen party. We have our arms wrapped around one another, and our faces are glowing with first love as we stare into each other's eyes.

God, we were so young.

So clueless and naïve.

We had no idea what was lying in store for us.

I love he still has the photo and it's the first thing he sees when he wakes.

It speaks volumes, and I just love him even more.

Redirecting my attention to the sleeping man beside me, I smile as I drink him in. He might be tired and stressed, but he's still so fucking gorgeous. The scruff on his face is thicker than usual, and his hair is all mussed up. My fingers twitch with a craving to touch him, but I don't want to disturb his precious sleep. He looks beautiful, and I feel the urge to pinch myself because I can't believe he's finally mine.

Sliding my hand under my head, I stare at him like a bona fide creeper, marveling at the ink on his chest and his arms and salivating over his nipple piercings. My mind wanders, and I visualize licking and sucking his nipples and tugging on the titanium barbells with my teeth as he hisses with the sting. Invisible hands roam lower, examining every dip and curve of his toned abs, before tangling in the line of dark hair leading—

"I want to know what dirty thoughts are going through your head," Jared says in a sleep-drenched tone, interrupting my sexy daydream.

I lift my head from his lower torso to this face, licking my lips and squeezing my thighs together. I only have my panties on under the clean shirt he gave me to sleep in last night, and it doesn't do much to hide my desire. My hard nipples poke through the thin material, instantly drawing his attention.

Jared's nostrils flare, and his eyes darken as they linger on my chest. In a fast move, his arm darts out, hugging my waist and pulling me in close. "Answer me, baby." His voice is thick with lust as he rubs his thumb across my lower lip. "What were you just thinking?"

I see no need to lie. "I was imagining sucking your nipples and tugging on your piercings with my teeth."

Jared yanks me flush with his hot semi-naked body, and I squeal. "Say the word, and I'll turn that fantasy to reality." He nips at my earlobe, and liquid lust gushes between my legs.

"I've never been with a guy who had nipple piercings." I plaster myself to his front and stare dreamily into his eyes.

"They're not my only piercings." His eyes flash with smug pride.

I wet my dry lips and thrust against the hardness between his legs. "Do you mean?" I drag my lip between my teeth as my vagina throws a party.

"Take a look for yourself." Lying flat on his back, he keeps one arm curved around me as he presents his glorious form for examination. "My body is yours to do with as you please." He smirks again as he pulls the covers back, revealing the full extent of his male gorgeousness. I love the playful glint in his stunning blue eyes, but I love the massive bulge in his boxers even more.

My eyes are out on stilts as I stare at his manhood. "It looks much bigger than I remember."

Jared barks out a laugh. "Baby, I was only a kid then." He cups his junk. "I'm all man now, and I can't wait to prove it."

My tongue darts out, wetting my lip again as I tuck hair behind one ear. "Are we really doing this now?"

His expression turns somber. "You set the pace, Syd. You know that." He secures my hair behind my other ear and gazes adoringly into my face. "I want to make love to you. I want to feel as close to you as humanly possible. After last night, I need it even more."

I slowly nod, understanding it fully. "I love you, babe." I brush my lips fleetingly over his. "But I need the bathroom first." I hop up out of bed. "I'll be right back." I toss him a flirty grin over my shoulder as I saunter to his massive en suite bathroom, feeling his eyes glued to my barely covered ass the entire way.

I pee, splash water on my face, and give myself a little pep talk in the his and hers bathroom. I want this. I want Jared moving inside me again, but I'm also a little nervous, which I guess is to be expected.

What if it's not good?

What if we're not compatible sexually?

What if we've built the attraction up in our heads and it's not all that?

"Stop overthinking it." Jared comes up behind me, staring at me through the mirror.

"I'm nervous."

He sweeps my hair over my shoulder and lightly brushes his fingers against my neck, eliciting a rake of fiery shivers all over my body. "I'm nervous too, but I'm going to take care of you." He plants a slew of drugging kisses on my neck while grinding his hard-on against my ass. "I'm going to erase every man who's come before, and the only name ever leaving these lips in the throes of ecstasy will be mine." One hand cups my pussy, and his eyes flare with heat as I watch him through the mirror. "This is mine." His fingers crawl under my shirt and up to my boobs, cupping one heavy breast. "These are mine." His lips curve in a smile. "It seems my dick isn't the only body part that got bigger."

"Thank fuck. My tits were practically nonexistent when I was fifteen," I say over a moan as he tweaks my nipple.

"You've always been perfect to me, Syd." His hand moves to the center of my chest, in between my breasts, and he holds his palm there. "This has gotten bigger too." Our eyes meet in the mirror, and emotion is evident in his gaze. "You've always had a huge heart, Syd, but it's grown even bigger. The way you love me blows my mind. Your inner strength and your survival instinct is strong. I know you don't believe that, but the things you went through shaped you into the woman you are today. I'm in awe of that woman, and I plan to spend every day for the rest of my life showing you."

"Is that a promise?"

"Absolutely." He spins me around in his arms. "I know the timing isn't right, but I'll be putting a ring on your finger soon. I've waited a long time for our happy ever after, and I'm fucked if I'm going to waste more time. Tell me you're on the same page?"

So much for me setting the pace, but I'm not going to disagree. Marrying Jared and starting a family with him has been my dream for as long as I can remember. "I want that with you too."

"Thank fuck." He moves to kiss me, but I shove him away.

"I need to brush my teeth."

He yanks me back to him, muttering, "I don't give a fuck," before he slams his lips down on mine. I'm putty in his hands as he pushes me back against the counter while he devours me. I whimper into his mouth as he rotates his hips and thrusts his long thick shaft against me through my panties. I'm not going to last much longer because the need to feel him moving inside me is all I can think about.

Jared abruptly pulls back, grinning savagely at me. "Brush your teeth, babe, if you want, but if your sexy ass is not in my bed in two minutes, I'm throwing you over my knee and spanking the shit out of you."

"You say that like it's a threat." I smirk as I line toothpaste up on his toothbrush.

"She likes spanking. Duly noted." Jared flashes me a wicked look as he shoves his boxers to the floor and takes his cock in his hand.

My jaw trails the floor as I rake my gaze over his very impressive erection, fixating on the horizontal silver barbell piercing the tip of his cock. "Holy fuck. That thing will never fit."

He lazily strokes his throbbing flesh while fighting a grin. "It'll fit." He reaches around and turns the faucet on. "Tick-tock, babe. You're nearly out of time." We take turns brushing our teeth, and I race out of the bathroom to get in the bed while J takes a piss.

I'm naked under the covers when he reenters the bedroom, swaggering toward me with a predatory look in his eyes. I can't drag my eyes away from him. He's fucking magnificent, and I'm ready to be ruined. His body is a work of art. An ode to immense dedication in the gym and a career as a drummer. From his broad shoulders to his firm chest, ripped abs, toned biceps and arms, his muscular thighs, and his magnificent cock, he is all man.

And all mine.

"This won't last long if you continue looking at me like that," he says when he reaches the bed.

"I don't care. I have nothing planned today except staying in this bed and fucking until we both collapse from exhaustion."

He sits on the edge of the bed and leans down to plant a tender kiss on my lips. "Sounds like a perfect Sunday." He sweeps his fingers across my face. "Are you okay with this? It's what you want?"

"Yes." I sit up, letting the covers slide down my body to pool at my waist. His eyes flare with wanton need as they lock on my bare breasts for the first time.

"Fucking hell, Syd." He grabs both breasts in his hands. "These are fucking perfect." He kneads my sensitive flesh, and the ache in my core intensifies. "Let me see the rest of you," he commands, his eyes seeking permission as his fingers curl around the top of the comforter.

I nod, watching his reaction as he peels the covers back fully, exposing my naked body. There's no hiding now. His gaze is laser focused as his eyes roam steadily over every inch of my skin, and I'm so turned on I could probably come with a couple of quick rubs on my clit.

"Part your legs, and show me my pussy."

His gaze is trained on the apex of my thighs as I slowly open my legs, fighting a bout of uncharacteristic nervousness. Sex is a means of release for me mostly. I enjoy it and don't ever put too much thought into it.

But this is different.

This is Jared.

He's my one true love, and I want it to be different.

Special.

There is more resting on this than any other sexual encounter, and what he thinks matters.

He crawls up the end of the bed, his nostrils flaring as he eyeballs my pussy like a lion lining up its next meal. "You're exquisite, Sydney," he says, helping to settle my anxiety. "My every desire come to life." He lies flat on the bed in between my thighs and parts my folds with his thumbs.

"What are you doing?" I ask over a nervous laugh.

"Gazing on perfection," he purrs before shooting me a devilish grin. "I'm also committing this to memory for the spank bank." He presses a kiss to the top of my inner thigh, and my legs quiver. "We don't have the luxury of taking sexy pics like most people. I won't ever trust that someone couldn't get their hands on them. As much as I'd love to film us fucking and take pics of every inch of your body, I would never risk it." He moves up over me, softly brushing his fingers against my lips. "After what was done to you, I would never ask it of you."

"I trust you." I palm his cheek. "I have never let anyone take pics or videos of me, but I'd trust you to do it." It's the truth. I know Jared said we have to learn to trust one another, and we do, in a way. But in another way, that trust is already ingrained in me from years of loving the boy who is now this man. It's more a case of remembering how to trust one another. It doesn't need to be earned because Jared has done nothing to lose that trust.

"I love you so very much, Sydney. I wish I had the words to properly convey how my heart feels when I'm with you. When I look at you." He leans down and kisses me. "When I kiss you." His hands sweep lower over my body. "When I touch you."

"We don't need words, J. I see it in your eyes every time I look at you." I drop a kiss on his lips.

"Then let me show you with my body."

Chapter Thirty-Four
Jared

"Do I need a condom?" I ask as I settle in between her legs. We've spent ages tangled in the sheets, exploring one another with our mouths, tongues, and fingers, and her fantasy became a reality when she toyed with my nipple piercings and played with my ampallang piercing. I could have gone for the Prince Albert, like Linc, but the ampallang enhances sex by stimulating nerve endings in the vagina, clit, and anus, ensuring it's a better sexual experience for my partner.

I like pleasuring my woman, and Sydney won't ever leave my bed unless she's fully satisfied and struggling to walk with the insistent throbbing between her legs.

My thoughts smolder as I stare at the sexy woman writhing underneath me on my bed. The time for foreplay is over. If I don't get inside her stat, I'm going to explode.

She shakes her head. "I'm clean, and I have an IUD."

Not for long if I have anything to say about it.

"I'm clean too." I lower my body against hers as I kiss her.

I can't stop kissing her.

I can't get enough of her.

I meant what I said earlier. I need this to quell the raging storm brewing inside me after last night's revelations and the gut-wrenching pain that flays me on the inside every time I think of Sydney pregnant with my baby and it being ripped from her body by monsters. I force thoughts of those men aside because they have no place in this moment.

"The only woman I have ever gone bareback with is you." I want her to understand she has always been on a different level for me.

"I've never gone bareback with anyone but you."

The beast inside me loves that. "I'm giving you that orgasm now, and then I'm making love to my woman." I've been edging her a little, wanting her first orgasm to be earth-shattering. I situate myself between her legs and dive in, lavishing her with my tongue and my fingers.

"Oh fuck, J, that feels so good." Sydney whimpers as I curl three fingers in her pussy and hit that magical spot.

"Ride my fingers and my face, baby," I say as I suck and lick her swollen clit.

Her thighs grip my head as her legs dangle over my shoulders while I eat her out. Her pussy is like manna from the heavens, and I'm addicted to the taste and the smell of her. She's perfect in every fucking way. I thrust my fingers in and out of her at a more urgent pace when I feel her pussy clamping around them.

"Don't stop, J," she pants, fearful I'm going to pull back and deny her again.

But I'm done denying both of us.

I drive my fingers in and out in a punishing rhythm, working her clit until I feel she's close, and then I graze my teeth over her swollen bud, and she virtually skyrockets off the bed, screaming my name repeatedly. It's music to my ears, and

I'm dry humping the bed as I milk every last drop of her climax, more turned on than I've ever been.

"Ready to have your world rocked?" I say as I straighten and line my cock up at her entrance. It's cheesy as fuck, but I don't give a shit.

"Always." Syd wears her heart in her eyes as I push into her, keeping my gaze glued to hers as we finally become one again.

It takes effort to ease inside her slowly, but I want our first time to be slow and sensual. Then I'm going to spend the rest of the day fucking her brains out.

"Jesus, fuck." Sydney pants, her eyes widening a little in alarm as she watches my thick cock disappear inside her warmth.

"You feel incredible," I murmur, my heart swelling behind my chest as I seat myself inside her and stop. I'm feeling so much. I'm overwhelmed with love for this golden goddess staring at me like I put the stars in the sky. "Love you," I say before kissing her passionately.

"I love you too." Her fingers wrap around the back of my head, and she tugs on my hair. "Now make love to me."

"Happily." I slide in and out in slow languid strokes while I kiss her lips, her jawline, her neck, suctioning on that sensitive spot just below her ears, almost coming undone with the moans emerging from her mouth. Sydney's hands roam up and down my back, and she grabs handfuls of my ass, silently pleading for me to go harder, faster.

But I want to enjoy this.

Savor it.

Memorize it.

So I continue kissing her, lavishing attention on her body, her tits, her nipples, before I take pity on her and pick up my pace, rutting into her deeply as my fingers move to her clit.

"Don't come until I tell you," I warn before leaning down to steal another kiss.

She shoots daggers at me, and I chuckle. Sydney has a fiery temper when aggravated, but ultimately, I know she wants to submit to me in bed. She wants me to take control of her pleasure and I'll happily oblige.

I flip her over and pound into her from behind as I grope her tits and explore her body. She presses her ass back against me and I'm bedded so deep it feels like I'm almost touching her womb. Angling my hips, I drive inside her in a way I know my piercing will heighten her arousal.

"Oh, fuck, fuck, fuck, Jared, that feels so fucking good."

Sydney curses a lot which shocks most people because she's an elegant woman and she carries herself with grace. She looks like an angel who sometimes has the mouth of a devil. It's a consequence of growing up in a house full of men and one of the things I adore about her. I love that she curses like a sailor and carries no shame for it.

"J." She looks over her shoulder at me.

"Yeah." I arch a brow, slowing down, concerned I'm hurting her or she's having second thoughts.

She pins me with a naughty grin. "I fucking love your dick, and I'm warning you now I'll need a daily fix. At a minimum."

I cover her back and bend down to kiss her. "It's not like you have a choice," I tease. "Now I've felt heaven on my cock, there is no turning back. I'm going to be worse than an animal in heat. I'm going to fuck you raw as often as I can."

Her eyes flash with heat, her lips curve into a smile, and her pussy clenches around me, almost squeezing my dick to death. "You won't get any complaints from me." Her features soften a little. "You were made for me, Jared. We fit perfectly together in every way."

"I know," I say, thrusting my hips and driving in deeper. "Now hold on because the ride's about to go faster."

———

"I think you broke me," Syd moans, turning over in the bed to face me.

I chuckle. "Sex is pointless unless you ache all over and struggle to walk after it."

"Jesus Christ," she pants, pushing knotty strands of hair out of her eyes. "I tied myself to a sex beast. I'll never be capable of walking straight again."

I wrap my arms around her, suctioning our sweaty bodies together. We've been making love and fucking for hours, only leaving this room to grab water and some fruit. We switched our cell phones off and shut out the outside world, and it was the best remedy. I don't care if the PR people are going crazy. I pay them to handle this shit, and they can deal with it for a day. I needed this. To swim in our love and drown in the feel and taste of the only woman who has ever mattered. I feel closer to Sydney than any other person in the world, and it's an addictive feeling.

"Don't worry, baby," I say, scooping her up. She shrieks at the unexpected move. "I will always take care of you."

We take a bath in my Jacuzzi tub, taking turns washing one another. It ends with Sydney climbing onto my dick and riding me even though I'm sure she's sore. I'm not sure who is the bigger sex beast of the two of us.

We dress in toweling robes and head downstairs where we make food side by side, listening to music, dancing, singing, and talking about mundane shit. It's so normal, but it's invigorating. I've never shared my life with any woman like this, and I know it's because I was waiting for Syd.

We take heaping bowls of creamy pasta into my living room and eat it on our laps, curled up beside one another on the couch, as we watch a few episodes of *The Vampire Diaries*. Another show from our past.

"I have something to ask you," I say, taking her empty bowl and putting it with mine on the coffee table. I reel her into my arms, and she peers up at me.

"Go for it."

"Move in with me."

She blinks successively before scrutinizing my face. "You're serious?"

I nod. "I know you love your house. I love it too, but it seems silly to have two houses when we spend most all our time in one or the other. Security is tighter here, and it's more private. We have the helipad and plenty of unfurnished rooms we can turn into an art studio for you." I wind my fingers through her hair. "But if you prefer to stay in your place, I'll sell this one and move in with you. I don't really care where we live as long as we're together and you're protected."

She nibbles on her lower lip. "Can I think about it?"

"Of course." I'm just glad she didn't tell me an outright no.

"I have made an important decision about my life," she adds, running her fingers up and down my chest through the robe. I encourage her to continue with my eyes. "I'm going to resign from my position at the museum and focus on my art instead."

My smile is instantaneous. "I love it. I want you to achieve your dreams, and I'll support you fully whatever you decide." I'm not sure what her financial situation is. She seems to have money, but I don't know how much. I know her father basically cut her off and she's surviving on the settlement she received from Sawyer and the income she's earned from her jobs, but I don't know how substantial that is. "I know you're independent, Syd, but what's mine is yours. If you need any financial support, just ask."

"I appreciate you offering, J, but I'm good. Having no money of my own for years actually taught me the value of saving and being selective with the things I buy. I put most of my savings into buying my house, but I have plenty set aside to cover me as I build my art business, and if I end up selling my house, my savings account will grow again."

"When we're married, my money will be yours, so if you need anything, just come to me. I never want money to be the cause of any arguments between us."

"I wouldn't let it," she says, toying with a loose thread on my robe. "I like being independent, but I'm not going to be stupid about it."

I tweak her nose. "Glad to hear it."

"I'll save our arguments for more important things." She flashes me a cheeky grin, and I slide my hand under her robe and pinch her ass. She jumps, and her eyes ignite with instant lust. Sex with Syd is fucking mind-blowing. Today was the best sex of my life, and I get to have it every day until I stop breathing.

Life doesn't get much better than this.

We still have shit to wade through. A lot of it. But I know we're going to make it because we have each other.

Chapter Thirty-Five
Jared

"Sawyer and Xavier will meet us at the private airfield," Sydney says, repocketing her cell after she ends the call with her ex.

"Good." I thread my fingers in hers as we buckle in for the six-hour flight to New York. "Did he give you any indication of what he has to tell us?"

She shakes her head. "He said it was better to go through it in person and Herman and Gladys need to be there."

"What about Toria?" I ask as the plane moves down the runway.

"He was a little evasive. All he said was he had news."

"Hmm." I scrub a hand over my jaw. My ex is giving me hell again. To say she isn't happy I'm with Sydney is an understatement.

I can't even attend the doctor's appointments anymore because she raised bloody murder last week and embarrassed herself and me in front of the doctor and his team. She got so worked up her heart rate elevated, and it's not good for the baby. The doc recommended I stay away. He has agreed to send me regular reports and to notify me immediately if there is any concern or risk to my unborn child.

Toria is seven months pregnant, so the end is in sight. There is no denying she's pregnant now. Her considerable baby bump is another source of anxiety for her, and of course, I'm to blame.

We petitioned the court for full custody after I offered her five million to amend the terms of our arrangement so the baby lives full-time with me and she has visitation rights, and she turned me down. She demanded thirty million dollars, confirming my bandmates were right.

She's in this for the money.

She must have sabotaged a condom to get pregnant on purpose.

I think everything she has done is an elaborate performance to make me think she's crazy so I'll do anything, pay anything, to get her away from my kid. Making the offer played to her agenda. I love my son, and I want him protected, but I'm not handing thirty million dollars to that nutjob. I thought about it for a while, but Sydney and John convinced me not to do it. If I start down that road, it will never stop.

Our best option is to go the legal route, but so far, the court refuses to grant anything but joint custody. When Toria messes up—and I know she will—the court will side with me.

So, I just have to bide my time.

But it's not easy.

I worry all the time she'll cause harm to my child.

Add that to the sadness and pain I feel for the baby I never knew and the ordeal Sydney went through, and my head is a pretty fucked-up place these days.

I'm only sane 'cause Sydney is by my side. She moved into my house a couple of days after I asked her to. She has quit her job, but she hasn't put her house on the market yet. She still needs a place to paint, and I walk her over to her house every morning before I go to work. I know she's committed to me and neither of us have plans to ever walk away from one another, but I think she needs that safety net for a little while longer, and I won't ever deny her anything she needs. It's probably for the best anyway. We have paparazzi, fans, and nosy neighbors out in force in the neighborhood, so showing a house in those conditions wouldn't be ideal.

I have hired contractors to build a massive art studio and storage warehouse for her at the rear of my house, and the work is already underway. She'll have a stunning view and lots of natural light.

I've been in L.A. a lot. Between laying down tracks, doing media interviews, and meetings with my lawyer, PR people, and the label, my life has been hectic. But I make sure I'm home every night for dinner.

Returning to a home-cooked meal and the love of my life waiting for me is the stuff of dreams. We rarely go out, preferring to spend our time in our house, wrapped up in one another, and I'm content being a homebody. I'm happier than I've been in a long time. When we're in our little bubble, not even Toria and the other shit we're dealing with can eradicate the happiness that radiates from deep inside me.

Sydney is my person.

My soul mate.

My life.

My love.

My forever.

Protecting her and what we're building is the main reason we are en route to The Big Apple now. We need to face the demons of the past and finally draw a line under it.

My desire to beat the ever-loving shit out of Herman Shaw has not dissipated.

I was tempted to fly to New York and deal with her asshole father on the down-low, but I promised Syd I wouldn't do it, and it'd be a shitty way of repaying her trust in me. She knows I need to confront him for my sanity. So when Sawyer called, we came up with a plan. I tricked Mom into traveling to New York, and we'll be dropping into her Manhattan apartment after we finish with Herman.

It should be an interesting day.

"Why don't you go back to bed?" I suggest when we're up in the air and Sydney is yawning. It's only four a.m., and both of us have had minimal sleep.

"I will if you come with me." She stands, offering me her hand.

I take it and let her pull me to my feet. "To sleep, babe." I press a kiss to her head before leading her to the back of the private plane. "As much as I'd love to lose myself in your body, we need to have our wits about us when dealing with that bastard you share DNA with."

"I agree," Syd says, sliding past me into the bedroom.

We strip out of our clothes in record time and climb under the covers in our birthday suits. We kiss for a few minutes, but I stop it when my dick hardens and need surges in my loins. I'm insatiable for Sydney and grateful she feels the same. We are fucking like rabbits, making up for lost time. "Sleep, darlin'," I say, turning her around so I can spoon her from behind. "I love you."

I tell her a lot. Compensating for all the times when I wasn't able to.

"Love you too." She curls her hand back around my neck and brings my mouth down to hers for a sleepy kiss. "To infinity and forever."

The biggest smile graces my mouth. We used to say that to one another all the time as kids after we became a couple. I squeeze her tighter as I whisper, "Infinity and forever," in her ear.

———

We land in New York at lunchtime. Sawyer Hunt and his business partner, Xavier Daniels, are waiting to greet us, as promised. They drove from their home in Boston last night and stayed at their Manhattan penthouse. I clasp Sydney's hand tight as we walk toward her ex-husband and his new husband, subtly taking the measure of him.

He looks like the quintessential well-groomed billionaire businessman in an expensive black suit with a crisp white shirt and a black and silver tie. He shields his emotions behind a neutral expression as we approach, giving nothing away. There is something guarded in the way he holds himself and the way he looks at me. His husband appears to be the exact opposite. Xavier's messy hair is dyed blue and green at the tips, he has an eyebrow piercing, obvious tattoos, and a wacky sense of style if the vibrant purple silk suit and red shirt he's wearing is any indication. A wide smile crests his mouth as he waves at Sydney and...winks at me.

"Did he just wink at me?" I ask in a low voice as we close the gap between us.

"Remember what I told you. He's a good guy. Just a little out there."

I'll say.

"Sydney, darling. You look amazing. Totally fuckable if I was into pussy," Xavier says, enveloping my woman in a tight hug. "Wow, babe. You're really rocking that outfit." He waves his hands up and down her body, and he's not wrong. My girl looks hot as fuck in her ripped jeans, silk blouse, blazer, and high heels. All that gorgeous hair falls in soft waves down her back, and she looks utterly stunning. I make a mental note to fuck her later in those heels.

In only those heels.

"Love really agrees with you," Xavier adds, pulling me out of my head. "You are positively glowing, and I'm sooooo happy for you." He hugs her again before releasing her and yanking me into a hug. "Look at you, Mr. Sexy-ass Rock Star." He releases me and stands back a little, grinning. "Who knew our Sydney was hiding such a big secret in her closet."

Sydney giggles as Xavier blatantly checks me out, and I don't know what to make of the guy.

"Yep, I'd do you," he proclaims a few seconds later. "What are your views on sharing?" He winks at Sydney. "I'm thinking the four of us could get our kink on later. What better way to celebrate after dealing with the crazies than some dick in your ass?"

Sydney convulses with laughter, clutching her stomach and bending over, while I'm tempted to tug on my ears, sure I must have heard that wrong.

"Jesus, Xavier." Hunt drags a hand through his hair, looking slightly ruffled. "Did you have to go there? This is your first time meeting the man, and you proposition him?"

"Chill out, Hunt, before you give yourself an aneurysm. Syd and Jared know I'm only teasing, and you know I'd never share you. I'm just trying to lighten the mood."

"Well, that was a stellar plan," Hunt drawls. "Everyone definitely looks relaxed now."

Syd palms one side of my face, still sporting a wide grin, with flushed cheeks and vibrant eyes, and it's a good look on her. Xavier has managed to distract her for a few moments, and now I know he wasn't serious, I can appreciate his wacky attempt at levity.

"You're such a party pooper, babe." Xavier rolls his eyes at his husband. "I can't even say you need to get laid," he adds, drilling him with a look. "Because you get laid plenty. Take that stick out of your ass, or I'll bend you over the car, remove it, and replace it with my cock."

My brows climb to my hairline as a burst of laughter rolls from Sydney's lips. She presses her mouth to my ear. "I told you Xavier was one of a kind."

"I see that."

"I apologize for my business partner," Sawyer says, stepping forward and offering me his hand. "I promise he's professional when it counts."

"I offer no apologies." Xavier tosses a disgruntled look at his spouse. "I am unmistakably me."

"And I love you for you." Hunt's features soften as he stares adoringly at his husband. "But we've discussed this."

"Sawyer, seriously. This is Sydney. She's practically family. You know I'm always professional with clients, but this is different."

"It is," Sydney agrees. "Don't stand on ceremony on our behalf. We don't need it."

"It's cool," I offer. "I'm not offended."

Hunt nods before turning his attention to my girlfriend. "It's great to see you so happy. You deserve it."

Jealousy rears its head when he leans in and kisses her on the cheek. I know Hunt is no threat, but try telling that to the caged beast who resides inside me.

I'm feral when it comes to Sydney.

If a guy even looks at her, I want to rip his eyes from his head so he can't do it again.

"It's good to see you, Sawyer. Love clearly agrees with you

too," she says, squeezing my hand. "We're grateful to both of you for your help."

"Any time, babe," Xavier says. "It's been an interesting investigation."

"We look forward to hearing all about it," I say.

"Let's make a move," Hunt suggests. "Your father is expecting us shortly."

Sydney and I share a look because that's news to us. We thought we were meeting Sawyer and Xavier for a debrief and then meeting alone with Herman and later with my mother. The guys said it was important we speak with both our living parents if we wanted full answers.

"We'll explain on the way." Sawyer opens the back door to a Lexus SUV with tinted windows.

As soon as the four of us are in the back, the driver takes off.

"We met with Herman last week," Hunt says, surprising us.

"Certain things were clear from the investigation," Xavier adds, "and it warranted a conversation with your father."

"We gleaned some additional intel. Your father has been gathering evidence for some time, and we were able to pool our efforts."

"I don't understand." Sydney frowns. "Gathering evidence of what?"

"I thought the whole point was to get answers from the past and to find evidence we can use to get him off Sydney's back for good?"

"That was the assignment, but it took an unexpected turn," Xavier says.

"Can you just quit with the cryptic shit and tell us," I grit out.

"It makes more sense to wait until we're with Herman. He has things he wants to explain in person. I agreed in exchange for his intel," Sawyer says.

"You could at least have asked me before agreeing." Sydney pins a sharp look on Sawyer.

"I knew you'd say no" is the unapologetic reply.

"You need to hear what he has to say face-to-face," Xavier adds in a sober tone.

The two men exchange a look.

Xavier reaches over and takes Sydney's hand in his. A pained expression washes over his face. "We know what happened to you when you were sixteen, and we're so unbelievably sorry."

I circle my arm around Sydney's shoulders, letting her lean on me for support.

"I know I should have told you," she whispers, looking directly at Sawyer. "But it's not exactly something one says over the phone."

"It's okay. I understand." Sawyer holds her gaze for a few seconds. "I wish you'd told me when we were married."

I barely trap my snarl. Thinking of her married to anyone but me, even if it was fake, really rubs me up the wrong way.

"Why?"

"Maybe I could have done more to help back then."

"You did plenty to help me, Sawyer, and I'm not your responsibility."

"You were hurting. I should have done more."

"It's water under the bridge now." Xavier releases Sydney's hand to hook his hand in Hunt's.

"Sydney told me all you did for her," I say, shoving my jealousy to one side. "I'm grateful you were there for her and you're helping us now. You don't have anything to feel guilty about."

Sydney turns and pecks my lips. "I love you," she says, not shielding the words from our audience.

I don't know what I did to warrant that reaction, but I'm

not unhappy about it. "Love you too, baby." I kiss her hard on the mouth.

"I want front row seats at the wedding," Xavier says, flashing me a perfect set of white teeth.

"Deal, mate." I really like Xavier. He is unapologetically himself, full of life, and it's infectious.

"I thought you were going to bargain for concert tickets," Sawyer says.

"Oh, those are a given already." Xavier leans back in his seat, grinning again.

"Whenever you want them, they're yours," I promise.

"Awesome. I've always wanted to see Ruminate live."

"We're only about twenty minutes out," Sawyer says, and Sydney's brows knit together. "We aren't meeting at Shaw Software." He answers her unspoken question. "We thought it best to meet somewhere private. A friend has a house close by, and he's letting us use it for the meeting."

"Okay. This is most unusual." Sydney leans back into me, and I hold her tight.

"I know we're being vague, but it'll all make sense when we get there."

"What about Vittoria?" Sydney asks. "Can you tell us what you discovered about her?"

Sawyer and Xavier exchange another look, and a sense of dread tiptoes up my spine.

"It might be better to wait until after to discuss that," Sawyer says, eyeballing me.

"I want to know now."

"This won't be easy to hear, dude," Xavier says, and I hate the look of pity on his face. His poker face definitely needs work.

Sydney turns in her seat, wrapping her arm around my front, clearly sharing the same instincts as me.

"Whether you tell me now or later won't change that fact."

"True." Sawyer runs a hand through his hair. "There is no easy way to say this."

"So, we'll be blunt," Xavier says. "Vittoria has been scamming you from the start. That baby isn't yours."

Chapter Thirty-Six
Sydney

You could cut the tension with a knife after Xavier drops the bomb. Jared is in complete shock, staring at Xavier and Sawyer in a daze. I hug him tighter and press a kiss to his neck. I'm in shock too. Though it doesn't really surprise me. Vittoria has shown herself to be completely conniving. There's a lot to process in that revelation, and now isn't the time to delve into it. We can't go into the meeting with my father at a disadvantage. I understand now why Sawyer wanted to wait until later to tell us this.

My heart hurts for Jared. I know how invested he was in the baby.

My hatred for that bitch elevates to new levels.

How fucking dare she do this to him.

She is going to pay dearly for fucking with us.

Jared is still staring into space, and no doubt, his mind is all over the place. I rub a hand back and forth across his chest as he clings to me, burying his face in my hair. He's shaking, and right now, I'm close to asking my friends if they can organize a hit on that manipulative bitch.

I clear my throat, my worried gaze bouncing from my boyfriend to the guys and back. "I'm not going to ask if you're sure because I know you wouldn't have said it if you weren't. But I want to know how you know this is true."

"She has a childhood sweetheart from Florence," Xavier begins explaining as the car takes a sharp turn up ahead. I'm assuming the driver is a trusted employee if we're discussing all this in front of him. I don't question the guys because I trust them.

"They came to the US together," Sawyer continues. "While Vittoria was riding your coattails, Antonio was bartending at a popular club in the city. He fell in with a certain crew, and one of the guys works at a DNA laboratory."

Jared's head whips up, and the trembling stops as realization dawns. "He got him to doctor the paternity test."

Sawyer nods. "We had a little chat with the guy, and he divulged everything while he was pissing his pants."

"We got the original results," Xavier confirms. "Antonio is the father. They must have concocted this plan together. To extort money is our guess, but you'll have to confront her to know for sure."

"I don't understand," I say. "Her career was going well, and she stood to make a lot of money in her own right. Why would she do this? She has sabotaged herself, and it doesn't make sense."

"Our little lab rat alluded to the fact her boyfriend is miserable here and he wants to go back to Florence. Vittoria's career is in the US. Seems like she had to make a choice," Sawyer says.

"So, she was going to marry me, probably try to do that without a prenup, then divorce me after the baby was born, bleed me dry, and go back to Florence after having broken my heart with the news the child wasn't mine," Jared says, wrapping both his arms around me and holding me tight.

"And when that plan fell apart, they worked out a Plan B," I say, grinding my teeth in anger as I consider what it could be. I peer deep into Jared's eyes as a light bulb goes off in my head. "They wanted money more than they wanted their child."

He slowly nods as he draws the same conclusion. "They were banking on me fighting for full custody and going to use that as leverage."

"They were going to trade their baby for cash, and you'd have raised a baby who wasn't your own."

"Sounds about right," Xavier says, looking thoroughly disgusted.

I dig my nails into my thighs as sheer rage filters through me. "She doesn't deserve to be pregnant. They both deserve to die." A red haze coats my vision. "All that pretending to not eat, faking being sick, and everything else she pulled is clearly an act, meant to keep you tied to her, stressed out, and concerned so you'd give in and pay her more."

"John was right. I never should have offered her anything."

Jared's shock has transformed to anger, and he looks down-right murderous. I can relate to the feeling. I'm actually a little worried he might take it out on Herman. I've spent the past two weeks trying to talk him off that particular ledge. It's not that I care what happens to my father. I only care about Jared not going to prison.

"I'm glad she was a greedy bitch. Now the only thing she'll get is a prison sentence." I lock eyes with Sawyer. "I want that stupid cunt to pay for this. Please tell me she can be charged and locked up for this?"

"You can go after her for paternity fraud for sure, but they don't tend to send women to prison," Sawyer says. "More than likely, she'd have to pay you compensation for stress and emotional trauma. You could probably tack on damage to your reputation and brand."

"I don't want her fucking money." Jared releases his hold on me, clenching and unclenching his fists. "I want her to pay a different price."

"There are ways we could help make that happen," Sawyer coolly says, sending shivers down my spine.

I could call my cousin. Ashley knows dangerous people. If we wanted them to die, we have the contacts to make it happen. After the innocent baby is born and given to decent humans who will appreciate the precious gift he is and not try to use him to extort money.

But I already know Jared won't do it. This is just anger speaking. The baby may not be his, but there's an emotional investment, and he would never hurt an innocent by depriving him of his mother. Personally, I'd be tempted. What kind of life will that child have being raised by those two lowlife bloodsuckers? We'd probably be doing the boy a favor eradicating those two, but it's not our job to play God.

"If we wanted their visas retracted and them kicked out of the country forever, could you make that happen?" I ask, churning other ideas in my mind.

"In a heartbeat," Xavier confirms.

"Let us think about it for a few days," I say, watching Jared with concern. He's staring out the window, his jaw tensing and his hands balled into tight fists. He's a live wire fit to explode, and it doesn't bode well for the rest of our meetings today.

"J." I softly touch his cheek, turning his head to meet my face. "Do you want to reschedule the meetings today? This is a lot to take in."

"No. Absolutely not. We came here to get all the answers, and I'm not leaving until we have them."

"We could stay here for a few days and—"

"I'm okay, baby." He takes my hands and kisses my knuckles. "I mean, I'm not." A wry laugh filters from his mouth. "But

I can do this. I want to get this over and done with and then get the fuck out of this city."

"Okay." Tears fill my eyes. "I'm so sorry, J. I know how much you wanted that baby."

"I did, but I also didn't want to be tied to that crazy cunt for life. I dodged a bullet." He kisses my knuckles again. "*We* dodged a bullet. I'm still in shock, and I won't deny I'm upset, but I'm also relieved. She's gone from our lives now. When the public finds out, we'll garner sympathy, and all the online abuse will stop. We can move forward without the stress of having to deal with her." His face crumples. "Fuck, that's really selfish, isn't it?"

"No, dude," Xavier says. "It's a natural human reaction."

"We both have a lot to unpack."

"But it'll have to wait," Sawyer says as the car stops at two wrought iron gates. "We're here."

Chapter Thirty-Seven
Sydney

"Sweet pea." Herman Shaw gets up from the leather tub chair he's sitting in as the four of us enter the large living room in the lavish house Sawyer and Xavier's friend owns. His face dissolves with emotion as he drinks me in while I stare in shock at the man standing before me.

I saw him last year at Doug's funeral, and he didn't look like this. He's thinner than I've ever seen him with spindly limbs and clothes hanging off his skeletal frame. He looks way older than sixty-eight, and I have a sinking feel I know why. His hair is fully gray and receding. Brown patches cover his hands, arms, and his face. Saggy skin droops from his neck and underneath his tired-looking eyes, and he's so pale.

"It's so good to see you." My father walks toward me as Jared slings his arm around my back and keeps me close.

"What's wrong with you?" I ask.

"I have prostate cancer," he says without attempting to sugarcoat it. "An aggressive kind. I ignored the warning signs, and now it's too late. It's spread to other organs. I don't know how much time I have left, but I needed to make things right with you before I go." His gaze dances between us as I stand frozen to the spot, shell-shocked at that revelation. "You look good, son."

"Don't call me that!" Jared snaps before snorting out a rough laugh. "Fucking typical. You ruin her life, and only impending death prompts you to make it right." His jaw locks, and fire blazes in his eyes. "You're lucky you're half dead, old man, because I want to throttle you with my bare hands for the part you played in splitting us up and the things you did to Sydney and *my baby.*"

"I don't blame you," he says without hesitation. "If I were in your shoes and it was the woman I loved, I would feel the same way."

"If that's supposed to make me feel better, it doesn't. You won't ever receive any forgiveness from me. The only reason I'm not putting a bullet in your skull is because Sydney doesn't want me to end up in a cell for your worthless hide."

"Fair enough, Jared. I can't argue with that."

He's being far too reasonable. That's not the man I know or knew. It's obvious his diagnosis has changed him. I still can't process the news or decide how I feel about it. I'm not close with either of my brothers, but I would have expected Tucker or Felix to have mentioned it. "Were you even planning on telling me or just letting me find out via the media when you were dead?"

"I was always planning to tell you, and I wanted to try to make it up to you before it's too late."

"Let's sit." Sawyer gestures toward a hard-looking burgundy leather couch.

Jared folds his arm around my shoulders as we sit on the couch while Dad reclaims the tub chair, Xavier perches on the arm of the couch, and Sawyer sits in another tub chair across from Herman.

Tension trickles into the air.

"This is your show," Sawyer says, eyeballing Herman. "I suggest you don't waste any more time."

Herman nods, taking a sip from a glass of water before clearing his throat. His eyes plead for understanding I don't possess. "I made so many mistakes with you, Sydney. I know that. But I was trying to protect you. Everything I did, I did out of love."

It would be easy to throw shit at him to disprove his words, but I didn't come here to argue. We came to get answers, and debating the motive behind his actions is pointless. He will never convince me he did those things for my own good or my protection. I will never believe it.

"We'll have to agree to disagree," I say, and I'm aware how cold I sound. "Just tell me what I need to know so we can leave."

Hurt flickers in his eyes, but he disguises it fast. "I loved your mother from the second I met her," he begins explaining. "It was most definitely love at first sight. At least it was for me." Sadness drenches his features as he looks off into space. "It was actually Amos and Gladys who introduced us. Amos had been seeing Gladys for a few weeks, and they set up a double date with Michelle and me." His eyes dart to Jared. "It was your father's first time meeting Michelle too, and I wasn't the only smitten one."

"That's a lie," Jared grits out.

Herman shrugs. "Maybe. Maybe not. I never confronted him about it, but I could see the way he looked at her. Michelle only seemed to have eyes for me, but I have since questioned whether I was blind. Whether anything went on between them in college."

"I don't understand what Amos and Mom have to do with how you treated me." I'm already growing impatient. I lean into Jared's shoulder as I stare at my father, willing him to hurry up and tell us what we need to know.

"Amos and Michelle are the crux of everything that happened," Xavier says, sympathy splaying across his face. "This is important."

I nod at my father, and he continues. "You know the rest. Amos married Gladys, and I married Michelle. Then Heather and your brothers came along. We were all the best of friends. Amos and I were busy building our respective businesses and not at home a lot. The girls were close, spending every day together and doing things with the kids. I know you think you were a mistake, but you were very much planned." His eyes move to Jared. "As you were. The girls were broody and wanted more babies. You two were conceived close together."

"Oh my God." Panic races through my veins as a hideous thought lands in my mind.

"No, sweet pea." Dad sits forward in his chair. "You and Jared are not related. You are mine and Michelle's, and Jared is Gladys and Amos's son. I verified that when the truth of the affair was revealed because I was worried for a while that maybe you weren't mine."

"Fucking. Hell." Air whooshes from Jared's mouth as we share a dazed look. I think he almost had a heart attack too.

"I worshipped the ground my wife walked on, but the second you were born, princess, I was a goner. You stole my heart the minute I held you in my arms. You were the apple of my eye, and I was determined to be there for you in a way I hadn't been there for your brothers. My business was more established, and I didn't have to be at the office as much. You probably don't remember as you were so young, but we did lots of things together. I left the office at three thirty every day so I could take you to the park. Some days, we walked from the house. Other days, you cycled. We spent an hour at the playground, and then I'd take you for a sneaky ice cream before we'd head back home for dinner."

He lifts a frail hand to his face, rubbing his smooth jawline. "I only found out later those were the times Amos visited your mother."

"How long was their affair going on?"

"From what I've been able to piece together, almost two years. That prick ended things when she got breast cancer."

Jared tenses beside me but says nothing. It's not like either of us can pretend that wasn't callous.

"How did you find out? Gladys said you found some hidden letters and photos years later."

He purses his lips, and a murderous glint appears in his eyes.

There's the man I know.

He's still in there, hidden under the veil of illness and impending death.

"That is true. That's how I found out. My initial inclination was to put a bullet in Amos's skull. I sat for hours at my desk looking at my gun, but I didn't want to make it easy for him. I wanted him to know what it feels like to have your entire world pulled out from under you."

"We already know that's why you stole his business and drove my family away," Jared says, his anger flaring again.

"No, son. That's not even the half of it."

Jared growls, and I wrap my arm around his front, offering him comfort. He presses a kiss to the top of my head, and a softness crawls over my father's face as he watches us.

"Continue, Herman," Sawyer says, ensuring we stay on track.

"I went to Gladys with the evidence. She was devastated."

His lips curl into a snarl. "But she came to me the next day and told me whatever I was planning she wanted in."

"No." Jared bolts upright, jabbing his finger in the air. "You are not going to implicate my mum in this."

"Jared, you need to let the man explain," Xavier says.

"You need to prepare yourself," Sawyer adds, drilling my boyfriend with a look. "Your mother is involved in this. We found some proof, and that's what led us to Herman's door. This will not be pleasant to hear, but Herman is telling the truth."

"Babe." I rub my hand up and down his chest. "Whatever it is, we'll get through it together. Just hold on to me."

Jared wraps his arms around me and eases back, but his body is still rigid, and he's wound tighter than a ball of yarn. I hug him close and nod at Herman to continue.

"Gladys and I had an affair for a year while we both plotted to steal Amos's company from under him. I was under no illusion. Neither was your mother. It was just revenge sex. There was no love or anything even close to it. Our hurt fueled us. One by one, your mother charmed the members of the board while I was stealthily buying up shares until I had a majority holding."

Herman's eye glaze over. "Our plan had been to show up at a board meeting, tell Amos his company was now ours, Gladys was going to divorce him, and his life would be left in ruins. But a couple weeks beforehand, Amos found a positive pregnancy test, and he came to me because he said it was evidence Gladys was cheating on him. Unbeknown to her and me, he'd had a vasectomy years earlier. Amos was a serial cheater. Gladys knew about some of his other women but not the vasectomy. I talked Amos off a ledge and then met with your mother." He stares at Jared. "That's when I saw her true colors. When I realized she was playing both of us."

Jared is visibly seething, and I hug him tighter. "What does that mean?" he asks in a clipped voice.

"She wasn't ever going to divorce your father. She was going to steal his company and take her share of the profits and hide it, but she wasn't ready to give him up. I was obsessed with my wife, but Gladys's fixation with Amos was on a whole other level. Amos was hers, and she wasn't letting him go. It's why she tolerated the affairs. She knew he was coming home to her every night."

"I don't get it. So why have an affair with you and plot to take his company if she planned to stay with him?" I ask.

"I believe she wanted the money so she had a way out should she choose one in the future. That money gave her back some control and power in her marriage. But mostly, she wanted him to suffer, and it was all payback for Michelle. She thought fucking his best friend would destroy him, that he'd finally realize her worth and change his ways."

A nasty chuckle tears from his mouth. "When Amos found out, he was angry but only because I'd bested him and stolen his company right out from under him. He couldn't give a shit I'd slept with his wife because he never loved her. Not the way he loved my Michelle."

Jesus Christ. This has got to be killing Jared.

"The stupid bitch thought the baby was Amos's. She thought a baby would cure all the problems in her marriage. When she discovered it was mine, she aborted it without telling me." He breaks out in a coughing fit, and Xavier walks to the table and refills his glass with more water, urging him to drink it.

"My mind is reeling," I whisper while Herman is composing himself.

"Join the club," Jared whispers back. Pain fills his eyes when he looks into mine. "I will never forgive my mother for this. I know we haven't heard it all, but I've heard enough. She's dead to me now."

"How did we end up with such shitty parents?"

"Rotten luck." He presses a kiss to my brow. "At least when we're parents, we'll know all the things not to do."

"Guys, we're ready to resume," Sawyer says, glancing at his watch.

"Things went to shit after that. I was furious with Gladys for the abortion and stabbing me in the back. When Amos confronted her about the pregnancy and abortion, she threw me under the bus. Said we'd been having an affair, which she had tried to end several times, but I was obsessed with her and wouldn't let her go. She tried crying and pleading, but Amos saw through her. Of course, she didn't tell him the part she played in taking his company from him. After he lost his business and went to England, I had proof of her treachery hand-delivered to him. I believe that's why he divorced Gladys."

"Jesus, Dad! Couldn't you have let it go? Enough damage had been caused."

"She had to pay. She still does. It's why I've been working for years to find enough evidence. I will fight to see justice done for my Michelle before I draw my last breath."

"What do you mean?" Adrenaline courses through my veins as I watch a myriad of emotions coast over Herman's face before it crumples.

"She knew," he croaks, grabbing what little hair he has left on his head. Tormented eyes meet mine. "Gladys had known about Amos and Michelle's affair for years and said nothing. She was too terrified of losing Amos, but after I discovered the truth and she knew I was going to retaliate, she had no choice but to join me or pay the price with Amos."

So much for her being obsessed with her husband.

"How did she know?" Jared asks, clutching me in a vise grip.

I watch in disbelief as tears roll down my father's face. I have never seen him cry. I'm sure he cried at my mom's funeral, but I was only five, and I don't remember it.

"Gladys took great delight in telling me how Michelle had confessed to her. My wife was trying to cleanse her soul before cancer came for her. I guess she planned to tell me too, but she didn't get the chance because she died that night at the hands of her best friend."

My heart thumps wildly in my chest. "What?" I whisper. "No. No!"

A strangled sound leaks from Jared's lips.

"Cancer would have killed your mother," Herman says, staring at me through blurry vision. "If Gladys hadn't smothered her with a pillow first."

Chapter Thirty-Eight
Jared

"You filthy fucking liar!" I hop up and lunge at Herman, my hands instantly wrapping around his throat. First Sydney and my baby, and now this? No. This fucker does not get to live.

I'm dragged off him a few beats later by Sawyer and Xavier and tossed back on the couch.

Herman is coughing and spluttering as Sydney watches with a horrified expression on her face.

"Is it true?" she blurts, looking up at Sawyer.

He nods as I slump on the couch. "What proof do you have?" I ask, trying to calm myself down.

"None," Herman says. "All I know is what she told me as she drove the knife in deeper."

"We're just expected to take your word for it?" I hiss as Syd reaches out and pulls me back in to her side.

"You need to get the truth from your mother," Sawyer says. "She has lied about a lot of things."

"I can't wrap my head around this," Sydney quietly says, curling against me.

"I know." My arms snake around her body, and I hold her close. We need one another now more than ever. I refuse to let what our parents did or didn't do affect us any more than they have. "Mum loves Sydney. She was her surrogate mother after Michelle died."

"Your mother is incapable of love, son. At first, I thought maybe her guilt drove her to step up after Sydney lost her mother, but I think she got some perverse pleasure out of taking the things Michelle had loved. It made her feel like the better woman to know Michelle's daughter loved her like a mother and she'd fucked her husband. But it's all conjecture. The truth is, Gladys King is a sociopath, and she has spent the last ten years trying to hurt you, Sydney."

We both just stare at him. Is there no end to this madness?

"Mum claimed you were trying to hurt me, and now you're claiming she was trying to hurt Sydney. I think you're both fucked in the head."

"We have proof of hits taken out on Sydney by your mother, Jared," Sawyer calmly says.

I blink repeatedly, wanting to wake up from this nightmare.

"It's why I insisted on bodyguards and enhanced security at the house and why I wanted you close. If you were at home, you were safe. I have a lot of powerful contacts, and they have helped me keep you safe over the years." Herman eyeballs Sawyer for a split second. "Ethan Hunt and his good friend Travis Lauder were instrumental in helping me protect you. I owed Ethan, and when his company was in trouble, I agreed to a merger on condition Sawyer married you because I knew you were drowning, sweet pea, and nothing I was doing was helping. I knew Sawyer was a good man. I hoped you'd fall in love and find peace, but I was wrong to force both of you into doing that. It's one of my bigger regrets. I owe both of you a big apology."

I think that ship has sailed, and judging by the deafening silence and lack of response, Sydney and Sawyer do too. "Why would my mother try to kill Sydney?" I ask, hurt, confused, and concerned in equal measure. It feels like I've walked into an alternate realm because this cannot be happening. There is no fucking way I'm meeting my mother at her apartment or leaving Sydney behind because I no longer trust the woman who gave me life.

"She's a fucking looney tune," Xavier says. "There may not be any logical explanation."

"Gladys acted all concerned when you two started dating because she said you were too young to get so attached. She manipulated me into trying to keep things PG between you. She was always planning on taking you to England after Amos lost the business because she wanted to keep you two apart. During our final conversation, she said hell would freeze over before she let Michelle's slut of a daughter trap her son into marriage and have history repeat itself. She warned me if I didn't keep Sydney away from you she'd kill her. I'd seen enough unhinged behavior at this point to treat the threat seriously."

"So you redirected my messages and calls and intercepted Jared's," Sydney says.

Herman nods, leaning forward on his elbows. "I never wanted you to know any of this, princess. I tried to protect you and shield you from the truth. It was a mistake. I see that now. But you loved Gladys like a second mother, and you had already lost one. I thought as long as I kept you safe and worked to find evidence to put her away for your mother's murder, I could protect you from the worst of the pain. I briefly considered telling you everything at eighteen, but you were out of control, and I was so concerned you'd kill yourself before Gladys ever had a chance to."

"You should have told me. Everything would have been different if I'd known the truth. It actually would have helped." She grips my arm tight. "Losing Jared sent me into a downward spiral. If I'd had him at my side, it would not have been the same."

"Why didn't you have her arrested for trying to kill Syd?"

"Son, you don't walk into the cops in New York and claim hitmen are trying to take out your daughter. The mafia own most of the cops, and most of the hitmen are paid mafia guns for hire. I'd have put a glaring target on both our heads if I'd done that."

"The mafia aren't the only ones who were involved," Xavier says from his cross-legged position on the floor. "The Elite have a lot of control in the major cities, and they had a hand in this."

"The Elite?" I inquire, wondering if I've sleepwalked onto a movie set or something because shit is getting even weirder.

"The Elite are a powerful group of wealthy, well-connected men with their hands in tons of shit they shouldn't. Killing people is a hobby for a lot of them," Xavier adds.

"The less you know, the better," Sawyer supplies.

"How were they involved?" I at least want to know that much.

"Dr. Mulligan was Elite," Sawyer confirms, rising from his chair. "The only way Herman got away with murdering him and those other sick fucks was because my dad and Travis Lauder helped him to pull it off in a way it couldn't be traced back."

"What?" Sydney splutters. "*You* killed the doctor? You told me you didn't believe me!"

Tears well in the old fucker's eyes. "Of course, I believed you, princess," he chokes out. "But I didn't want you involved or tied to any retaliation, and I didn't want you to remember. I thought if I convinced you it hadn't happened you'd start believing it. Forget it and put it out of your mind. But it's just another example of how I messed up."

He gets up and walks to the couch, dropping onto his knees in front of my girlfriend. He takes her hands, and she lets him. "I failed you, sweet pea. I failed you, and I hate myself for it. I should have protected you from every horror, and I didn't." His gaze drifts between us. "I need you both to know that I didn't sanction any abortion. I brought you to Dr. Mulligan, Sydney, as he came highly recommended. I wasn't happy you were pregnant so young, and I was worried what Gladys would do if she found out, but I would never kill an innocent baby or take that decision away from you. I took you there to get the best prenatal care. I was prepared to support you even if you insisted on keeping the child. That bastard told me the baby was dead and he'd had to perform an emergency procedure. I didn't doubt him when I should have. He should have asked my permission, and he didn't. It's no excuse, but I wasn't in a good place back then. I was in a very dark place, enraged over Michelle's affair and her murder and worried about you."

"Daddy." Tears stream down Sydney's face, and I'm struggling to contain my emotions too.

"I'm so sorry for what they did to you." Tears cascade down his cheeks, and there's no doubting his sincerity. As much as I want to dismiss everything he's said, I can't. Sawyer and Xavier are saying it's the truth, and it's written all over Herman's face. "I wished I could have tortured the bastards personally, but Hunt and Lauder told me I needed to stay out of it. They organized the fire at Mulligan's building and hunted down the other men until they were all dead. They also helped me to set up a specialist top-secret team within Shaw Software, and we got all the videos down. We wiped them from existence."

Nothing is ever really gone once it's out there, but with his skill set, I trust it's gone from the public domain. "You could have at least told Sydney that much," I clip out. "It's plagued her for years."

"I should have put your mind at ease. Jared is right. I have no excuse except I made a lot of bad decisions. Decisions that caused me to lose you, and I've paid the highest price." He breaks down sobbing, and it's uncomfortable to watch. He may not be guilty of all the sins we thought him guilty of, but he's still fucked up a lot, and I don't know if there is ever any way to forgive him for making it worse for Sydney, no matter the motive. Maybe Syd will find it in her heart to forgive him before he dies, but that's her call to make.

"I think this is a good point to bring our guest in," Sawyer says, pressing something on his ear as he moves toward the closed door.

"What guest?" I ask as Sydney whispers with her dad.

"Knowing what we did, we couldn't let you meet her alone," Hunt says, opening the door.

"Get your fucking hands off me, asshole," Mum shouts, thrashing around as two armed men, wearing head-to-toe black, grip her arms and escort her into the room.

Chapter Thirty-Nine
Jared

"Jared, thank God." Mum's eyes find mine first in the room, and she has the audacity to smile at me. "Tell them to let me go. There's been a mistake."

"You're lucky these men are honorable," Herman says, climbing awkwardly to his feet. "If I had my way, I'd be pumping you full of bullets, setting fire to your rotten corpse, and putting you through a grinder before tossing your ashes into thin air."

Wow. That's an incredibly specific plan, and I can tell Herman has been dreaming about killing her for years. After what I've heard today, I can't say I blame him.

Mum narrows her eyes at Herman. "Not if I beat you to it first," she hisses, her face contorting into an ugly scowl.

"Did you really try to kill Sydney?" I ask even though I already know the answer. I need to hear her say it. I hold my girl tight as I scrutinize my mother's face, watching for signs she's lying.

This has been a shit show of a day, and Sydney and I are

clinging to one another in matching shock, horror, and desperation.

"Don't listen to whatever these bastards have said." A mask goes over her face as she smiles at me. "I'm your mum, Jared. These people are lying to you to cause trouble."

"You're fucking certifiable if you think your son buys that bullshit," Xavier says, pushing her down into a wooden chair that's been placed in front of the couch. Sawyer bends down behind her, restraining her wrists and ankles together with zip ties and tying them to the chair.

"Is this really necessary?" she asks, sounding bored.

"You seem to have forgotten our little chat from earlier," Sawyer says, coming around to the front. He shoves a tablet in her face. "All your bank accounts are frozen, and our legal team is poised to transfer the deeds of every property you own into our names. If you want to lose everything, by all means, continue lying to your son's face."

Who the fuck are these guys? Sydney and I trade another shocked look, and it's becoming the norm.

"I'm not saying shit. You'll just take everything and murder me anyway."

"I already told you your fate lies with Jared. As much as others in this room might like to riddle you with bullets or have you locked away for the rest of your life, what happens to you will be your son's decision." Sawyer looks over at me, and I see nothing but the truth in his eyes.

I nod, spotting the relief creep over Mum's face as she watches us. It's more than a little premature. Right now, I'm close to wrapping my hands around her throat and choking the life from her myself.

"I want the truth, Mum, and don't even think about lying. You took me away from Sydney and tried to have her killed. I'm not feeling very charitable, and I have zero patience left. If you want to survive, you'll tell me everything and hold nothing back."

A brief glint of confidence flashes in her eyes before she conceals it. She doesn't think I have it in me to kill her. Maybe I don't, but if she is guilty of everything, I will not let her walk away unpunished.

"Yes, I tried to have the little slut killed, but it's not my fault. You can blame Herman because he failed to keep her in line."

I push all my emotions into a mental lockbox and pretend like my mother isn't my mother. It's the only way I'll get through this without going crazy. "Why do you not want me with the woman I love?"

"Because she's not worthy of you," she spits.

I rub Sydney's arm when I feel her trembling beside me.

"No offspring of that bitch could ever be good enough for my only son." Her features appear to soften, but I trust nothing about her anymore. "You were always destined for greatness, Jared, but you suffer the same curse as your father. You let your cock rule your life, and it's been disappointing to watch. First, this little slut, and then that crazy Italian bitch. I was protecting you from a marriage like mine. If you stay with Sydney, she'll only cheat on you, just like her cunt of a mother." Her eyes bleed with poison. "Michelle was my best friend! We did everything together. I confided in her about Amos's affairs and how much they hurt me. She urged me to leave him, but I would never do that. I loved him so much. Later, I realized why she was encouraging me. She wanted him all to herself! That stupid cow wanted me to divorce my husband so she could marry him. Well, fuck that. She wasn't having him, and her daughter wasn't having you. Don't you see, Jared? It was all for you! Everything I have done was to give you the best life and to ensure you ended up with someone worthy of you."

She sounds delusional and insane, and I wonder how I've never seen it before. Sure, there were occasions when I was growing up when she'd lose the plot. Screech and scream and throw things around, but I just put it down to her having a short fuse. I knew her relationship with my father was tempestuous as they often argued. But this is a whole different level of crazy.

"That's not your decision to make. You tore me away from the only girl I've ever loved, and I'll never forgive you for it."

"Don't forget to tell him about Anvil," Xavier says, sucking on a cherry-red popsicle.

"Anvil?" Sydney straightens up. "What about Anvil?"

"She was grooming him, and he did a lot of her dirty work," Sawyer says.

All the blood drains from my face as I stare at the woman who birthed me and realize she's a complete stranger.

"Fuck off looking at me like that, Jared. Of course, I didn't groom him. He wanted me." She smirks, obviously still believing she's in the clear because she doesn't think I have it in me to punish my own mother for her crimes. She'll find out in due course how wrong she is. "He couldn't keep his hands off me."

I almost vomit on the spot.

"Tell Jared how young he was when you took his virginity," Sawyer says.

"Anvil was always very mature for his age and very well endowed for a teenager."

"I think I'm going to puke," Sydney says, and I'm not far behind.

"He was thirteen," Xavier says, glaring at my mother as he noisily slurps his popsicle. It would be comical if there was anything even remotely funny about this.

"Age is irrelevant. He loved me. From the minute we

started having sex, he was fucking me any chance he got. He was my good boy and so eager to learn. Such a good pupil."

"Not according to the law, you sick bitch," Sydney says, and I'm glad she articulated it because I'm currently incapable of forming any words.

Gladys narrows her eyes at my girlfriend. "You're in no position to judge me. Junkie whore."

"You set it all up," I hiss. "You told Anvil to hit on her."

"I wanted him to seduce her so she'd leave you alone, but the fucking idiot couldn't even manage to do that. Though he did come in useful later with the photos." She laughs, and I see red.

I lunge for her, but Sydney holds me back this time. "She's not worth it, J. She's evil through and through, and she's going to get what's coming to her. You don't need her blood on your hands."

"My son won't hurt me." Her smug demeanor is sadly misplaced.

"No? What makes you so sure I won't hurt you the way you hurt me?"

"I've never hurt you, Jared. I've protected you."

She is legit insane, and I hope I inherited none of those genes. I already have a long mental list from today of all the ways she has hurt me. "You sent Vil to fuck Sydney and made him send me the evidence. It destroyed me."

"Quit with the dramatics, Jared, and he didn't fuck her. He was too loyal to cheat on me. He just made it appear that way." She snarls at Sydney. "If she hadn't been so high, she'd have known that."

I don't know if I believe her—Vil was definitely fucking Cay back then—but if it's the truth, it won't offer much comfort all these years later. We've already moved beyond that. I'm actually starting to feel sorry for my ex-friend. Thinking back on how he was, it seems clear Mum fucked his head up. She was raping him from the time he was thirteen. I feel ill thinking about it. Now her penchant for dating younger men after her divorce makes more sense. I never judged her for it, but maybe I should have. "Did you target any of my other friends?" I ask even though I'm not sure I want to know.

"I'm not a whore." She has the nerve to look disgusted.

"She fucked at least one other friend of yours we're aware of," Xavier confirms.

"We spoke with Anvil," Sawyer adds. "Your mother ruined his life. She messed with his head and then outed their relationship, so his father cut him off financially, and his family turned their back on him. All because Vil knocked a girl up at eighteen when he was heartbroken over your mother cutting her out of his life with no warning. You should talk to him. He feels bad for the part he played in splitting you and Sydney up, and he's pleased you found one another again."

"You're a disgusting piece-of-shit rapist," I tell her.

Her eyes narrow to slits as she glares at me. "You take that back! I'm your mother, Jared. I gave you life, and you will show me some respect!"

"You lost any respect the moment you raped his friend, broke us up, and tried to murder me," Sydney says, her voice devoid of warmth and radiating with pure hatred.

"Tell them the rest," Sawyer prompts.

"Why should I? He's just going to tell you to kill me."

"I won't," I say, and it's not a lie. Death would be too easy. I want her to suffer. To feel what Sydney felt thanks to the things she set in motion. "I give you my word."

That seems to be good enough for her. Maybe I'm her Achilles' heel. The only person she's gullible with. Or maybe she has some sliver of a conscience and she wants to get it off her chest.

"I organized Sydney's abortion." Her wicked smile confirms all of the above thoughts are completely wide of the mark. She just wants to dig the knife deeper.

"You did what?" Herman roars.

Sawyer gestures at one of the guards, and they quickly restrain the old man before he attacks her.

I watch the evil smile growing on her face with mounting horror.

It's true.

She *is* a sociopath.

She's getting off on this. She enjoys causing hurt and pain.

"Dr. Mulligan did my abortion, and I knew he was an evil man."

"I guess evil recognizes evil," Sydney snaps.

I pull her onto my lap because she's trembling so badly. I'm in a kind of numbed-out state now. I think my brain is over-loaded and it has shut down to cope.

"I called him and made him a proposal. He took one look at Sydney's pretty innocent face, and he readily made a deal. He had a contact of a contact slip Herman his details, and he took care of the rest."

I'm reconsidering my no-murder suggestion. Right now, I want to take a baseball bat to my mother's face and tear her limb from limb.

"You bitch," Sydney rasps. "That baby was your grandchild."

"I didn't want any grandchild with Michelle's conniving DNA," she screeches, straining against her restraints.

The irony is astounding.

"How are you so sane?" Xavier asks, looking almost perplexed. "Be thankful you seem to have more of your father in you."

"Which leads us nicely to the last segment of the day,"

Sawyer drawls, and it's official. My life has turned into a soap opera. "Tell Jared what you did to his father."

"Jesus," Syd whispers in my ear. "I don't think I can take any more."

I sweep hair behind her ears and kiss her quickly. "Tell me about it. I'm not sure I'll be able to walk out of here when we're done. My mind is reeling."

Mum scoffs, reclaiming our attention. "I murdered your father," she says in the same way one would comment flippantly on the weather.

I squeeze my eyes closed, and I think I may have reached my breaking point.

"What did you do to Amos?" Herman asks, disbelief threading through his tone. It's evident from his surprise that he didn't know about the abortion or this.

"It was his fault." She holds her head up high. "I told him if he ever divorced me I'd kill him. He was mine, and he lost sight of it."

"How did you do it?" I clip out, resting my face against Syd's arm.

"I injected him with medication that created an arrhythmia, lowered his heart rate, and induced cardiac arrest." Her evil laugh bounces off the walls. "It was so fucking easy. The coroner didn't find the injection site between his toes. Geriatric moron."

Slowly, I lift Sydney off my lap onto the couch and get up. No one stops me as I approach my mother and slap her across the face repeatedly. She deserves worse.

"What do you want to do?" Sawyer asks. "It's your call. If you want her dead, we'll make her disappear. If you want her charged for her crimes, we've been recording her confession, and I have an FBI contact friend on standby. He can have a team here within the hour."

"Don't you dare, Jared," Gladys threatens.

"I need to think about it," I say, reaching for Sydney.

She takes my hand, and I pull her to her feet. We are silent as I lead her out into the hallway and close the door behind us. "What do you think I should do?" I ask, leaning back against the wall and pulling her into my arms.

"The part of me that aches for our lost baby wants to gut that bitch from head to toe and feed her remains to sharks."

"But death is an easy way out."

"Yeah."

I'm not surprised we're on the same wavelength.

"But it's more than that. I don't want her death on your conscience, J. Although we have justifiable reasons for killing her, that's not who we are. Who you are. We'd be no better than her if we start making life-or-death judgment calls. I say we hand her over to the FBI. Let them throw the book at her."

"It will garner global interest because of who I am."

"We'll handle it. It'll be a shit show with this and the Vittoria news, but then it will die down, and hopefully we can live out the rest of our days without drama."

"I think we've used up a lifetime's quota today."

"I'm in complete shock and in a lot of denial," she admits.

"I'm the same. I don't know how I feel about most of it."

"It's a lot to process. I thought my dad was behind everything."

"But it was my mum." I hold her head in my hands. "I'm so sorry, baby."

"You are not apologizing for that psycho!" Her eyes flare with anger. "You are not going to assume one ounce of guilt over this, J, because this is all on your mother. It's not on you. Look at all the damage she's caused."

"Heather is going to take this so hard." My sister is close with Mum.

"She'll be horrified." She rests her brow against mine. "God, Jared. Your mother murdered our baby, and she murdered your father and tried to have me killed. I can't wrap my head around it."

"I know. The guys won't believe it when I tell them."

"Neither will Cay. She's been firmly anti-Herman for years."

"Your father isn't blameless either even if his heart was in the right place and his motivations were protective."

"I know. I don't know if I can forgive him, but he's dying."

Shouts emanate from the living room, and it's time to face the music. "Let's pick this up at home. We have lots to think about, but right now, getting that evil bitch behind bars is priority number one."

We walk back into the room hand in hand. Sawyer and Xavier walk toward us. "What have you decided?"

I glance over their shoulders at my mother. "We should kill you. A slow and torturous death, but that would only make us as bad as you. You deserve to suffer."

"I hope your life behind bars is the worst hell on earth. It's the least you deserve," Sydney says.

"Are you very sure?" Sawyer asks, eyeballing both of us. "You don't have to be the one to do it," he says in a lower tone. "We can handle it and keep you out of it."

"We're not killers," Sydney says as a shout rings out, and then a shot is fired.

We all drop to the floor on instinct as the smell of gunpowder swirls in the air.

"Welp, that's one way of handling it," Xavier quips, climbing to his feet alongside Sawyer as I help Sydney to stand.

We stare at the fresh hole in my mother's skull. Her head is tipped back, and her empty eyes stare at the ceiling.

"I'm sorry, Mr. Hunt," one of the guards says. "He unclipped my gun before I realized what was happening."

"It had to happen like this," Herman says, handing the gun back to the man. He walks toward us, and I swear it's as if a huge weight has visibly lifted off his shoulders. "She couldn't live, son." He clamps a hand on my shoulder. "She might have found a way to get to you or Sydney from jail, and I couldn't take that risk. This way, an old man can die in peace knowing his little princess is safe." He squeezes my shoulder with more force than I considered him capable of. "I'm entrusting Sydney to your care, Jared. Worship her. Love her. Cherish her. Support her. Protect her."

"With everything I have."

"Give her lots of babies because my sweet pea was born to be a mother."

"I plan to give her all the babies she wants," I say, tucking a teary-eyed Sydney under my arm as he drops his arm and releases me.

"Love big and live hard, sweet pea." He plants a kiss on Sydney's brow. "I'm proud of you, princess. You're a survivor, and you didn't let what happened to you erase the most important parts of who you are. I'm just sorry there isn't enough time to make it all up to you."

"Oh man." Xavier slaps a hand dramatically to his brow. "The emotion in this room is stifling. I need to cry, fuck, or have a drink." He shrugs. "Maybe all three at once."

"I vote for alcohol," Sawyer says, ignoring the instant pout on his husband's face.

"I'm down with that plan," Sydney says.

"You go with Xavier, and I'll meet you in a while. I'll just wrap things up here."

"Thank you," I say. "While today has not gone how we thought it would, we came here for answers and got them."

"I'm sorry they weren't the ones you were hoping for, but at least you can draw a line under it now," Sawyer says.

"When we walk out of here," Syd says, looking into my eyes. "we're leaving the past firmly in the past."

"Amen to that, baby." I kiss her soft lips. "Now we get to live the life we always wanted."

Epilogue
Sydney – Seven Months Later

"You got a glorious day for it," Cay says as the makeup artist puts the finishing touches to my bridal makeup.

"I couldn't have asked for better," I agree, peering out the window of our master suite and smiling at the assembled crowd in the near distance on the beach.

"The media took the bait," Zeta confirms, topping off my flute. We're drinking nonalcoholic champagne in honor of Cay because she's six months pregnant.

Jerry and Cay's December wedding was magical, and they discovered they'd made a honeymoon baby seven weeks later. I'm so happy for my bestie. I've never seen her so content, and I can relate. I'm the happiest I've ever been in my life.

Especially today when I get to marry the man of my dreams.

It's been a very rocky road to this moment, but we made it.

"I can't believe you had to stage a fake L.A. wedding and hire actors to pretend to be guests just to ensure privacy on your special day. I still can't believe how invasive the celebrity world is. It's freaking nuts," Cay says, sipping the bubbly liquid.

"It's been a steep learning curve," I say as subtle pink blusher is applied to my cheeks.

"You had a baptism of fire, girl." Zeta sits on the window seat looking pretty in her bridesmaid dress.

Cay and Zeta are wearing the same burnt-orange silk dresses but with different styles. I'm honored Cay chose to return to her dark roots for my wedding, but I would have picked a different color dress if she wanted to keep her purple locks. She said it was time for a change and a lot of women choose not to dye their hair during pregnancy. Cay opted for an empire line short dress, which is flattering with her bump, while Zeta is wearing a fitted dress that molds to her envious curves and hits mid-calf. The top is a halter neck, and her back is bare.

"I did. Those first few months severely tested my sanity." The initial days after the shock revelations were spent at home trying to dissect it all and figure out our feelings. We both attended therapy, individually and as a couple, as we needed some additional help. Of course, no one knows Gladys was murdered by my father. Sawyer disposed of her body and arranged for a fake accidental drowning in the middle of the Atlantic Ocean while on vacation. Her body was never found, assumed eaten by sharks. That news dropped a month after it all went down with Vittoria.

Jared and I confronted her and her baby daddy together. As long as I live, I will never forget the look on that bitch's face when she realized the game was up. I was a little petty, groping and kissing Jared in a near replica of the time in the gallery. Even though she is supposedly in love with Antonio, she couldn't conceal the envy and rage on her face. I think she probably did pick up feelings for J. Maybe she hoped their marriage would work out and she'd cut her childhood sweetheart loose. We'll never know. We didn't bother asking.

We stood outside her apartment and watched as the authorities arrived to arrest both of them for paternity fraud and visa fraud. Jared waived his right to compensation in return for ensuring neither of them were ever allowed into the US again. At the same time, he sold his Florentine home, and we drew a firm line under that episode of our lives.

Cameras were at the airport when they were escorted in handcuffs onto a plane bound for Italy. The world's media lapped it up, and we garnered enormous sympathy. Jared is even more revered now, and fans have openly embraced me, happy to see he's happy even if they wish it was with them.

We have settled into our new life with ease because it was always meant to be like this.

The guys' new album dropped recently, and it was an instant number one on the charts. The album cover was a hit too, and I have more requests for commissions than I can handle.

Jared offered to buy me a gallery as a wedding present, but I don't want the hassle of running one. I love the enormous airy studio he built me here, and I'm content painting commissions and working at a schedule that suits me.

It will be even more important in the near future.

A wide smile graces my mouth as I consider the news I have to tell my fiancé. It's been killing me keeping it a secret this week, but it's going to make the best wedding present. I can't wait to see his face.

"You're glowing, girl," Zeta says, pinning me with a knowing look. I think she's figured it out, but I'm saying nothing until I've told my baby daddy the joyful news.

"I love seeing you so happy," Cay says with tears in her

eyes. She's a big ole hormonal mess, but I love the bones of her. She's my sister in all the ways that count.

"I have dreamed of this day from the time I was a little girl. I can't believe it's finally happening or that it was possible to be this happy."

"You went through hell to reach heaven. Embrace it, babe." Cay leans in and hugs me as the makeup artist packs up her stuff.

"Knock, knock," Felix says, poking his head through the door.

"You're supposed to do that before you open the door," I tease. "I could have been naked."

My youngest brother rolls his eyes as he walks into the room with my nephew and Jared's niece.

"Oh my God, look at you two," I squeal, loving how adorable they are in their flower girl and page boy's outfits. "You look so pretty, Carrie, and you're very handsome, Jamie."

I made my peace with my father before he died, and I was at his bedside with Tucker and Felix as he passed away. Dad made us promise to make more time for each other, and I had a big heart-to-heart with my brothers after the funeral. They were aware of some things and not others. Tears were shed, apologies offered, and promises made. So far, we are making time to get to know one another, and I'm enjoying spending time with my nieces and nephews. The time difference and distance between us doesn't help, but we've visited them in New York, and they've come here a couple of times, and we're making it work.

I didn't think I needed family in my life, but I'm glad to be proven wrong.

Heather and Jared have grown even closer after the revelations. Jared chose not to tell Heather the truth about how their mum died. She believes she drowned on vacation and that it was karma at play.

"Give Auntie Sydney her gift," my brother says, encouraging his son and Heather's daughter to come toward me.

"This is from Uncle Jared," Jamie says, handing me a Tiffany's bag.

"And this is from my mom," Carrie adds, thrusting a plain white bag in my lap. I know it contains a blue garter because Heather told me she had one.

"Thank you so much." I kiss both of them on the cheek, rubbing my lip gloss from their soft skin before they leave with my brother to get ready to walk down the aisle.

"Oh, wow," I say, opening the large Tiffany box to find a stunning diamond and emerald necklace with matching earrings and bracelet. Jared has such good taste. These will look fabulous with my dress. I open the accompanying card and tears instantly stab my eyes.

> For my beautiful bride. I cannot wait to call you my wife. I've been dreaming about you walking down the aisle to me my whole life. I'm so proud to call you mine and so honored to get to share my life with you. I love you so much, Sydney. Thank you for giving me a second chance.
> All my love,
> Jared.

"He's so romantic." Cay swoons as she reads over my shoulder.

"Songwriters have a special way with words." Zeta smiles

as she reads it. "Jared reminds me of Ryder in a lot of ways. They both love big."

"That they do," I say as I pin the earrings to my ears and put the bracelet on. Zeta clasps the necklace around my nape, and I shimmy the garter up my leg, securing it in place. Then my bridesmaids help me into my dress.

"Fuck, babe. You're already making me cry." Cay hastily swipes her tears as I twirl in front of the mirror.

"I'm so happy I could burst," I admit, loving my reflection. At first, I wanted a big princess style dress because it's what I always dreamed of. But when we settled on a beach wedding at our house in June, I knew I had to adapt my plans or risk sweating the whole day. I found a local dress designer who makes custom dresses, and we designed one to suit my needs. It's made of white chiffon with a lace overlay. It's strapless and fitted at the bust, and then it flows out in a full skirt from my waist, ending at my calves. Pretty ribbons tie it in place at the back, and I bought gorgeous silver stilettos and a matching bag to complete the look. The expensive jewelry and little diamonds embedded in my hair add the perfect finishing touch.

Jared had a temporary path, deck, and gazebo erected this morning on the beach for the ceremonial part of our wedding. At least this way, I can wear heels, and our guests can avoid getting sand in their shoes. After we're married, we're heading to the house for a champagne reception on the terrace followed by dinner, drinks, and dancing in a large marquee on the grounds.

As it's hot today, I chose to wear my hair in an elegant chignon with a braid wrapping around the front. After dinner, I'll take my hair down for the dancing portion of the night.

A loud rap on the door is quickly followed by a booming voice. "Are you ready, Syd? Your man is getting antsy," Jerry says, and I smirk.

Cay strides to the door to let her husband in.

"You look beautiful, honey," he says, his eyes lighting up as he lets his gaze roam his gorgeous wife.

"You look so handsome in your suit." She straightens his tie.

"You look beautiful too, Zeta," he says before his eyes pop wide when he looks at me. "Oh, wow, Sydney. You are stunning. Jared will be falling to his knees and worshipping at your feet."

"As he should," Cay says. "He's a lucky bastard."

"He more than knows it."

The guys have become good friends, and Jerry is almost like the fourth member of Ruminate at this point. If he had any musical talent, I wouldn't be surprised if they'd rope him into joining them.

Jerry offers me his arm. "Ready to claim your man?"

I considered asking one of my brothers to give me away, but it didn't feel right. It was a toss-up between Linc and Jerry in the end, but I went for my bestie's husband because I've known him longer. "I was born ready." I beam at him. "Lead the way."

Epilogue 2
Jared

"I didn't think you'd be nervous," Linc says as he stands beside me with Wilder on his other side. The assholes scrub up well, but it took bribes to get them to agree to wear a dress suit and shirt. We got custom navy suits with white shirts, no ties, and brown shoes.

"It's not like she's going to ditch you at the altar," Wilder adds.

"That girl is crazy about you," Linc says. "I'm really happy for you, man. You got the girl."

"I did, didn't I?" I can't keep the grin off my face.

"Sydney is an amazing woman," Wilder says. "Watching you two together makes me realize I want that too."

"Any man who says he doesn't want that is a goddamn liar," Linc agrees as I catch Anvil's eye.

His nine-year-old daughter is his date today, and she looks cute as a button. I spotted Angelica playing with Ryder's daughter Etta as we were making our way to the top of the aisle a short while ago. They're close in age, so it's no surprise they've made friends.

After some soul searching, therapy, and many discussions with Sydney, I reached out to Anvil at the start of the year. We met up in New York and had a long conversation, thrashing everything out. My mother messed him up pretty bad, and he's carrying a lot of baggage from the things she did to him when he was still a child. He has struggled to accept it as rape when he felt like he wanted it at the time. But it was obvious from speaking to him that she brainwashed him to a certain extent. It was also obvious he needed help, and I couldn't walk away from him.

He apologized to me for the part he played in splitting Sydney and me up. He has since apologized to Sydney too. We made the decision as a couple to forgive him and to help him.

He knocked up his now ex-wife when he was high, strung out, and down on his luck. In many ways, he said his daughter saved him. His family refused to help, so he got a job, married the girl, and tried to make a go of it. But they were ill-suited, and he was miserable. He found out she was cheating on him just before I came back into his life, and he was living in a shitty motel and fighting her for joint custody of Angelica.

I couldn't stand by and do nothing. With John's help, we hired him a kick-ass lawyer in New York who handled his divorce and won him joint custody. Sawyer and Xavier put him up in their Manhattan penthouse, which was lying idle at the time, and they refused to take any rent.

After his ex fled overseas with her rich lover, abandoning their daughter, he went to court and was granted sole custody. Then Ryder stepped in with an offer of a job as a backing singer with the label. Anvil moved to L.A. in April, and things are working out great for him and his daughter. Torment Records is even paying for Anvil to attend a part-time sound engineering course.

My Bel Air house was empty, and I offered it to him. He

refused at first, but I insisted he move in until he's saved up enough for his own place. The property market in Cali is a nightmare with people leaving the state in droves. I don't want to sell my house as we still need an L.A. pad for when we're in the city, and it makes sense for him to stay there. As far as I'm concerned, he can stay there for as long as he likes. But Anvil is proud, and he doesn't want to rely on me for everything. He's told me often how grateful he is for our help, proving he's a much different person from the cocky, hotheaded, rebellious guy from high school.

We stay at the house when I'm needed in L.A., and I had an art studio built for Sydney as well as an outdoor playground for Angelica.

I'm hoping one day our kids will join her on the playground. I plan to talk to Sydney on our honeymoon to see if she's ready to get rid of birth control. I won't force her, but I'm dying to have kids with her. We're twenty-seven, and I feel it's a perfect age to start a family.

"Dude, you've zoned out." Linc snaps his fingers in my face, drawing me back into the moment.

"I did."

"What were you thinking about?"

"Tossing Syd's birth control."

Wilder chokes on a breath, and I smirk. "You don't mind if we bring kids on tour, right?" The US leg of our tour kicks off in ten months, so it's possible we might have a baby on board by then.

"I fucking love kids," Linc says, surprising the shit out of me. "We can get you your own tour bus, and we'll equip it with all that baby shit and stuff."

Wilder and I stare at him like he's grown horns.

"What?" He looks upset. "You don't think I'm a family man? As soon as I find the right girl, I'm on that shit."

At least he seems to have moved past his fixation on Presley Kennedy, which I'm counting as a win.

"Maybe you need to quit the groupies," Wilder says as my gaze wanders over the ground.

I smile at a host of familiar faces. All the owners of Torment Records are here with their families. Our assistants, PR people, and other business associates are here too. My lawyer has proven invaluable this past year, so he scored an invite. It was nice to meet his wife and adult kids.

I nod at Sawyer and Xavier as they chat to Ashley and her husbands Ares, Jase, and Chad. Sydney's brothers are here with their families as is my sister Heather with her husband and kids. Gemma and Francesca, from the gallery in Italy, both look starstruck as they sit beside Ryder and his kids.

I invited a small number of celebrity friends because we chose to keep the wedding small rather than have a massive one. I let Sydney make all the decisions though I was still involved. Like with all the modifications she made to the house, Sydney wants our decisions to be jointly made. We're a real team in every sense of the word, and I really hope she'd hurry the fuck up and get here so I can marry her already.

The thought has only just popped in my head when the wedding march starts, signaling it's showtime.

A hush settles over the crowd as it kicks off. Oohs and aahs ring out as Carrie and Jamie walk down the aisle. Jamie is carrying the ring cushion, and Carrie is having great fun throwing rose petals from a basket. Next up is a glowing Cayenne. Pregnancy and marriage really suit her, and it's good to see her happy. She's spoken with Anvil, and they cleared the air over the past. I spot him smiling at her as she walks past.

Ryder's gaze is locked on his wife as Zeta walks down the aisle next, but I barely notice her because Sydney and Jerry have appeared at the end of the aisle, and my beautiful bride is all I can see.

My heart is pumping like crazy, and the vein in my neck is throbbing as I drink her in. She's the most beautiful woman I have ever seen and sexy as hell.

"Wow," Wilder says. "She's stunning."

"You're a lucky bastard," Linc says.

I can't even form words. She looks like a real-life princess. Regal, graceful, and beautiful, wearing a glorious smile, her joy obvious to everyone. A messy ball of emotion clogs my throat as I watch my bride walk toward me.

The instant our eyes connect, butterflies go crazy in my chest. I'm feeling so much as she approaches, and I hope I can find my voice to make our vows. This is the culmination of every fantasy I've ever had about my wedding day, and life really doesn't get better than this.

"Hi." Sydney beams at me when they reach the altar.

"You are so fucking beautiful," I say, pressing a soft kiss to her lips because I cannot hold myself back. My gaze roams over every inch of her as Jerry places her hand in mine. "How did I get so lucky to call you mine?" My voice cracks, and tears well in my eyes.

"You look sexy as fuck," she says with matching tears in her eyes. "I love you."

"Not as much as I love you."

"Stop it. You're going to make me cry," Jerry says. He kisses Sydney on the cheek. "Be happy, girl. You deserve it."

"Thanks for looking after my girl."

"Anytime, *mate*," he teases before walking over to take his seat.

The celebrant clears his throat as we turn around, holding hands and grinning like lovesick fools.

"Let's begin."

"Come with me, Mrs. King," I say, snatching my wife's hand and dragging her away from the champagne reception on our terrace. We were married fifty-six minutes ago, and I can't wait any longer to fuck my bride. We've been chatting with our guests and accepting congratulations while enjoying the glorious sunshine, some delicious canapés, and expensive champagne.

"J," Sydney hisses. "We can't leave our guests."

I pop a quick kiss on her lips. "Yes, we can. They'll be calling us for dinner soon, and I cannot wait until later to feel you around me."

"Jesus. You're insatiable."

I drill her with a look. "I've three words for you. Pot. Kettle. Black." Sydney has been jumping me nonstop lately. I have zero complaints.

"Oh, well, when you put it like that." She grins, urging me forward. "Let's hurry."

Five minutes later, she's standing with her hands against the wall in our master suite, her ass in the air and her dress hiked up to her waist, as I drive inside her.

"Goddamn it, baby, you feel incredible. I'm not going to last, wifey."

"J." Her soft tone has me stalling for a moment. She looks over her shoulder at me with tears in her eyes.

"What's wrong?"

"Absolutely nothing." She smiles at me. "I just want you to know how indescribably happy you've made me today."

I lean in and kiss her passionately. "Same, baby. I love you so fucking much. Sometimes, the intensity of it scares the shit out of me."

"We were made for one another, and I love our life. I'm so excited for our future."

"Same, baby."

She arches a brow.

"What?"

"Did you forget you're inside me?" She pushes back against me.

"Not fucking likely," I say, thrusting in deep.

"Good," she moans, throwing her head back. "Go faster. Deeper. Harder. I want to feel you between my legs when we go back downstairs."

"You're perfect, Syd," I say, pulling out and slamming back in. "So fucking perfect."

The only sounds in the room after that are the sound of skin slapping against skin and our mutual groans and whimpers. When the tingle starts moving up my spine and I feel my balls lock up, I reach around and rub her clit in time with my thrusts, and it's not long before we're falling over the cliff together. I hug my wife from behind for a few seconds before slowly pulling out.

My spunk seeps down her legs, and I'm tempted to shove it back up inside her, but there's no point. She's still got an IUD. "Stay like that, baby. I'll get a cloth and clean you up."

When I return to the bedroom, the sight of my wife with her wedding dress bunched up to her waist and her ass jutting up instantly hardens my dick. It'll be a problem unless I can get it to calm the fuck down before they call us for dinner. I press soft kisses to each of her ass cheeks as I clean her up. Then I help her fix her sexy lingerie and dress back in place.

Sydney's cheeks are flushed, and her eyes are swimming in emotion as she turns to me. "I love you so much, Jared. Thank you for making me the happiest woman on the planet today."

She kisses me tenderly before reaching for her purse. "I want to give you your wedding gift now."

"You mean that wasn't it?" I joke.

"No." Her eyes fill with tears. She's been extra emotional today. But I get it. I'm the same. There were many years when I thought I'd lost all this. To finally have it come true, especially after all we've been through, is magical.

"Close your eyes," she says, and I do what I'm told.

I know my place.

She places something cool and light in my hand.

"Open them now," she whispers.

I stare at the stick in my hand in silence for a few beats. When I lift my head, I can hardly see her through my blurry vision. "You're pregnant?" I choke out.

She nods, biting the corner of her lip.

"How?"

She snort-laughs. "Um, we fuck like rabbits all the time, J. Do we need to have a conversation about how these things work?"

I reel her into my arms and swat her ass through her dress. "I'm going to spank you for that later." A wide grin lets loose. "Is this real? Has the best day of my life just become even better?"

"Yeah, babe. We made a baby. I had my IUD put in at sixteen. I forgot they only last a maximum of ten years, but I went for a routine checkup on Monday, and the ob-gyn confirmed my pregnancy, and he safely removed the IUD."

Panic rears its head immediately. "Is the baby okay?"

"Yes, all is perfect. Don't worry." She pats my chest.

"So, we've been having unprotected sex the entire time?"

"Yup."

"You'd think my swimmers would have hit the target before now." I pout, feeling a little insulted.

She cracks up laughing. "Although you can technically get pregnant at any time after the IUD expires or is removed, it takes most women months to get pregnant afterward."

We look down at her flat stomach at the same time.

"I can't wait to see your belly swollen with our child," I say, placing a reverential hand over her stomach.

Syd puts her hand over mine. "Me either. I want lots of babies, J. Lots of mini Jareds."

"I'm so fucking happy I could burst."

She circles her arms around my neck. "I knew you would be, and I am too. I can't wait."

"Are you feeling okay?" I ask as a million concerns instantly flood my mind.

"Apart from ping-ponging emotions, I'm fine. No nausea or tiredness yet."

"I'll find the best doctor, and you'll have the best care."

"I know." She beams up at me.

"Thank you." I lean down and kiss her stomach. "This is the best wedding gift."

"We couldn't have planned it better if we tried."

Lifting her hand to my lips, I stare in amazement at my incredible wife. As I press a kiss to her knuckles, I offer silent thanks for the life I've been given, and I vow to never waste a moment or ever take it for granted. "To infinity and forever."

Sydney kisses me before pulling back and smiling. "Infinity and forever."

THE END

Want to read more angsty romance? I've got you covered! Check out my *All of Me Series, Inseparable, When Forever Changes, Always Meant to Be, Still Falling for You,* or *Incognito.* All are available FREE with Kindle Unlimited. Also available in paperback and audio (Audible, Amazon, iTunes.)

The One I Want

Stuck in a limbo state, I was falling apart while trying to be strong for my boyfriend.

Then *he* entered my life. The hot, slightly older guy who looked like a cross between a tatted biker and a billionaire businessman.

Beck understood me, and our situation, in a way no one else could.

As a friend, he held me together and helped to piece back the shredded fragments of my heart.

I didn't mean to fall in love with him—it just happened.

No one understands, least of all me.

Now my heart is split in two, and I don't know what to do.

Is my first love my one true love? Or do I belong with the man who brought me to life?

Available now in ebook, paperback, alternate paperback, and audiobook.

About the Author

Siobhan Davis is a *USA Today, Wall Street Journal,* and Amazon Top 5 bestselling romance author. **Siobhan** writes emotionally intense stories with swoon-worthy romance, complex characters, and tons of unexpected plot twists and turns that will have you flipping the pages beyond bedtime! She has sold over 2 million books, and her titles are translated into several languages.

Prior to becoming a full-time writer, Siobhan forged a successful corporate career in human resource management.

She lives in the Garden County of Ireland with her husband and two sons.

You can connect with Siobhan in the following ways:

Website: www.siobhandavis.com
Facebook: AuthorSiobhanDavis
Instagram: @siobhandavisauthor
Tiktok: @siobhandavisauthor
Email: siobhan@siobhandavis.com

Books by Siobhan Davis

KENNEDY BOYS SERIES
Upper Young Adult/New Adult Contemporary Romance

Finding Kyler
Losing Kyler
Keeping Kyler
The Irish Getaway
Loving Kalvin
Saving Brad
Seducing Kaden
Forgiving Keven
Summer in Nantucket
Releasing Keanu
Adoring Keaton
Reforming Kent
Moonlight in Massachusetts

STAND-ALONES
New Adult Contemporary Romance

Inseparable
Incognito
When Forever Changes
No Feelings Involved
Still Falling for You
Second Chances Box Set
Holding on to Forever
Always Meant to Be

Tell It to My Heart
The One I Want

Reverse Harem Romance

Surviving Amber Springs

Dark Mafia Romance

Vengeance of a Mafia Queen

MAZZONE MAFIA SERIES
Dark Mafia Romance

Condemned to Love
Forbidden to Love
Scared to Love
Mazzone Mafia: The Complete Series

THE ACCARDI TWINS
Dark Mafia Romance

*CKONY #1^*
*CKONY #2^*

RYDEVILLE ELITE SERIES
Dark High School Romance

Cruel Intentions
Twisted Betrayal
Sweet Retribution
Charlie
Jackson
Sawyer
*The Hate I Feel^*
*Drew^*

THE SAINTHOOD (BOYS OF LOWELL HIGH)
Dark HS Reverse Harem Romance

Resurrection
Rebellion
Reign
Revere
The Sainthood: The Complete Series

DIRTY CRAZY BAD DUET
Dark College Reverse Harem Romance

Dirty Crazy Bad - A Prequel Short Story
Dirty Crazy Bad # 1
Dirty Crazy Bad #2

ALL OF ME DUET

Angsty New Adult Romance

Say I'm The One
Let Me Love You
Hold Me Close
All of Me: The Complete Series

ALINTHIA SERIES

Upper YA/NA Paranormal Romance/Reverse Harem

The Lost Savior
The Secret Heir
The Warrior Princess
The Chosen One
*The Rightful Queen^*

SAVEN SERIES

Young Adult Science Fiction/Paranormal Romance

Saven Deception
Logan
Saven Disclosure
Saven Denial
Saven Defiance
Axton
Saven Deliverance
Saven: The Complete Series

^Release date to be confirmed